‖‖‖‖‖‖‖‖‖‖‖‖‖‖‖‖‖‖‖‖‖‖‖

☑ **W9-CBV-918**

"Hello?"

"What the hell do you want?" wasn't exactly the response she'd expected, but it was clear and to the point.

"My name is Antonia Stonewright. I'd like to talk to you about selling your work in my gallery." That should work. She'd never met an artist who didn't want to make a bit more money.

"My agent's Robbie Peterson. Contact him!"

Damn mortals! She watched him bend over as his strong arms and broad shoulders eased trays of unfired pots into the open kiln. "I certainly will, but I would like to see some of your work first."

He looked up, straightening as he turned toward her.

Something inside her did a little skip.

Unbidden, her tongue slowly licked her upper lip as the gums around her fangs tingled.

BOOK YOUR PLACE ON OUR WEBSITE AND MAKE THE READING CONNECTION!

We've created a customized website just for our very special readers, where you can get the inside scoop on everything that's going on with Zebra, Pinnacle and Kensington books.

When you come online, you'll have the exciting opportunity to:

- View covers of upcoming books
- Read sample chapters
- Learn about our future publishing schedule (listed by publication month *and author*)
- Find out when your favorite authors will be visiting a city near you
- Search for and order backlist books from our online catalog
- Check out author bios and background information
- Send e-mail to your favorite authors
- Meet the Kensington staff online
- Join us in weekly chats with authors, readers and other guests
- Get writing guidelines
- AND MUCH MORE!

**Visit our website at
http://www.kensingtonbooks.com**

ROSEMARY LAUREY

Keep Me Forever

ZEBRA BOOKS
KENSINGTON PUBLISHING CORP.
www.kensingtonbooks.com

ZEBRA BOOKS are published by

Kensington Publishing Corp.
850 Third Avenue
New York, NY 10022

Copyright © 2006 by Rosemary Laurey

All rights reserved. No part of this book may be reproduced in any form or by any means without the prior written consent of the Publisher, excepting brief quotes used in reviews.

If you purchased this book without a cover you should be aware that this book is stolen property. It was reported as "unsold and destroyed" to the Publisher and neither the Author nor the Publisher has received any payment for this "stripped book."

All Kensington titles, imprints, and distributed lines are available at special quantity discounts for bulk purchases for sales promotion, premiums, fund-raising, educational, or institutional use.

Special book excerpts or customized printings can also be created to fit specific needs. For details, write or phone the office of the Kensington Special Sales Manager: Attn. Special Sales Department. Kensington Publishing Corp., 850 Third Avenue, New York, NY 10022. Phone: 1-800-221-2647.

Zebra and the Z logo Reg. U.S. Pat. & TM Off.

ISBN 0-8217-7928-1

First Printing: April 2006
10 9 8 7 6 5 4 3 2 1

Printed in the United States of America

Chapter 1

"This is it!" Antonia Stonewright announced, opening the wide front door. "What do you think?"

Elizabeth Connor looked around the beautifully proportioned hall; the wide, curved staircase with its shallow, broad steps; and the airy drawing room just visible through the half-open door to her right. "It's absolutely lovely. No wonder Dixie hated to leave."

"Part of me thinks it a shame to use it for base money-making activities, but heck, we've tried for a year to rent it out with no luck. Seems the locals consider it tainted."

"That oily estate agent said as much."

Antonia creased her high forehead. She'd been as unimpressed with Mike Jenkins as Elizabeth had. "Nasty little snirp, wasn't he? Mind you, he was helpful—dealing with painters and electricians and so forth. No doubt made a little on the side, but it's done." She walked across the polished floor and opened wide the double doors into the drawing room. "This is going to be one of the main sales rooms."

The only furniture was the built-in corner cabinets. "When are the tables and other stuff coming?"

"In the next couple of weeks. Sooner, if we're lucky. We've still got the outside work to do. Dismantling some old buildings and removing an air raid shelter left over from the Second World War and expanding the stables to make the tearoom."

"And when will that get done?"

"Right away, now that I'm here."

Elizabeth didn't doubt it. Vampires had a way of getting what they wanted. "Want to unload the computers and so forth?"

"Might as well. We don't have an audience, so we can work at our own speed. We can set up our office in the breakfast room."

Elizabeth threw open the back doors of the van. It was packed to the roof with desks, computers, a printer, and filing cabinet, everything Antonia deemed necessary to set up a temporary office. "We should have taken sleazy Jenkins up on his offer to come out to the house with us. He could have helped heave this little lot. He did offer to help whenever we needed, didn't he?" Elizabeth couldn't resist a grin. The man had fairly oozed at them. "We could call him over. He'd make dinner for you."

"Spare me! I'm particular where I put my fangs."

Antonia was particular about everything, including the exact positioning of desks to avoid direct sunlight from the French windows. And she was not happy that the promised phone line was not connected. "Make that the first priority in the morning," she told Elizabeth. "That and internet connection. I'm getting this show on the road if I have to throw glamors over half the population."

They had everything set up in time that would have left mortals blinking. Antonia surveyed the room with grudging satisfaction. "At least it looks as if we mean business. I'll drop you at the car hire place, and we can meet back at the hotel."

"Let me see the attics Dixie mentioned first." Antonia obviously didn't like the idea. Too bad! It hadn't been that long since the entire vamp colony had been very happy to have a witch on their side.

Antonia followed her into the kitchen and up the narrow staircase, concealed behind a door. At first sight they were in two attics with pitched ceilings and tiny windows overlooking the garden, but . . . Elizabeth looked around. The shelves were bare, but in the middle of the floor sat three packing cases addressed to her. She pulled one open, delved in the shredded packing, and pulled out a jar with spidery, dark handwriting on a yellow label. She was actually looking at mandrake root. Bless Dixie! She had it all packed up as promised. Elizabeth pulled out half a dozen jars—some almost empty; others containing shriveled contents, ground powders, desiccated leaves or petals—before realizing Antonia was watching with a wry expression. "I've never before had a chance to actually go through an old-time herbalist's storeroom."

"Don't forget the lot you inherited this from were more than little old lady herbalists."

"I know, but not all of this is harmful. Look, this is arnica. Used to heal bruises and aches." She set the jar on the table and smiled at Antonia. "You'll be telling me next that your mother kept all this on her kitchen shelves."

Antonia smiled. "No, ghoul. My father had a skilled herbalist in his service. My mother spent her time trying to convert my father to her newfangled Christianity."

That was a conversation for another day. "What am I going to do with all this? Have it sent on to Tom's, I suppose." They were eventually converting these attics and the kitchen into the caretaker's accommodation.

Not often Antonia laughed, but that tickled her funny bone. "Better warn him first. On the other hand, since he's sleeping with a witch, he can't be too put out at . . ."

"Stow it!" Inelegant, yes, but really, vamps did have a tendency to intrude.

"You mean you're not sleeping with him?" Antonia deserved a shove in the ribs for that, but no point in risking
breaking an elbow. "We don't actually sleep that much,"
Elizabeth replied with a grin. "I only need a couple of hours
a night, assuming I feed, and talking about feeding, I really
need to before I go meet the Collins's. Don't want to get
dizzy driving."

"Think you can last while we check the rest of the house?"
She could.

They went through every room: The long drawing room
with sliding doors that gave onto a parlor that looked over
the back garden and caught the morning sun. The dining
room paneled in exquisite pear wood with beautiful built-in
china cabinets and a vast mirror in the overmantel that Antonia
avoided. Upstairs were five rooms, and the old book room still
lined with shelves. "We can take those out if we need too,"
Antonia said, "but I keep hoping we can find a bookseller to
join us."

They ended up in the kitchen with its vast Aga and delft-
tiled fireplace. "We are keeping those, aren't we?" Elizabeth
asked. Seemed a shame to yank them out.

"Yes, but not here. The Aga will be a feature in the tearoom. Not sure what to do with the tiles." She frowned a little as if thinking. "I knew a potter once. Dutch. Refugee.
Odd people, potters." Elizabeth was tempted to ask when
and a refugee from which war? But Antonia ran her hand
through her short hair and said, "Let's grab something for
you to eat and then get you a car."

They were heading for the door when the bell chimed.
Antonia opened the door to a smiling, bright-faced young
woman in the advanced stages of pregnancy. "I'm Emma
Gordon," she said. "One of your neighbors. I nipped in to
say hello and bring you a basket of goodies. I thought with
moving in, you'd like something to nibble on."

If the fates were kind, there would be meat in the basket

of goodies. "How nice of you," Elizabeth said. "You live close?" This had to be the Emma Dixie had mentioned.

"Next door but two. Just past the new semidetached. That's us. I thought you could use a cup of tea. There's a thermos in there and cups. I know what it's like moving. We just moved half our stuff next door, and it took me ages to find spoons and spare socks."

"Won't you come in and join us?" Antonia asked. "We've not much furniture, but we've desks and chairs."

It didn't take long to unpack Emma's basket of goodies and pour tea.

"You moved next door?" Elizabeth asked. Seemed odd.

"We needed the space. Where we are used to be a terrace of four cottages. Then they got converted into two houses. We bought ours when Peter was born. This"—she patted her bump—"will be numbers four and five. Plus I run a catering business—you've got a few samples there." She nodded toward the basket. "So, when our next door neighbor moved away, we got a truly frightening mortgage and bought the other half. It's brilliant. We have bedrooms and to spare, and a wonderfully massive kitchen for the business." She smiled, her eyes twinkling. "Ian says I have the shortest commute to work in history: downstairs and turn left."

Elizabeth took a sip of tea. "The catering business sounds fantastic, but a heck of a lot of work. How old are your children?"

"The eldest is in school. The other two in a play group this afternoon, and when they're not, I have a wonderful au pair, Nina from Sweden." The scent of meat from the basket was getting close to overwhelming. Steak, from what it smelled like. "She's fantastic, and the sprogs love her, and even better, listen to her," she paused. "That's enough about me. If you ever need food for a party or dinner, my phone number and price list is in the basket."

"I've heard great things about your food." Elizabeth said.

Emma stared. "Was it Mike Jenkins?"

"No." Might not be the moment for this, but who knew? "It was Dixie." She went on in the face of Emma's shock. "Dixie LePage."

"You know her!"

Elizabeth tamped down the guilt at causing shock to a pregnant woman. "I met her in the US, by chance as it happened." That much was true. "We got talking, and she mentioned she had a house in the south of England she was trying to sell. I knew Antonia was looking for somewhere near here, so here we are. She told us a lot about Bringham and mentioned several names, including yours." Hopefully prolonged shock wasn't harmful to pregnant women.

"I'll be blowed!" Emma let out a little gasp. "You're American too, aren't you?" At Elizabeth's nod, Emma went on. "Talk about a small world. I've so many questions to ask, I don't honestly know where to start but . . . Is she alright?"

More than alright, but Emma didn't need to know all that. "Fine. She's living in Ohio and running her own business. Gave us a lot of helpful information about Bringham. I got the impression she had mixed feelings about selling, this being family property."

Emma jumped right on the hint. "I'm not surprised. She loved it here, but after all that happened . . ." she broke off. "I shouldn't really gossip, but . . ."

"Yes?" Antonia prompted. "She mentioned a spot of bother."

Emma rolled her eyes. "'Spot' doesn't begin to describe it. Honest. While she was here, we had the most excitement in Bringham since a German bomber pilot parachuted onto the common back in the middle of World War II." She paused to take another drink of tea. "In a nutshell, we had arson, murder, a mysterious disappearance, and one of the village worthies going bonkers and accusing himself and half the village of heaven knows what. Some of it turned out to be true. Most of it got written off as lunatic ravings. You wouldn't believe some of the tales that got out. Witches, vampires . . ."

Elizabeth met Antonia's eyes. They had no trouble believing. "All settled down now though?" Antonia asked.

Emma nodded. "Pretty much. Did cause a lot of upheaval though. Disturbed a few lives. My neighbor Sally moved after Sebastian, the solicitor who went loony, accused her and a number of others of helping to murder someone. Nothing was ever proven, but it was a nine days' wonder while it lasted."

"I bet it was," Elizabeth said. "Anything interesting happened since then?"

"Not much," Emma replied. "One of the school teachers broke her leg on the ice last winter; there was a big debate over the new sign in front of the Barley Mow, and a couple of people claimed to have seen the Surrey puma."

"The Surrey puma?" Antonia asked.

Emma laughed. "Our local big wildcat. Frankly, I think it's a stray dog or sheep. Heck, it's been seen at intervals since my mum was a girl. I doubt pumas in the wild live that long. Every so often, someone sees a stray dog or a sheep, usually at dusk when visibility is poor, and Bob's your uncle, everyone digs up the old stories, and off we go again." She stood up. "I must go. Only popped over to say hello. Enjoy what's in the basket."

"Thanks for the goodies," Elizabeth said. "They really are welcome." More than this mortal could ever guess.

"Enjoy. It's really just a not too subtle way of pushing my wares. Oh, is it true you're opening a craft market and center here?"

"Yes. We plan to open in September and be in full swing for Christmas. We're going to be selective, but if you know any local artists or craftspeople who might be interested, spread the word."

"I will." She frowned as if thinking. "The vicar's mother-in-law does watercolors of kittens and puppies, but I don't think they're the sort of thing you're after." Antonia tactfully nodded. Emma went on, "There's the Misses Black. Old, old ladies—one's almost blind, but they do knitting. Some of it is beautiful. And you might want to contact Michael Langton. His stuff has been in galleries and shows in Town."

"A painter?" Antonia asked, not recognizing the name.

"A potter. Lives out on the edge of the common. A bit of a recluse, but he does make beautiful stuff. Someone gave us one of his lamps as a wedding present."

"We'll check him out," Elizabeth said.

"Bye."

As the door closed on Emma, Elizabeth made a pounce for the basket. A baguette filled with slices of rare steak and a packet of chicken goujons disappeared as she wolfed them down. "Sorry," she said, wiping her mouth on one of the neatly folded napkins tucked in the side of the basket. "The smell was driving me crazy. Hadn't realized how much I needed food."

Antonia gave her a wry look. "I'm glad you managed to contain yourself. Might have put Emma off a bit, finding her nice new neighbors gnawed their food."

"Darn tasty—for cooked meat, that is. Mind you, who are you to talk? Good thing she didn't peek in the cooler you have in the kitchen."

"True," Antonia agreed. "With people coming in and out, we'd better get a fridge and keep it in the attics over the kitchen. We can leave those rooms untouched for a while."

Elizabeth nodded as she gathered up the remains of the picnic basket: fruit tarts, some sort of pâté and crackers, and a generous bowl of salad. "Pity we have to toss these. If Sam were here, he'd make short work of them."

"But since he and Stella aren't due for another week . . ."

"I know, I know. It's just Adela did such a job on me about

not wasting anything in the Universe." Elizabeth sighed, thinking how much she really missed her stepmother.

"Out of curiosity," Antonia asked, "was the food good?"

"Yeah! Very good, in fact. I'm not that great on sausage rolls, but those were good, and the chicken was delicious."

"Good enough to consider for our tearoom?"

Why not? "Definitely. She does catering after all, and heck, this would be convenient for her."

"Better keep her in mind." Antonia glanced out of the French windows. "Assuming it ever gets built."

"It will! Use your vampire mind control if they drag their feet."

That got her a raised eyebrow. "Isn't it time we checked into the hotel? Let's do that, then go over to Collins Car Hire. I need transport."

"Monica's gone to get the boys from school," the gray-haired woman said, watching Elizabeth with sharp, intelligent eyes. "She left the keys and the forms for you to sign. I can take care of it if you'll give me your license."

Elizabeth put her license and credit card on the counter—her real ones, now recovered at long last—and waved at Antonia through the open door. If she had fridge buying to do, no point in waiting, and besides, on her own, Elizabeth might find inclined to chat a bit.

"You must be Ida Collins."

The woman looked up from studying the license, raised a gray eyebrow, and nodded. "I am. This was my son's business. I help my daughter-in-law with it now. American, aren't you?" Elizabeth agreed, she was. "You bought Orchard House?"

"No, my employer did. I'm just going to be working down here, so I'll need a car."

"Is your employer American?"

"Antonia? No, she's British." No need to say just how ancient a Briton she was.

Ida copied down the license number. "After the previous owner, I wondered. She was American, you know?"

"I do. It was through Dixie that I learned about the house being on the market."

"I wish your employer better luck than the last owner." Ida pushed the license back across the counter. Elizabeth closed her hand over the plastic rectangle and hesitated, hoping Ida would say more.

She didn't.

"Dixie didn't talk much about Bringham. Said just that she'd inherited the house from distant relatives and they sounded like local characters."

"Characters!" Ida almost spat it out. "Nasty, tightfisted, spiteful old bisoms they were." She paused as if about to say more. Elizabeth waited, but Ida had gone silent.

"Dixie mentioned finding books on herb lore and Wicca in the house."

As a conversational probe, that wasn't much help. Ida nodded. "Those two were always up to something."

"And according to Dixie, they blatantly ignored the Reede to do harm to none." That earned her a sharp look, but nothing more. Ida just finished filling in the forms and reached over to a hook for a set of keys. "My stepmother is a practicing Wiccan. She taught me a fair bit, and I wondered if there's anyone around who practices the old ways."

The keys jangled as Ida slapped them on the countertop. "You're new here. If you're planning on staying around a bit, don't mention witches, Wiccans, or whatever you call them to anyone. No one wants to hear anything about that. Not now!" She turned the paper around so it faced Elizabeth. "Sign here and here and initial those three boxes. You've got the car for a month. If you want it longer, let us know."

She'd been fishing for a response and certainly caught one. Interesting. "Thanks."

Ida separated the back copy and handed it to Elizabeth with the key. "The car's the red one. Fred'll show you." She called behind the service center, "Fred, customer's ready for the red Fiat."

"Thanks," Elizabeth said. "Sorry if I offended you."

Ida acknowledged the attempt at conciliation. "You weren't to know. I doubt Dixie told you all that happened here. Come to that, she couldn't. Half the trouble was after she left, and I don't blame her running off the way she did. Must have scared the willies out of her. Someone tried to kill her."

And finally succeeded, but that was by the way. "How terrible! What happened?" Tom and Dixie between them had told her everything, but Ida's slant on it might be illuminating.

"The bastard got my only son instead. That's why I'm working here. I moved back to Bringham to help out Monica. She wanted to keep the business going for her sons, but it's too much on her own, and that useless mechanic . . ." she paused. "Fred! Customer's waiting for the Fiat!" For a septuagenarian, Ida still had fine voice projection.

"Coming!" a voice called from outside.

"Thanks," Elizabeth said to Ida. "Sorry again if I said the wrong thing." Ida smiled and waved it off, and Elizabeth went out into the June sunshine with Fred.

The car was a zippy little compact with a hatchback that might well come in handy. After listening patiently to Fred demonstrating windshield wipers and automatic windows, Elizabeth drove off. Following Fred's sketchy directions, she headed back toward Bringham.

As the car pulled out of sight, Ida reached for the phone, punching in the numbers with a shaky finger. "Emily Reade.

It's important." While she waited to be transferred, her free hand tapped on the counter. This was bad news. Why did these darn Americans have to keep on turning up and causing trouble? Not that this one had done anything yet, but Ida trusted her instincts, and her instincts sensed upheaval and disharmony.

"Emily," she all but snapped when Emily finally answered. "We have to meet. Soon. Very soon. I've just spoken to the woman who bought Orchard House. She's a friend of Dixie's and knows far too much. Dixie told her about the house, her aunts, and I don't know what else! Even dropped hints about us! Too darn nosy for her own good. We have to do something. We can't risk any more trouble."

Emily was not about to argue. They both knew she'd kept her job in the bank by a slender chance. "Better warn Mildred then," she replied. "We'll meet at my house tomorrow after I get home. Six o'clock. Will you tell her?"

After Emily rang off, Ida dialed another number and caught Mildred Rowan at home. "Mildred," Ida said, her voice shakier than ever. "We've run into a snag."

Chapter 2

When Elizabeth waved from the open door of the little office, Antonia took it as 'All's well,' waved back, and drove down the lane. Elizabeth seemed set, and no doubt, would have a nice time chatting witchy stuff to Ida. The thought didn't give Antonia as much of the creeps as it would most of the colony, or at least the newer members. She remembered the days when the old religion still held sway in the woods and around isolated campfires. Still, she wondered how Tom, raised when witches were publicly tried and burned, quite handled getting intimate with one. Not that it was any of her business really, but one couldn't help thinking about it.

Still, if Gwyltha as leader of the colony accepted Elizabeth, who was she to question it? Besides, she liked Elizabeth and needed her skills to get set up, and the prospect of working closely with someone and not having constantly to conceal her nature was more than welcome.

And meanwhile . . .

Antonia covered the few miles from the Collins's in Horsley to the outskirts of Bringham in a short time. After pulling to the side of the lane to consult Dixie's lists and maps, she drove through the village, turned right at the church, took the next left, and parked in front of a modern house. The vast Victorian rectory that had housed former vicars and their offspring and servants was now an old people's home. The current incumbent had far more modest and vastly more comfortable surroundings.

A glance at the immaculate rose beds and lush hanging baskets showed someone in the house was a very eager gardener—or they hired one. Might be handy to get the name and add it to her list. They'd need help with the wilderness around Orchard House. The lawn cutting service didn't extend to weeding or pruning.

Hoping someone would be in—it was the vicarage after all—Antonia rang the bell.

The genteel ding-dong-ding of the chiming doorbell was drowned out by what sounded like the baying of a wolfhound. The gray shape that appeared through the reeded glass in the front door pretty much confirmed it.

"Hush, Pansy! Hush!" a woman's voice called, and as the dog quieted, the door was opened by a fresh-faced young woman. "Yes? Can I help you?"

"I was hoping so, but is this an inconvenient time?"

"No worse than any other. I'm afraid Mum's out if you wanted her."

"If your mother's the vicar's wife, yes. I had hoped to speak to her. I just moved into the village. My name's Antonia Stonewright.

"Oh! You bought Orchard House and are turning it into a B and B." She gave the dog a yank back as it tried to sniff at Antonia. "Behave yourself, Pansy!" She looked back up and smiled, "Sorry. Excuse my manners." She held out her free hand. "I'm Judy Abbott. Dad's the vicar here, and I just got down from Uni. Come in."

Antonia stepped over the threshold. Pansy decided she

was persona definitely grata and started sniffling and licking her hands.

"Want a cup of tea?" Judy asked as she led the way back to a large kitchen filled with sunshine and overlooking a back garden every bit as immaculate as the front. "Oh, Pansy, leave her alone!" Judy gave the dog a gentle nudge, and then Antonia noticed that Pansy wasn't merely large and fat, she was expecting. After Emily this morning, Bringham appeared to be a font of fecundity.

Pansy lumbered her bulk into a vast dog bed and, after turning around several times and scratching the pillow, settled, but kept her eyes on Antonia.

It was a darn good thing animals didn't really react to vampires the way they did in some fanciful fiction. "She's a beautiful dog," Antonia said. "My father had several wolfhounds."

"Several?" Judy looked around from filling the kettle. "I hope you had a bigger house than this one!"

It had been a hall: vast, draughty, dark, and large enough to sleep a hundred men. "It was."

Judy plugged in the kettle and reached for the teapot. Antonia would have sighed if she still could. Another cup of tea! Better get used to swallowing them if she planned on knocking on doors. After all, at her age, she could ingest gallons of tea without ill effect. She hoped. "Mum should be back soon," Judy said. "If you want to wait, that's fine, or if I can help . . ." She walked over to the table and cleared away a heap of sewing and a workbasket. When the kettle boiled, she took two mugs from a row hanging beneath the countertop. "Tea bags alright?"

"Perfect." The mugs caught Antonia's eye—souvenirs of the London Dungeon and the All England Tennis and Croquet Club just didn't seem to mesh exactly. But who knew how mortals viewed these things?

Judy filled each mug and swirled the tea bags around. "So

you need help? About the Bed and Breakfast? If you need staff, Mum can spread the word, but an ad in the local paper might get better results." She squeezed out the bags, added milk without asking, and handed Antonia the London Dungeon mug. "Sugar?" She put a small pottery bowl of sugar on the table.

"No, thanks." The tea was hot, so it had better sit. Swallowing boiling liquid tended to get noticed. "Actually, it's not a B and B. I'm opening a small art gallery and craft center. We plan to open in September and be in full swing for Christmas. What I was hoping was your mother might be able to help me find someone. I was given a name, but can't find him in the phone book."

"Maybe I can. If not, Mum or Dad might. Who is it?"

"A potter. A Michael Langton."

"Oh! The reclusive potter!" Judy smiled and shook her head. "He's hard to find, ex-directory and ex just about everything. Beats me how he runs a business, but he seems to sell all over the place. I've never met him. Dad has. When we had a silent auction to raise money for repairs to the church, Michael Langton donated a really beautiful soup tureen and plates. Told Dad he was happy to contribute as long as he didn't have to come. Odd sort, but his stuff was beautiful."

"You have any?"

Judy shook her head. "It all went and got a good price, too. Someone from Effingham bought it and thought they got it for a song. Seems he's known all over the country. As for where he lives," she paused, "let me call Sylvie, who edits the parish mag."

Judy picked up the phone and speed dialed a number. After enquiries about Sylvie's Dad's health and how much he was looking forward to two weeks in Brittany, she wrote down what was either a long address or extremely complicated directions. "The address is Manor Farm cottages, but you can't get there from Manor Farm Road." She handed Antonia the paper. "Here are Sylvie's directions verbatim. If you get lost, I've written her number at the bottom. Call her. She's been there to deliver parish magazines."

The paper was covered with large, loopy handwriting, but it was legible enough. Antonia tucked it into her pocket. "Thank you so much; you've been really helpful."

"Glad I could be. The odds were I couldn't have as I'm gone more than I'm here, but it so happened I remembered Mum and Dad talking about him." She paused. "Want Mum to spread the word in the village you're looking for people for craft sales? Or do you have particular requirements, nonamateur stuff and so forth?"

"I'll be very selective." Abel help her, she was going to have to be. "But I've nothing against amateur. It's quality and originality that matter. I hope to use mostly local people. Do you know anyone else?"

"Only two old ladies, the Misses Black. A pair of sisters who live in the Council Houses up by the main road. They knit and have for years. Mum had them make a marvelous poncho for me for Christmas. Their work is really good. A whole lot better than the sort of stuff we get for church bazaars."

"Someone else mentioned them. Do you have an address? Phone number?" Judy had both. Antonia downed a mouthful of tea. "Sorry to run, but I'd like to try to find the elusive potter before I go home."

"And," Judy went on, half-hesitating, "I do embroidery and collage. I sold a few cushions to an interior decorating shop in Oxford. Made myself some extra dosh to eke out my loans."

Might be hideous but one never knew. "Do you have some work handy?" Antonia glanced at the heap of sewing Judy'd pushed aside earlier.

"That one's still at the planning stage," she replied, following Antonia's gaze, "but I do have a couple I gave Mum and Dad for Christmas. Let me get them."

While she nipped upstairs, Antonia took the opportunity to tip the contents of her mug down the drain to save her body the effort of absorption. She was sitting back down, empty mug in front of her, when Judy returned, clutching two large pillows.

Antonia had to stop herself from gaping. They were almost bed pillow size, a glorious mix of colors and textures and embroidery. Both had foregrounds of skeletal winter trees. One background was bright oranges, yellows, and reds; the other was done in pale blues and whites with pink and lilac streaks. "Sunrise, sunset?"

"Yes. Dad's a night bird, Mum's a morning person. My brother and I nicknamed them Sunset and Sunrise when we were little. I made these for them for their silver wedding."

"They're incredible but hardly economical. There must be hours of work in these."

"Weeks and months actually. The ones I sold were nowhere near as intricate."

"Could you make up a few samples? I think they'd sell for Christmas or wedding presents. Maybe as special orders." Antonia turned the pillows over, inspecting the piping and finish. "I'd love to sell them. We just have to work out prices that cover the work involved."

"No prob." Judy took them back as Antonia stood. "We know where to find each other. Give me your mobile number, and I'll leave a message when I have something to show you."

Antonia drove away from the rectory and turned down the lane toward the station and the common. She'd check out these two Misses Black. Having seen Judy's work, she was ready to accept her word that maybe the two knitting sisters would fit into the center. But what she really wanted was a couple of nationally recognized names, and if Michael Langton was as well-known as everyone claimed, he'd be a good one to start with.

The lane curved by the station; Antonia consulted the written directions and turned right onto a narrower lane that skirted the common. Antonia drove until the lane narrowed even further and, after several minutes, degenerated into a rough track with grass growing down the middle and over-grown hedges that brushed the car on both sides. No question the man lived in the back of beyond.

Potholes and ruts now joined tufts of grass as scenic additions to the lane. It wasn't quite as bad as roads she remembered from centuries back, but it would definitely have been easier on horseback. Just as Antonia was thinking of turning around—or would have if there had been any sign of a gate or field to reverse in—the lane came to an abrupt end in a graveled, open area where she could reverse comfortably. As she turned sharply to the right, ready to turn around, she noticed a battered van parked under an overhanging tree and a narrow bridge.

Footbridge, she amended to herself. A couple of stout planks to be more exact, held down at each end with rough boulders. On the far side, a narrow footpath led to a group of buildings that resembled sheds or dilapidated warehouses.

This couldn't be where he lived. She must have missed another turning. How could anyone, even a recluse, run a business here? Impossible to receive deliveries, and potters needed vast amounts of clay and minerals for glazes. What about food? Even back to nature self-sufficient sorts surely needed milk delivered. And how in Abel's name did he fire the kilns? He couldn't have electricity or gas this far out, could he? Hard to imagine coal or coke lorries venturing up that road. She wasn't even sure her car would make it back.

Antonia locked her car. Foolish really. Hardly likely to be

any sneak thieves around here, but city habits died hard. She crossed the narrow bridge. It was more of a small river than a stream—about three meters wide and running fast. The water shone clear and clean as it flowed over the bed of pebbles and sand. The afternoon sun glinted on shoals of silvery minnows as they darted back and forth. It would be fun for Sam to come fishing. Right now, she might as well see if the potter was at home.

The mortal appeared to inhabit a series of shacks—rough buildings, some mere lean-tos, clustered round a paved courtyard. Antonia passed each building until she found a mortal heartbeat, albeit a rather slow one, inside a long shed.

When a knock on the wooden door got no reply, she rapped harder before opening the door and calling out, "Hello?"

"What the hell do you want?" Wasn't exactly the response she'd expected, but it was clear and to the point.

"My name is Antonia Stonewright. I'd like to talk to you about selling your work in my gallery." That should work. She'd never met an artist who didn't want to make a bit more money.

"My agent's Robbie Peterson. Contact him!"

Damn mortals! She watched him bend over as his strong arms and broad shoulders eased trays of unfired pots into the open kiln. "I certainly will, but I would like to see some of your work first."

He looked up, straightening as he turned toward her.

Something inside her did a little skip.

Sweet Abel! She was far, far too old and cynical to fall for a mere mortal. Even one as godlike as this specimen. They were a good three or four meters apart, but who could miss the dark, bright eyes; the unruly sandy hair; the wide shoulders, and the sheen of sweat across his face.

Unbidden, her tongue slowly licked her upper lip as the gums around her fangs tingled.

"My work's on display in the Sewell Gallery in Guildford."

And if she possessed a modicum of common sense, she'd
be in her car, headed for Guildford. "Fine, but I doubt it's
open late on a Tuesday night, and I really do want to see your
work. I don't want to interrupt, and I don't mind waiting
until you've stacked your kiln." Watching those shoulders as
he reached and stretched wouldn't be any hardship either.
Here was a mortal definitely worth visiting in the dark of the
night.

He raised one full eyebrow. "Might take me a while."

"Doesn't matter. I should have called before coming, but
I was on my way home and . . ."

"You just happened to be passing?" His wide mouth
twitched at the corners.

"No. I just happened to think it was only half a mile out
of my way, and by the time I realized my mistake, I had no
way of turning around."

The twitch became a rather twisted smile. "You could
have reversed on the open patch across the river."

"I could, but I'd come this far, and I do want to see your
work. I'm opening a gallery and craft center in the village."

"I don't make souvenir ash trays or milk jugs with 'A present from Bringham' on the side."

"I should hope not. I didn't wreck my car's paintwork and
suspension for tourist tat."

His dark eyes lit a little as his smile broadened. "Since
you're here, you might as well wait." He angled his head to
the racks behind him. "I've two more trays to pack. Go into
the cottage next door and wait. I've a few samples on the
shelves. They're not for sale at any price, but you can look.
I'll be along in a half hour or so once I get this packed and
going."

He hadn't thrown her out, something she'd half-expected
after his initial unwelcome. Seemed, recluse or not, he had
more sense than to rebuff a potential sales source.

Lingering just long enough to enjoy the view as he hefted

the next tray of pots, Antonia stepped out of the kiln room
and into the courtyard. The first building to her right looked
more like a henhouse than human habitation. The next,
while as shabby as the rest, did have windows and a recently
painted front door. A glimpse through the curtain of a table,
a sofa, and shelves of pots confirmed her assumption.

She grasped the doorknob—a loose one, missing a screw.
Home maintenance was obviously not one of his priorities.
She opened the door. She could see the array of pots on the
shelves across the room but couldn't cross the threshold. His
casual 'go in and wait' wasn't an invitation to enter.

Drat! Nothing for it but to wait. Once he did actually in-
vite her in, she'd be able to enter as freely and as often as she
wanted to, and Antonia Stonewright was certain she would.

It had been a while—at least several decades—since
she'd felt this strong a pull to a mortal. But it hadn't been so
long that she'd forgotten the sensation, and just thinking
about the taste of his skin on her tongue had her gums tingling again.

She sat down on the step; stretched her legs out in front of
her; and watching the sun sink through the trees, thought
about the potter.

She could hear him moving in the other building, lifting
trays, shifting pots, muttering under his breath, and once or
twice uttering a muffled curse. But they were the only sounds
apart from the river a few meters away. Odd really that she
didn't hear any birds. It was too early for them to be nesting
for the night. Maybe the fumes from the kilns kept them
away. Odd he didn't have a dog too. Most recluses or back to
nature sorts tended to have cats or dogs for company and
conversation, but seemed bedworthy Michael lived solo.

Good. She'd have to stay away if he had a wife or girl-
friend. Antonia was strict with about that. After her own experience with betrayal, she'd never poach on another's
territory.

Damn! Even in the sylvan vastness of the Surrey hills, she had to think about Etienne Larouseliere. Damn and double damn him! But his infidelity and betrayal she'd turned to her good. Learned not to give her heart away and to find friendship among the vampires of her colony and sex and sustenance from humans. Worked so much better all around. If a mortal betrayed her, death would put paid to their duplicitous ways. All she had to do was wait.

Antonia leaned against the door, closed her eyes, and wondered if Elizabeth had learned anything from Ida. Antonia hoped not. As far as she was concerned, the scattered coven was best kept that way. What earthly good could come of encouraging witches to mischief? True, Elizabeth was loyal, noble, and trustworthy, but she was an anomaly.

"Didn't you go in and look around?"

The tone struck her more than his words. This was one prickly mortal. She smiled. "No. I'd rather see your work with you. Always helps to see your reactions and hear what you have to say about it." Wasn't entirely a lie either.

"And why would I even want to do business with you when I have a perfectly good agent to handle all that nuisance for me?"

"Maybe you don't." And maybe she didn't, but she'd driven this far, waited this long, she was entitled to at least a good look at his work. She stood up. And smiled. Mortals tended to fall for her smile. "You won't really know until we talk, will you?"

He didn't exactly fall at her feet, but he did nod and open the door for her. "Might as well come in then."

He wasn't straining himself with graciousness, but it was all she needed. Seconds later, Antonia stepped into the house, barred to her before his invitation, and almost gaped. A bit ramshackle it might have been from the outside, but inside, it was a showcase of comfort and efficiency. Including, she noticed, a state of the art security system. There was no mistaking the touch pad beside the door. He'd want to protect the collection of pots on the shelves from burglars.

What had looked interesting through the window was incredible close up. Not waiting for further invitation—hadn't he expected her to barge in anyway—Antonia crossed the generous sitting room cum kitchen to the dark wood shelves on the far wall. As she reached them, Michael must have flicked a switch. The shelves were bathed in concealed light.

His work wasn't good, it was incredible! Assuming . . . "They're all your work?"

"Every last one."

Yes, a definite edge to his voice there. Not that she blamed him. An artist of his caliber was entitled to be possessive.

Antonia stopped an arm's length from the shelves. She so wanted to touch the pots, run her fingers over the voluptuous curves, and test the muted glazes against her fingertips, but she satisfied herself with gazing at the full shapes, the wide shallow bowls, and the wonderful subtle blues and greens and soft grays. "You use all wood glazes?" As she spoke, she turned and caught the surprise in his eyes. Hm-m-m, so he hadn't expected her to know that much, had he? Michael Langton might be in for a bit of a surprise.

He nodded. "For my best pieces, I save ashes all winter. I don't have enough for all I produce, and I do a line of shallow dishes and bowls with enamels." He paused. "Want a cup of tea? We can go into the warehouse later and look at the mass production pieces if you like." He smiled, his eyes sparkling as they creased at the corners. For a second, she almost forgot he was mortal.

"I'd love a cup of tea." A lie, but she knew better than to refuse the offer of hospitality. Some things hadn't changed in fifteen centuries. Besides, he was definitely mellowing . . . might as well encourage it. She turned back to his pots ranged side by side. "They almost ask to be touched."

"They were made to be touched."

She heard water running and the ding of a lid being put on the kettle, but making tea was a mortal occupation. She had far more fascinating prospects in mind. Reaching out both hands to the round base of a tall pot that resembled a giant water lily bud, she stroked the firm curves, running her fingers up to the narrow neck and over the smooth edge. Beside it, another rounded shape had a wide neck plus a handle and a spout. He obviously intended it as a water jug. But it was the brilliant, bloodred glaze that caught her attention. Beside the muted blues, greens, and grays, it stood out like a flash of heat and passion.

"How utterly beautiful!" she whispered but Michael Langton appeared to have incredible hearing.

"It's the one and only," he replied, crossing the room with almost silent steps. "A fluke really. Years back, I was experimenting with Raku—reduced firing," he added after a slight pause. "Most come out with interesting glaze effects, but this one . . ." He reached out and touched it, his finger a bare inch or less from hers. "This one I'd packed in the dead center of the kiln, and somehow it came out this magnificent color. I tried a score or more times to replicate it, but never could." His strong fingers eased up the spout. The pad of his index finger caressed the rim before he stroked back down to the base. She found herself staring at his work-worn hands. "I decided to accept this as a gift from the gods and not demand a repeat." He shrugged. "But I held on to this one. I don't ever intend to part with it." His closing words held a note of finality, almost a gentle threat.

"I can't imagine how you could." She took her hand away. Almost touching fingertips was something she was not yet prepared for. Nipping a vein yes—that was sustenance—but intimacy of any sort was not a wise idea. "I'm flattered you let me see it, and the others." Her gaze went over the beautiful shapes, the shallow bowls and the tall, smooth urns. She turned to look at him. He was close. Far too close. She caught his scent: healthy male with a light touch of fresh sweat and something else, a wild, almost feral scent.

She gave herself a little shake. Rural vastness was doing things to her mind. "You've shown me what you won't sell. What about the work you will?"

That smile was beyond mortal. He angled his head to his right, and a couple of sandy curls shifted over his right eye. She was letting a mortal male have far, far too much effect on her. Attractive, yes; a fine specimen, definitely, but having the blood in her veins tingle at his nearness was utterly ridiculous.

"I keep the stuff to sell in my warehouse. Want to look before or after tea?"

Brushing aside the suspicion that sharing anything with Michael Langton, even a cup of tea, was injudicious, she smiled back. "How about you show me? Then we'll settle business over a cup of tea."

Was she pushing too hard? He certainly hesitated but, in the end, shrugged. "Over here." He opened a heavy door and stood aside to let her enter.

Appearances were deceptive. The apparently ramshackle wooden building between the pottery and his cottage was a modern metal building, almost hygienically clean, with finished pots stacked on shelf after shelf and several packing cases sealed and ready to ship.

As she studied the rows of shallow bowls, lamp bases, and mugs, she couldn't help considering the contradictory exteriors and interiors of Michael's setup. Odd really, but what the heck. He was an artist, after all, and she'd known enough artists over the centuries not to be surprised at anything one of them said or did.

Right now, just keeping up with Michael Langton was enough.

That and his work, of course. "What's your lead time for

orders?" She picked up an oval shallow bowl that was the color of a robin's egg.

"Depends. Rush orders I can do in a week or so, but I prefer four to six weeks. Better to pace myself and work in with standing orders."

"You have a price list?"

"Of course." She didn't need to look his way to know that his wide mouth was curling just so at the corners and his dark eyes had a glint of amusement . . . or perhaps something else that right now might not be a good idea. Or was it? "I'll print you out one. Any particular products you're interested in?"

"Depends on prices. I'd like a quantity of the small bowls, mugs, and dishes. Assorted glazes will be fine, and say three, no, four, of the large lamp bases and urns." She glanced up, and he nodded. "I've found, as a rule, that smaller items sell better if there's an expensive item on display."

He grinned. Watching with fascination was a big mistake. "I see. Sneak selling, eh? Hook them on the pricey stuff they can't afford so they permit themselves a consolation purchase."

She grinned back. What the hell? He'd started it. "It's not infallible, but works quite nicely most of the time."

Michael reached over her shoulder for a shallow dish with a pale turquoise glaze. "Take it as a sample," he said, putting it in her hand. "Let's go back into the kitchen and have tea while the price list prints out."

She closed her hands over the smooth, cool glaze and walked back into the house as he stepped aside and locked the door to the warehouse after them. He was very security conscious for someone living this far from civilization, but he did have his livelihood in that small warehouse.

She put the dish on the counter beside her as she sat on the stool he held for her and watched as he reached for two mugs from hooks under the shelf.

He'd made the mugs himself, of that she was sure—the outsides showed wide marks from his hands on the wheel. Inside and outside, they were covered with a white glaze that let the darker clay show through on the wide curves. "Milk?" he asked.

She nodded. "Please, but no sugar." Not that it tasted any different to her, but why put refined sugar in her body when it had no use for it?

He poured the tea, passed one mug her way, and offered a tin of biscuits. She refused, but he took four chocolate-covered digestives and proceeded to munch on them with particularly white and strong-looking teeth. He swallowed and looked at her. "Okay. What sort of commission are you charging?"

Better talk business than dwell on luscious, dark eyes. Better discuss delivery dates and returns than wonder how his sandy curls would feel against her face or how his tanned skin and rich blood would taste on her tongue.

Later. She could and would return, but for now, she had a deal to hammer out.

It was twilight before she was ready to leave.

He walked with her across the footbridge to her parked car, hesitating as he offered his hand. "Bye," he said. "I'm sure I'll be hearing from you."

Her fingers closed over his, his eyes registering surprise at the strength of her handclasp.

She smiled. "We'll keep in touch. Once I have storage space ready, we'll firm up the consignment." She dropped his hand and stepped away, fighting the temptation to step closer. He was mortal. She'd visit him, yes, but . . . "Goodbye!"

"Bye, Antonia," he replied. "Be careful reversing."

She drove back down the lane, half of her determined to

return and feed and give Michael Langton a night of dreams to remember, while some deep instinct insisted that with this man she was biting off more than she should. Her mouth twisted at the unintentional pun. Sweet Abel! What did it matter? She'd never harm him. Couldn't. Wouldn't. But she had no question in her mind. She'd return. Soon.

Michael Langton stood listening until there was no sound of her engine and even the scent of motor oil and petrol had faded.

He should have thrown her out of his pottery at first sight. Yeah, right! He could no more have done that than change his nature. Antonia Stonewright fascinated him. Women were danger, trouble, and traps for the unwary. But about Antonia he sensed something different. True, she'd been all business, but he'd need to be devoid of all five senses not to catch her interest: the glimmer in her eyes, the scent of her skin. Odd, he hadn't noticed a quickened heartbeat, but her smile and her voice had been enough.

She shared his interest.

The prospect was a recipe for disaster. He hadn't cultivated the reclusive artist persona to have it breached by a good-looking woman down from Yorkshire.

Pots and bowls—yes, he'd send them on consignment. But never, ever could anything more than business exist between them.

He looked up at the sky. Two, three hours before dark, with moonrise a couple of hours after that.

He returned to the house, rinsed out the mugs they'd used, and walked over to the pottery to check the progress of the new firing. The kiln would be at temperature by dawn, and he'd be back long before then. He wedged several pounds of clay, slicing it with a twisted wire, before dropping each segment on the remainder, turning, cutting, and dropping again, until the clay was smooth and free of air bubbles. Satisfied, he wrapped it in a wet cloth and heavy plastic.

He washed his hands and took off his clay-covered smock and hung it on the hook by the door. Back in the house, he unzipped his jeans and left them, and the rest of his clothes, in the bathroom. He set the security system and closed the door behind him. Naked, he walked out into the moonlight. Standing in the shelter of a cluster of trees, he looked up at the full moon, threw back his head, and let out a deep, feline howl. Minutes later, a large, dark shape ran on all fours toward the open fields.

Chapter 3

James Chadwick stared at the papers spread on the leather-topped satinwood desk. He'd checked three times and scoured every single paper in the deed box. This was all there was. The pile spread out in front of him included his own birth certificate and those of his mother, uncle, and grandparents. Marriage and death certificates for his grandparents and death certificates for his great grandparents. Heck, even a stack of outdated passports and driver's licenses and his parents' marriage certificate dated six months before his birth. Interesting! But most interesting was reading his parents' names: Rachel Stephanie Amy Caughleigh and Roger Alexander Chadwick. Amy, spinster, aged seventeen and Roger, retired solicitor, aged sixty-six. Crap almighty! May and December wasn't in it. What wouldn't he give to know the story behind that? A rushed marriage with Sebastian putting leverage on his younger sister? Or was it his grandparents? They had still been alive then. Just. They'd both died in a car crash a year after the shotgun wedding.

James let out a slow whistle. Seems the Caughleighs had a couple of eventful years. His parents' marriage, his father's death from heart failure five months after his birth, his grandparents' accident, and then his own mother's death.

Except that as punctilious as dear Uncle Sebastian had been about record keeping, Amy Chadwick's death certificate was missing. Odd. Extremely odd.

James thought back to the little he remembered about his mother. She was fun; she laughed and played with him. Why not? She'd been not yet eighteen when he was born and twenty-four when she'd disappeared, and only a few months after that, he'd been told she was dead, and Uncle Sebastian had left him with old Sarah Wallace when he went off to the funeral in . . .

Damn! He could not remember. He had to have been told, surely? But at six, he'd scarcely grasped what it meant that his mother was dead. Never to come back. Ever.

Odd, thinking back, but ole Uncle Sebby had never been inclined to speak of his sister. The few times James had asked, he'd been brushed off. Not really surprising. Sebastian always brushed off anything he didn't want to be bothered about. It had only been a year later that Sebastian had yanked him out of the village school and packed seven-year-old James off to boarding school.

James couldn't resist a dry chuckle. He'd been so lonely for a few weeks, he'd even missed miserable old Sarah and the moustache that tickled when she kissed him good night. He'd spent half his childhood making up tales of his mother returning. She'd been snatched by fairies, been off visiting the King of Siam, or been captured by pirates and unable to escape.

Wild, childish hopes and dreams.

But why the missing death certificate?

Was she not dead? Had she run off and stayed away? Life with Sebastian had to have been pretty confining for a young woman, but damn it—why leave him behind? He remembered it so clearly. She'd kissed him, tucking a Penguin in his hand as a treat for being a good boy, and promised to be there when he came out of school. Every other day she'd been waiting at the gate. That day she wasn't. Where the frigging hell had she gone? And why?

James twisted the swivel chair from side to side, frowning to himself. It was enough to send him back to the bottle, but he'd sworn off the stuff a year ago after he'd woken up, on his back, in the middle of a field with no idea how he'd landed there and suffering the worst headache of his life. His sudden temperance earned him a ribbing for a while at the Barley Mow, but hell, that little incident had scared him sober.

And now . . . What had happened to his mother? Might almost be worth a visit to ole Uncle Sebby, except James knew before he even dismissed the idea that even if Sebastian were in one of his sane moments, he would tell James nothing.

But there were ways of finding out . . .

He pondered the wisdom of contacting one of the private agencies Sebastian had used from time to time but decided he had better plans for Sebastian's money now that he had power of attorney, when the phone at his elbow rang.

"James?" He recognized the panicky tones of John Rowan, a member of Uncle's erstwhile coven. "We need to get together. There's trouble. These damn women."

"What damn women?" Given that he'd just decided his mother had abandoned him, the adjective seemed apropos to the entire sex.

"Emily, Ida, and Mildred!" Ah, John was having wife problems again. Stupid man should give her bingo money and shove her on a bus to Leatherhead.

"And you expect me to do something?" Let alone even care. Old biddies!

"Listen, James, this is serious. Ida's got them all steamed up. They're all up in arms over the new people at Orchard House."

"And . . ."

"Ida says the one she spoke to is a witch, and Ida thinks she's here to take over the coven. Ridiculous I know, but with all the trouble last year, we need to . . ."

"John, I don't give a flaming damn what you or the rest of the blasted coven do. I want nothing to do with you. Do you understand?" His voice rose, echoing in his ears, but he didn't care. "Whatever does or does not happen to any of you is no concern of mine. I wash my hands of the lot of you! Don't ever call me again. Understand?"

He slammed down the receiver with shaking hands. Those old fools! He was having nothing more to do with them. Ever. It was Sebastian's association with the coven, starting with those old crones down at Orchard House, that had him fixating on power and magic. The obsessions that drove him loony in the end.

Come to that, his mother had spent hours up there. Seemed half the trouble in the world started in that house and the damn coven.

James stood up. Might as well go out in case John called back—or even worse, decided to come racing over, hell-bent on dragging him back into the coils of the blasted coven. Never!

Locking the door behind him, James strolled down the drive and turned right toward the village. A good walk and a bit of fresh air might help clear his whirling thoughts.

"Hi"—Elizabeth looked up from the computer as Antonia opened the kitchen door—"been on a tour of the entire Mole Valley?"

"Never left the village." Antonia pulled out the other chair and sat down. "But I did find two potential clients. Both great."

Elizabeth listened. Attentively at first but as Antonia

waxed lyrical about the potter on the common, she couldn't hold back a grin.

"He sounds tasty in every sense of the word."

"For Abel's sake! He's not just a handy vein! He's a wonderful craftsman. We'll be damn lucky to handle his work. He's . . ."

"Decorative? Worth the bother?" Elizabeth ignored the raised eyebrows and frown. "Bedworthy?"

"Like to live dangerously, do you, ghoul?"

"No, just picking up clues. I've gotten pretty good at reading vampires the last few months."

Antonia rolled her eyes. She'd have sighed if her lungs still worked that way. "He's . . . interesting and, I can't deny, attractive. A nice, healthy mortal who won't miss the odd pint or two."

No point in getting squeamish. She was a ghoul who was pretty much committed to another vampire, and her dining habits weren't exactly the sort to get herself invited to Buckingham Palace. "You really are serious."

Antonia nodded. "Why not? I'd do better to keep the blood bags for emergencies. He lives in the back of beyond. I can visit unobserved. I'll not harm him, Elizabeth; you know that."

She did. Why was she objecting? Something about the light in Antonia's eyes suggested this Michael whatever his name was might be more than sustenance. And if so, why not? Antonia was certainly old enough to look after herself. "I know. Look, while you've been gallivanting over the common, I've been working. Tom called with all sorts of wonderful advice I may or may not follow." Much as she loved the vampire, he had to get used to the idea that they were not joined at the hip. "And best of all, Stella called. Seems Sam's cricket coach broke his leg and won't be coaching Sam after all, so they are on their way . . . or will be in the morning."

"I've got a job for her already—finding and interviewing

staff. Can't wait to see her." Neither could Elizabeth. One disadvantage of setting up house in London with Tom was not seeing Sam very often. She'd developed a big soft spot for the ten-year-old. "Anything else?" Antonia asked.

"I need to eat. I've eaten everything we brought with us, except your blood bags, and I don't much fancy liquid dinner. Let's try out the Barley Mow. Wouldn't mind the walk either. I've been glued to this chair all afternoon." She pushed back the chair and shut down the computer. "Want to come?"

"For the company?"

"So we can both order large, rare steaks for me."

The Barley Mow was pretty much as Dixie had described it—an old, tile-hung building with low ceilings, beams, and horse brasses all over the place and a wide, now empty inglenook fireplace. The bar filled one corner, the menu was written on a blackboard in neat handwriting, and a well built man with salt and pepper hair polished glasses behind the bar.

"Evening," he said, nodding in their direction. "What can I get for you ladies?"

"Are you Alf?" Elizabeth asked.

"Right you are." He inclined his head and smiled. "You have the advantage of me there."

"I'm Elizabeth Connor." She held out her hand. "Dixie LePage told me about this pub."

His rosy face broke into a grin. "Well, I never! You'd be American, too, I gather."

"Oh, yes." Might as well get that straight. "Dixie said to say hi and told me you'd have something great for dinner."

He gave her a questioning glance. "You ladies wouldn't be more vegetarians, would you?"

Little did Alf dream . . . "No way."

"I'm not either." Antonia obviously decided it was time to chip in. "I'm Antonia Stonewright. I just bought the house from Dixie."

Alf reached over and shook her hand. "Well, I never. So you're the two ladies opening the souvenir and gift shop."

She sensed Antonia's wince. "A craft gallery. We're still getting organized."

Alf chuckled. "That old place has been needing work since the 1960s. Dixie cleaned it up a bit, and there was a new roof put on back in the spring, and of course, you'd be the one having the painting done these past weeks. Well, welcome to Bringham, and what can I get you ladies?"

"How about a nice steak?" Might as well get it clear right off that she was a definite carnivore.

"We've got a nice Porterhouse or, if you want something smaller, a nice fillet."

"I think I'll have the fillet. Rare." Elizabeth carefully pronounced it fill-it like Alf did. "And . . ."—she eyed the board on the wall—"how about a side salad and a jacket potato?"

"Right you are." Alf turned to Antonia, "And what about you, madam?"

"The same."

He called the order back to someone through the open hatch and turned back to take their drink orders. He seemed disappointed that they only wanted sparkling water, encouraging them to pick a bottle of wine. "We've a nice line in California wine you might be interested in."

If he'd offered Oregon wine, Elizabeth might have been tempted, but it really wasn't worth the heaviness in her head that resulted from drinking alcohol. "Maldon water will be fine."

Taking their glasses, they settled in a corner table by the empty fireplace, nodding to an old man sitting on the opposite side of the inglenook. He sat deep in a wing chair and looked as if he inhabited the spot permanently. In front of him was a half-empty tankard of beer and an open packet of crisps. At his feet lay a shaggy black spaniel that raised its head and growled softly as they passed.

"Easy, Parsnip, easy," he said, patting her head to calm her. "It's just two ladies. Nothing to get het up about." He looked up, returned their "good evening," and gave his attention to his crisps and beer.

Antonia took a sip of her water before setting the glass down on the polished tabletop. "Can't see the point, paying through the nose just to get bubbles in it."

"It's called fitting in. Something Tom has lectured me about endlessly. It's most unchic to drink tap water these days."

"I know, I know. I paid a ridiculous amount every month to get twenty liter tanks of drinking water delivered to the gallery in York. But one has to cater to them, after all."

By them, Antonia meant mortals. Sheesh, vamps could be terrible snobs at times. "They have their uses though, don't they?" She couldn't resist the jab. "Like a certain potter?"

"Behave yourself, or I won't share my dinner with you."

Elizabeth grinned "What are you going to do with it then? Feed it to Parsnip here?"

Antonia cackled. Several customers looked their way, curious but not altogether interested, and returned to their drinks and conversation. "So much for being unobtrusive. Ghoul, you're a disturbing influence."

"Sorry about that." Big lie really. Antonia needed to laugh once in a while. She was too damn serious about everything. "Tell me more about the potter."

"His work is good. Very good. I'm not sure I totally convinced him we'd be a good outlet for it, but I'm not giving up. Having his stuff and those incredible cushions from Judy, the vicar's daughter, will start us off with quality articles. Set the standard, so to speak. My one dread is having all sorts of handicraft nuts wanting us to sell their crocheted loo roll covers or candlesticks made from wooden cotton reels."

No point in telling her cotton thread now came on plastic reels. "I think you can handle that, Antonia. We just need to accept work slowly. We ought to talk to Emma, sound out her interest in taking over the tearoom once it's finished. How long do you think that will take?"

"Judging by the work on the gallery in York—twice as long as the contractor estimates. Demolition is the easy bit. Once that's done and everything cleared away, then comes the slow work. We'll open without it and hope to have it done by October or November. We also need to decide what to do with the garden. We have to find space for a car park, and a picnic area with tables might be a good idea."

Elizabeth had definite plans for one particular part of the garden, but she'd pick her moment to share them. "We still need internet connection. Once we get that, I can set up the web site."

"You'll see to that?"

"You bet! I'll start on it tomorrow." Would be nice to get connected. Would be even nicer to have Tom here to work with her. She was already missing him, and it hadn't even been twenty-four hours. Vamps did really get a hold on one. "I might need to talk to Tom about it . . ."

Antonia let out a deep chuckle. "Missing him already, are you? I thought you wanted time on your own to put space between you?"

"I thought so too."

Antonia must have inferred more than she'd intended. "If he means that much to you, why did you ever leave him?"

Darn good question. She took a drink of the sparkling water. "When I'm with him, I feel as if I'm being absorbed into him. I can't describe it. We make love and I'm utterly content, but then I yearn to be single, alone and self-sufficient again. And when I'm on my own, like now, I miss him like hell."

Antonia's mouth twisted at one corner in a wry smile. "I think it's called being in love."

"I'm sure of it! Just never thought it would be this complicated."

"Oh, it is, Elizabeth. It is." She grinned. "But at least you have a good man. He might drive you batty, but he'll never be unfaithful."

Did Antonia still hurt? Obviously! Dumb question. Good thing she'd kept that thought to herself. "If he were, I'd cut the offending part off."

"Doesn't work with a vamp. It just grows back."

Elizabeth spluttered expensive bottle water down her nose. Most undignified, but when she wiped her eyes with the napkin Antonia handed her and had her breath back, she asked, "You are speaking from experience?"

"Oh, yes! When I caught Etienne with that floozy, I grabbed his own knife from the bedside table and amputated. If he'd just been feeding, I'd not have given it a second thought, but he was going beyond the bounds of mere sustenance."

Didn't pay to wrong a vamp. Not that she planned to any time soon. But she had to ask . . . "Didn't he fight you?" She could just imagine two angry vamps locked in combat, one hell-bent on revenge, the other defending his manhood—literally!

"He tried, but it was approaching dawn, and he was half asleep—he's different from us—his bloodline sleeps during the day. Plus, I'm several centuries older and much, much stronger." She paused to sip her drink. "I don't think he's ever forgotten or forgiven."

"I met him, remember?"

"And Tom had a fit, if I've heard rightly."

"He didn't need to. Frankly, the smooth, smarmy sort doesn't appeal." Not that anyone did, not that now she had Tom.

"Not to me now either, but . . ." She shrugged. "I was

younger then. Amazing what a century or so can teach you."
She looked up, and Elizabeth followed her gaze. A young
black woman with a shaved head and a silver barbell through
one eyebrow stood by their table, a plate in each hand.
"You're the ladies who ordered fillet steaks?" She set the
plates on the table and reached into a pocket of her apron for
cutlery rolled in linen napkins and salt and pepper. "Anything
else I can get you? Worcester? HP Sauce? Ketchup?"

It was hard to think of a reply with the heady aromas of
meat fogging her brain, but Elizabeth managed, "No, thanks.
This is great." Barely registering Antonia's, "Thank you, this
looks lovely." A lie if ever there was one.

"Right you are then. I'm Vickie; let me know if you want
pudding later."

She'd barely stepped away before Elizabeth grabbed her
knife and fork and attacked the steak, cutting it into eight
pieces and swallowing three of them right away. It was good
and nicely bloody. The edge off her hunger, she ate the rest
at something more approaching human speed before looking
up at Antonia, who was watching with open fascination.

"Amazing," she said. "It still smells much as it always
did, but I honestly can't remember what cow or bull tastes
like. It's been so long."

"You miss it?" Tom claimed he didn't miss eating solid
food, but Stella unashamedly hankered after chocolate chip
cookies and rocky road ice cream.

Antonia shook her head. "Not really. I don't remember
mortal food ever giving quite the same pleasure as warm
blood from a willing vein."

And if she were still mortal, that would have put her off
the rest of her dinner! As it was, the immediate interest their
entry stirred had settled, and everyone was back to playing
darts or watching snooker on the TV. Elizabeth reached over,
stabbed her fork into Antonia's steak, and shifted it to her
own plate.

Her movement caught Parsnip's attention. The dog sat up and cocked her head expectantly. Her pink tongue lolling to one side, presumably to give the impression of being half-starved. Her sleek coat and plump body made a lie of the attempt.

"Oh, Parsnip! Give over!" her owner said. "Leave them alone. Sorry," he went on to Elizabeth. "She can be a right pest if you let her."

"She is beautiful though." Elizabeth put down her fork and stroked Parsnip's sleek head. "Mind if I give her just a taste?"

"Spoil her you will but . . ." A smile creased the wrinkled face. "She'll love you for it, but mind you, she'll never forget. She'll expect it every time she sees you."

"I can spare a mouthful. Here, Parsnip."

Elizabeth cut off part of the fringe of fat and offered it. Parsnip took it, her dark eyes gleaming as she wolfed it down.

"That's enough, Parsnip; you lie down now." With the closest thing to a canine sigh, Parsnip lay down, resting her nose on her owner's boots.

Elizabeth took care of the rest of the steak.

"You'd better stock up at a local butcher," Antonia said. "You'll literally eat all our profits if we come here for three meals a day."

Good point. "I intended to today, but after I had such an odd experience when I picked up the car, I wanted to come back and think about it."

"What happened?"

Elizabeth gave her the gist of her conversation with Ida.

"She might just be cautious. I bet they had the place over-run with reporters last year."

"She knew I wasn't a reporter. I mentioned Dixie and you buying the house. Heck, I called a couple of weeks ago to book the car. It was as if . . ." she paused, "she was scared.

Afraid. Though why she should be afraid of me, I don't know."

"She no doubt has her reasons."

Antonia was right but . . . "I know. It's just . . ."

"You'd counted on her for introduction to the coven."

Elizabeth nodded. "I know you lot don't really understand, but I want to meet fellow witches. Meg Merchant and her coven welcomed me once she got over Tom being a vampire. She invited us into her home. The coven was small, but they joined with me in defeating Laran. It was a shared venture based on our common faith. But Ida was downright unfriendly. I could try contacting Emily Reade, the other name Dixie gave me, but I don't even know if she's still in Bringham. I need to ask around."

"Maybe the coven has completely dispersed. You might have to look further afield."

"At least you're not telling me to forget it like Tom did."

"I'm trying to be broad-minded. Also, I go back further than Tom. When I was girl, the old ways were still observed, often alongside the newfangled Christianity."

"I thought Gwyltha said the witches all moved west. You grew up in the south, right?"

"The Druids moved west, mostly into Wales, and took their magic with them, but old practices remained, and wandering Druids and Merlins kept customs going. They were chased out in the end, but Gwyltha was one at the time—she was part of an envoy sent by King Aramaugh to negotiate an agreement to fight the Saxons."

She'd learned more history hanging around with Tom and his lot than in twelve years of compulsory education, four years of college, and a couple more of grad school. "Was she always so imperious?"

Antonia nodded. "She was, but she had reason to be: she spoke for the king. Her reputation preceded her as a powerful woman. A couple of days into the negotiations, I learned

I was part of the agreement." Elizabeth waited, hoping she'd go on. "I was to be married to Aramaugh's second son."

"You agreed? Or did you have no choice?"

"I could have refused. My father, Vortax, would never have forced me into marriage; at least, I don't think he would have. I was sixteen. I had reached puberty a year earlier. I knew I was expected to marry sooner or later, and my agreement meant increased defense for my father's lands. And I was clearly informed that the union had the approval of the High King, Arthur."

"So you married King Aramaugh's son?"

Antonia nodded as she took a sip of water. "In two weeks, I was married to Bram. Less than a year later, I gave birth to twin boys." She paused, her eyes going misty as if looking back over the centuries. "They were heralded as a wondrous omen. The king's eldest son's wife was barren. My baby boys were considered the hope of the kingdom. They were less than two years old and had only been walking a few months—I still hadn't weaned them—when they were slaughtered in a Saxon raid. I tried to hide them, but a group of raiders dragged me off them and beat their brains out on the ground. Then they cut my throat, as if anything more could hurt me.

"Gwyltha drove them off. Killed a few of them, I think, and carried me off into the woods where she transformed me. She told me, when I came to, that I had the chance and the power to avenge my children and my husband. That was the first I'd heard for sure Bram was dead, but I knew in my heart he was.

"I'm sure you can imagine the havoc one new-made, vengeful vampire can wreak. Between us, Gwyltha and I and two others I never dreamed were vampires dispatched our share of Saxons to hell. For some years, they avoided that part of the coast. Declared it was invaded by evil spirits. We were next to unstoppable, impossible to slay. Driven by hate."

"Excuse me, you want pudding or something else?"

They both stared at the waitress as if she were a being from another planet talking in an alien tongue. In a way she was. Elizabeth had been transported back to fifth-century Britain, and Antonia was there with her, reliving ancient pain.

"Thanks," Elizabeth managed as the girl cleared away the plates. "We'll skip pudding tonight."

"Right you are. Brill, thanks." She grinned as she pocketed the tip Elizabeth handed her. "Hope to see you back in here again some time. Okay?"

She walked back to the kitchen, and Elizabeth hoped Antonia would continue her story. She didn't. Couldn't blame her. Elizabeth had had some nasty experiences she'd rather not dwell on, but nothing to match Antonia's horrors. She drained her glass of water in silence and had just opened her mouth to ask Antonia if she was ready to leave when a tall man lurched up to their table, grabbing the edge and knocking Antonia's water onto the floor.

Chapter 4

Elizabeth froze, for a moment unable to comprehend what was happening. Antonia reacted faster, straightening her overturned glass and looking the man in the face. "Excuse me," she began, turning toward the bar to get Alf's attention. "We need a cloth here."

"You need to get out of Bringham!" the man snarled in her face, turning his head to give Elizabeth a share of his scowl. "Get out. Go back where you came from, and stop upsetting everyone."

"Who are you?" Elizabeth managed.

"Wouldn't you like to know?" he snapped back, giving her the full benefit of the alcohol on his breath. "But I know what your lot are doing: causing trouble, bothering people. We don't need you here!"

"Come along now, John!" Alf appeared at the man's elbow as a knot of customers gathered at a discreet distance. Elizabeth could almost see their ears flapping. Whatever was going on—and she'd love to know what exactly it was—was much more interesting than darts or snooker. "You leave these ladies alone now." He met Antonia's eyes. "Sorry about this."

"I'm not!" The man called John wrenched his arm free. "Let them leave us in peace. Coming here. Stirring things up."

"I believe, sir," Antonia said in her best daughter of a chieftain voice, "you are mistaking us for someone else."

"I'm bloody well not! I heard you tell Alf you'd bought Orchard House. I know exactly who you are."

"That's enough, John Rowan," Alf took one of his arms and pulled him back. "On your way. You're not having any more to drink tonight, and you're not staying here to bother customers."

"You!" John Rowan, lunged forward and grabbed Elizabeth by the arm. Her blood stirred, and she willed her face and hands not to shift. Now was not the time to turn ghoul.

She didn't need to worry. As he lunged, Parsnip growled and sank her teeth into his calf.

He screamed, flailing his arms and completely overturning the table. Another man joined Alf, and together they pulled John away while Parsnip's owner tugged her lead. She wasn't giving up that readily. Having adopted Elizabeth as friend, she was defending her source of tidbits.

In the midst of another table overturning; a chair going flying; Parsnip's owner shouting, "Give over, Parsnip! Give over;" and Alf telling John Rowan to settle down, the door opened. A burly, gray-haired policeman came in, followed by a younger, dark-haired one.

"Spot of trouble then?" the older one asked, his quick eyes assessing the situation with a resignation born, no doubt, from experience. "Oh, John Rowan! Not you again." He stepped forward. "Come along quietly then, and we'll take you home."

The appearance of the law calmed things considerably.

John stood and scowled but left the rest of the furniture standing. The crowd dispersed, and the snooker semifinals once more became the center of attention. As the door closed behind the policemen and a still mumbling John Rowan, Alf and his helper straightened tables and chairs, and Vickie appeared with a towel and mopped up the mess.

"I'll get you each another Maldon water," she said. "On the house."

"Don't bother—" Antonia began.

"No, let me. Alf will feel guilty if I don't. Your first time here and all," she went on. "Don't know what got into John Rowan. He gets miserable and moans about everything, but I've never seen him go for anyone like that. People here don't think like him. Honest. Most are glad you're opening up the house and giving people jobs."

"Vickie, love. Go get two Maldons." Alf turned to Antonia and Elizabeth. "How about pudding? On the house. Just to show no hard feelings. So sorry about this; really, I am."

"A fresh drink would be lovely," Antonia said, "but nothing more to eat for me."

"I'll skip too, thanks," Elizabeth added. She was about to ask who exactly this John Rowan was when the younger policeman came back and headed straight to their now tidied table. "Everything alright now?" he asked. When assured that yes, it was, he nodded. "No one hurt? Either of you ladies want to press charges?"

Every eye in the bar might be looking at the TV, but Elizabeth sensed every ear flapping for their reply. Even Parsnip had picked up her head. "Of course not," Antonia replied. "He was drunk. It happens."

"He is alright, isn't he?" Elizabeth asked. "There won't be trouble over Parsnip? She was just trying to protect me."

The policeman smiled. "What? Trouble with old Parsnip?" Her ear cocked at hearing her name, and her tail thumped the carpet. "Doesn't look like a dangerous dog, does she?" He shook his head. "We'll take John home, see he doesn't cause any more trouble." He shrugged and turned to the door.

The sound of the departing car came though the open windows. Everyone deciding the entertainment really was over, the darts game resumed. Alf arrived with two fresh drinks and lingered, repeating his apologies and assuring them that John Rowan did not speak for Bringham.

"Any idea why he feels so anti us?" Antonia asked.

Alf paused as if considering how much to say. "Don't rightly know exactly, but since you know Dixie, you heard about the trouble here last year?"

They both nodded.

"Dixie mentioned about the arrest and the bombing," Antonia said. "Rather upset she was as she felt that prevented her selling or letting the house. She was pretty open about it and gave me a very good price. Seems a shame as property in this part of the country usually goes for much more."

Alf picked up. "You're right there. Now, I'm not one to gossip, but after what just happened, seems you have a right to know. John Rowan has had brushes with the law over the years, and he and his wife were among a half dozen or so that Sebastian Caughleigh named as accomplices. They got questioned by the police and let go. Nothing in it. Caughleigh was bonkers. Killed my helper Vernon—that much they did prove—and maybe more, but he did confess, and seems he most likely did do in the old ladies, Dixie's aunts. Mind you, he claimed he killed Dixie too, and she's still alive and well, right?"

They both nodded. Dixie was well and happy, if not exactly "alive."

"No doubt your coming wound John up. Half the crowd in here were talking about your plans for Orchard House.

Must have touched off a sore spot if you ask me. It's not like him really—he's more sneaky than confrontational—and I'll see it never happens again. You have my word."

He ambled back to his position behind the bar, and a few minutes later, Antonia asked Elizabeth, "Ready? Perhaps you should leave before you risk ghouling everyone."

"I'm okay, but yes, let's go." Elizabeth paused to pat Parsnip on the head. Her owner nodded and smiled over his beer. "She's a good dog," Elizabeth said, half to herself.

"That she is," he replied. "She knows her friends and the other sort." He looked up at her with eyes milky with age. "There's some in this village would rather things were as they were before. Better watch for them, ladies. Good night."

The evening air was fresh and welcome. "I'm glad we walked," Antonia said. "I'll walk back with you, and then I'm going for a run."

Elizabeth could make an educated guess about exactly where Antonia was going to run. "What do you think that old man meant? Talk about ancient inhabitants uttering cryptic warnings. Like something out of a gothic novel."

"I think," Antonia replied as they set off down the lane, "it was an expansion of what Alf told us. The chap had to have heard."

"You mean that John whatever his name was was one of Sebastian's bunch?"

"John Rowan was his name, and yes, that's exactly what I think. Might be worth keeping our ears open for mention of him and his wife Mildred. Never hurts to be careful."

"Might be worth giving Dixie a call. See if she remembers the name."

"A little project for you while I hunt."

"It's hardly hunting when you already know what you're after."

"It's always hunting, Elizabeth."

Not entirely. She'd learned that much from firsthand experience. "It's not always hunting. It can be seduction."

With Antonia off hunting, Elizabeth stayed in Orchard House, wandering through the echoing rooms, absorbing the voices and spirits. There was evil and unkindness here—that she sensed, even without knowing all Dixie told her—but under that was more: happiness, births, love, tears and loss, all part of the fabric of the house and its inhabitants. In the kitchen, she sensed the most. "Must be five, six hundred years old," the architect commented on one of his early visits. "They tacked the house onto an old farmhouse, I imagine."

The age of everything was hard to conceive. The "new" part was "only" a couple of hundred years old or so. Life in the older part seemed to reach back forever: the air full of mysteries, sorrow and happiness, and comings and goings.

And Antonia and she were about to add another layer.

Brushing aside her reverie, Elizabeth dug into her pocket book for her phone and speed dialed Dixie. She wouldn't talk long given the absurd rates for transatlantic mobile calls. She got Dixie's voice mail at home before she remembered the five-hour time difference. At the shop, Dixie answered with her still unmistakable southern accent. "Vampire Emporium."

"It's Elizabeth. Can you talk?"

"Elizabeth? You bet. Hang on."

A clink of the phone being put down, a pause, and . . . "Okay now. Just locked the door and turned the sign to 'Closed.' We can talk now."

"Didn't mean you to close the shop!"

"It was empty, and besides, I could do with a chat. Christopher is off on a buying trip for a few days. When he gets back, there will be a bunch of new stock arriving, so here goes. How are things in Bringham?"

How were they? At the price this was per minute, better get to the point. "Fine, busy but looks good so far. Antonia's already recruiting craftspeople, but I really called because . . . Did you ever, over here, come across a John Rowan or his wife, Mildred."

"No." She sounded pretty sure. "Did they say they knew me?"

"Not exactly." She gave Dixie an abbreviated version of what had happened.

"Odd." In the ensuing quiet, Elizabeth almost heard Dixie thinking. She certainly pictured the crease between her eyebrows. "When you meet Ida Collins, ask her."

Another explanation needed. "Brush-off is a polite word for her reaction."

"I tell you, Elizabeth, I don't know, but I'd be leery. Sounds as though either that coven has disbanded, or they don't want a soul to know they haven't. You could try talking to Emily, but I always found Ida more willing to chat." She was quiet for a moment. "Was he really threatening?"

"He meant to be, but really, how much can one mortal threaten a ghoul and a vampire?"

"Don't underestimate that lot. They almost finished off Christopher. Even if Sebastian is out of the way, there's the rest of them. I'd be careful. Where's Antonia?"

"Out alley catting with a potter she fancies."

"Oh Lordy, do tell."

Elizabeth told. Chatting was good, and after hanging up much later than she'd intended, she called Tom to reassure him that she was fine but omitted mention of John Rowan. His threats might not gel with Tom's definition of fine, and she promised that yes, she would get the train back on Friday for the weekend.

It was only after she hung up that she remembered what she'd intended to do once Antonia was out of the way.

She rummaged through her bags until she found a dark blue silk pouch. Unrolling it, she took out a beeswax candle and from another bag, a small bottle of scented oil. She'd prepared it herself a few days earlier, dropping cinnamon, patchouli, frankincense, and juniper into grapeseed oil. Taking bottle, candle, and a box of matches, she walked out to the garden.

Old outbuildings and roofless stables were hardly the setting she sought. She walked round the back of the house, pausing where the lights from the kitchen windows threw irregular rectangles on the newly mown grass.

Sitting cross-legged, she anointed the sides of the candle with the oil; scraped out a small hollow to help the candle stand upright in the grass; and striking a match, lit the wick. It sputtered and flickered in the night breeze but soon burned steadily. As Elizabeth focused on the light beam in the dark garden, she prayed for success of their venture, and as she sat there at peace in the quiet, she added a prayer for Tom's safety.

After a few minutes of calm, the flame sputtered out in a sudden breeze. Gathering everything together, Elizabeth stood up. And realized she wasn't alone. Eight, ten feet away was a dark shape. A large dog. A very large dog. For a second, she thought of wolves but reminded herself this was the Home Counties, not the wilds, and hadn't wolves been extinct in the British Isles since the Middle Ages?

Was it a dog? It moved as she did, turned away, moving soundlessly like a cat, until with a leap, it bounded over the low hedge that separated the lawns from the rose gardens and disappeared into the night.

So much for local fauna. Odd. Had to be a trick of the light, magnifying an ordinary household cat into an extraordinarily graceful creature the size of a Labrador. She hesitated a moment or two, the July night tempting her to explore the gardens further. She still hadn't seen the magic garden, but the night was dark and the light from the house only penetrated so far. Too bad she hadn't brought a flashlight.

Might as well go down to the hotel, take a shower, and curl up in bed with a book. She had the latest Anita Burgh sitting in her suitcase.

Antonia ran through the night, down the lane and toward the common. Fast as she ran, she'd be just a blur to mortal eyes, if anyone happened to be peering out their windows or wandering home from the Barley Mow. Knowing the way, she kept up speed as the lane narrowed, heading onward, driven by hunger and a deep, burning need to see Michael Langton again. Nutty really, that. She was far too old to view a mortal as more than a pleasant source of sustenance and intimacy, but there was something about his dark eyes and that little twisted smile.

Maybe she'd make him smile in his sleep.

If he was asleep.

If he wasn't, she'd be patient. Something told her Michael Langton's dreams would be worth waiting for.

As she approached the last curve in the lane and the footbridge over the stream, she slowed to almost mortal speed. His van was still parked under the trees, and every light was out in both house and workshop. He was the hardworking early to bed and early to rise sort.

She jumped the river just for the heck of it and covered the last few meters in seconds. At the door she hesitated, listening, then slowly walked around the house, senses alert. By the time she returned to the front door, she was frowning, trying to ignore the deep and heart-stinging disappointment. He was not in. No doubt about it. There was no heartbeat.

Hardly likely he'd died since she last was here. He'd been far too healthy and hale for that. Foul play? No sign of anything untoward, but she still needed feeding. Kit had managed for years on local livestock while he lived here. Might as well follow his example.

A half mile across country brought her to a riding school. Twelve nicely groomed horses and ponies slumbered behind neat stable doors. Antonia went for the first one, calming the white mare with her voice and stroking the strong neck gently as she felt for a vein with her other hand. Not quite what she'd hoped for, but the mare's blood was rich and abundant. Taking just enough to restore her, Antonia eased away, licking the wound closed. The mare seemed contented enough, even nuzzling Antonia's shoulder and whinnying as she left. "Don't worry," Antonia whispered as the mare picked up her ears. "I might well be back some other night." Closing the door behind her, she noticed the name Madam stenciled over the doorway.

Who knew, she and Madam might get to be close acquaintances.

The night was too fine to go home. Energy and strength renewed, Antonia ran back toward the common at an easy lope. She debated taking a short cut through the grounds of a large house to her right but instead veered left across open fields. She'd gone a couple of hundred meters when she saw the animal ahead. It was the size of a large dog, but it moved with the sinuous grace of a cat. She slowed, wanting to keep her distance and not scare it. Unlikely it would hear her, but if it caught her scent . . .

It appeared not to, or perhaps the wind was in her favor. She drew closer, fascinated by the strength in the animal's shoulders and the smooth grace of its pace. Running diagonally to put distance between them, she drew level, but it seemed the creature sped up. Not that she had any trouble keeping up. It leapt a hedge; she followed easily, barely breaking her stride.

It was then the creature turned and looked her way. She

froze, watching, waiting to gauge its reaction. If it attacked, she could easily outrun it, or attack back, if need be. Seemed aggression was not on the animal's mind. He just stared, watching. *Mutual risk assessment*, Antonia thought to herself and smiled.

What the heck was it? She'd seen wolves in her youth and foxes and wildcats more recently, but this was far too large for either, and Abel help her, it was watching her. Even met her eyes. No wild creature did that voluntarily. Why? How? She wasn't exerting any power other than the ability to stay stock-still.

Turning its head both ways as if to catch the wind or her scent, the creature set off across the field at a racing pace.

Curiosity overtaking caution, Antonia followed.

Chapter 5

She had to be, in Sam's words, barking. Here she was, Antonia Stonewright, vampire; daughter of King Vortax, one of Arthur's chieftains; wife of King Aramaugh's younger son, running around in a cow pasture, following a big cat. Barking didn't even begin to describe it, but something compelled her, and in fifteen centuries, she'd learned to follow her instincts.

It was an easy pursuit.

The cat moved silently and swiftly, keeping to the shelter of the hedges unless crossing fields. Quite amazing, really, how much open countryside was so close to London. She followed him a good fifteen minutes, moving at pretty much mortal speed. The creature never looked back, just continued at the same steady pace as if stalking an invisible prey, until it disappeared.

One instant it was there, moving silently along a field of yellow mustard plants, then it was gone.

Sweet Abel! It had been a long, long time since she'd been shocked like that. Given that cats, no matter how large, were unlikely to levitate, where was it? How had it crossed

the ten or so meters to the trees so swiftly? There was nowhere else it could be concealed; Antonia ran for the fringe
of woodland. She could move faster than any cat and would
soon catch up.

Minutes later, she was through the trees and in a narrow
lane. A lane looking surprisingly like the one leading up to
Michael Langton's and no doubt similar to forty or fifty
miles of twisting thoroughfares between here and Guildford.
Looking around, she sensed life to her right and ran down
the middle of the lane. In seconds, she saw Michael's van
parked by the stream, and with a leap, she was back in the
woods. Watching. She moved forward cautiously, still in the
shelter of the trees.

Then she saw him.

Michael Langton. Standing in the wash of light from his
wide-open front door. Tall as ever. Naked apart from a pair
of jeans that looked as if they'd been pulled on in haste. The
zip was fastened, but not the metal button at the waist, and
his waistband hung open.

Sometimes, vampire sight was a questionable advantage.

Seeing Michael like this—tall, beautiful, his bare chest
gleaming in the night—underscored her earlier disappointment and her desire. Madam had not satisfied her needs one
iota.

He lifted his head as if sniffing the air, looked slowly
from side to side, then looking straight in her direction,
asked, "What are you?"

She shivered. A reaction she hadn't known in centuries.
She half-suspected she was blushing, or would be if such an
action was physiologically possible. He knew. Something.

She stepped out of the trees. Making herself move at
mortal speed. For now. "I'm vampire."

Before she had time to debate the wisdom of that bit of
foolishness, he took a step in her direction. "What?"

She moved toward him. "What are you?" His question seemed purely academic.

He smiled, his dark eyes gleaming in the moonlight. "I'm the local legend."

Another Samism, "clear as mud," came to mind. Why, oh why, had she revealed her nature? Why was she standing an arm's length from him? Why was she wanting those arms around her?

"You were here earlier," he said.

"You weren't." At this rate, it would be dawn, and they'd still be trading facile utterances.

He nodded while she tried to think of a good reason not to turn and run. Preferably back to Yorkshire. But the prospect of walking away from such a perfect specimen of maleness, warm skin, sweet muscles, and firm chest, to say nothing of the warm blood coursing through his veins, was an impossibility.

For better or worse, probably worse, Michael Langton had her mesmerized.

"Since you're here, want to come in for a cup of tea?"

She couldn't hold back the smile. "It's not my beverage of choice."

His laugh was full, rich, loaded with amusement and sheer and utter confidence. Obviously facing a vampire didn't disconcert him in the slightest. She'd no doubt be very wise to run. Fast.

She stepped forward.

"Come in then."

One look at his eyes told her he wasn't inviting her in for a quick cuppa. His whole body appeared taut with need, wanting, and arousal.

That made two of them.

"Why?"

It was the grin that convinced her. That and the feral

gleam in his dark eyes. "You tell me. Why were you here earlier?"

"I was hungry." If she was being incautious, might as well do it thoroughly.

He motioned her to enter with a graceful movement. His bare, muscular arm was covered with a sprinkling of soft, golden hair that gleamed in the light.

Antonia paused midstep, met his almost feral eyes, and smiled, her chest tightening and every nerve ending in her body thrumming with anticipation. In three good strides, she was over his threshold, turning to face him as he pulled the door closed behind him. He grinned, resting one broad shoulder against the jamb, as he folded his arms across his magnificent chest.

He was damn lucky she wasn't grabbing him by the neck and throwing him to the floor. What sort of man toyed with a vampire? Unless, of course, he thought her insane, or he was some sort of fanatic.

His weren't the eyes of a fanatic.

No fanatic had wide lips that curled at the corners, setting a dimple in his left cheek. "Fancied me for dinner, did you?"

"Just fancied you, really."

Again that glorious laugh. A rich peak of amusement, excitement, burgeoning life, and a tinge of the unknown.

What in Abel's name was she waiting for? Her gums, tingling earlier, now burned. Hunger and need stirred deep. How in Abel's name had she thought a horse would satisfy? Her mouth curled at the memory of docile Madam. This man she ached for was feral.

She stepped close, felt his living breath ruffle her hair, heard his heartbeat and the steady rhythm of lifeblood flowing. Caught the sweet scent of fresh male sweat and the restrained need that thrummed off him in waves. Need that primed her own arousal.

This was insane, but perhaps she'd been sane for far, far

too long. Strong, poised, self-possessed, always in control. Laughter rose deep in her belly, bursting in a great peal of joy as she reached out across the centimeters that separated them and touched his arm.

His hand closed over hers, meshing their fingers. If she were mortal, her heart would race and her blood pressure mount. Her heart might not pound, but her chest tightened just as if she were being laced into one of those damned corsets she'd had to wear a century or so ago.

As he lifted her hand to his mouth, she pulled away, uncertain, irritated at his assumptions. Even if they were spot on. His grip tightened, and he drew her hand upward, never taking his eyes from hers, he whispered, "Oh, yes." And brushed his lips on her knuckle.

Make that knuckles! All one hundred ninety-nine of them! Very, very slowly! His touch sent wild messages to her brain and other, far more sensitive parts. His lips seemed to burn against her skin. As he pulled her to him, she splayed her free hand on his chest to maintain space between them, but he pulled her tight, chuckling as he wrapped his arm around her, trapping her hand against the hard muscle of his chest. He smiled and brushed his lips on hers.

Sweet nights and bat wings! What was he? Who was he? And did it matter a mortal cuss?

As his mouth pressed gently, almost tentatively, her lips parted. Heat inflamed her mind as she met his kiss touch for touch, pressure for pressure, tongue to tongue, as she leaned into him.

He responded by angling his hips against hers. There was no mistaking his interest. Arousal was not the word for the iron hard cock pressing against her belly. Insane, crazed, or just plain moonstruck, his need matched hers. Oh! How they matched! She smiled under the onslaught of his mouth. As he eased the kiss, probably to catch his breath the way mortals were wont to, she reached up, pulling his head back down, mashing her lips on his, invading his mouth with her tongue, and willing his need to meet hers.

He wasn't complaining.

Not in the least!

Sliding his hands down her back, he eased under her shirt and ran his warm hands over her skin. Involuntarily, she shivered.

"Cold?" he asked, his eyes almost glazed as he pulled his lips a breathspace from hers.

"Not in the least."

He replied by unsnapping her bra and smoothing his hands up to her nape and back down to ease his fingertips inside her waistband. She had it easier—nothing but hot male skin fore and aft—and as he explored, she mirrored his actions.

"You've got cold hands," he murmured.

With good reason. "I did warn you."

"You didn't tell the half."

She might feel cold to his touch, but his warmth leeched into her bones. Heat flared between them. One hand held her still as his other eased around to cup her breast, causing her to shudder with pleasure. She felt his erection even stronger as his eager fingers found her nipple, tugging gently as it hardened with need.

Forget reason or sanity! Damn caution! Grasping his shoulders, she wrapped her legs around his waist. They were now eye to eye. His hands abandoned their caress and grasped her bottom, pulling her even closer, rubbing his erection where she wanted it most, or almost the most. She wanted his hard heat deep inside.

"Sure?" he asked. For a second, she fancied he'd read her mind. "Mean it, do you?" He rocked her against his erection. "Because I'm pretty much at the point of no return."

She was impressed. How many mortals resisted her this long? "I'm certain." She smiled. "I hope you are?"

"Hell, yes," he muttered, his voice as ragged as the jerky movements of his chest. Plastering his mouth on her, he carried her across the room. She was going backward through an open doorway, until he tipped her and they both bounced as they hit the mattress. "Got you where I need you!" he whispered. "All I need now is to have you naked."

He stood up, spreading her legs with his strong hands.

"I need more than just me being naked," she said, sitting up and reaching for his zip. He moved faster. Impossible, but it happened. Grasping her knees, he lifted her legs and, stepping back a little, pulled off her shoes and socks before wrapping a strong hand round each ankle and placing her feet on his chest.

She bent her knees, intending to push him away and reestablish who was stronger, but he took the advantage. Leaning over as her knees bent, he opened her shirt, pushing aside her bra and cupping her breasts with his hands.

Darn it! That horse had to have been doped! It was impossible that Michael was strong as she. It violated the laws of nature and reason, but nature and reason scarcely mattered as his lips closed over her breast. She let her legs sag open and cried out as his erection pressed against her.

They both had too many damn clothes on.

He was starting on her other breast when she reached for his jeans, trying to fumble with his zip. She moved to make it easier but instead, he shifted off her just enough to grab her by the waist and yank her zip down, pulling her slacks and panties down to her knees. He paused a moment, gazing down at her. She smiled. Vanity aside, she was in darn good shape . . . for her age.

"Pleased with yourself?" he asked, grinning down at her.

"Not yet. I haven't seen all I want to."

"It'll have to wait!"

As she debated the wisdom of ripping her slacks off, he bent over and breathed between her legs.

She almost left the mattress, crying out as his heated mouth covered her. It was wonderful, incredible, but not enough. Was he intending to string this out, to make her wait, to make her beg? He'd go begging!

His mouth was magnificent, but she wanted, needed more. Much more. And he knew it. Wrenching her legs apart, she ripped her slacks. That rather distracted him a bit. "What was that for? I was about to get there!"

"I'm disinclined to wait," she replied, sitting up enough to kick off the remnants of her slacks and pull off her shirt, tossing it aside.

He seemed happy to stand and watch. Extremely happy going by the convex zipper on his jeans. Tossing aside the last shreds of clothing, she leaped up and stood beside him. "You've had your eyeful. Now it's my turn. She twirled him around, tipped him back on the bed, and unzipped and yanked down his jeans faster than he had time to argue. Not that that was the least likely.

Standing back, she took her time admiring. Beautiful was not the word. His skin was a wonderful golden shade, highlighted by the tawny hair across his chest and the cluster of darker curls at his groin. Fixing her with his dark eyes, he waved his cock as if saluting and, darn his arrogance, settled his hands behind his head and grinned.

Antonia deliberately focused her entire attention on his chest. Not much of a hardship, really. She knelt between his legs as she trailed her fingertips over his chest, down to his navel and just a wee bit lower, skipping the darker curls to stroke the flat of her hand down his thighs. Sweet Abel! The man had muscles. Potting must be harder labor than she'd imagined, or the man worked out like a maniac. It had been decades, maybe centuries, since she'd encountered a mortal body this firm, this . . .

She met his eyes. "Nice," she whispered, letting her mouth twitch a little as she trailed one finger up the inside of his thigh, pausing just a hairsbreadth from his balls. "Very nice, in fact." Brushing them softly, she ran her finger up the side of his cock. "Extraordinarily nice, really."

So darn nice, it was ridiculous to prolong this any longer.

Moving fast, she straddled him. Positioning herself just a centimeter or two above the tip of his magnificent cock, she ran her hands over his chest and across his shoulders. Hard bodied was not the word. He was as firm as one of his pots warm from the kiln.

And the best part of him would be . . . she waited no longer and lowered herself. Slowly.

He let out an almost agonized sigh of sheer and utter joy. That much she read in his eyes as she tightened around him and rocked gently.

"Dear saints in heaven!" he gasped. "What in creation are you?"

"I told you!" She laughed, lifting herself just enough to ease half off him before lowering back down, all the time holding him tight. Wondrous was not the word. Magnificent was utterly inadequate. He was . . . Michael! It was the only word to describe the wonder deep in her cunt.

She murmured his name. Repeatedly. In rhythm with her body, holding his eyes with hers, not by will but by mutual desire.

As her climax rose, a distant part of her mind dimly registered that never had she known a man so strong, so virile. He was her match. Had to be something in that horse's blood that slowed her, but now was not the time to ponder that.

Sensing him peaking inside her, she leaned down, brushing her breasts against his chest and setting her lips on his skin. He smelled male, alive and horny, and for this moment in time, he was hers. Her desire surged as she eased her lips up to the base of his neck and the richness of his life pulsed against her tongue.

His arms encircled her, holding her, embracing her. Her

body sang with need, heat, desire, anticipation of the right-ness of his lifeblood, and the rising power of her climax.

She rubbed her fangs over the skin above his vein. Sensed the pulsing heat beneath them as she gently bit.

His body bucked with the power of his orgasm. Wild, gut-tural feral groans rose from deep in his gut. His hand raked her back, each scratch intensifying her own climax. His hips rocked; his back reared up, and with a tremendous surge within, he rose, turning so now she was underneath. He leaned into her, the weight of their bodies digging his nails deep into her back as her fangs held tight. She was lost in sensation, drowning with sheer and utter blinding pleasure as her body rocked with his and her being absorbed the power of his mighty climax, engulfing his strength in her own soul-rending peak.

Seemed they clung to each other for an eternity, joined in the after-ripples of ecstasy, drowning in wild pleasure and the total joy of their mutual possession.

He was gasping, great breaths that expanded his strong chest and flattened her breasts between them. He was hot, damp with sweat and their bodies melded together. Joined as their minds and emotions had linked a while earlier.

Slowly, sadly, she felt him soften inside her and ease out. She bit back the whimper of disappointment. She was vam-pire. She was not showing mortal female weakness. Instead, she rolled on her side, and resting a hand on his shoulder, leaned up and licked the wound in his neck, stanching the al-ready slowing flow of blood. Just the taste of him on the tip of her tongue roused a surge of lust. Better restrain herself. She wasn't leaving him helpless.

She curled up against him, luxuriating in his closeness and maleness. Her eyelids drooped with satiation when he whispered in her ear. "You weren't kidding about the vam-pire line, were you?"

Darnation! Sweet Abel, help her! How could she have

been so indiscreet? But she had. Easy to take care of. Just take his memory away.

Her hand resting on his chest over his heart, Antonia ran her lips up his neck, pausing just long enough to appreciate the sinews and muscle under his skin, then rested her lips on his forehead and focused on the mind within. Nothing. Utter silence, like a shuttered room or a deserted landscape. Lifting her lips, she looked down at his eyes. Oh, they were intelligent alright. Hazy with the aftermath of sex, but alert, clear, contented.

Was massive brain damage possible? No, he'd barely function in that case, and Michael Langton functioned very nicely. "What are you?"

He smiled up at her, brushing the hair off her forehead. "I told you, the local legend."

Damn him! So he was the village stud, and she'd fallen for him like a simpering mortal. "Of course you are," she replied. Fast as she could move, she got out of bed and reached for the remnants of her clothing.

"Hey!" Michael said, jumping out of bed and grabbing her arm. "Where are you going?"

"Home!" Or at least the closest approximation nearby—a nice country house hotel.

"Not yet," he said. "Stay. You can't walk away like that. Not after what happened between us."

Whether she could or couldn't, she was going to. "I must go."

"Stay, and I'll cook you breakfast. You can be back home early, and no one will know you stayed out."

As if that were her prime concern! "I think at my age, my reputation can stand a late night."

"Then why go?" He was centimeters from her, not touching, but the heat of his body came at her in waves. And he was hard again. Naked women did that to mortals.

She leaned in to kiss his forehead. He moved and took her

mouth with his, cupping the back of her head with his hand. Darn it! He all but marked her—opening her lips with his, taking her tongue deep into his mouth, rekindling wild sensations deep inside her, sending shivers over her with his fingers, and leaving her mind racing and her reason fogged. But not completely.

"See?" he said, lifting his mouth off hers. "Wouldn't you rather stay?"

What she'd rather do and what she was going to do were two very different things. "I never stay."

A flash of hurt crossed his dark eyes. "Never's a very long time."

As if any mortal really understood the meaning of "a long time." But she couldn't just walk out, not after . . . not after the most incredible lovemaking she'd known in centuries, if ever. "Michael, I have to go. I just do. No reflection on you, or . . ." she paused, "what we just shared. I just don't ever stay the night."

He nodded but said nothing, as if biting back words. She discarded her ripped underwear but pulled on the two ripped halves of her slacks and looked around vainly for something to run through the loops and hold them together.

"You're not really going out like that?"

"Since I didn't bring a change of clothes, yes."

He made an exasperated sound. "Hang on. If you insist"— he rummaged in his drawers—"wear these." He handed a folded teeshirt and a pair of well-worn but clean workman's overalls. Too big by far, but unlikely to fall off. "Put them on, and I'll take you home."

"That isn't necessary."

"Put them on, dammit, and I am taking you home!" He tossed them on the rumpled bed and rested his hand on her shoulder. "Turn around."

"Ever thought of saying 'please'?"

He took a deep breath. It made his cock jerk. "Please turn around."

"Why?"

He gave a long, exasperated-sounding sigh. "I want to look at your back. I think I scratched it."

She remembered his nails raking her back, but any marks were long healed. "I'm alright."

Without asking again, he spun her round and succeeded. Hand on her shoulder holding her steady, he licked up her back, his tongue warm but rough. What shocked her most was the realization that her back *was* scratched and the scratches unhealed. She felt them close as his tongue traced them. Three, four times he licked and then brushed a couple of smaller spots.

She was hallucinating! Had to be. She was vampire. She healed on her own! How could a mere mortal do what he did?

"Better get dressed," he said, stepping away and taking his warmth with him. "Before I throw you back in bed."

He left her alone while she put on the borrowed clothes. She looked around for her discarded shoes. Stepping onto them, she noticed they were caked with mud. Hardly surprising given the fields and woods she'd crossed.

So Michael Langton was taking her home. How mortal! She had other ideas. She opened the bedroom window wide, leapt out, and, in seconds, was running at vamp speed toward the village.

Chapter 6

Antonia was comfortably perched on the roof of Orchard House cogitating on her recklessness, idiocy, and uncharacteristic unbridled lust when Michael drove up. He pulled up right in front of the wrought iron gates and got out of his van, standing in the lane and staring up at the darkened house for several minutes before climbing back in the van and pulling away to park in the shadows under the sycamore tree on the corner.

Lying in wait for her, was he? Poor chap was going to be there a long, long time. She was tempted to nip down to the hotel, change, wait until he eventually fell asleep and deposit his borrowed clothes on the passenger seat with a thank-you note. But in fairness, she really should wash them.

No! She was not thinking detergent and rinse cycles. Not with her body still humming from Michael Langton. If she could exhale to sigh, she would right now and maybe call on the heavens to restore her reason. There was just too much that didn't make sense. It wasn't possible that he was as strong as she was. It defied reason, but he had rolled her under him, and he turned her around by the strength of his arms. Good upper body strength from hauling bags of clay and hours spent turning pots didn't account for that. Her fears that something in the mare's blood had weakened her had been allayed once she tried running. She was as fast as ever—the trip home reassured her of that. Then how had he overpowered her?

She could tie her brain in knots over that one. Better make up her eternal mind how to cope with their next meeting. She looked back to where he waited, a dark figure hunched over the steering wheel. He could wait if he wanted to. She had a nice, comfortable bed down the lane.

It was the damn dawn chorus woke him. He'd have been more appreciative of the glories of the morning without the crick in the neck, the stiff legs, and sore shoulders. Michael Langton eased his cramped limbs as best he could and got out of the van to stretch properly. He hadn't slept that long. He clearly remembered the clock on the church steeple chiming three. Why he'd hung about even that long was beyond him. She must have gone home via the common and fields and across some private gardens and nipped in the back way. He'd covered the only road.

Why the bitter disappointment? Why the burning need to see her again? Why the sense of loss that she'd refused to stay the night?

He was losing it after all these years. He did not need the complication of a woman in his life. If he let her get close, sooner or later, she'd discover his other nature. He'd been stupid just telling her he was the "local legend." Silly, risky and downright idiotic—no doubt she thought he was boasting of his sexual prowess.

For two pins, he'd march up that drive, hammer on the door, and ask her.

But since he didn't have two pins, he'd get in the van and

drive home. He had a kiln to unload, if it wasn't ruined. Sooner or later, he'd run into her again. In a village this size, it wouldn't be hard. Wouldn't be hard at all. Even if he was.

"I've had it." Elizabeth ran her hand through her hair. "Don't think I can take it anymore. So much for the peace and quiet of the countryside."

"It's progress," Antonia said, her voice almost drowned out by a colossal thump outside. "Besides, it was your brilliant idea to demolish the sheds and outbuildings and add on to the old stables to make a tearoom and café."

She must have been demented! "If only it had been done when the rest was."

"The builders had to wait for planning permission."

Very true, but . . . Elizabeth shrugged. "The noise is driving me nuts. I want to check out the walled garden by daylight, and I need to run a few errands." Including another visit to Ida Collins.

Antonia looked up from the computer. "Go ahead."

She'd been a bit terse all day, brushing off Elizabeth's inquiries about the potter on the common. Obviously refreshed with new blood, she didn't look exactly renewed by the encounter. "Don't forget Stella and Sam are arriving."

A furrow appeared between Antonia's brows. "Are they coming straight here?"

"No, Stella said she'd check into the hotel and get settled. Then call us. I'll be back by then."

"Fine."

Antonia looked, and sounded, distracted. Elizabeth actually considered staying, but wanted to explore the garden.

The lawns did look different in the daylight. No sign of giant paw prints either. In the twilight, her mind must have magnified an ordinary household moggie.

She wanted to give the magic garden a good look over

and then descend on Ida again. Elizabeth pulled open the old door—might as well get the builder's men up here with oil or new hinges while they were here—and stepped into the enclosed space. Dixie had likened it to Mary finding the secret garden. Not too far off! The chamomile lawn in the center showed no signs of Dixie's deprecations with a can of kerosene. Nature had taken back hold on the entire garden. The enclosed space held an air of mystery and ancient rites, not the menace Dixie sensed. But the four mossy obelisks marking the four points of the sacred circle might have looked like granite penises, and Dixie had no knowledge of the significance of the symbols carved into the panels in the stone walls. Elizabeth trod the uneven paths, stepping over cracks and ridges. In each corner grew a tree: a mountain ash, a yew, a holly, and an oak that looked ready to lift up a huge section of the path with its roots. Sacred trees, all of them, and among the rampant growth in the unkempt beds was, Elizabeth was sure, a wondrous collection of ancient plants and herbs. If only Adela, her stepmother and mentor, could see this. But Adela was off in Oregon on a house swap, admittedly keeping on eye of Elizabeth's invalid father.

There had to be members of the coven who knew these plants and their significance. Ida was not wiggling away this time.

Elizabeth spent the better part of an hour walking the paths and examining the stone carvings. Later, she'd make rubbings and send them to Adela. How old was this place? Far older than the house for sure. The walls were gray stone, not brick like the walls around the rest of the garden. Whatever statues or images once filled the niches on the north and south walls were long gone. Where? Were the long ledges on the east and west wall altars? This was certainly a sacred space. All the more blasphemous that it had been used for intended harm. Must have been the inspiration of the Goddess that roused Dixie to save Kit.

But fascination with the garden aside, she'd better get going if she wanted to catch Ida. Just one last circuit of the old walls, and . . . but as Elizabeth paused by the western altar, she noticed a tuft of fur hanging from the wild rose that straggled over the path. She pulled the soft, yellowish fur off the thorn that snagged it. Rubbing it between her fingers, she frowned. It wasn't human hair. Wrong texture. It was some sort of animal's fur.

"I'm none too happy about all this, Justin!"

Justin smiled. Safe to do when Tom was at the other end of a phone rather than across the room. "But you let her go."

A splutter sounded interesting when distorted by fiber optics. "As if I could stop her! You know that as well as I do!"

Tom was learning. That was definite progress. Justin bit back the sarcasm. "True, and your Elizabeth has more than her fair share of common sense."

Slight pause while Justin imagined Tom nodding in acknowledgment. "That's well enough, but she's also got much more than her fair share of bullheadedness and courage. I can't get it out of my mind that she's going to barge into that crew of witches and get hurt."

"Alright, Tom; think about it. We all know about Elizabeth's power. You witnessed it yourself. Even Gwyltha was suitably awed, and we both know how much it takes to make any sort of impression on our fearless leader. That given, I doubt many can overcome Elizabeth. Bear in mind, that lot down in Bringham are hardly skilled. Their one go at magic was foiled by Dixie, who had no knowledge to counter them other than her own gut instinct. The real harm they did cause they managed by employing human agencies. Whatever the lot remaining can come up with, I bet Elizabeth can handle. Assuming there is any harm left there. Seems to me the architect of all the trouble is where he can do no harm."

"You're right." Justin could picture a little smile and a shake of Tom's head. "But I can't help worrying."

"Of course you can't, lad. You're in love. Worry comes with it—it's a package deal."

"At least I see her this weekend. She promised, and if she doesn't come back, I'll go down and fetch her."

"Stella and Sam are on their way down as we speak."

"You're not worried at them going?"

"Of course I am! But I know Stella will do nothing to endanger Sam and . . ." he paused, letting a little chuckle escape. "Having them down there, I have a perfect excuse to visit them whenever the fancy takes me . . . as do you."

Silence suggested that thought was new to Tom. "Right, we do, don't we?" He laughed. "Here I am worrying myself to hunger pangs, and no doubt she and Antonia are up to their ears in work, planning, and builders with no time to get into trouble."

Elizabeth parked in the car park in Horsley village and walked toward Collins Car Hire. Arriving unheralded when the office was empty was what she had in mind. Feeling a bit silly but telling herself it was all for a good cause, she waited at the bus stop, one eye on the timetable and the other on the Collins's forecourt.

To all intents and purposes, it looked quiet. No customers in the middle of the afternoon. A station wagon pulled out of the driveway—Monica picking the boys up from school. Ida was alone in the office.

Squelching the niggle of guilt over deliberately accosting a solitary old lady, Elizabeth crossed the road.

Ida looked up as the door opened. "Trouble with the car?" she asked.

"Not at all. The car's great. I came to talk to you."

"Oh!" Ida drew her shoulders back and looked Elizabeth in the eye. "What exactly do you need to talk to me about?"

As if they didn't both know. Elizabeth smiled. Ida didn't. "I want to make contact with other witches. Why did you deny knowing any when I asked yesterday?"

Ida paled, then flushed. A direct approach was one thing. Giving an old lady a heart attack hadn't been part of the plan. "Why would I not?" The old voice came sharp and bitter. "You are a friend of that Dixie. She brought trouble down on us."

Yeah! Right! Blame Dixie for being in Bringham and getting herself nearly killed. Skip that. "My stepmother taught me the way. I have some skill of my own but was hoping to connect with like believers while I'm living here." She paused . . . might as well fire all the ammunition in one go. "Dixie lent me her great aunts' notebooks."

Talk about attention getting! Ida was hooked. "All of them?" Her eyes positively gleamed with interest and excitement.

"Some were destroyed." Along with just about anything that could do real harm.

"Who destroyed them?" Snippy old lady, but at least she wasn't denying anything . . . yet.

"Dixie, I think. I'm not sure she knew what she had."

"She was a skeptic. An unbeliever."

That was hardly relevant right now. "She knew I studied herb lore and thought I'd be interested."

"And you follow our way?"

Trick question perhaps. She certainly wasn't into blackmail or sacrificing vampires. "I follow the Goddess's path and do harm to none."

Ida was silent a good several seconds. Outside, a car changed gear as it rounded the bend and accelerated into the distance.

A phone rang in the room behind and was picked up by the answering machine.

Elizabeth waited.

At length, Ida asked, "What do you really want from us?"

"I just want to meet other believers."

Another pause, but not quite as long this time. "There's not many of us left. We had trouble. Terrible trouble, and the coven scattered." No point in admitting she knew every single detail of the so-called "trouble." "I'll call you. After I talk to the others. You're living at Orchard House?"

"I work there." Elizabeth pulled a business card from her pocket. "I'm staying at Bringham Manor Hotel. Here's my mobile number."

The old eyes scanned the little rectangle of card. "Orchard House Center," she read. "Local arts and crafts. Special commissions undertaken." She laid the card on the counter. "So that's what all the work there has been for."

"Yes. We'll be opening early in the fall, if not before."

"Don't disturb that old house too much. There are secrets there that are better left sleeping."

After unjamming the printer for the third time, Antonia admitted her mind was not on the job. The entire compass of her perception was focused on mortal sex—or more specifically, sex with a particular mortal. For centuries, she'd been amused at mortal angst over "the night before." Now she understood what it was all about.

Not that she regretted it. Not in the least! The encounter had been incredible, and his blood rich and sweet. And she was beginning to think, addictive. She craved him. Throbbed between her legs at the thought of him and shivered as she remembered the touch of his warm, oddly rough tongue on her skin.

Shivered? Ridiculous. She was vampire. Vampires did not get goose bumps. Did not need any mere mortal. She had no reason to yearn for a pair of warm mortal arms about her. Absolutely did not need to spend time remembering the taste of his sweet blood on her tongue or the feel of his wondrous cock deep inside her.

This preoccupation was unacceptable.

She needed a break, a change of scene. Elizabeth had been right. The noise of falling buildings was a distraction. Better take a few hours off. Go into Leatherhead, talk to the newspaper, and see about a nice little bit of coverage in the local press.

With that thought in mind, she steered the van down the drive and all but collided with a red BMW turning into the gate.

Chapter 7

Antonia pulled the van hard over to the left, brakes screeching as she came to a standstill. Mortals! This one obviously harbored illusions of invincibility. Or maybe not, judging by the pale face that emerged from the open door. A bit wobbly on his pins too. Obviously didn't take close calls well.

But he made it over to where she was standing and had the grace to look worried. "Look, I'm really sorry. Never thought you'd be coming out of the gate just there."

"It is my house!"

That wasn't the answer he'd been expecting if the dropped jaw was anything to go by. "You bought it?"

If it was any business of his. "Yes, I did before I knew it was dangerous to venture out of my front gate!"

He had the grace to look embarrassed. "Sorry. I didn't do any damage, did I?"

"No." If she'd been mortal, it might have been different, but as it was . . . "No damage." Though why had he been heading for her front drive? "You were looking for me?"

He shook his head. "Looking for Jeff Wellow actually. I

heard he was working up here today." He paused. "I'm James Chadwick."

"I'm Antonia Stonewright." She offered her hand, rather regretting it when she encountered his limp handshake.

"Okay if I nip in and have a word with Jeff then?"

She didn't need vamp powers to know this Jeff was a figment of his imagination. She smiled ever so helpfully. "Might as well save yourself the bother. He left after doing some measuring, said he'd be back tomorrow early. Drop by about eight, and you might catch him." She almost laughed at the look on James's face. Nothing like hoisting someone on his own fabrications.

"Oh!" His brows creased over his pale eyes as he tried to dredge up a good comeback. "Well then, tomorrow. Early, you said?"

He did give up easily. Antonia smiled sweetly—a facial expression she'd perfected over the years and one guaranteed to rile. "Want me to watch as you reverse? You don't want to scrape your car, do you?"

Concerns over scrapes or not, she hadn't left him with much alternative. With questionable good humor, James got back in his car while she oh so solicitiously directed him out. Once his tail pipe disappeared, Antonia got back in the van. Frowning. Yes, she'd expected to encounter him sooner or later, and he'd been pretty much as Dixie described him, but what in the name of Abel the Father was he doing lurking around the house? Always assuming it hadn't been legitimate, and there really was a Jeff Wellow among the crew busy demolishing the coal bunkers and the old garage.

Now that was a thought. Unlikely. Leopards didn't change their spots, and anything James was up to had to be nefarious, but she'd put paid to whatever it was, at least for now. Time to head into Leatherhead and beard the local press.

* * *

James gave her ten minutes, then doubled back. This time, he took the narrow, unpaved lane beside Orchard House and parked twenty yards down it. He didn't even really need to go past the house. There was the door in the wall and the inevitable gaps in the old hedge. As neglected as the garden was now, he'd have no trouble getting in. But darn, the woman was sharp! Tossing back his Jeff Wellow in his face. Okay, it was a lame tale, but most would have fallen for it. Who knew the names of workmen anyway?

Miss Stonewright had a brain behind her good-looking face. James grinned. Dear Uncle would have loathed her, just as he had Dixie. James had to confess to a passing admiration. But right now, he had a gap in the hedge or the old door to find.

He found a gap first. Smaller than he'd hoped for, but he squeezed through after going back and leaving his jacket in the car. He crossed the overgrown kitchen garden and the ankle-deep grass in the orchard until he finally stood in front of the walled garden and the half-open door. Who'd been in here? The Stonewright woman? Perhaps the other one? Hell, he'd forgotten her name, if he'd ever known it. The one who had Mildred and John all up in arms.

So what? She wasn't here now. The builders were unlikely to venture this far from the work site, and he was here. Alone.

He stepped through the door and bent down to run his hands over the unkempt chamomile lawn. The scent took him back to his boyhood. Thinking about his mother yesterday had brought him back here today. He could all but feel her with him here. He was six years old again, and her hand was soft as she held his.

"There's so much to learn, Jimmie," she said. "The Misses Underwood are teaching me. That's why I come down here when you're at school. I'm going to learn all I can, and when you grow up, I'll teach you."

"Teach me what, Mummy?" he'd asked.

"The wisdom of the ancients. The old ways of power and knowledge," she'd replied. She died just a few months later.

And he'd never learned. The Underwoods were senile by the time he was old enough to be taught; the other old biddies in the coven never trusted him; and as for Uncle, all he ever shared were orders and insults.

And his mother was gone—dead—taking the lore with her.

He walked over to the closest wall, tracing his fingers across the worn carving of the Seal of Solomon. Almost hearing his mother's voice explaining that the upright point denoted fire, the downward one, water. Odd that he remembered that after all this time. Odd too that he remembered she called the five-pointed star on the next wall a Druid's foot and that the carving on the far wall was the Green Man.

There was so much here that Sebastian had ignored. James walked down the uneven paths, avoiding the center of the lawn. That incident was sure proof of ole Sebastian's insanity. Insisting they had to sacrifice a vampire, of all things, to draw his powers. Looking back it was nuts, but everyone had believed the old, crazy man and gone along with it!

So had he. To his shame. If he'd really known what Sebastian had intended with Marlowe and that cripple Vernon, would he have opposed him? That was a question that had caused a few bouts of insomnia. Okay, Marlowe got away somehow. Who believed that vampire crap? But Vernon had died in the fire, and the poor sod Marlowe had been blamed. At least Uncle Sebastian got his comeuppance.

He shook his head. And now what?

Hell if he knew! The old biddies twittered about herbs and potions. John was all up in arms about the new woman stirring up trouble, and all he, James, wanted was a quiet life. He wandered along the path, avoiding a wildly overgrown wild rose, and perched himself on one of the stone ledges. It was quiet here and utterly peaceful. He shut his eyes and tried to remember his mother's voice.

"Doing alright, Mum?"

Stella wasn't sure whether to sigh or chuckle. Sam was truly getting Britished or was it Britishised? With an "s" of course! She should be happy he'd adjusted so readily. She'd worried so about making the move from Ohio to Yorkshire, but Sam had settled in as if he'd been born in Havering. She was the one who felt the pull of home and the unease of the new.

Heaven knew why. She had a wonderful life, a husband and the lover of her dreams. And she was alive, thanks to Justin, rather than a moldering corpse. She was content. Happy. But sometimes she hankered for thin bacon that cooked up to a crisp and rocky road ice cream, and she was still unsure about driving on the "wrong" side of the road. Today wasn't too bad. Once on the motorway, you just followed the rest of the traffic hurtling south, but there had been a few occasions on deserted country roads that she'd ended up on the right-hand side until she met a lumbering tractor or an incensed motorist.

"I'm fine, Sam. Shouldn't be much longer once we get off the motorway." And then the fun would start. She had to find her way through a small town and a couple of villages. All, she just knew, full of narrow, twisting, and congested streets and roundabouts. Would she ever get used to roundabouts?

"Can't wait to get there, Mum. And, Mum, do you think Angela will like the present we've brought her?"

"Of course she will, and, Sam, try to remember to call her Elizabeth. That's her real name."

"I will, Mum. I keep forgetting. I just knew her as Angela for so long."

All of a few months or so! Stella smiled. Time was different for a kid. And a mortal. And for a kid who had vampire parents? She couldn't worry about that and drive at the same time.

"Look, Mom." Sam pointed at the road sign ahead. "Leatherhead. That's where we get off the motorway."

Once they would have "exited the freeway," but now . . . "I see, Sam." She flipped on her turn indicator and eased into the slow lane.

"Why's it called Leatherhead?"

Good question. "No idea, Sam. Maybe we can find out while we're down here."

"All the place names are odd—Leatherhead, Bringham, and what about Dorking?" He gave a dirty laugh. "Do they know what a dork is?"

"Maybe it has a different meaning here."

"I think they're just odd!"

"And Havering isn't? Or Pickering? Or Scagglethorpe?"

He wasn't quite ready to agree. "I'm used to them."

She slowed as she left the motorway and followed the directions Sam read out. So far so good. They bypassed Leatherhead, the signs agreed she was headed for Bringham, and the road was even reasonably straight. Ahead was a petrol station, just when she needed one. She pulled over, filled up; and, leaving Sam in the car, went in to pay. Just her luck, there were three people ahead of her. While she waited, she picked up a couple of Penguins for Sam—he'd become quite hooked on them. She didn't altogether blame him—chocolate cookies filled with chocolate cream and covered with chocolate were almost enough to tempt her to try a bite.

Must have been a good five minutes before she walked out, receipt and snacks in hand, just in time to see her car pull out of the petrol station.

Damn all Justin's cautions about concealing her powers before mortals! One glimpse of Sam's scared face as the car pulled away, and Stella ran. Faster than a mortal eye could register. Fast as a stolen Jaguar on a country road. Faster than a stolen Jaguar. The car had to follow the roads. She could leap hedges, cut off the curves and bends, and overtake it. Overtake and jump on the hood. The driver swerved in shock. Stella braced her knees against the windshield and reached over to open the door. The car swerved and skidded into a hedge; she kept her balance, jumped down and yanked open the door, and grabbed the driver.

He was shaking and pale. He deserved to be. She dragged him out and shook him. "How dare you! How dare you! This is my car and my kid, and don't you ever think you can do this again!"

"Mum! Mum!" Sam called. "People are coming behind us."

Damn! What now? They were, not fifty meters or so back. She threw the would-be thief over the hedge and then jumped back in the car. The keys were still in the ignition—her stupidity and carelessness. A mistake she'd never make again. It was a matter of seconds to restart the engine, back up, and drive off.

She was shaking, but knew she had to put space between them. Directions forgotten, she just drove, calling out to Sam that it was fine and he was to sit tight. She took turns, went round bends, bumped over a level crossing, and finally stopped in the entry to a field. Sam leapt over the back seat and into her arms. He was a bit too big to hug in the confines of a front seat, but they managed.

"I was so scared, Mum. He told me to sit still or he'd put my lights out, but I knew you'd come and rescue me."

She had, hadn't she? Probably injured the would-be robber, but that possibility left her completely free of guilt. He'd tried to run off with her baby. The felon deserved what he got. She hoped he'd landed in cow shit.

"Mum, hadn't we better get going?' Sam asked at last.

They had. Once she figured out exactly where she was, and . . . "Let me have a look at the car, Sammy, okay?"

"Okay." He got out with her. "Wow, Mom! You really messed it up."

"I didn't, dear; the carjacker did."

"Yeah! But it's not coming off his insurance."

Frankly, she didn't give a proverbial damn, but when she walked around, she had to concede Sam had a point. The right fender was smashed and both headlights were done for. Just as well that it was summer and light late into the evening, and she was close to getting there. At least she hoped so. She was, at a guess, five or ten miles from the crash scene and a good few more from the petrol station. If she kept to the back roads and followed signs, surely she'd get to Bringham?

They did almost an hour later after asking for directions a couple of times—her wild chase and drive had been in the opposite direction from Bringham—and being on the receiving end of several pointed comments about the state of her vehicle. She was going to have to call Justin and the insurance and get it fixed. Tomorrow. Right now, all she wanted was to get to Bringham Manor Hotel, see her friends, and hug Sam again. Tightly.

After judiciously stopping in Horsley, Effingham, and the village so as not to get too much attention over vast meat purchases and engineering a strong possibility of a meeting with the old coven, she'd done a good morning's work, Elizabeth decided.

The workers were still enthusiastically wielding picks and shovels and loading the mountain of debris onto a skip in the lane beside the house. Antonia had also given up on working through the noise and confusion according to the note on her desk.

What now? Back to the hotel to wait for Stella? First, another visit to her garden. She was thinking it was "hers," and why not? Antonia was unlikely to get proprietary about it, and once restored, it would be one more attraction for visitors.

On the other hand, did she want tourists tramping over sacred space? Good question and one for later.

The garden was as peaceful as always: birdsong and the rustle of branches were the only sounds, apart from the odd faint clunk and distant shouts as the workmen loaded up the last of the debris. She walked almost all the way down the right-hand path before she noticed the man sitting in the shade of the yew tree.

Who was he? Did other villagers use the space as their own? He was unmoving, eyes closed, at peace. She was half-tempted to retreat and leave him to his meditation, but something made her step closer. "Excuse me . . ." He opened his eyes with a start. "I'm sorry to interrupt you but . . ." But what? Do you trespass here all the time? Were you one of the lot trying to do Kit in? "Do you come here often to pray?"

He was about her age. Tired-looking. Nervous. Fair enough—she had rather jumped at him.

"No," he replied, shaking his head. His eyes were pale, and his dusty blond hair disheveled, but he was neatly dressed in slacks and a sports shirt. "No, I don't come here often," he paused. "Years ago, I used to come here with my mother."

Odd. Weren't Dixie's only relations old ladies? Deceased old ladies at that. "She lived here? In Orchard House?"

He shook his head as he stood up. "No, not here. She died when I was a child."

"Oh!" That she understood. "I see. We're going to be working in here soon, weeding, pruning, tidying up, but if you want to come in another time, just let us know, okay?"

Why the heck had she made that offer? He didn't seem vicious or dangerous. More like pathetic and helpless. "Don't wander in without asking first, okay?"

He nodded and obviously possessed enough gumption to take the hint to leave. "I'll be sure to, and thanks." He took a step away, looking around where the trees cast shadows on the lawn. "It was so different when I was little. Seemed so much bigger too. It was like a hidden world." He nodded and turned to leave.

Elizabeth made a point of following a couple of minutes later. He went out the side gate. Altogether odd she decided as she locked up the house and drove away. Strange young man—he'd seemed almost vulnerable. Or maybe she was a hopelessly soft touch.

Ten minutes later, Elizabeth pulled up in front of Bringham Manor Hotel and hadn't even turned off her engine when Sam opened the driver's door. "Hello, I'm so glad to be here. Oh, Angela! I missed you!" He clung to her, almost overbalancing her as she tried to stand.

She hugged back. Tight. In a couple of years, he'd be too macho to spare hugs for his old baby-sitter. She'd take them while she could. "Sam, it's great to see you. Your mother's here?"

"Yeah! She's checking in. We just arrived."

What perfect timing! "Had a good trip down?"

"You can't guess! Honest, you can't! Oh, Angela—I mean, Elizabeth. We got carjacked! Or rather, I did. Mum was paying for petrol, and I was reading in the back seat and—

"Hush, Sam!" Stella came running out. "We'll tell Elizabeth everything in a minute. Not now."

Obviously something she didn't want broadcast to the village. Interesting.

"Okay, Mum, but I bet she'll want to know what happened when she sees the car."

At that, she had to take a peek. Sam was right! "Sheesh! What happened?"

"Later," Stella said. "Every time I stopped to ask directions, I got comments about that. Please don't start. Help us get unloaded first."

"I've got a brilliant room," Sam said. "Next door to Mum's, and there are horses in the stables down the lane, and I can have riding lessons if I want to. We're going to have fun here. Heck . . ." he giggled. "We've already had an adventure."

"Looks as though the car had one too!"

"That," Stella said, "is the least of it. I swear I might just defy my nature and get gray hairs after today."

Now Elizabeth was itching to know about it. But if Stella wanted discretion, so be it. "Where are you getting the car fixed?"

"It can wait." She unlocked the trunk. "Give me a hand; thanks." Elizabeth grabbed one case. "Sam," Stella said, "get your books out of the front, please."

Stella and Elizabeth had made it to the glazed entryway when Sam called, "Mum! Come and see!"

Ghoul reflexes were almost as good as vampire ones. Elizabeth was only a footstep behind Stella as they raced back to the car. Sam stood by the open passenger door. Staring. "What's that, Mum?" he asked, pointing to a leather carryall on the floor.

"Hell if I know, Sam."

That earned her a sharp "Mum! you swore!" from her shocked son.

"Sorry, Sam, but it's been an afternoon and a half."

"Think the robber left it, Mum?"

Elizabeth sensed she'd missed the vital first episode. "What is going on?"

"Not too sure," Stella replied, "but I think it might help to have a look in this." She grabbed the leather bag. "Heavy." She hefted it. "Let's get it, and everything else, upstairs and have a look."

Elizabeth had to admire Stella's self-discipline. She really did make Sam wait until everything was upstairs before she locked the door and picked up the leather bag.

"Better tell Elizabeth what happened, Mum," Sam suggested.

Stella nodded and, in a few sentences, aided by Sam, explained how her car lost two headlights and mangled its front fender.

Elizabeth swallowed. "Sheesh! Weren't you scared, Sam?"

"You bet! But once I saw Mom catch us up, I knew everything was going to be alright." He grinned. "It's like having Wonder Woman for a mother."

Stella's face suggested a different interpretation of the incident. "I suppose I should worry about harming a mortal, but frankly, if Gwyltha ever starts on at me about that, she'll hear about it."

"Might be just as well to keep it under our hats," Elizabeth replied. "Whoever he was, he's hardly likely to go around telling everyone a woman overtook the car he was stealing, threw him out, and tossed him over a hedge, is he?"

"He's probably still wondering what hit him!"

Sam interrupted. "Now Elizabeth knows everything, can we look in the bag? Might be treasure."

"Could be a bomb," Elizabeth suggested.

"Please!" Stella entreated. "I get enough wild imagining from Sam; don't you add any."

"If you just open it, we won't have to imagine," Sam pointed out.

Stella pulled down the zip, and the bag fell open to reveal several cloth-wrapped bundles and a leather case. Stella picked up the case and untied the tapes. It unrolled like an old-fashioned sewing kit, but it didn't hold needles and scissors.

"What are they?" Sam asked.

"Unless I'm very much mistaken, house- and safe-breaking tools." Elizabeth replied.

"How come you know?" Stella asked.

"I once got locked out of my apartment and had to call a locksmith. He had a set of lock picks. And aren't safecrackers supposed to use stethoscopes? They do in the movies anyway."

"Hey," Sam's voice burst with excitement. "Think he really was a thief?"

"He certainly stole my car!" Stella said.

"What's this?" Elizabeth put aside the set of picks and unwrapped the first bundle.

A mass of jewelry spilled onto the bed, cut gems and metal glittering in the light.

Sam whistled.

Elizabeth and Stella just stared.

"Good heavens!" Stella managed at last.

"He was a thief!" Sam sounded jubilant that he'd been right. He reached for a glittering diamond and ruby bracelet. "Is it real?"

"One way to find out." Elizabeth picked up a diamond brooch. "Let's see if it cuts glass. Aren't diamonds supposed to?"

Diamonds did.

All three stared at the tiny cut in the corner of the bathroom window.

"It works!" Sam said.

"Yes." Stella sounded much less enthusiastic. She walked back into the bedroom and stared at the pile on the bed a moment before unrolling the second bundle. If anything, it held more than the first. "Seems we acquired someone's loot."

"What the heck are we going to do?" Elizabeth asked.

"I think we should call the cops," Sam said. "It's all stolen goods anyway."

"You're right, son, but for one little detail—how exactly am I going to explain that I ran after the car and yanked the carjacker out?"

"Shit!" Elizabeth muttered. "Sorry, Stella. Just came out."

"I've heard that word before. Lots of times," Sam replied. "I know what it means too!"

"No reason to use it," Stella told him.

"What are you going to do, Mom?"

"Call Justin."

"What do we do about all this?" Sam asked, pointing to the glittering heap on the bed.

"Cover it up," Stella said, pulling down the bedspread and doubling it over. "There, nicely hidden now. Let's go to the bar downstairs. Sam, you can get a Coke or Tizer. We'll get . . . something or other, and I'll call Justin."

"While we're at it," Elizabeth said, "I might as well call Tom. He'll hear about it anyway."

"Pity Antonia isn't here. She'd know what to do. Where is she by the way?" Stella asked.

"Off talking to the local press, and then . . . well. She might be back soon or maybe later. She has found herself a . . ." she paused, glancing sideways at Sam. "*Un bel ami.*" She wasn't sure Stella knew any French.

Sam did. "Does that mean she's got herself a fella?"

"It means you're poking into what doesn't concern you." Stella told him. "You keep your mind on stolen jewels; that should be enough to keep you busy." The ridiculousness of that statement hit her, and she and Elizabeth laughed out loud.

Chapter 8

Antonia had done what she could with the local press. A little mind nudging, and she had a promise to come and interview her and add a few photos of the house. Taking the reporter's suggestion that including names and works of a few local participants would increase readers' interest, Antonia called Judy and asked if she'd be willing to be interviewed. She'd have called Michael, but he'd been elusive over details like phone numbers.

She'd just have to visit him in person. Again.

Who was she deceiving?

It hadn't been outside noise and walls falling down that distracted her from work. It was the wild memories in her irresponsible body. Somehow, a simple need to feed had morphed into an obsession.

She'd tried. She really had. She was vampire and not susceptible to mortals no matter how bedworthy and delicious, but heading her van toward Bringham, she acknowledged the truth. She hungered for Michael Langton, and the best way to appease a hunger was to sate it.

Halfway there, she pulled over in a car park beside an olde worlde tea shop and asked herself what exactly she was doing?

Easy one that—running after a mortal. But what a mortal! In centuries, she'd never felt this way about anyone. Apart from the confusion and the bewilderment, it was an experience to savor. She grinned and chuckled aloud. Just as well there was no one around to see her. She turned on the ignition and headed for the common, and the man she couldn't get out of her mind.

He wasn't home!

Alright. She had no right to expect him to be twiddling his thumbs waiting for her. But a vamp could dream, couldn't she? The place was empty and had been for some hours. There was warmth from the kiln shed, but that was that.

Or was it?

It was broad daylight, and she was not standing in shadow. But at her age and on her native soil, why the sense of uncertainty? That was the wrong word. The air was alive, or rather, nearby there was a shifting of power. It had been centuries since she'd been aware of a change of nature. Old magic was stirring. Power was in the woods and the ground under her feet. This was what she'd sensed last night but not recognized.

Magic power. How and why?

Were those witches gathering more power than they'd ever imagined? No. This was not mortal magic. This was ancient power. She sensed it, and then it was gone. Like the passing scent of blossom on a breeze. Now there was nothing. Nothing at all.

She gave a grim smile. Michael Langton was playing with danger. Or perhaps danger was playing with him.

She spun around as she sensed life behind her, and there he was, just emerging from the woods. "You came back then."

Perceptive of him! Oh, she was getting snappy. "I don't have your phone number."

He raised an eyebrow and grinned. "How remiss of me. Good thing you knew where to find me."

Now he was getting on her nerves. "I wanted to talk to you."

"Talk?" She was tempted to turn on her heel at his arrogant, self-assured macho grin.

She didn't. Abel alone knew why not. But she was not retreating. She was vampire. Powerful. Strong, and, darn it, she was in dire physical need and tempted to throw a glamour over him and drag him indoors—or better still, not even bother with the last step. Nothing wrong with alfresco sex. "We need to talk about what you have and what I want." Abel take her! Had she actually said that?

Yes! He raised a sandy eyebrow as he took a step closer. "Vases and slipware dishes, I presume?"

It was the realization his feet were bare that did her in. This man walked the woods in bare feet! Feet she wanted, no needed, to feel against her legs. "No. Not slipware dishes or vases. I left too early last night."

His eyes gleamed. Both eyebrows lifted. "I did ask you to stay."

"My mistake."

"And mine for letting you go." Michael stepped forward. Why had he been such a fool? He should have stopped her leaving, tied her to the bed, kept her. She'd been on his mind all day, distracting him. This wild woman who joked about being a vampire! Siren more like. Soaking into his reason, leaving him obsessed with her. "I followed you home."

"I know."

"Where did you go?"

"Home—I know a fast way."

Damn the van! He should have followed her in puma

shape. "I'll remember that next time. But since you are here." He reached out and closed his hand over hers. She was so cool, but he'd have her warm and aroused before long. He could smell the need on her. This was utterly foolish. Detachment had been his path to survival all these years. But what the hell? He meshed his fingers with hers and moved in, sweeping her up in his arms and heading for the door. He nudged it open with his knee and carried her inside.

She made not the slighted protest.

Good.

If she did, he'd be hard-pressed to let her go.

That thought had him grinning. He slid her down the front of his body; might as well let her know just how hard-pressed he was.

She leaned into him, and he felt her need in every fiber of his being. This wild desire, this desperate need made no sense. It was dangerous, foolish, reckless, but he was not the only one wild with need.

He brushed the dark curls off her forehead and kissed the cool skin. "I'm going to strip you naked," he whispered, "and carry you into my bedroom, and we're going to make love until we both collapse."

Her hand closed over the button of his shorts. "Who's going to strip whom naked?"

He'd be a fool to argue. Her cool fingers flipped his shorts open and had his zip down in seconds. A shift of his hips, and his shorts were round his ankles, and he showed her exactly how glad he was to see her.

Her hand around his cock had him groaning. Time to get her naked, but as he reached for the tiny pearl buttons on her blouse, she moved.

Damn! The woman was fast, but he'd not complain. She was on her knees and brushing her lips against the tip of his cock. He took a deep breath, clasped her dark hair with his hands, threw back his head, and let out a low howl. What she did to him! Her mouth eased up the head of his cock. Sweet woman's touch against his heat as her tongue caressed and her lips enveloped him. He was close to losing control, feeling the animal in him ripple up his spine and his cat pelt rise under his human skin. Not now! No!

With a gasp, he pulled her mouth off him. He hated to shatter the moment, but he'd never loved in cat form, and wasn't about to start any time soon. Hands gently clasping her upper arms, he raised her to her feet. "The floor is hard and cold," he said, brushing his lips on hers. "I can think of a softer and warmer place for this." Not waiting for her reply, he lifted her in his arms and covered the few feet to his bedroom in seconds.

He laid her on the bed and settled astride her, just in case she had ideas of taking over again. He grinned down at her wide eyes and upturned face. "I assume this is what you had in mind?"

"I'd planned to be on top."

"Not a hope, love. You're right where I want you." He reached over and slipped open two buttons on the blouse. "And I'm keeping you here until you're too worn out"—he undid another button—"to sneak out on me again." The last button taken care of, her blouse was open to her waist. He pushed the two halves wide open.

He smiled. A nice bra, but it was in his way. Easing his hand under her back, he took care of the hooks with a flick of his fingers. The pale blue lace hung loosely around her full breasts, but not for long. It joined her blouse on the carpet. He took a few moments to stroke her heavy breasts, rubbing his thumb over her nipples until they rose hard and ready for his mouth, but he let her wait, ignoring her sighs of need as he yanked off her slacks, panties, and shoes.

Now he had her just as he'd wanted her. As he'd imagined

her all day long: Naked in his bed. Naked and hot for him. Naked and needing him, and this time she would not leave before he was ready for her to leave. Which might just be never.

Smoothing his hands up her thighs, over the voluptuous curves of her hips and her soft woman's belly, he eased his fingers over her rib cage until he cupped her luscious breasts. She smiled up at him, folded her hands behind her head, and shifted her chest to press her breasts into his hands.

Other than that, she was so still he'd have sworn she wasn't even breathing. Playing games, was she? He knew how to get her moving. He bent over, grabbed a full nipple in his lips, and teased it with his tongue before grabbing it hard with his mouth, pulling just enough to cause her to arch her back. "Please . . ."

Since she'd asked so nicely, he repeated the gesture with her other breast.

She groaned. "That's so good!"

He lifted his mouth just enough to whisper, "Yes, you are good, my love, but this is just the beginning."

He kissed a line down to her navel just to savor her sweet woman's smell, her sighs and little moans a treat to his ears. Strange she was so cool to the touch but so hot in her soul. He could smell her arousal, sweet and sexy, as he brought his mouth lower.

Her entire body responded to his tongue. He felt the shudders, the shivers, her ripples of pleasure deep in his gut. Never in his century of life had he met a woman this responsive, this sexy, this demanding. As his mouth worked her, she finally moved her arms, bringing her hands down to run her fingers through his hair and hold his head. She was strong. As strong as he was. A deep, distant part of his mind wondered what she ate or where she worked out, but the thought dissipated in the rising tide of his own need.

But he could wait. He wanted her panting and begging

first. Wanted her bonded to him so she'd never leave his bed before morning, if then.

He raised his head, and she muttered in complaint. "Patience, sweet Antonia," he said, letting a little feline growl enter his voice. "I'm not finished with you yet."

He breathed onto her wet, scented flesh, opening her with his fingertips to view the sweet secrets deep in her femininity. To savor her loveliness and relish her need, a need he was only too contented to sate.

His mouth came down as he pressed two fingers inside her, reaching deep before curving his fingertips upward, searching for her tenderest spot deep inside. And found it.

Her entire body shook at his touch, shuddered as he applied pressure and pulled on her sensitive nub with his lips. She was twisting, moaning under his touch, her shoulders and hips lifting as her body arched with her rising climax.

His heart soared with joy at the thrill of conquest. To have the woman of his dreams groaning and shuddering at his efforts was enough to make him cry out. Any sound he made was muffled by her sweet core and the soft curls that pressed against his face.

Not much longer! He sensed her growing need, her peaking desire as her cunt tightened around his fingers and her hidden flesh grew damper with passion. She gave a great scream, shouted his name to the ceiling, and with a wild thrust of her hips, she climaxed.

She was his. Almost! While she still shook and gasped with the after-ripples of her climax, he knelt up, opening her legs farther. Smiling at the view of her now rosy cunt and holding her steady, he pressed in deep.

She gasped, crying out it was too much, too soon. She had to wait, and she needed more, much, much more. She wanted him deeper. She could not stand it. It was marvelous. He was marvelous. She could never get enough of her magnificent lover. He drove deeper, working his cock inside her until he could barely contain himself. She reached out, grabbing his arms, begging for more and harder. Her hair was tousled, her eyes misty with heat and passion, and her face flushed with pleasure,

It was his turn to cry out, drawn into her joy as his climax heightened. As the wild after-ripples of her climax caressed his cock and the sweet shudders eased, her muscles tightened, drawing him deeper into her core, pulling him along with her reawakening need. As her body thrashed under his grip, he let his own passion rise and burst.

Wild cascades of pleasure flooded his mind and soul. His entire being and reason focused on the incredible woman under him, the superb, passionate creature who now locked her legs around his back and drew him even deeper. As he sagged, he braced his arms to hold himself off her, but she wrapped her arms around him and pulled him down onto her.

"I want you close," she told him. "I want to feel you deep inside me. I want your body on mine. Your weight on top of me. Your heat within, and your wonderful, hard cock touching my heart."

"I'll stay right here," he told her. "With me on top like this, you can't go anywhere." But he couldn't. Not for long. She was strong, but he'd crush her. Not that she was complaining, and as long as she was content, so was he.

Might have been ten minutes, twenty, thirty, an hour, ten hours. He lost touch with time, but slowly, as his erection subsided, he slipped out of her, and at her muttered and sated complaint, whispered, "I'm not going anywhere, and neither are you."

She didn't argue. Definite progress! To keep her with him, he reached down for the duvet and pulled it over them. She nestled close and said his name. His heart fluttered at the sexy way she whispered into his chest, but as they lay together in a loving tangle of legs, arms, and hands, he realized she wasn't even warm. She should be sweaty and hot after their decidedly athletic sex. Instead, she was as cool as ever.

She also had no heartbeat.

Impossible! He snuggled closer, resting his head between her breasts. What he'd missed in the frenzy of his driving passion was all too apparent—either he was losing his hearing, or she kept her heart somewhere other than beneath her left breast!

His mind was trying to work its way around that impossibility when he heard her whispered, "You are incredible, Michael. I really am tempted to stay the night."

He leaned up and stared her in her eyes. "Tempted?"

"Yes," she agreed, "very tempted."

"I thought staying the night was part of the agreement."

"If I do, it will be the first occasion in a very long time."

"Time to do it right then, Antonia, my love."

She smiled up at him, her face flushed and her beautiful blue eyes misty with sated passion. She still hadn't agreed, but she was close, but first . . . "You're staying, dear. You know you are, but please, darling, tell me, what are you?"

If she'd had a functioning heart, it would have stopped there and then! Antonia looked into his dark eyes, deep with question, and the face of the lover who'd just taken her to ecstasy and back. A face that would pale with shock at the bald truth. Or would he? She might not be mortal, but he was more than he was revealing. Might as well play for a little time and string him along a bit. "What do you mean? I'm an art gallery director trying a new business venture."

He gave a snort of disgust. "A gallery director? Hm-m-m?" He raised one of those sexy eyebrows, but this time, it alerted every survival instinct she'd honed in her fifteen centuries of existence. "Why do you have no heartbeat then?"

Damn! She should have made it thump a few times in his ear. She had the strength and power to, but had been too caught up in the heat of her needs. "What do you mean?"

"Don't toy with me, Antonia. Your heart doesn't beat." He rested his hands on her left breast. "Nothing." A bit too late to fake it, but how the hell had he noticed? "You don't even sweat, my love. What are you?"

"Talking of heartbeats—Why is yours so slow? After athletic sex, yours is slower than any mortal's resting heart rate. What are you?" Attack wasn't the best defense, but his shock gave her time to think.

She should run—flee and never come back. But she couldn't leave him, not after the love they'd shared. Sometimes being a woman really got in the way of being vampire. "What are you, Michael Langton? And don't fob me off with the "local legend" balderdash. As far as the village is concerned, you are the reclusive potter out on the common, not the local Don Juan."

He threw her a look of utter hurt. Maybe Don Juan was unfair, but he had claimed to be the local stud. "Are you sure you really want to know what I am? I don't think you do."

She sat up at that. "How, by Abel, do you know what I want?"

His mouth curled in a sexy, lopsided grin. "Haven't managed too badly so far, have I?"

"Stop trying to distract me with sex. You started this 'what are you?' business. It's not a good idea." Time for a little vamp glamour. "You don't want to know, Michael; you really, really don't. It's best not to ask these things."

His eyes flashed. Sparks of light in the depths of dark brown. "Who are you trying to fool?"

She felt her jaw drop. And immediately closed her mouth. He was something more than mortal. No one had ever resisted her mind control. He stood up, magnificent in his maleness—their current debate had not lessened his interest in her one little bit. "So, Antonia whatever in heaven you are, you want to know what I am, do you?"

He threw his head back, let out a low howl from deep in his throat. The air around them vibrated, sizzled with power. She knew it for magic, remembered it from her mortal days when the remnants of the Druids still summoned their waning power. Just as she recognized the sizzle in the air for what it was, Michael shifted. Like waves washing across a beach, power rippled through him: his back arched; his face changed; golden pelt rippled over his skin, and in minutes, her lover was gone, and a large wildcat stood beside the bed, fixing her with his dark eyes.

It was the eyes that all but did her in. They were human eyes, dark, intelligent, the same eyes that had met hers as Michael brought her to pleasure.

What she had just witnessed was as impossible as vampires.

She reached over and tentatively stroked the smooth fur on his raised head. "Alright, Michael, you showed me. Now it's my turn." He pressed his muzzle against her hand, butting it away, and shook his head. "You want me to wait?" Tricky this, if he couldn't speak in animal shape.

Lifting his head, he rose up on his hind legs and shifted back, taking longer than before and grabbing the side of the bed as he finally regained man form.

She reached out to steady him. "Are you alright?"

"Yes."

The exhaustion in his voice made a liar of him, but she kept her opinion to herself. "Better get back in bed then."

He smiled. An emotion that looked strangely like relief flickered across his face. "You don't mind sharing your bed with an animal?"

So he doubted her, did he? "Since it's your bed, come on in." He darn well needed to. He was wobbling. She grabbed his hand and yanked him close. Seemed he was too weak to resist as she jumped out of bed and all but lifted him back in, pulling the covers over as she nipped in beside him. "Don't you dare tell me you're fine, Michael; I can see you're not!"

"I'm weak, that's all. I don't usually change back and forth like that."

He'd only done it because she'd insisted. "Well, you made your point. Shift often, do you?"

"When the need to run free consumes me or"—he wrapped his arm around her chest—"when I need to confront a pushy woman with reality."

And that last, she suspected, rarely, if ever, happened. At a hunch, most mortal women would run screaming into the night. She was not mortal. She leaned into him, catching now the animal scent that had first drawn her to him.

Now it was her turn. He'd trusted her with his secret. "You confronted and convinced me. I've got a few questions like full moons and so forth, but you want to know what I am."

"Yeah, I do," he agreed, fatigue shading his voice. "The full moon business is an old wives' tale. I shift when I want to. Now, what are you?"

"I'm a vampire, Michael."

His eyes widened as he let out a slow whistle. Incredulity, shock, disbelief, and then utter shock, such truly mortal emotions, crossed his handsome face as his human mind processed three, ultimately relationship-shattering words.

"A vampire!"

She nodded.

He was silent for five of his slow heartbeats, then let out a quiet whistle. "You weren't kidding last night, were you? Would be a bit trite to say something about not realizing they were real, wouldn't it?"

"Yes, it would."

"Won't do it then." He exhaled with a long, weary sigh. "What about shifters? Did you believe in them?"

She nodded. "Yes. I encountered one once. A while back."

He perked up at that. "How long ago?"

"About a thousand years."

More amazement. He was really so easy to read. "You're older than a thousand years." She nodded. "How much older?"

"I born in the early part of the fifth century."

Another slow whistle. They really were quite sexy now that she came to consider it. "So I've really picked an older woman."

"'Fraid so. Does it bother you?"

"If me going furry when the mood takes me doesn't bother you, I can handle an older woman. An older dead woman."

Better put him straight there. "I'm not dead. I'm a revenant. I live beyond death."

"Okay . . ." She suspected it wasn't but let him go on. "So you're a vampire. Any more of them around?"

"Not locally."

"But others who aren't local?"

Sticky this but . . . "I'm not the only one in England, let's put it that way."

He accepted that. At least for now. "What about your assistant? The pretty, blond one with the long hair?"

When had he seen Elizabeth? "What about her?"

"She's not a vampire?"

"No, she's not." This was not the time to discuss ghoulishness.

"But she knows you are?"

Lucky guess perhaps. "That's between us; how do you know about her?"

He gave a lopsided smile. "I saw her one evening as I was taking a feline stroll through your grounds. She was sitting on the grass and very quiet. I think she was praying."

She was? What the heck. She had more important things

on her mind than Elizabeth's nocturnal devotions. "Her religion is rather nature based by today's customs."

"A tree hugger eh?"

"I don't think she'd appreciate the description. Besides, what's she doing in bed with us?"

"Beats me."

For all his nonchalance, his exhaustion would have been evident even to a mortal. To her eyes, he approached collapse. She drew him close, resting his head on her breast. "You need to rest. We can talk later." A long, long conversation.

"Can't sleep, love. I've got to watch a kiln."

Damn kilns, but they were his livelihood. "You haven't been watching it the past few hours."

He chuckled. "Damn right there!" He lifted his head to glance at the clock by the bed. "I've got to turn off the kiln in a couple of hours."

She knew very little—alright nothing—about shapeshifter recovery, but at a guess, he'd be out cold in a couple of hours. "Sleep," she suggested. "I'll wake you in two hours."

He pondered her offer for all of ten seconds. "I knew there was a reason why I loved you. Two hours, promise? If I leave them, they'll be ruined."

"You have the word of an ancient vampire."

He accepted it.

He was asleep in her arms in minutes, his slow heartbeat reverberating against her silent chest. She eased him onto the pillows and settled the duvet around him.

Talk about hormones taking over! She should be long past all that mortal frailty, but she obviously wasn't. Now she'd exposed herself, risked the colony, and maybe put Elizabeth in danger, and drat! Stella and Sam were due to arrive any minute. What about them?

And what about Michael and her?

What about them? He was sleeping the restful, sound

sleep of a shapeshifter. She choked back a wry laugh. The local legend indeed!

There was a computer in the other room. Maybe she'd borrow it. She needed to research Michael a bit.

Chapter 9

"Where's Antonia?" Stella asked. Elizabeth shrugged, casting a glance in Sam's direction. Stella got the message. Antonia's whereabouts were less pressing than stolen jewelry.

Dixie was right. Life in Bringham was anything but dull.

Elizabeth's phone buzzed the *Pink Panther* theme. She flipped it open and after a very brief, "Hi. Okay. Yes, we will." snapped it shut. "That was Tom. Seems Justin is on his way there. Transmogrifying because it's not yet dark. They'll come down together. We're to 'sit tight' and 'do nothing' until they get here."

Elizabeth obviously enjoyed "sitting tight" as much as she did. "Any idea when they'll arrive?" Stella asked.

"It'll be a while yet. Justin's going to have to feed when he arrives, I imagine. Then they have a drive down in Friday evening traffic. Could be ages."

"Meanwhile, we're sitting on a fortune of someone's stolen loot."

"We could watch the news and see if anything is reported stolen," Sam suggested.

"You're a smart kid," Elizabeth said. "It might give us some clue." But it didn't take long to discover Bringham Manor Hotel didn't get satellite news.

"If we had a police scanner, we could listen in," Sam suggested.

"I don't think your mother remembered to pack one," Elizabeth said with a bit of a smile. "I know I forgot to."

"I was just suggesting," he replied, a hint of affront in his voice. "Tell you one thing though," he went on. "Two things actually: I'm getting hungry, and I bet you, Elizabeth needs to feed. Why don't we get dinner now? Two of us can cover for Mum not eating, but I doubt we can cover for three vampires."

"Good point, son," Stella said. "What's the second one?"

"We can get a map and try to figure out where we were when the car was taken. The robbery has to have been somewhere close if he walked there and grabbed the car."

"Smart kid," Elizabeth said. "Very smart kid, in fact. Good thinking."

Sam grinned. "I try."

"Tries me other ways sometimes, too," Stella said, but she didn't hide the pride in her voice. "A plus for brilliance, Sam. Would you do something for me now?'

"Sure, Mum."

"Wash your hands, get presentable—you are pretty much already—then go downstairs, ask how soon we can have dinner, and see if they have a map we can borrow."

"Sure, Mum."

The minute the door closed behind him, Stella all but pounced. "Okay, time out from jewel heists. Tell me, what's going on with Antonia? Is she okay?"

"As far as I know, yes."

"Where is she?" Stella didn't need a disappearing vampire on top of carjacking and the attempted abduction of her child.

"I don't know, but I can make an educated guess."

"And that guess would be?"

Elizabeth was obviously bursting with it. "Seems a bit trivial compared to everything else going on." She cast a glance at the pile in the middle of the bed. "But unless I'm very much mistaken, Sam hit it on the head. Antonia has found herself a fella."

"You're certain?"

"Not one hundred percent certain, but she went out yesterday afternoon and came back waxing lyrical about this incredible potter she'd found. Last night, she goes out hunting—okay, she needed to—but this morning she came down glowing like a virgin who's discovered sex. Didn't say a thing, but I have eyes in my head, and she was only half with it all day. When I got back from running errands, she'd left. Tried to call her a couple of times, and either she's out of range, or the mobile's turned off."

"You think she's safe?"

"I doubt there's many creatures could best Antonia. She's over fifteen hundred years old. Almost as powerful as Justin."

True. Antonia was old enough to take care of herself. It was just odd to have her disappear like this. "She just met him yesterday? A bit sudden, isn't it?"

"I don't know. Sometimes it happens fast."

True, her heart had gone kerflooey the moment she met Justin. Still hadn't settled down, for that matter, and part of her hoped it never did. "So, we manage without her until she turns up." Thank heaven Justin and Tom were on their way. Much as she hated to admit it, Stella sensed this was not anywhere near over, and a fortune in stolen gems could only mean trouble in capital letters.

"Between us, I think a vamp and a ghoul and Sam can hold the fort until reinforcements arrive."

"I hope they get here soon. Sam's liable to think he can do everything Justin can."

"He's got what—" Elizabeth's phone chimed out the *Pink Panther* theme again. Drat! What now? Tom again? She flicked open the phone. "Hello?"

"Miss Conner, this is Ida Collins."

"Yes?"

"I spoke to Emily, we both talked to Mildred, and we're willing to meet you this evening. Come to Emily's house in an hour. We can talk there undisturbed. It's Bower Cottage, just across the Green from Orchard House, the house with the yew hedge and the white-painted gate."

Darn, exactly what she'd hoped for, exactly when she couldn't go. "Ida, Mrs. Collins. Not tonight. It's impossible."

"You said you wanted to meet us!"

"I did, and I do. But something urgent has come up. How about tomorrow?"

"Doubt we can. Mildred has bingo on Saturday nights."

Elizabeth resisted the urge to spit and snap. She'd finally managed this meeting, but no way was she walking out on Stella.

"I'm truly sorry; can we do it Monday?" Surely by then, all this mess would be sorted out.

"I don't know about that, I'm sure. I'll have to talk to them."

"Please do, and give them my apologies."

Elizabeth fancied there was an affronted sniff just before Ida hung up. Too bad. There'd be time to mend fences later.

"Trouble?" Stella asked.

Unsure of how Stella regarded witches, Elizabeth shook her head. "Not really. Just a bit awkward. I'd been a pushy American to get a group of local ladies to meet me, and now they give me an hour's notice. They'll wait. They'll have to." Stella accepted it with a nod. Good. No need to explain any more. "Think we'd better go down and see what Sam's arranged for my dinner?"

Mention Sam, and Stella let everything else go. "Lets."

Stopping only to wrap up the stash, shove it back in the zip bag, and conceal it in Stella's suitcase—no point in surprising any chambermaids who came in to turn down the bed—they locked the door behind them and went down to the wide, airy, marble-floored entry.

Sam had been busy.

He waved them over to his seat at a window table in a lounge just off the deserted bar. On the table in front of him, a map was spread open, and two uniformed waitresses and the barman appeared to be hanging on his every word.

"Mum!" he called as he saw them across the room. "I found a map." He also appeared to have found a glass of Tizer and a packet of crisps. "There's all sorts of neat things around here and lots of things to do. There's an old Roman villa in Leatherhead Dad might like to see. It's all buried but never mind, and there's the Devil's Punch Bowl and the Hog's Back and Leith Hill, which is a mountain if you count the tower on it, and a castle in Guildford. Lots and lots of places, and Mr. Miles"—Sam smiled toward the doorman who manfully held his post in the front hall—"says I can borrow this map so we can look for places to go to. Isn't it great, Mum?"

He was overdoing the enthusiasm a bit, but she couldn't resist his smile or the gleam of success in his eyes. "Thanks, son." She looked around at the adults hanging on her son's every word. "Sure it's okay if we keep it a couple of days?"

"Of course, madam," an obviously besotted, curly-haired waitress replied. "We've got a supply. Let Master Sam keep it."

Heaven help her! If Sam got this sort of adulation at ten, what would she do when he was seventeen? "Thank you so much."

"It's a pleasure, madam, and whenever you're ready to order dinner, just let us know. Master Sam said you were expecting visitors and wanted to eat early."

If the poor girl knew what sort of visitors, she'd be out cold on the carpet, but since she never would know . . . "That would be great. We never had lunch, and I can see Sam has already started."

"Oh, Mum! It was just a pack of crisps!" Less than a year ago, it would have been a bag of chips. Her son adapted fast.

Settled in a table in the bay window overlooking the lawn, rose beds, and an herbaceous border worthy of showing up on a calendar, they ordered, or rather, Sam and Elizabeth ordered and Stella just echoed, Elizabeth's "steak, very, very rare, please."

The whole switch and chew went far easier than Stella had expected. Vampires switched plates faster than a human eye could register, and besides, with just three of them in the dining room, they were pretty much alone most of the time.

"Good steak, nicely rare," Elizabeth said as she wolfed down the last of the second one.

"You practically aspirated the first, and the second wasn't much slower," Stella said.

"Thanks to the little delay with your "adventure," I haven't eaten for nearly four hours."

"And Mum says I eat her out of house and home," Sam said with a little smile.

"And is she wrong there?"

Stella and Sam turned, and Sam squealed with delight at the voice, and both all but jumped out of their chairs.

"Justin!"

"Dad!"

And beside Justin was the man, or rather the vampire, who had Elizabeth running across the room. "You got here, Tom! Thank you!"

"M-m-m," Tom replied, "Couldn't wait to gallivant off on your own, but get into a spot of bother, and who do you need?"

He deserved to get shoved where it would hurt, except it

wouldn't hurt him. "Now you're here. Let's hope you live up
to all your promises."

"When have I ever let you down?"

They both knew the answer to that one. As a little smile
twitched a corner of Elizabeth's mouth, Tom grinned with
triumph.

Sam, caught in a double hug between his mother and
stepfather, turned his head and laughed. "Better kiss her
now," he advised, "while she's smiling."

Tom did as suggested, then muttered, "By Abel! I'm getting relationship advice from a ten-year-old!"

"Pretty good advice if you ask me," Justin said, his arms
firmly around the crux of his contentment.

"You two behave yourselves!" Stella said, pulling back a
little and frowning at Tom. She wasn't sure which two she
meant but . . . "We've had dinner; let's go upstairs and explain what's going on.

"We saw the car," Justin said.

"That," Elizabeth said, "is a minor detail."

"You're both alright though?" Justin asked, still keeping
hold of Sam and Stella.

"We're fine," Sam assured him. "I wasn't at the time, but
I am now. But dinner's not over. I haven't had any pudding."

"Dinner's over," Stella assured him.

"How about I ask if they do takeaway puddings?"

"Try your luck, son," Justin suggested.

"He'll have luck," Stella said as they watched Sam cross
the dining room toward the kitchen door. "He has the entire
staff eating out of his hand."

"While he's negotiating pudding, how about you catch us
up with everything that happened," Justin suggested.

That seemed the best idea. Elizabeth grabbed the borrowed map from the table, and everyone went up to Stella's
room, closely followed by Sam bearing a double serving of
blackberry pie and cream.

"How did you get here so fast?" Stella asked. "We thought the traffic would slow you."

"So did we. Once I arrived at Tom's and resumed human shape, we drove to the City Airport, and Jude brought us by helicopter. He landed near Leatherhead and had a car waiting."

Stella hoped they had as simple a resolution to their hot gem problem. "Talking of cars, mine is going to need fixing."

"Agreed." He smiled at her. "At what point did that happen?"

"It was the hedge or rather the raised bank the hedge was growing out of. At least it's still driveable."

"Barely. I called Jude to send someone to get it first thing in the morning. The sooner it's out of sight the better."

She wouldn't argue there. "Thanks, love."

"My pleasure," he paused. "Do you remember what you did with the carjacker slash jewel thief?"

"Mum threw him over the hedge," Sam said. "She just grabbed him, and he was gone."

Justin reached out and pulled Sam to him. "She did, did she? Good for your Mum!"

"I think so," Sam said. "And you know, I'm not sorry if he broke his neck falling in a cow's pancake. He scared the shit out of me!"

He barely paused at Stella's shocked, "Sam!"

"Sorry, Mum, but he told me he'd knock my lights out for me if I made a sound."

Justin let out a low, feral growl and held Sam even closer. "Don't worry, Sam. We'll see justice is done."

"Like you did back in Columbus?"

"If we can." He sounded grim.

"Funny really, isn't it? We keep finding money and jewels but can't keep any of it."

"It's all stolen, Sam," Stella reminded him, "and I sincerely hope this is the last and final time we come across stolen goods."

"Talking of the loot, let's have a butchers at it," Tom said. "Happen to have it handy, do you?" Stella opened the suitcase and reached for the leather grip. "Hold on, Stella; put these on." He handed her a pair of thin rubber gloves. "I know you've touched it already, but no point in leaving more fingerprints than we have to."

She'd never thought about leaving fingerprints. Where had her brain been? "Can't we just wipe them all off?"

"And wipe off the thief's prints if there are any?" He shook his head. "A few stray, unidentified prints will pass unremarked, but a cluster all the same . . ."

He had a point. One she should have thought of earlier. Stella took the gloves, pulling them on while Tom handed round gloves to the others. With the grip on the bed, she tugged the zip and once again watched everything spill out. Justin stepped forward, put aside the tools, and unrolled the first bundle of jewels.

They were every bit as impressive as last time. Sam even ignored his blackberry pie to gather round the bed and gape. Wasn't often vamps were struck dumb.

"By Abel and all his offspring!" Justin muttered.

"Looks like the ruddy Crown Jewels," Tom said.

"You really think they are?" Sam asked.

"Sorry to disappoint you, son," Justin said, "but I don't think so. On the other hand, it's more than you'd find in your average jewel box."

"Maybe from a jewelers?" Tom suggested.

"I don't much care where it came from," Stella said. "I want it gone. Just looking at it gives me the willies."

"It's a bit like hidden treasure," Sam said. "A pirate's hoard."

"You might have hit the nail on the head, son."

Sam looked at Justin. "Really? Pirates?"

"Not literally. Not in Surrey, but perhaps a combination of several burglaries or thefts."

"Assuming they are all real," Tom said.

Stella stared at the gems winking and glittering on the bed. Even without their little test on the bathroom mirror, who could doubt it? "I think they are, and I want them gone."

"They will be," Justin promised.

They were.

Once Sam was asleep, much against his protests, and the moon was up, Justin and Tom set out, launching from Stella's bedroom window and heading for Leatherhead. They knew the way to the police station from an earlier excursion.

"Getting to be habit, this," Tom said as they both perched on the roof and peered over the edge.

"Hush!" Justin muttered. "Want to announce our presence to the mortals?"

"They'd never believe their own eyes or ears anyway."

"Best not take any chances. Kit nearly got caught by a police helicopter once."

"Kit Marlowe flirts with danger."

Justin couldn't hold back a smile. "And what are we doing? Hanging about the coppershop with a rucksack full of hot jewels because our women need help!"

"Knowing Elizabeth, she's put out that she isn't here with us."

"Damn good thing neither of them can fly. Once Stella develops the power, there'll be no holding her."

"Talking about holding—how much longer are you holding onto the loot? I'd like to dump it and get back."

Justin smiled. So Tom itched to get back. A couple of days or so apart, and he was missing Elizabeth. Justin knew how it was. If Stella hadn't called him, he'd have been down by morning anyway. "What I'm thinking is that dropping it here is a bit too obvious. Even a crook with a conscience wouldn't walk up here and dump their ill-gotten goods on the front step. Or the back step, come to that."

"What do we do with it then? I'd like to see Stella's face if you walk back in with it and say you changed your mind and want to keep it!"

"No, I have a better idea. Let's leave it on the vicarage front lawn."

"You jest, Corvus! What if the milkman steals it?"

"The back lawn then! It's a good place. No one will suspect the vicar of having nicked it. He'll call the police right away, and the local sergeant lives just down the road. Recovering it will be a nice kudos for him."

Tom caught his drift. "You mean, take it back to Bringham?"

"Why not? It was stolen somewhere between there and here."

"Know where the vicarage is?"

"Yes, I once went there with Dixie when she was making her spurious goodbyes."

"Let's get going then. Knowing there are cells below gives me the willies."

Understandable, given what Tom had once endured. "Follow me then."

They flew pretty much in a straight line until they reached Bringham. Justin headed for the church and then skimmed the trees and landed. Fifty yards or so down the lane from the original, eighteenth-century vicarage was the twenty-first century replacement. It was a matter of minutes to approach from the woods and leave the leather bag sitting on the back doorstep.

Job done, they jumped the fence and ran for all they were worth down the lane, across the Green, and toward the common until they finally slowed as they reached the drive to Bringham Manor Hotel.

"What now?" Tom asked as their feet scrunched on the gravel drive.

"Don't know about you," Justin replied, "but I'm going to keep my woman warm."

She was waiting, curled up in bed in the red satin nightgown he loved—and particularly enjoyed taking off her. She smiled up at him, her eyes sparkling with anticipation. "Sam's asleep, but we'll have to be quiet. I'm not sure how thick these walls are."

Thick enough. "Two vampires should have enough control to keep their voices down."

Stella nodded. "They should."

They did, but it was rather touch and go when she got under the sheets and kissed her way up his legs from his ankles to his thighs, stopping only to wrap her sweet lips around his cock. She was definitely testing his vampire control.

And won, but as he collapsed onto the pillows, pulled her to him, and caught the scent of her arousal, her so ready need stirred his desire, his desire to satisfy the woman he loved. She was willing and loving, and his own hunger for her burned like a Beltane fire. He drew her close, raining kisses over her soft flesh, stroking her breasts as he positioned himself between her thighs.

Her skin was always vampire cool, but inside, she was hot and welcoming. He eased himself home, knowing he would never cease to praise the day he'd found Stella. Holding her steady and covering her mouth with his—to muffle his cries as much as hers—he brought them both to climax.

They lay snuggled like two spoons in a drawer, content, relaxed, and sated.

"Do you need to feed?" she asked.

"I can wait until morning," he replied. "Where do they keep the spare blood?"

"In Orchard House. They thought it was safer than here."

He smiled into her hair. His vampire was learning.

They were half-asleep when the urgent rap came at the door and Justin caught Tom's whispered, "Let me in!"

Chapter 10

Antonia looked up from the computer, feeling a bit as if she'd be prying, but she'd only Googled and read the numerous entries and web sites for the Surrey puma. Michael hadn't been kidding when he'd called himself the "local legend."

What intrigued her, apart from his varied descriptions, was the supposed sightings in Yorkshire. Had he lived up there? Was it possible? She might have passed him on one of her runs or while hunting and never realized it. Except she was darn cracking certain she'd never pass Michael by without noticing. He'd caught her eye both as human and as the beautiful cat prowling the common.

"What the frigging hell are you doing?" Michael, wearing those impossibly formfitting jeans and not much else, was striding toward her. Highly irritated.

It probably did look as if she'd been snooping but . . . "Researching you."

He loomed above her, peering over her shoulder at a screen showing two blurry photos and an account of a reported sighting in 1967. "Oh, that!" He sounded disgusted.

Whether still at her or the decidedly unflattering photos, she couldn't tell.

"I was curious," she told him, "so I thought I'd see what I could find out. You're quite a wandering phenomenon."

He rested his hand on her shoulder, his touch warming her skin though her shirt. "You don't want to believe everything you read."

She smiled, sensing his anger dissipating. "You're telling me! Think about the drivel that's been published about vampires."

He reached for a kitchen stool and pulled it up beside her. "Learn anything interesting?"

"Lots! Tell me—" It did feel good to have him so close. "Have you really been all over Yorkshire, Devon, and the Midlands, or are there scores of shapeshifters all over?"

"There's a few of us. Some stay in animal form most of the time. We say they've 'gone feral.'" He smiled. "Most of us live human and shift as the urge takes us. And yes, I've been in Yorkshire and Devon, the Midlands, Kent, East Anglia, and even Scotland for a time in the eighties. Since we live much longer than humans and appear to age slowly, we can't stay anywhere for too long."

"We have the same problem."

"Yeah!" It was obvious that thought had never struck him before. "I bet you do! Is that why you moved here?"

"Yes. I ran the gallery in York for nearly twenty years. Hated to leave it, but there's only so long you can claim the youth-preserving virtues of yoga or meditation."

"From purely selfish motives, I'm darn glad you had to move." He wrapped his arm around her shoulders and brushed his lips on her cheek. "Very, very glad."

"So am I." She was. There was a massive snarl of complications ahead for both of them. Gwyltha would no doubt throw a wobbly at an alliance with a shifter, but Gwyltha was up in Yorkshire. She, Antonia, was in Surrey with a man who'd professed his love and had a warm bed waiting for her. Whenever he finished whatever he had to do with that kiln of his.

She kissed him back. "I intended to wake you in ten minutes."

"I think I'm programmed to my kiln." He took her hand. "Come in and see what I'm doing."

If she were mortal, she'd have been sweating from the heat of the room; as it was, her body warmed, or maybe that was just proximity to Michael. Waves of hot air radiated from the sealed kiln in the middle of the room. How hot did it have to be inside? This was a far cry from the hand-built brick kilns she remembered from her girlhood or even the vast bottle kilns she'd seen in Stoke-on-Trent a century or so ago.

Michael was peering through a peep hole in the door. He turned to her. "Have a look."

She glimpsed curves, edges of what had to be mugs, or vases, or whatever. "It's all red hot."

"Yes, it heats up in there," he replied. "See the little cone?"

"You mean the thing curling over. I thought it was something broken off."

"No." He shook his head. "That's my gauge, my measure. When the little cone bends right over, the kiln has reached temperature, and I turn it off."

"And that's it?" Couldn't be.

"That's the beginning. After I turn it off, we go back to bed. We can sleep or . . ." His hand on her breast rather implied the "or" would be more to her fancy. "Then, in five hours' time, round about three A.M., I think, I come out and you keep me company while I open the door just a crack, and then we either go back to bed or get up and have breakfast early. Round about midmorning, I open the door wider, and by suppertime, they'll be cool, and we'll empty the kiln together."

It sounded so enticing, another ten, twelve hours or more in his company. And why not? There'd be no work on the house over the weekend. Elizabeth could hold the fort if needed, and Stella . . . Damn! Stella and Sam were arriving—no doubt had arrived. Oh, well. She'd see them in the morning. Elizabeth would take care of them.

This was her time.

"Something the matter, love?" He'd been watching her cogitations, it seemed.

"Not really. I just can't stay all day. Wish I could, but I've invited a friend and her child to stay with us."

Whatever he'd expected by way of excuse, this hadn't been it. He looked at her, a little frown between his eyebrows. "Oh, I see."

She bet he didn't. "I'll stay until morning. If I can get back later to help empty the kiln, I will. I can't walk out on guests."

"No, you can't. Fair enough, Tonia. It's just I can't quite square you being a vampire with having friends who have children. Silly but . . ."

Now was not the time to mention that the friend was also a vampire. "Elizabeth, my assistant, used to baby-sit Sam when he was younger. We're all pretty good friends."

Sounded reasonable enough, and he bought it. "So come back to bed and cuddle, and in the morning, I'll cook breakfast . . . if you eat breakfast, that is. Do you?"

She shook her head. "No, dear; my diet is pretty monotonous."

He sat down on a bench, rattling the stack of mugs and dishes on the end. "You know, Tonia, this is unreal. I'm in love with a woman who sucks blood for breakfast."

"Coming from someone who shifts back and forth to feline, that's a bit rich."

He threw back his head, his tawny hair shaking as he laughed. "You're right, love; if you saw me feed as a puma, it would probably put you right off me."

"As of now, I'm rather 'on' you."

He grabbed her hand; perhaps he was afraid she'd change her mind.

Back in his bedroom, Michael was unbuttoning her blouse when he paused. "What is it?" she asked, seeing the hesitation on his face.

"I just thought about how you feed."

"Yes?"

"Was what I thought was a love bite yesterday a vampire bite?"

She nodded. "It adds to the pleasure and intensifies the climax." For the space of a few terrible seconds, she feared she'd repulsed him.

Until he raised a sandy eyebrow and smiled, his dark eyes glinting. "Want to intensify my pleasure again?"

She didn't waste words replying. Just unbuttoned her blouse herself.

"Tom, it had better be good," Justin muttered as he opened the door a chink after grabbing his trousers just in case a chambermaid or guest also lurked in the corridor.

"It's important."

"It really is," Elizabeth said.

Justin opened the door wide. They both trooped in, and Stella pulled the sheets up to her chin. "Hush," she said. "Sam's asleep."

"Sorry to disturb you," Elizabeth said. "But we thought maybe you hadn't watched the eleven o'clock news."

"To be honest, I'm surprised you did," Stella said, ignoring Justin's shocked look. As if Elizabeth and Tom couldn't figure out exactly what they'd been doing.

"You'll want to hear this," Elizabeth said.

Justin closed the door behind them, standing against it, arms folded on his naked chest. Better get her mind on whatever Elizabeth claimed was important. "Sit down and tell us."

"Seems there was a jewel robbery in broad daylight near Leatherhead this afternoon. Someone is helping the police with their inquiries—I love the way they put that—but there is no trace of the stolen goods, which included a collection of jewelry intended for an auction in London next week."

"It has to be connected, right?" Stella said.

"Seems unlikely there were two robberies at the same time in the same area," Tom said.

"So what now?" Stella asked.

Justin moved to sit beside her and motioned the other two to grab a seat. "I make sure Jude takes the car away first thing in the morning. Once that's gone there's nothing to connect you with this."

"Unless," Tom added, "anyone saw you."

"Saw me do what? Run down the road at fifty miles an hour? If they did, they wouldn't believe their eyes. It was out in the country anyway, and by the time I stopped it, we were halfway in a field."

"Nothing to worry about then. Jude will bring a new car down tomorrow, and we can spend a weekend taking Sam to Hampton Court and Windsor Castle." Justin looked at Tom. "Thanks for filling us in with the news, but things are set. I suggest you two go and get some sleep."

"Not too sure about sleep," Elizabeth whispered to Stella as she stood up and headed for the door.

* * *

Antonia wanted to sing to the stars overhead. Staying and waking beside Michael had its appeal, but running through the night with him was only a few steps down from love-making. They'd run north across the common, leaping the rail-way cutting, crossing open country, skirting Stoke d'Abernon, and heading almost to Cobham.

She'd run through the night countless times, but to run with her lover beside her, a lover who ran as fast and as long as she could, was a pleasure she'd all but forgotten. In puma form, Michael raced beside her, leaping when she leapt and tearing across open fields with her to jump hedges and gates together. If she had a heart or circulation, it would be pound-ing or racing; as it was, her mind and heart soared with the joy of the race.

They turned back, taking a more roundabout way home, neither wanting to end the companionship of the chase. As they neared the edge of the common and approached the graveled drive that led to the hotel, Antonia stopped. How exactly was she getting into the building, at whatever hour of the morning it was, without rousing half the hotel?

She stood on the drive. Michael couldn't talk in puma form, and she could hardly ask him to shift and stand naked in the driveway just so she could ask about getting into her room without ringing the bell. Darn it, she'd just follow him home, drive back, and call Elizabeth on her mobile and ask her to open a window for her.

The unmistakable sound of mortal footsteps on gravel came across the clear night air. Michael heard it too; his ears twitched, and his dark eyes scanned the drive. She motioned him to the hedge as she silently moved up the curving drive.

There were four cars parked in front of the hotel; Stella's Jaguar and Elizabeth's little hired car she recognized; the others she didn't, but she did see the man trying Stella's door. Abel help us! Was nowhere safe nowadays? No time to contemplate the increase of petty crime in the countryside.

Antonia leapt forward, noiselessly landing a foot behind the would-be thief and tapping him on the shoulder as he slipped a lock pick into the door handle.

He turned around in horror, snarled, and brought a knife up in his other hand. An ambidextrous felon! Interesting, but not interesting enough to stop her. Moving faster than he could ever see, she grabbed his knife and threw it in the air so it embedded itself in the trunk of a nearby tree fifteen or so feet above the ground.

"What exactly do you think you are doing?" she asked.

"Bitch!" he muttered, looking sideways to gauge his chances of outrunning her. She pinned him back against the car with her flattened palm on his chest. Squirm as he might, kick as he tried, he wasn't going anywhere.

"Oh yes, absolutely!" she replied, her smile probably wasted in the dark. "You don't belong here. Go!"

Since that was the thought foremost in his mind, she didn't need to make a second suggestion. He fled the minute she released him, casting a terrified look behind him and screaming as Michael leapt out of the hedge and snarled. As the sound of a motorbike faded down the lane, a light went on in one of the windows overhead.

Drat!

Taking discretion as the better part of valor, she followed the thief's trail down the drive and, with Michael at her heels, raced toward his house.

He shifted and followed her inside. Yes, staying was a temptation, but after this little incident, she wanted to get back to Stella and Elizabeth. In the dark, her vampire vision had noticed the damage to Stella's car, and she wanted to make sure no one was hurt.

Michael had other ideas.

"He won't come back; things there are fine. Wait until morning. You can even nip on me for breakfast."

It was a tempting suggestion given he pronounced it in all his naked glory, but . . . "I'm going back, Michael. I have to. I need to know what's happened to my friends. Stella's car was damaged; it looked as if she's had an accident. Perhaps Sam is hurt or something."

He nodded. "You're right, but better give it a little while. That yob's scream might have awakened the entire establishment. You don't want to walk into an uproar."

Not a good idea. "I'm going to give it time to settle, then call Elizabeth." Assuming she hadn't turned her phone off for the night.

She hadn't, but it took several rings before she answered. "Antonia?"

"Is everything alright?"

"Well . . ." The pause was a bad sign. Antonia heard Elizabeth say, "It's Antonia," then she was right back. "It's okay for now, but we've had a few problems, or rather, Stella and Sam have."

The car! "They weren't hurt?"

"Sam was more shaken than he'll admit to, I suspect, but they are fine. It's a bit involved. Justin and Tom came down. They were getting worried about you."

So that was whom Elizabeth had spoken to. Made sense. "I'm fine." More than fine in fact. "Look, sorry to disturb any tender moments, but . . ."

Elizabeth snorted. "What do you need?"

Bless the ghoul! "I want to get into the hotel without rousing everyone. Can you let me in?"

"No prob. I'll draw back the curtains, turn on the light, and open the windows. Will you be long?"

"Give me ten, fifteen minutes."

It took her nearly that long to part from Michael. Leaving

was not easy. "Remember you promised to help unload the kiln," he said.

She did not remember actually making any such promise, but the idea held great appeal. "If all's well with my friends, I will be here."

He nodded. "Fair enough." After pulling on a pair of slacks, he walked her to her van and watched as she drove away. An odd pang tugged at her heart as she rounded the corner and no longer saw him in the mirror.

There were no two ways about it; she had fallen for a wild puma.

Elizabeth was as good as her word. She stood at the open window, silhouetted in the night, and Tom Kyd waited on the lawn.

"Thought you might need a hand."

Chivalry was all very well, but expecting Tom with his crippled hands to help her was a bit over much. "I can manage."

"Don't talk wet, Antonia."

She could have fought him; she was several centuries stronger, but she smiled and let him. She'd have other points to make later. Choosing one's battles was a wise course.

Ever the gentleman, he let her climb first, following right behind, and echoed Elizabeth's, "Are you okay?" with a slightly less courteous, "Where in Abel's name have you been?"

She was tempted to say, "Having wild sex with a shape-shifter," but on balance, decided the timing was not right. Instead she replied, "Chasing off a car thief who was about to break into Stella's car."

That certainly got their attention, and a catechism as to the hows, whys, whens, and wherefores before they filled her in with the earlier installment.

She was glad she was sitting. "Think it was the same man?"

Tom shook his head. "Unlikely; not after Stella tossed

him over the hedge. We were getting a bit worried about her having injured him, but Justin insists she had provocation. He threatened Sam."

Antonia smiled. Colony rules aside, she couldn't imagine any vampire censuring Stella for protecting her child. "What are we doing about it?"

"Justin has it under control."

She bet he did, and one glance in Elizabeth's direction confirmed she had her own ideas, as, no doubt, did Stella. "I hope he has." Not that she doubted Justin wouldn't raise heaven, earth, and the seven seas for his stepson. "I certainly missed the excitement."

"Bet you had plenty of excitement of your own," Elizabeth said with a grin.

She was not in the sharing mood, not with Tom half-frowning at her. "Better get myself to bed then."

Elizabeth handed her the key. "I nipped down after you phoned and nicked it from the front desk."

Thank goodness for small mercies. "Thank you."

Antonia locked the door behind her, kicked off her shoes, and dropped her clothes on the floor. Acrobatic sex, wild runs across country, and disposing of car thieves rather wore one out.

Across the woods and fields, James lowered his eye from the telescope and shook his head. He knew he wasn't drunk, and he was pretty darn sure he wasn't hallucinating, but he had seen a man climb down the side to the Bringham Manor hotel and then climb up with a woman. Interesting. He'd heard of people skiving out early without paying hotel bills, but skiving in? Odd, very odd.

Chapter 11

Margaret Abbott tied the belt of her seersucker dressing gown and went downstairs without waking her husband or Judy. The house was quiet apart from Poppy's enthusiastic wet-nosed greeting. Wasn't often a vicar's wife had time to herself. Margaret had learned to cherish those moments. She opened the door and let Poppy out, put on the kettle, and retrieved the milk and paper from the front step. After scanning the headlines in the hopes there would be good, cheerful news for a change, she put a slice of brown bread in the toaster and measured tea into the pot. Out of the corner of her eye, she saw Poppy racing around the back garden, growling and dragging something brown in her teeth.

Judy must have left out one of her packing boxes. Too bad! She could tidy it up when she finally got up. If Poppy chewed it the shreds, then maybe Judy would learn. The kettle boiled. Margaret filled the pot, caught the toast as it popped up, spread it liberally with marmalade, and carried the lot to the table. Flipping the paper to the crossword, she settled for a peaceful half hour.

When Poppy scratched at the door, Margaret opened it

and refilled Poppy's water bowl. It wasn't until Poppy shoved her muzzle in the dish, slurping water as usual, that Margaret noticed the jeweled hat pin caught in the dog's fur.

Darn Judy and her college theatricals! What else was in the box? Now no doubt spread all over the lawn. She really should be more careful. "Could have hurt you, old girl," she said as she disentangled the pin from Poppy's fur. "What if you'd trodden on it?" She put the hat pin on the draining board and then picked it up again. A nice piece, reminded her of ones her grandmother used to wear. The weight and quality of the setting were not that of cheap paste. She was almost certain it was real. A lucky junk store find perhaps? Judy was always looking for odds and ends for the collages and embroidery.

What else had Poppy tossed about the back garden?

Margaret opened the door.

Parishioners sometimes left fruit and vegetables, even eggs and loaves of homemade bread, but jewelry scattered over the lawn was something new.

She retrieved the brown leather bag from under a rose-bush and piled most of the dumped contents back in, but the sight of a chewed on stethoscope had her frowning. Judy had had a few wild moments, but this was impossible. Who among all the villagers had dumped this on the back step?

It was more than any vicar's wife should have to cope with single-handed. Leaving the lot sitting on top of her half-finished crossword, she went upstairs and roused her husband and daughter.

While Simon called the police, she put the kettle back on. Sergeant Grace never said "no" to a cup, and darn it, she needed another. Funny really, when they'd moved here six years ago, she'd labored under the misapprehension that village life was quiet and dull. She'd erred!

* * *

Tom and Justin were conferring outside, no doubt lamenting the injuries to Stella's car, as Elizabeth took a place by the window for breakfast. Sam joined her minutes later, saying Stella was skipping breakfast. She wasn't too surprised at Antonia's absence either, but she would have welcomed the two extra breakfasts. One could hardly order rare bacon and raw sausages, and cooked meat just didn't sustain the same. Thank heavens for her stash in the fridge at Orchard House.

As she and Sam watched, one of Jude's minions drove up in a brand new gray Mercedes and traded it for Stella's bashed-in Jag. There was no doubt about it—vampires had life organized.

"You know what we're doing today?" Sam asked between bites of toast.

"What?" Kids really amazed her. Not a day earlier, he'd been all but kidnapped, and this morning, he was devouring sausages and planning the day ahead.

"We're going to Windsor to see the castle. Then we're going on a boat ride down the river and having a picnic."

"Have fun."

"Want to come with us?"

It was tempting, but . . . "Another time, Sam. I have things to catch up on." Like getting back in touch with the coven.

"I know," Sam nodded, smirking a little with youthful knowledge. "You want to spend time with Tom, right?"

Darn! She'd overlooked that complication. He was down here for the entire weekend. Forget meeting the coven. "That's right, Sam. You going to eat that last sausage?"

"You have it. They'll bring me more."

A leisurely, but substantial, breakfast and chatter with Sam, who, Elizabeth realized, she missed a great deal, and she was ready for a nice romantic day with Tom. They could explore the countryside, perhaps go into Guildford, maybe even wander the antique stores in Dorking. In fact, she was rather curious about visiting a town called Dorking.

It didn't quite work out that way.

She'd barely had time to clean her teeth when Tom popped his head round the door. "Any plans for the weekend?"

She grunted while she spat. Trust Tom to pick an undignified moment to start a conversation! She rinsed again, straightened, and wiped her mouth. "Thought I might spend it with you." Or at least most of it.

He came closer and rested his twisted hands on her shoulders. Despite his injuries, or maybe because of them, he had the gentlest touch. "I've missed you, Lizzie."

"I've missed you, too." Truth indeed. "But it's been busy."

"And unsettling. Justin keeps thinking we've taken care of the carjacking-jewel robbery business, but something tells me it can't be that simple. That attempted break-in to Stella's car last night . . ."

"How did they know where she was?"

"Not that hard. How many cream XJ8s do you see around here? I bet half the village knew there was a cream-colored Jaguar with a bashed bonnet and headlights parked here."

True. "Poor Sam and Stella. So much for a nice break in the country."

"Stella handled it. Sam doesn't have much to worry about with her and Justin to take care of him." He pulled her close. "Much as Justin is a good friend and I really like his wife and child, I didn't come down to talk about them. We've sorted things out. Once the vicar finds the jewels, he'll call the police, and it will all be in their hands. Meanwhile, we have the place to ourselves."

"What about the others?"

"Justin and co. are off for a day of tourism and history. Antonia appears to have some commitment to discuss work with a local potter." Elizabeth just managed to hold back a grin. Things were getting interesting in that department. "So it's just us, Miss Connor, and I thought we could see about getting married."

"Getting married?"

"Why not? We've talked about it."

"Yes, and we agreed to wait a bit."

"We've waited a bit. I haven't changed my mind; have you?"

"Not in the least."

"Fine then. We want to get married. Toby has things in Oregon well in hand. No need to worry there. Let's do it!"

"Today?"

"We can get a marriage license at least. Set a date, buy a ring. Sounds like a full day to me."

"Sure I'm the ghoul for you?"

"Never doubted it for a moment. My only concern has been getting you to agree."

"What about Gwyltha and the rest of the colony?" Heck, as leader, Gwyltha pretty much had the last word about everything.

"Considering, my love, that you disposed of a rogue vampire who had all but bested her, I think she holds you in high esteem and respects your power. Anyway, she agrees; I told her I was marrying you."

"Before you asked me?"

"Didn't want any silly bureaucratic delays once you said 'yes.'"

"I haven't said 'yes.'"

"You will. You're mine, aren't you?"

Something inside flickered and spread warmth to every fiber of her being. She was scared, thrilled, delighted, wired, anxious, elated, and a little terrified, but one thing she wasn't was uncertain. "Yes, Tom."

It was a leap into the unknown. Marriage! To Tom, and

soon if he had anything to do with it. "I'll still work here with Antonia."

"Of course; you can commute or stay down here once in a while. We'll work it out."

It wouldn't be that easy. It hadn't been so far, but who cared? A complicated life with Tom was infinitely preferable to a serene one on her own, and in all fairness, when had her life ever been serene? "So I'll be Mrs. Tom Kyd."

"You bet. Now while we still agree, let's go shopping."

"I've got to make a call first."

He rolled his eyes and yanked her close. "What for? It's the weekend. Antonia can work if she wants to; you don't have to."

Antonia wasn't working, but if she wanted the others to believe she was, fair and good. "Not work exactly," she paused. Why? Tom was marrying her knowing she was a witch, and hadn't he just said that Gwyltha, the leader of the colony, respected her? "I'm trying to make contact with the local coven. I finally got them to agree by being a pushy American, and I was supposed to meet them last night but canceled because of Stella's trouble. I really need to call back and apologize at least."

It said a lot for how much he loved her that Tom merely nodded and fetched her cell phone from the dresser. "Don't take too long and do watch your back. They are an odd lot here."

"I won't be long. I'll be ready in a jiffy."

"We don't have to go out. We could just stay here . . ." The corner of his mouth twitched.

"No way! You promised to take me ring shopping!"

She had the car hire number on speed dial, but Ida wasn't there. She tried the house and waited while the lad who answered the phone called for "Grandma!"

"Who is it?" Ida asked sharply.

"Elizabeth Connor." Soon to be Kyd. "Sorry about last

night. A friend had a problem, and I couldn't leave her. Can we fix another time?"

Seemed like an endless pause before she replied, "Alright, I suppose. I'll have to talk to Emily." She paused. "We're having tea. We'll meet you, too." No mention of Mildred, the third one, but what the heck? "What about the Copper Kettle at four?"

Heck, no! But could she put them off again? They'd never take her seriously. But damn it, she was busy today getting engaged. "How about later? Six?"

"Alright, where? We can't sit in the Kettle for two hours!"

"Let's meet in the Sacred Garden behind Orchard House."

Pause. Heck, she could almost hear Ida mulling that over. "Alright."

"Great! I'll see you there at six!"

Now, to explain that to Tom.

No need.

"A meeting of witches?" He had an odd, wry smile.

"Yes. I made it later. Wanted plenty of time with you . . ."

"Good thinking. The old magic garden?" She nodded. "Good. I'll be there too."

"No, Tom, please. They're skittish about meeting me as it is. And what if one of them is like Meg and can read your aura?" Or rather, his lack of one.

He shook his head and grinned. "Think I'm really thick, don't you? I'll be there. Up in a tree, feathers on, listening to every word. If one of them makes a move toward you, I'll be on them in all my naked glory!"

How he could make her laugh! "Tom, no one is going to hurt me. These are two old ladies, and remember the Wiccan creed?"

"Yup, and I remember what this lot did to Kit. These are not your nice, benign witches, Lizzie. These are murderers."

Tom shook his head. Had he really called witches "nice" and "benign"? What was this woman doing to him? But if she thought she was meeting that lot alone, she'd better get her ideas straight! "I'll be there, love. Be sure of it."

She nodded. "Okay."

He almost dropped from shock at her ready acquiescence, but he wasn't going to question when he was ahead. This morning had all gone his way. Fine with him. "Ready to go then?"

"Oh, yes." She grabbed her bag. "Let's get going, Tom. The maid must be waiting to make the bed."

"All the better for us to rumple it when we get back!"

After pretty much scouring the county, they found an antique ring with a square-cut ruby flanked by two diamonds in a small shop in Richmond.

"You're mine now," Tom said, "for good! Pity we don't have time to see about the license. Took you forever to make up your mind."

"I should think so too! It's not every day a ghoul gets engaged!"

"Don't you think we overuse that pun?"

She shook her head. "You fell in love with a ghoul, better get used to it, love."

She kissed him on the cheek, just a brush of her lips, but he felt it down to his cock. So he was hard—nothing new in that, he'd been that way most of the day. Not that he was complaining, and they'd be home soon, once Lizzie had her meeting with the witches. She'd need strength for that. "Think we'd better stop by Sainsbury's and get you a steak, or six, and head back. You can gnaw while I drive."

She did, chomping her way through three sirloin steaks between Richmond and Esher. Not that he was in any position to comment on eating habits. Living with Lizzie had reintroduced him to butcher shops, which had improved vastly from the insanitary establishments of the sixteenth century, and forced him to enter supermarkets, places he'd had little or no use for until now.

"Tom," she said as they passed through Cobham and headed toward Bringham. They were on country roads now, but it seemed half the population of Surrey was out for an afternoon drive. "Would it bother you if I took my ring off?"

What was she thinking? She was going to wear that for eternity. "Why?"

"I don't think it's a good idea to wear it for my meeting. No point in drawing attention to either of us. If one or another of those old ladies notices my ring, the first question will be to ask, 'Who's the lucky man?'"

She had a point. A good one. "Put it back on when it's over, alright?"

"You bet. I'm going to flaunt it!"

But first back to Orchard House.

He picked a back room that overlooked the garden. "Be sure to leave the window open, Lizzie; I want to be able to get in. The neighbors might look askance at a naked man running around."

"I'm not shocked at the sight of you naked." Her wicked grin was a definite enticement. Did she know what it did to him? Yes, darn her, she did.

"Want some help?" She eased one finger between two buttons on his shirt.

"You can help when I'm getting dressed. Now I need to concentrate." He'd never before—at least not that he remembered—tried to transmogrify with a hard-on. This was his chance to find out what a sexually aroused owl looked and felt like.

Elizabeth stood back and watched him transmogrify. One minute, he was Tom, beautiful, naked, and definitely very happy to see her. There was a tingle, more of a tremor, in the air around, and Tom became a blur of color and movement, and then a long-eared owl was perched on the window ledge. He turned his head. Two dark owl eyes looked her way, and he was off, wings spread, headed across the garden. Her personal avian bodyguard, vampire lover, and fiancé.

She took a deep breath—just thinking the word fiancé gave her goose bumps of excitement. But still . . . she straightened the shoes he'd kicked off, tucked a sock in each one, and hung his shirt and pants on the closet doors. She permitted herself a touch of his shirt on her face and the brief indulgence of letting his scent stir her. Then she was out the door and down the stairs. She wanted to be in place in the garden when the other two arrived. A few minutes alone—okay, alone with a sentient owl bodyguard—to meditate, and she would be ready.

She sat on the grass under the rowan tree. Tom had perched in the large oak in the other corner, but now he'd moved. Most likely overhead. She was not going to look up. She didn't need to. She could sense him close by and basked in the feeling of security.

The day's heat radiated off the old brick walk. She leaned against the tree and watched the bees on the lavender bushes buzzing back and forth, some of them flying drunkenly, their pollen sacs so full it skewed their balance.

She understood the feeling. She was a bit off balance herself. Not a good way to feel at any time, and especially not now.

Perhaps she should have made tea or had something to offer them, but it was too late. All she had in the fridge were blood bags or raw meat.

"Hello!"

Elizabeth turned in the direction of the chirpy voice. Ida approached with a short, dumpy woman with tightly curled hair.

She stood. She should have brought out chairs she supposed, but that too was too late. She walked toward them, smiled at Ida, and offered her hand to the other woman. "You must be Emily Reade. I'm Elizabeth Connor."

It was a loose, wiggly handshake.

"Delighted to meet you," Emily said. "Ida has told me all about you."

Not exactly. Ida didn't know all about her, but . . . "Thank you for meeting me, and I do apologize again about last night. A friend had a bit of a problem." Sheesh! She'd been here too long! A "bit" of a problem. It had been a full-blown crisis!

"Nothing serious, I hope," Ida said, her eyes agog with curiosity.

"A minor car accident, but she was shaken up." That was part of the truth.

"Oh, it's terrible the drivers on the roads these days," Emily said. She shook her head, but her curls stayed firmly lacquered in place.

Yeah! And the carjackers were a damn nuisance too. "We got it taken care of." She hoped. "But Stella really needed the company."

"Well, I'm glad that's settled," Ida said. "Now, let's talk."

"I thought there was a third person you mentioned before."

Ida shook her head. "Mildred Rowan couldn't get away. John is difficult sometimes."

That was one way to explain the scene in the Barley Mow.

"Let's sit under that lovely tree where you were before," Emily suggested. "Such a beautiful spot!"

"Would you like chairs or something to sit on?" Though the Goddess knew what sort of "something" she could produce.

"We're fine!" Emily insisted, striding across the chamomile and plonking herself down near where Elizabeth had been sitting.

If Tom now possessed an owl's metabolism, Emily was in danger of attack. Did he? She'd have to ask him later. She waited for Ida to settle herself—she was nowhere near as agile as Emily, but she was probably twenty-five years older, if not more. With both of them settled, Elizabeth sat between them.

"So," Emily said—it seemed she was the appointed spokeswoman—"shall we salute the Goddess in her sacred garden?" She held out her hands. Ida took one, Elizabeth the other, and then Ida and Elizabeth joined hands. Ida's hand was thin, worn, and old, but warm. Emily's felt cold and hard, and unease spread up Elizabeth's arm. Unease, discord, and tension that increased as Emily began to chant.

Ida joined the chant. Unfamiliar with the sequence, Elizabeth intoned quietly. Her unease grew. All Adele's lectures on misuse of power came rolling back. She took a deep breath. And another, and all but sighed with relief as Emily finished and dropped hands.

"Praise to the Goddess!" she said.

"Praise to the Goddess," Ida repeated, and Elizabeth joined in on the tail of her response.

In the ensuing quiet, the peace of the garden settled around her. The bees resumed their dance among the lavender. From the crushed chamomile where they sat, a fresh, sweet scent rose in the warmth. In the shelter of the old brick wall, the air was still, warm, but none of the beauty and warmth quite dispelled the sense of unease she felt at Emily's proximity.

"So, you wish to join our coven," Emily said, her voice clipped to the point of combativeness.

"Perhaps." That got a couple of raised eyebrows. "I have studied the craft for ten years. My stepmother first taught me. I've been curious about The Way here in England. I knew from Dixie that Ida was active in an old coven here. Since I'm working here for a while, I contacted her."

"Is that why you hired the car?" Ida asked.

"I hired the car because I needed transport and Dixie recommended you."

"Forget the car!" Emily snapped. "We need to decide if Elizabeth will make a suitable candidate."

If Elizabeth decided she wanted to join them. "Perhaps you could tell me a little about your group."

Emily drew herself up. "We are an ancient coven. Older than you can imagine as an American." Really? Given she was marrying a four-hundred-year-old vampire, she had a pretty good notion of "ancient." "We can trace our roots back five hundred years." Okay, they had a bit of an edge, but . . . "We had members burned for their craft and have endured persecution and trials." She looked at Elizabeth. "Can any coven in America make that claim?"

It was hardly a matter for competition. "None that old that I know of."

"Thought so." She smiled. No, she smirked. "You have to understand how things are in a coven such as ours."

She was understanding pretty fast. "Who is your leader?" It was hard to see either of these two leading anything.

"We—" Ida began but Emily interrupted.

"Our leader is not with us now. He, too, is, one might say, persecuted."

Elizabeth nearly choked. Sebastian Caughleigh persecuted! He was a murderer! Okay, an insane one, but still . . . She looked at Ida and fancied she was rolling her eyes. Interesting all around.

"So, without a leader, how do you function?"

"By the Goddess's good graces and our own commitment to our leader's ideals," Emily replied.

Elizabeth groaned silently. This had not been one of her better ideas. "I understand that you both are skilled in herb lore." A change of subject was always a good idea.

Perhaps not. The two women exchanged glances. "We have skills," Emily agreed. "Is that what you want to study?"

"Maybe." A put off, but she was not about to commit to anything, not when Emily sent snakes of unease down her spine. "You mentioned the coven being old. You knew Dixie's aunts?"

"I knew them," Ida said.

Emily snapped, "The whole village knew them."

"I worked for them," Ida said. "Started working for them when I was fifteen, right after I left school. Hard they were."

"Oh, Ida! You do go on." Emily pursed up her mouth and creased her eyebrows.

"I know." She looked right at Elizabeth. "I worked there four long years, ten, twelve hours a day sometimes, one day off a week, and a pittance of a wage as I lived in. When Peter Collins started asking me out, I welcomed him as my escape, and when he asked me to marry him, I loved him for getting me out of the house."

"Did they introduce you to the coven?" Seemed reasonable, but . . .

"Yes, but that was later. After Peter married me and I moved out, they couldn't find another girl stupid enough to live in. I finally agreed to come in and clean one day a week. Did it for eight years until I got pregnant with Stanley."

"I think it was to keep me on, they started sharing their herb lore with me. Then they introduced me to the coven. It didn't keep me. When Stanley came and Peter's mother was getting on and came to live with us, I gave up cleaning, but I did stay with the coven."

Interesting, and the longest speech she'd ever heard from Ida. It had left Emily quiet too.

But not for long. "So," she said, "are you ready to join us?"

"Not yet."

Emily's jaw sagged, and it took several seconds for her to close her mouth. "What do you mean?"

"Just what I said. I'm not sure." A lie, as she was getting surer by the second. "I wanted to talk to you, make contact. That's what I told Ida. I'm not sure an organized coven, even one as historic as yours, is where I belong. I just needed to meet like-minded people."

Emily let out a noise that sounded like "pffft!" "Wasted our time, did you?"

"I hope not." Now, it was her turn to get starchy. "Thank you for coming. And Ida, thank you for bringing Emily. It's been good to meet you."

"Do you have the old ladies' books?"

Emily's question sent Elizabeth's caution sense to high alert. "Their books?"

"You told Ida you had them. Records, grimoires, papers, spell books, recipes. You know what I'm talking about."

She did. "I told Ida I'd seen them. Dixie took them with her when she left the country." Most of them anyway.

Emily shook her head. "What we could have done with them!"

What harm, no doubt! "Would you like Dixie's address and phone number to ask her?"

Emily shook her head. "No need." And stood up. "I'll be off."

Elizabeth gave Ida a hand to help her stand. "Thank you," Ida said, brushing down her floral print skirt. "You're a good girl." She lowered her voice. "Should have listened to me. You did insist."

She had. "Thank you."

She'd planned on walking with them through the door and toward the house, assuming they'd parked in the drive, but instead, Emily headed for the far end of the garden, Elizabeth following with Ida. Was Emily going to pause by one of the empty niches or an altar? Neither. She walked toward the oak tree. As they neared, Elizabeth noticed what she'd thought was a buttress or support was an extension of the wall covered with ivy and vines. The path here was covered with overgrown plants, but it veered behind the wall, to another door.

How had she missed this? Goddess only knew, but she hadn't exactly clambered over plants to inspect the walls. The door opened onto a narrow strip of land that gave onto the lane.

So that was how they had come into the garden without Dixie knowing. How many other doors were there? She'd check or, better still, get Tom to. He'd literally get a bird's eye view.

But as she stepped back into the garden, a dark brown shape, wings spread, headed over the wall and toward the house.

She'd see him soon. And he'd no doubt say, "I told you so."

Chapter 12

Ghouls were no slouches when it came to moving. Elizabeth ran across the lawns and the overgrown kitchen garden toward the house, but vamps had the edge when it came to speed. By the time she reached the back door, Tom was waiting, already dressed, a curious light in his eyes.

"Satisfied?" he asked.

Not in the slightest! "That was one of the oddest conversations I've ever had."

"Want to talk about it while I grab a couple of bags?"

No doubt he needed them after transmogrifying. "Okay." Not that there was much to talk about. She waited as he nipped up the narrow stairs and came back down a few minutes later, two empty bags in his hand. "Where do you dispose of these?"

"Wrap them in newspaper first, then put them in the rubbish compactor." She nodded to the gleaming appliance sitting in the corner. "Antonia bought it just for that."

"Nifty little gadget," Tom said after he set the machine in motion. "Maybe we should get one"—He gave her a sideways look—"when you come home."

"You're the one who needs it, not me."

"What about all those steak bones and chicken carcasses you leave in the wheelie bin?"

Good point. "Next weekend. We'll look in Selfridges."

"If you don't have another crisis to bring us both down here."

"I think we've had our excitement for a while. Stella's problem was one of those freak things." Nasty; scary; okay, panic-inducing, but all taken care of.

"I hope you're right." He came close. "I worry about you, Lizzie. This village . . ."

She kissed him. "Is fine. Two vampires and a ghoul can take care of most things. We're going to put the house to good use and cleanse it of any negative energy."

"I hope you're right" He raised her hand to his lips. "Where's your ring?"

She took it out of her pocket and slipped it on. "You know why I took it off."

"Yeah. Going to keep it on now?"

What the heck did he think? And why was he so prickly? Or was it she who was touchy? She let out a long sigh. "You heard everything, Tom. I wasn't imagining they were a bit strange, was I?"

"Love, they are a pair of addled old women."

"Emily isn't that old. Forty-five, fifty at the most."

"And all caught up with malicious ambition and misuse of power. Darling,"—he drew her close—"don't start the 'harm to none' line to me. I know you live by that. I know Adela does. This lot don't. If they were led astray by Caughleigh, they agreed to follow." He kissed the top of her head. "Know what I think?" he asked as she looked up at him. "If you'd told them you had the old ladies' recipe books and the contents of their herbarium upstairs, they'd have welcomed you into the fold. As it was, they decided you had nothing to benefit them. Stay clear of them."

Everything he said confirmed her own impressions, but . . .
"I had so hoped to meet others."

"You will in time. You found Meg, didn't you?"

"Meg is in Devon."

"Give her a bell. She might know someone. Look beyond Bringham. With that little car, you can travel."

Goddess bless him! Elizabeth knew how much this cost him. "I knew there was a reason I loved you, Tom."

"I'll keep giving you reasons, Lizzie, my love."

Fine by her.

"That was a waste of time," Emily said as she headed her Honda down the lane and onto the main road.

"Not necessarily," Ida replied. "We know she's sincere in following the way, even if she is an American, and we had confirmation that everything was destroyed."

"If she's telling the truth!"

"Why would she lie? I, for one, think they are all destroyed. Nothing has come to light. Dixie is gone, and why would this young woman care what happened years ago? Just give over worrying. The old women are dead. We're better off. The whole village is better off with all their papers destroyed."

"I'm not talking about that!" Emily snapped. "Dixie did us all a favor there, but what about the rest of it? They had to have records, recipes, notes. No one could keep all that in their heads. If we had their old books, think what we could do with their herb lore at our fingertips."

"Maybe, but we don't have it, and we won't." Couldn't Emily face facts?

"Mildred isn't going to be happy about this."

"Mildred should have come with us." Ida let out a snort. "Can't believe how that woman waits on John hand and foot."

"He does have a dislocated shoulder."

"And no doubt got it falling down drunk! That man's been a burden to Mildred since the day they were married."

Emily gave her a nasty little smile. "Don't like him, do you?"

"Why should I? He's trouble. Been in jail three times and brought nothing but grief to her."

"He's been straight almost five years. He even has a job these days."

"But for how long? He won't stick to it long if you ask me."

"Nobody asked you, Ida. Let Mildred be."

"I'm not saying anything about her. I've known her since she was born. Her mother and I were girls together. Mildred was sharp as a wagonload of monkeys as a girl, but now . . . You don't understand, Emily."

"Oh, yes, I do!" She glanced at Ida and scowled. "Mildred knows John's up to no good. That's why she wouldn't leave him. That shiftless brother of his is out of jail and is staying with them. She's scared Dave will get John into trouble again."

"What did I tell you?"

Emily slowed. "We're here now. No point in upsetting her. We'll just tell her we have nothing and leave it at that."

Inevitably, it wasn't that simple.

As Emily pulled the car into the kerb, Mildred came running out the front gate. "Come in the back gate. We'll sit in the garden. They're in the front bedroom. They mustn't hear us."

Ida restrained a snappy reply. Mildred had a cross to bear with John, and there was no sense adding to her troubles. Wouldn't do any good either. Mildred stuck to John through thick and thin. Silly woman!

"We'll have a seat in the garden," Emily said, locking the car.

"Good." Mildred was whispering now. "I'll make some

tea. Just need to take a cup up to them first. Then we can talk."

"Why does she do it?" Emily asked, keeping her voice low, as Mildred nipped back into the house. "She runs after him like I don't know what."

"He's all she's got," Ida replied. "Some women think any man is better than no man."

Emily let out a choked laugh. "Yes, well, some women . . ." she shook her head. "Did you hear what happened at the Barley Mow the other night?" Ida hadn't, but she was willing to be informed. "John was drunk by all accounts. Made a scene and got brought home in a police car." Emily shook her head.

"Stupid man! He's scared the coven might get active again and Mildred might have something more than him to occupy her twenty-four hours a day."

"He was with us before."

"Only because Sebastian wanted a thug as an enforcer and found John's underworld contacts useful. Look at the trouble all that brought us."

"Here we are." Mildred came out with a tea tray and a plate of jam tarts. She handed cups around. "Now, tell me," she said, offering the tarts on small plates. "Exactly what did we learn from this American girl?"

The "we" grated on Ida, but she let it pass. "Nothing." Ignoring Mildred's raised eyebrows, she went on. "Not a thing. She claims to be a witch, says her stepmother taught her. Maybe she did, but what can an American know about these things? Learned it from books, no doubt! There's nothing she has to offer us. Not the Underwoods' books. Nothing. Elizabeth got to look at them a bit, that's all. Then Dixie destroyed them."

"Good thing too, if you ask me," Mildred replied, taking a sip of tea.

"What did they have on you then, Mildred?" Emily asked.

Oh, she could be spiteful!

Mildred flushed.

"Not as much as they had on you and your precious Sebastian!" Ida said, taking satisfaction in Emily's reddening face. "They had something on everyone, most of it of their own making. It's a good thing it's all destroyed."

"And she destroyed everything? Even the herb and recipe books?" Mildred asked.

"So it seems," Ida said. "You know these Americans—no appreciation of things that matter!"

"What now?" Mildred's face was back to its usual pasty pale.

"Now?" Emily replied. "Now we lie low and work among ourselves. We are not drawing attention to ourselves one little bit."

At least she had a bit of sense. Ida nodded. "We can slowly let out the word that we have herbs and remedies. Slowly, mind you. And only to people we know."

"We'll be careful," Emily said.

Ida looked at Mildred. "How's John, Mildred?"

"Mending slowly. I believe a dislocation is far, far more painful than a break. He's had a hard time of it."

And so, Ida bet, had Mildred.

"He fell?" Emily asked.

"So he says. Says it was at work, but his clothes, they look as if he fell in a field. I had to take his jacket to the cleaners."

So even Mildred didn't believe his fabrication. "If it was at work, they should have called an ambulance right there and then, not have him get a taxi home."

"That's exactly what I said. Told him I had a good mind to call them and tell them so, but John got all wound up and wouldn't let me. And now his brother is up there with him, and they're having words."

"What about?" Emily asked.

"How would I know? When I went up to ask if they wanted tea, John was telling Dave that he was useless, and Dave . . ." Mildred shook her head. "Look, you'd better go before they notice you've been here. John's really upset about something."

"Must be the pain," Ida said.

They left as they had come, by the side gate. "I don't know why we bother with her," Emily said as they drove off. "She won't even plug in the iron without John's permission."

Ida sighed. Emily wasn't far wrong, but . . . "Her mother and I go back a long way." She frowned. "Enough of that. Get me home."

James wasn't sure why he was going to the Barley Mow Saturday night. He knew it would be crowded, and he wasn't the least in the mood for conviviality, but he was hungry, and neither cornflakes nor tinned soup much appealed. It was such a clear night, he decided to walk. The exercise would do him good. Part of him often regretted selling Sebastian's hunter—riding would have been good exercise, except the animal was a brute, with a temperament suited to Sebastian.

Remembering to shove a torch in his pocket for the walk home in the dark, he set off, taking the the shortcut across the edge of the common, rather than going down the drive and round the lane. A hundred yards or so along the path, the gorse and bushes to his right rustled, and a large cat ran across his path.

Cat! It was the size of a sheep or a large dog! James stood rooted to the spot as the animal ran off and disappeared in a clump of trees.

He started walking again and was another fifty yards further on when the thought hit him. Damn! That was the puma! So it wasn't a myth after all. And he'd scoffed a few times over the years when locals had claimed to see it.

Cripes! He'd heard stories about the Surrey puma all his life, had long ago put it in the category with Father Christmas and the tooth fairy.

Well, he'd certainly have something to add to the conversation at the bar when he got there. If anyone believed him. Damn! After all his scoffing, he expected to be disbelieved.

The Barley Mow was as busy as he'd expected.

"We can have you a table for dinner in twenty minutes or so," Alf promised. "Shouldn't be too long."

While he waited, James ordered his usual: ginger beer served in his own tankard.

As Alf pushed it across the counter to him, he asked, "Heard the latest, have you?"

"What is it?"

"The whole place has been buzzing about it since lunchtime. Seems the vicar's wife got up this morning and found a bag of jewelry on the back step."

"An anonymous donation to the new roof fund?"

"Nah!" Alf chuckled. "Police think it was stolen."

"Stolen?" A man to James's left asked. "What makes them think that?"

Alf reached for another glass. "Supposedly, it's items reported stolen." He put the glass on a tray and reached for a bottle under the counter. "What they want to know is who put it there."

"Easier said than done," the man said. "Unless they've got fingerprints or anything. Did you hear?"

"I heard lots," Alf replied. "Everyone has a theory, and you know what? A couple of them mentioned you, David Rowan!"

Interesting how faces went red when roused. This one actually went closer to purple. "Why you!" he snarled. "Who the hell do you think you are?"

"This is my pub," Alf replied. "And no need to get so aerated, I'm just telling you. People are talking."

"Right! Pick on me because I just got out!"

James didn't miss the balled-up fist. "Hey," he said. "Alf wasn't picking on you. Just passing on gossip. More like a friendly warning. You know what the police are like—if they're watching, then best be unobtrusive." Once the man sneered, James recognized him. Yes, he had been out of circulation a few years.

"Fine, I'll be unobtrusive elsewhere. This ain't the only pub in the village!"

As he left, Alf reached for his phone and muttered a few words, snapped it shut, and went on filling glasses.

"Nasty customer, that," James observed.

"You said it," Alf replied. "I tell you, Mr. Chadwick, you can't afford, in this business, to turn away paying customers, but ones like him aren't worth the little they spend. What with John Rowan going for those two ladies the other day, and now Dave back in town. The Blue Anchor is welcome to their trade, but," he added, "I thought it best to warn Tom Smith what was coming his way."

James took a sip of ginger beer. "What happened with the two ladies?"

"Oh!" Alf shook his head as he tipped a glass under the draft ale and eased the handle toward him. "The ones redoing Orchard House. Nice ladies: one's American, friend of that Dixie who was here last year, and the other from up north somewhere. They were eating dinner over there by the fireplace, and John Rowan goes up to them, yelling and going on, and overturns their table. Proper carry on it was. I called the police. I'm not having that here. Right mess it was to clean up too, as if Vickie doesn't have enough to do."

James felt a flush across his face. Once he'd been the cause of an upset table in here, and he doubted Alf had forgotten. "I met one of them the other day. She seemed a nice woman."

"You're right there, and more jobs in the village can only

help us all." Setting the glass on the bar, Alf looked across the room. "Okay," he said with a nod and turned to James. "They've got a table for you. Said it wouldn't be long, didn't I?"

"How are you tonight, Mr. Chadwick?" the waitress asked. "Anything special going on?"

"I saw the puma on the common walking here."

"Well, I never! And you did hear about the fortune in jewels found on the vicarage lawn, didn't you?" James agreed that yes, he had. "Amazing, wasn't it?" she went on. "Would you like the soup or the shrimp cocktail for your starter? The pâte's good, too."

James ordered the pâte. So much for his bursting news. The Surrey puma was old hat. Diamond tiaras and pearl necklaces on the vicarage lawn were something new.

But as he waited for his soup, he did wonder if the sudden appearance of the stolen jewelry had any connection with the odd sight he'd witnessed at the Manor Hotel last night.

Monday morning, and Elizabeth was wondering if staying in Bringham was really her best choice. Work was not a substitute for Tom. Antonia was off talking to her potter again, Elizabeth was working on the web site, and Stella was trying to call applicants in for interviews.

Trying being the operative word. After a series of resounding crashes from outside, Stella put the phone down in disgust. "I'm giving up. How can I have a conversation if I can't hear myself think?"

"Friday it got so bad I left the house. Give up on the phone, and come over here. I'll show you how to set up a web site."

Stella rolled her chair across to Elizabeth's computer and watched, fascinated.

She'd always imagined web sites were complicated, scientific efforts, but watching Elizabeth click away and seeing pictures and graphics appear as if by magic entranced her. "Can I have a go? I know it can't be as easy as it looks."

"This bit is straightforward. Here." She pushed over the mouse.

Following Elizabeth's directions, Stella brought up a picture of hand-crocheted lace and cut and pasted the copy that went with it. "That's incredible." She stared at the screen. "I never thought I could do that!"

"Stella, love, there isn't much you can't do! Here . . ." She clicked again and brought up a new screen. "Try adding the photo and copy for the handmade wood toys."

They were both so engrossed—Elizabeth with teaching Stella, and Stella with amazement at her efforts—that they never noticed the noise outside had stopped.

They didn't even look up when the door opened, but Sam's worried-sounding, "Mum?" caught Stella's attention.

"Hello, love. Had a good time exploring the gardens?"

"Mum." He looked pale and scared. "There's a dead body outside."

"Hi, Sam, " Elizabeth said. "What is it? A bird or something?"

"No!" His voice shook. "It's a girl!"

Stella was out of her seat in an instant. "What do you mean?" It couldn't be what he thought. He'd made a mistake.

"Mum, it is. She was there when they pulled down that old earth building."

"The air raid shelter?" Elizabeth asked.

"Yeah. When they got the side off, inside was a dead girl. All wrapped up, but some of the covers fell off, and—" He gave a sound like a hiccup. Stella pulled him close. He seemed so certain, but surely . . .

Mark, the foreman, appeared in the open doorway. "Beg pardon for interrupting, and sorry the boy had to see it. But, ladies, I have to call the police."

Elizabeth handed him her mobile.

The day went to pot from then on.

By the time Antonia arrived, looking, Stella had to admit, as if she'd spent a delightful morning, most likely in bed, the place was overrun with police, detectives, and a crime scene team. And half the garden, it seemed, was marked off with blue and white police tape.

"Sweet Abel!" Antonia muttered, half under her breath. "What happened?"

Sam told her.

Seemed even ancient vampires could get shaken and shocked, which reassured Stella a bit. But not much.

They were all sitting in the office, the police having strongly suggested they not watch outside. Sam didn't hide his disappointment. "The most exciting thing I've seen, and I can't watch!"

"Sam!" Stella snapped. The tension really was getting to her. "Don't be so ghoulish!"

"Excuse me," Elizabeth said, her sharp tone eased by her smile.

"Sorry!" Stella said. "Just came out."

"It's okay, Mum. Elizabeth was just teasing," Sam said. He looked at Elizabeth. "Weren't you?"

She nodded.

"I'd like to know," Antonia put in, "how, Sam, are you sure it's a girl?"

He screwed up his face. "She . . . it . . . the body was on a sort of ledge, and the cover was off her face, or skull, really. She had long hair, very dirty but long, and it looked like a girl. Gross—really, it was. Steve—Mark's helper—he said, 'Oh, my gawd!' and threw up in the blackberries."

Boys' sensibilities definitely differed from adults'. "Sam, that's enough."

"But Mom, Antonia asked."

"It's still enough." Sheesh! Rural living in England wasn't without its rough moments. At least there weren't any rogue vampires around Surrey. Just carjackers and dead bodies.

The door opened. Everyone looked toward the tall man who strode in. "Good afternoon, ladies," he said. "Sir," he added with a nod to Sam. "I'm Detective Inspector Warrington. Sorry to keep you here, but we had the crime scene people outside, and I wanted to talk to the work crew before they left."

"They've left already?" asked Antonia, standing up.

"Yes, Madam, and you would be . . .?"

"Antonia Stonewright. I own this house."

"Miss Stonewright." He offered his hand. "Sorry to disrupt things, ladies, but work will have to be suspended for a few days. We need to go over the scene and may need to dig wider. One's never sure what will turn up."

"What about the body?" Stella asked.

"We're in the middle of moving it."

"It was a girl, right?" Sam asked.

"From what we can tell, yes, son," the inspector said. "You the lad who was there when they found her?"

"Yes!" Stella bit back a groan at his enthusiasm.

"Mind telling me what happened?" He looked around. "Is one of you this young man's mother?"

"I am," Stella said, stepping to stand close to Sam.

He nodded at Stella. "Alright if I talk with him a bit? Just to cross-check?"

"Okay." Sam seem eager enough, and could she actually refuse?

The inspector squatted down 'til he was eye to eye to Sam. "What's your name, son?"

"Sam. Sam Corvus."

"Well, Sam. Mind telling me what happened and when?"

"I was out watching them take down the old shelter thing and . . . " Sam went on, repeating what he'd told them earlier and describing the unfortunate Steve's upchucking in colorful detail. Obviously, detective inspectors had stronger stomachs than mothers. He listened as if nothing had ever interested him as much, and when Sam finished, he stood and shook hands.

"You're a good observer, Sam." He glanced over to the door and the younger detective who'd been taking notes. "Got all that, Jeffers?"

Jeffers nodded. Sheesh! She'd been writing it all down. Oh well. Sam had seen it all, and . . .

"Any of you ladies see anything?" Warrington asked.

"We were working in here until Sam came and announced they'd found a body. Then Mark Gould came in and called you." Elizabeth said.

"Sorry again about the disruption. Should all be over in a week or so, and you'll have your work site back. Remember, no one steps over the police tape. Any questions?"

"Yes." They all looked in Sam's direction. "How will you find out who she is?"

Seemed detective inspectors didn't often deal with ten-year-old boys. Stella's mouth twitched as she waited to hear him answer that one. "Sam, first we do a postmortem to find out how long she's been there and how old she was. They have tests they use. Once we have a date, we go back and look up any missing persons around that time who match the age and description. Then we spend a lot of time checking and investigating."

Sam frowned as he took this in. "Was she murdered? She has to have been, right?"

"We don't know for sure, but it looks like foul play." Stella went cold inside. "We'll find out exactly."

"Can I watch the policemen when they work?"

"Best not, might make them nervous, but you can look when they finish. Just promise not to cross the tape."

"I wouldn't." Sam shook his head. "But I will make

notes, so I remember everything. We have to write an essay about our holidays, and I'm going to write on this."

Stella bet that would be a first for his next year's teacher.

"I'm sure you'll do a grand job, too, Sam." Warrington shook hands all around and thanked them again, promising to let them know what transpired.

"Sweet Goddess!" Elizabeth said as the door closed behind him and the silent police constable. "What next? This has been one crazy weekend!"

"There were a few high points," Antonia said. "Like you getting engaged."

Elizabeth laughed. "You're right!"

"You've been looking pretty relaxed all weekend," Stella said.

"Not as relaxed as Antonia. She's had a great time with her potter."

"What potter?" Sam asked. "You mean her fella?"

"Never you mind," Stella said. "Let's go and have lunch now that we can leave."

"When are you and Tom getting married?" Sam asked Elizabeth as they crossed the Green toward the Barley Mow.

"Soon," she replied.

"Do I get to come?"

"Of course. I'll need someone to give me away. Could you do it? My father is too ill to travel." And would no doubt have another stroke if he ever realized his only daughter was a ghoul and was marrying a vampire.

Sam stopped in his tracks, eyes wide. "You really mean it? You want me to give you away?"

"Sure."

"How do I give you away? Tell secrets?"

"Not like that," Stella said. "Remember when Justin and I got married and Tom gave me away?"

Sam nodded. "Hey, I get to give you to Tom then?"

"You bet."

He gave a long chuckle. "I'll tell him he better be nice to you or I'll take you back!"

He would too. Elizabeth didn't know what she'd started. "Aren't you hungry, Sam?" Stella asked.

"Yes, I am! I could eat a horse!"

"Let's get going then. It's already nearly two!" The day was half-gone, and what a day! For a peaceful life, she should have stayed in Havering. In fact, Justin was perfectly capable of insisting they all return after this. He'd strongly suggested it on Sunday, and now . . . Heck! She'd worry about that when she called him. Which she'd better do right after lunch.

A few months earlier, she'd have been fascinated by the Barley Mow, but by now, Stella wasn't quite as intrigued by interesting old buildings. The lunch crowd had thinned out. Presumably, most honest, hardworking villagers were back at their jobs.

The tall, well built barman greeted Elizabeth and Antonia like old friends. "Good to see you back. Had a spot of trouble at the house?" Stella could almost smell the curiosity of the few customers scattered round the bar, but what did she expect? Who could miss the flashing blue lights and parked police cars? "Something wrong?" he went on, obviously eager for firsthand news.

"We found a dead body!" Sam announced to the world. Stella could have sworn she saw ears wagging. It was news, after all.

"A body, young man?" the bartender asked. "And you were there?"

Stella groaned inwardly. Not the sort of publicity they needed, but this was a village, and the gossip lines might as well start off with the right version. Speculation over an unearthed corpse would safely obliterate any casual memories of her arrival in a smashed car.

"I saw it all," Sam said. "I was watching them pull down the old air raid shelter. One of the workmen threw up all over the bushes."

"Well then, after all that excitement, I bet your Mum and her friends need a nice quiet lunch." He nodded at Stella. "I'm Alf, landlord of this here pub. Met your two friends the other day. Glad to see you back, and"—he held out his hand to Stella—"welcome to Bringham and the Barley Mow."

He had a good strong handshake, and Dixie had called him a friend. "Stella Corvus and my son, Sam."

"Well, ladies, what can I get for you?" They ordered steak, steak, and steak, all rare, but Sam went for scampi and chips. "It might be quieter for you in the dining room," Alf said, nodding toward the open doorway. "No one else there right now, and you'll have more space."

And much less likely to be the center of attention. Stella was tempted to hug Alf but settled for a smile.

"Thanks," Antonia said. "We have some talking to do."

"Everything else going alright? Apart from your trouble this morning, that is" Alf asked as he poured a Tizer for Sam and reached for three bottles of Malvern water. They must seem like boring drinkers.

"Other than that, yes," Elizabeth said. "We're busy."

"Any new venture will be," he agreed. "You've done a lot for that old house. Needed it, too," he paused. "Funny how things happen there, though."

"Not just there," said a man who'd wandered over to the bar. "What about the goings on up at the vicarage?"

"The vicarage?" Elizabeth asked.

Stella swore her throat went dry. Impossible but . . .

"Oh, yes," Alf said. "You didn't hear? Saturday morning, the vicar's wife found a load of stolen jewelry scattered over the back lawn."

Either Justin and Tom had been messier than intended or . . . "It's been a busy weekend for the police," she said.

Alf nodded and put the four glasses on a tray. "It was."

"Anything else exciting happen?" Sam asked.

"Something else?" Alf asked. "A dead body isn't enough excitement?"

"Oh, it is, but Mrs. Zeibel, our old next door neighbor, used to say things came in threes."

"M-m-m-m." Alf frowned as if thinking. "She did, did she? My old mother used to say the same thing, and you know, now I come to think of it, Mr. Chadwick up at the Grange saw the puma."

"What puma?" Sam asked.

Chapter 13

Alf shook his head as he handed the Tizer to Sam. "You haven't heard of our puma? What do they teach you at that school of yours? The Surrey puma is famous."

"Really? Famous like the Loch Ness monster and Bigfoot?"

Antonia smiled. So Michael hadn't been exaggerating the "local legend" bit. Alf nodded as he tilted a clean glass against the neck of the bottle and filled it with sparkling water. "More famous round these parts."

"Where do you see it?"

"Now, that depends. You don't see the puma much. She's shy and hides in the woods but sometimes people like Mr. Chadwick see her when they're out walking. Every so often, someone takes a blurry picture, and it's in the paper. she's even been on the TV a couple of times."

"Does she hurt anyone?"

Alf shook his head and placed the glass on the bar. "Not that I've ever heard. Once in a while, a sheep gets mauled, or some farmer's chickens get killed, and they blame the puma, but heck, she's got to eat something, and besides, who's to say it wasn't a fox? They're getting to be a real problem these days."

"Have you seen her?" Sam was getting into this. If he but knew . . .

"No, not me, but you come in of an evening, especially near closing time, and you'll have several who claim to have."

Sam grinned up at the man. "You think they're kidding?"

"I dunno, might be true. Might just be talk. But they've been talking about the puma since I was a boy. Now how many wild animals live fifty years or more?"

Sam pondered the point. "She could be a special animal. A super-puma perhaps?"

Antonia listened, amused at the sex ascribed to the puma. There was nothing in the least feminine about Michael! And as for Sam, how could a mortal child be so perceptive? Although a child who had the courage to save a vampire from extinction was no ordinary mortal.

"Come on, Sam," Stella said. "Let's find a table." Thank you, Stella. Time they put an end to this line of enquiry.

They settled by the window of the dining room. They were alone except for a pair of old men playing dominoes at a table in the sun and rows of geraniums along the window ledges. Antonia brushed one on purpose to catch the odd, sharp smell of the leaves.

Once they were seated, an odd silence settled. Antonia thought about Michael and Alf's words and wondered just how much anyone, besides her, knew. Sam had come close, but it was only a boy's guess, fueled no doubt, by comics and TV. The other two were subdued. Even Sam drank quietly and frowned to himself.

Hardly surprising. Finding a dead body was a shock to anyone's peace of mind.

"Who do you think she is, Mum?" Sam asked. "The girl, I mean."

Stella was silent a moment. Elizabeth stared. Antonia had her mouth open to answer when Stella said, "Someone whose family missed her but never found her."

He creased his brow. "Sad, isn't it, Mum? Think we should tell Dad?"

"Yes, dear, after lunch." She sounded as if she wanted lunch to last several hours.

And why not? It had taken some effort on both Stella and Elizabeth's parts to convince their respective men that staying here was a good idea, that the car incident was a long-shot occurrence, and that everything was fine. A dead body would put their macho protective instincts into overdrive. Come to that, she suspected Michael wouldn't be overjoyed when he heard.

One more obstacle in a very, very long life.

When the food came, they ate in silence. Elizabeth's hunger was intact. She took care of all three steaks, and Sam tucked into his scampi and chips with the enthusiasm of a ten-year-old. For her part, Antonia rather looked forward to a couple of bags or Michael's warm neck.

"Think I could have pudding, Mum?" Sam asked as he all but wiped the glaze off his plate,

"Go see what they have." Stella handed him a couple of folded up notes. "And get us each another water, please."

As Sam passed out of earshot, she gave a desperate look. "What the hell am I going to do? We come down for a nice break, and so far we've had a carjacking; an attempted kidnapping; stolen jewels; a car crash; an attempted break-in on what was left of the car, and now, a dead body." She shook her head as if to clear her mind. "And I thought crime was bad in our old neighborhood!"

"I'm beginning to compare it to the turmoil of the Saxon invasions!" Antonia said.

Elizabeth sighed. Lucky ghoul—she still could. "I'm not sure what to compare it to," she said, "but it has to get better, right?" She looked at them both as if trusting the vamps to know the answers. She was likely to be disappointed.

"Saying 'yes' might be pushing our luck," Stella said. "My instinct is to grab Sam and hightail it back to Havering, but suppose they want him as a witness or something?"

"There are plenty of others," Elizabeth said. "Mark, his workmen. They won't want Sam at the inquest."

"If they do, I can certainly change their minds," Antonia said.

At least that got a smile. "Of course!" Stella said. "I keep forgetting what we can do."

"Don't," Antonia said. "Who knows when we may need our powers? I suggest we have a long, long lunch and take the afternoon off, and by the morning, the police will have cleared the poor girl away."

"Sorry, son," Alf said to Sam. "You can pick something from the menu, but your mother or one of the other grown-ups has to pay for it."

"You mean Elizabeth, or Antonia, or Mum could buy it, but I can't?"

"That's right. Sorry, but you're just not old enough. If it were up to me, you'd be welcome to that treacle tart, but . . ." Alf gave Sam a nod. "Run and ask one for them to pay for you."

"Okay."

Sam had turned to go when a man standing the bar said, "Excuse me, but would that be Antonia Stonewright?"

Growing up in rough streets had taught Sam caution. He hesitated, but the man looked nice, he didn't exude menace; and two vampires and a ghoul were stronger than any bad guy any day of the week. "Yes, it would." he replied.

"Ah!" The man went thoughtful. "I tried to find her at Orchard House, but I missed her, they said."

"You've been to the house?"

He nodded. "I heard you'd had a spot of trouble up there and wanted to make sure Antonia was alright."

"We found a dead body."

He looked as shocked as a grown-up would be expected to. "Someone from the village?"

"I don't really know how they can figure out who she is, but the policeman said they would."

The man wrinkled his eyebrows as if thinking. "But Antonia and all of you are alright?"

"We're fine. Just had lunch. I think Mum and the others wanted to get me away because they thought it might upset me."

"Did it?"

"Sort of. It's pretty mean to hide someone away like that for years and years and years, but I'll have lots to write about when I get back to school."

"You will indeed. What's your name, lad?"

Sam held out his hand. "I'm Sam Corvus."

The man had good eyes, and his hand felt right. "Michael Langton, Sam. How do you do?"

"Oh, you're Antonia's potter!"

Sounded like a laugh from behind the bar. Alf's face was steady, but he looked as if he'd just swallowed a bee.

"Yes, Sam," Michael Langton said. "Antonia has been talking to me about taking my work in her new gallery."

"Actually, it's a craft center," Sam said. "Won't just be pictures and things. Anything local that's good quality and salable." At least that's what Elizabeth and Antonia had said umpteen times.

"I think Antonia and her craft center are just what the village needs." Michael Langton paused. "Tell me, Sam. Do you think your mother would mind if I paid for that treacle tart? Would save getting her in here."

Would she? The man knew Antonia, and Alf seemed to

think he was okay. "Should be fine, but they also want three more sparkling Malvern waters."

"I'll take care of it." He passed a bill to Alf, who reached for glasses.

"Down here to stay?" Michael Langton asked.

"No, we live in Yorkshire." He gave Michael Langton a good, long look. "Do you like Antonia? I mean, really like her?"

"Yes, I do."

Sam wanted to jump and say whoopee very loud, but he was indoors so . . . "I'm so glad because I think she really, really likes you."

"Would you like clotted cream with that treacle tart?" Alf asked.

Sam looked at Michael. He was paying after all.

"Would you?"

"Please!"

"Why do you think she really, really likes me?" Michael asked.

Sam grinned. "When she talks about you, she looks all happy. She's really nice, but she used to be really grown-up and serious. Now she sort of acts the way Mum did when she first met my Dad, my stepdad, I mean. All soppy but happy."

"I see."

So did Sam. "You're in love, aren't you?"

"Here you are!" Alf said. "Three sparkling Malverns, treacle tart with clotted cream and . . . Want another drink yourself, Sam?"

"No, thanks. I've still got some left."

"Right you are." Alf handed Michael the tray.

Michael hefted the tray. "Okay, Sam, you lead. I'll follow."

Michael couldn't hold back a grin at the look on Antonia's face. The other two women—the brown-haired one Sam went to, bursting with the news he'd just met "Antonia's friend," and the fair, stately-looking one—he barely glimpsed out of the corner of his eye. But Antonia, wide-eyed, mouth open, and the flush of sheer pleasure on her face—a look he'd happily noticed on other more intimate occasions—Antonia held his attention.

"What are you doing here?"

"Delighted to see you too," he replied, deliberately kissing her cheek. "I heard there was a phalanx of police cars converging on Orchard House. I came to see if you were alright." He pulled a chair over and sat next to her—forget waiting to be asked. "I see you are."

"More or less," she replied.

"Sam told me what happened." He looked at the other two women and offered his hand. "I'm Michael Langton."

They both smiled and exchanged very pregnant glances. He could almost hear them think "Antonia's Potter." Not that he minded being Antonia's in the least.

"I'm Stella," the darker one said, "Sam's mother."

"Elizabeth Connor."

"She used to be my baby-sitter," Sam announced. "Mum, Michael paid for the pudding and drink."

"It's Mr. Langton," she replied briskly. "And what were you . . ."

"Michael's fine," Michael replied, "and Sam wasn't cadging or anything. We got talking, and I realized he was with you. I was looking for Antonia, so you might say Sam did me a big favor."

A very big favor now that he was right next to Antonia. "I'd been worried there was an accident."

Even the look in her eyes did him in, and he was hard just sitting by her. He was in deep, but what the heck. She had secrets too. The two nice women sitting with her would no doubt pass out if they knew. And as for letting her son sit next to a vampire . . . "I'm relieved to see you're alright."

Zebra Contemporary

Whatever your taste in contemporary romance – Romantic Suspense... Character-Driven... Light & Whimsical... Heartwarming... Humorous – we have it at Zebra!

And now Zebra has created a Book Club for readers like yourself who enjoy fine Contemporary Romance written by today's best-selling authors.

Authors like Fern Michaels... Lori Foster... Janet Dailey... Lisa Jackson...Janelle Taylor... Kasey Michaels... Shannon Drake... Kat Martin... to name but a few!

These are the finest

contemporary romances available

anywhere today!

But don't take our word for it! Accept our gift of FREE Zebra Contemporary Romances – and see for yourself. You only pay $1.99 for shipping and handling.

Once you've read them, we're sure you'll want to continue receiving the newest Zebra Contemporaries as soon as they're published each month! And you can by becoming a member of the Zebra Contemporary Romance Book Club!

As a member of Zebra Contemporary Romance Book Club,

- You'll receive four books every month. Each book will be by one of Zebra's best-selling authors.

- You'll have variety – you'll never receive two of the same kind of story in one month.

- You'll get your books hot off the press, usually before they appear in bookstores.

- You'll ALWAYS save up to 30% off the cover price.

SEND FOR YOUR FREE BOOKS TODAY!

To start your membership, simply complete and return the Free Book Certificate. You'll receive your Introductory Shipment of FREE Zebra Contemporary Romances, you only pay $1.99 for shipping and handling. Then, each month you will receive the 4 newest Zebra Contemporary Romances. Each shipment will be yours to examine FREE for 10 days. If you decide to keep the books, you'll pay the preferred subscriber price (a savings of up to 30% off the cover price), plus shipping and handling. If you want us to stop sending books, just say the word... it's that simple.

If the FREE Book Certificate is missing, call 1-800-770-1963 to place your order.

FREE BOOK CERTIFICATE

Yes! Please send me FREE Zebra Contemporary romance novels. I only pay $1.99 for shipping and handling. I understand that each month thereafter I will be able to preview 4 brand-new Contemporary Romances FREE for 10 days. Then, if I should decide to keep them, I will pay the money-saving preferred subscriber's price (that's a savings of up to 30% off the retail price), plus shipping and handling. I understand I am under no obligation to purchase any books, as explained on this card.

NAME _____

ADDRESS _____ APT. _____

CITY _____ STATE _____ ZIP _____

TELEPHONE (____) _____

E-MAIL _____

SIGNATURE _____

(If under 18, parent or guardian must sign)

Offer limited to one per household and not to current subscribers. Terms, offer and prices subject to change. Orders subject to acceptance by Zebra Contemporary Book Club. Offer Valid in the U.S. only.

Thank You!

CN046A

THE BENEFITS OF BOOK CLUB MEMBERSHIP

• You'll get your books hot off the press, usually before they appear in bookstores.

• You'll ALWAYS save up to 30% off the cover price.

• You'll get our FREE monthly newsletter filled with author interviews, book previews, special offers and MORE!

• There's no obligation – you can cancel at any time and you have no minimum number of books to buy.

• And – if you decide you don't like the books you receive, you can return them. (You always have ten days to decide.)

Be sure to visit our website at www.kensingtonbooks.com.

ll..l..lll....ll.l.l.l..l.l..ll.l.l..l.ll.l..l.l..lll..l

Zebra Contemporary Romance Book Club
Zebra Home Subscription Service, Inc.
P.O. Box 5214
Clifton NJ 07015-5214

PLACE
STAMP
HERE

"We are," Antonia replied, "but some poor, unidentified woman isn't, and Abel knows how long this will hold up the building, but . . . can't be helped. We have other projects, and we'll manage."

"How about coming back with me? I wanted to show you a couple of samples."

"I see." Her smirk suggested she knew what samples he had in mind. "Well . . ." she glanced at the other two. "How about we take the rest of the day off?"

"Good idea!" Stella replied. "Sam wanted to see the maze at Hampton Court, and we never got there over the weekend. Coming with us, Elizabeth?"

The blonde shook her head. "Thanks, but I want to go back to the garden again. If we can't work on the buildings, perhaps we can start renovations outside."

Didn't take much to persuade Antonia to leave first. He didn't just want her in his bed; they needed to talk. What he'd heard the other night had been worrying him ever since; when he'd heard about the panda cars at her house, he'd feared the worst.

Detective Inspector Warrington tossed his jacket on the passenger seat and headed back to the station. They'd carted the corpse off, and now it was all up to the crime scene team. He'd done all he could until the reports started coming in.

Something nagged at him. It wasn't the dead body. He'd seen enough of those, although once he read the report, he'd feel his customary rage at the perpetrator. But, truth be told, apart from the feeling he'd missed something, his foremost sensation was hunger. He stopped to buy a takeaway sandwich, and he was tempted to take it down to the river to eat, but he had a stack waiting on his desk, and he wanted to talk to Helen Adams, the crime desk clerk. She was local, had been to school in Effingham. She might know what he was missing.

She came in as he was getting a cup of tea.

"You wanted me?"

"What does Orchard House, Bringham mean to you? Past happenings, gossip, scandal, you name it."

She thought a moment. "Wasn't that where they had the car bombing a year or so ago? Local man killed, and the bomb intended for the owner?"

That was it! "Can you get me the case? Bring up anything you have on it."

"Of course, and now I come to think of it, wasn't it involved in the Caughleigh case?"

Interesting. "Get me what you can, will you?"

What she dug up was interesting. The bombing case was still unsolved, but everything had been sent up to the bomb squad. Sooner or later, there'd be a match. But Adams had been spot on: a local man had died in the car bomb intended for the owner of the house, who had gone back home to America shortly afterward. And what was really curious was that Caughleigh, in his crazed confession, claimed to have had the bomb planted and later to have killed her in Yorkshire, but she had turned up alive and kicking a week or so later.

And now a long-interred body.

Dangerous place, that Orchard House.

What else had happened there over the years?

"Got your car with you?" Michael asked as he closed the door of the Barley Mow behind them.

"I left it at the hotel. I can walk, you know. Sore feet aren't a problem for me."

He gave a worried smile. "We'll drive. I brought the van, and there's something . . ." he paused. "Let's just get in."

Talk about a bone shaker. His van looked a bit decrepit.

Inside, it was derelict. How did he ever pass the MOT with this wreck? Or, perhaps shape shifters had their own unofficial papers system like vampires. Good thing she didn't have to worry about dying if the brakes gave out. "Where are we going?" They were certainly not heading for his place.

"You've got a bit of time; I thought I'd take you to one of my favorite spots."

She hadn't much patience for cryptic comments. Less for getting bounced over country roads in a vehicle of torture. "What if I have work to do? Some of us do, you know!"

"Most of us do, Antonia. I've been worried about you and your friends since last night, and after this morning . . ." He sighed. "Hearing there were cop cars and flashing blue lights all round your place had me imagining the very worst."

"There aren't many things worse than murder!" Ungracious, snippy, but by Abel, his "come with me when I tell you to" attitude rankled a bit.

"Yeah!" He all but grunted it out. "Thinking the woman you love had been hurt or murdered!"

"I'm a bit past getting murdered!" Unless circumstances were really, really unbelievably weighted against her. "What was that other bit?"

He glanced at her, still frowning. "Dammit, Antonia, you know I love you. Haven't I told you enough!"

Yes, but . . . "Lots of men have told me that over the centuries." And a few actually meant it.

Drat! He took that hard. She swore she felt the spasm of hurt clutch his heart. He scowled over at her. "Lots of men, eh?"

Abel help her! Men were all the same: touchy, jealous, possessive, and often liars, but Michael Langton was more. Much more. She hoped. "Hundreds actually, maybe thousands, and some perhaps meant it, but there were precious few that I ever loved back."

His brakes needed work. They squealed like a stuck boar when he slammed them and yanked the van to the side, all but pruning a branch from an overhanging tree.

"What did you say?"

Rhetorical questions were thoroughly irritating. "Are you telling me that with your superior-to-human feline ears, you didn't catch what I said?"

He let out a very feline hiss. "I'm in human shape now with human ears." Frowning, he grabbed her and yanked her close. His mouth came down with a kiss that might well have smothered a mortal.

It energized her. Wrapping her arms around his neck, she held him even closer, her vampire strength all but plastering his body to hers. Between them were a gear stick and the hand brake, but she ignored such insignificant mortal impediments. Wrapping her leg over his hip, she ground herself against him. As his tongue found hers, she felt her soul meld with his.

An impatient hoot behind them reminded them they were blocking a narrow lane.

Pausing only to whisper, "I love you," while she disentangled her leg from the gear stick, Michael waved rather cheekily at the irate motorist behind them and drove on.

Michael hummed as he drove, and Antonia felt a remarkably stupid grin creasing her mouth.

She was nuts! In love! Hadn't she learned? This was different! Michael was open, honest, and honorable, nothing like a certain French vampire of her misguided acquaintance.

"That's one thing taken care of," Michael announced with a trace of understandable smugness. "Once we get there, I'll tell you the rest, and then I'll take you home and make love to you until we both wear out."

"Where are we going?"

"One of my favorite spots in the entire county."

"I hope it's secluded with lots of privacy. Then we won't have to wait until we get to your place."

His downright sexy grin lit up his dark eyes and added to her anticipation. "Do vampires think of anything but sex?"

"Once in a while, but we are renowned in literature for our prowess."

"So the slavering hacks got something right!"

"Lucky guess probably. What do any of them know, really?"

"Same could be said about shifters."

"True, all that full moon nonsense."

"Just as well, if you ask me. Who wants the others knowing all about us? Discretion is survival."

How nice to talk about these things with a man who understood! Not that she'd ever broached the subject with one who didn't, and she wasn't likely to, but . . . "Michael, how old are you?"

"Not as old as you, but you're not robbing the cradle. I was born in 1903."

"Just over a hundred. I can live with that."

"Good, because you're going to!"

"Certain about it, are you?"

"Totally and absolutely. Do I hear any objections from the passenger seat?" None from her, but Gwyltha was likely to throw a wobbly. "What's the matter?"

By Abel! How could he read her silences so well? "Nothing, just a bit stunned. After all, it's not every afternoon I get professions of love from shapeshifting large cats."

"Come to that, I don't meet vampires most days of the week." But more often than he knew. "Damn glad I met you though, Tonia. Want to move in with me?"

She understood exactly what he was offering: not just sharing his delightful bed, but his secrets too. He was entrusting her with his safety. "Later, Michael. Right now, I need to get things settled with the business, and with this corpse complication, who knows how it will hold things up?"

"You'd rather live in a hotel than with me?"

"No, I don't mean that, but I have commitments. Elizabeth and Stella came down to help, and between us, we're getting things going. I can't walk out on them."

"They're friends, not just employees?"

"Right." She sensed where this was leading.

"Known them a while?"

"A couple of years."

"They know what you are?"

Moment of truth, or at least part of the truth. "Yes, they know I'm a vampire, a revenant."

"Very trusting of you."

"They also know that the oak stake to the heart and frying in sunlight are myths. They are friends, Michael."

"Good friends, too, and that Sam is quite a character."

"Isn't he? I love him dearly." Good idea to switch the conversation to the one mortal in the list. "Bright too. He's Stella's pride and joy."

"She doesn't feel any qualms about him being around a vampire?"

"Michael,"—better get this straight—"Stella knows I would never, ever do anything to harm Sam, or anyone else, for that matter. I'm a vampire, not a bloodsucking monster."

"Your kind does rather have an image problem though."

"Only among the ignorant, and let me tell you, I'm not in the habit of announcing my nature to all and sundry. You want to know something, Michael? I've seldom even told my lovers."

"You told me that first night."

"Yes, and spent the next twenty-four hours thinking what an impulsive fool I'd been. Of course, that was before you mentioned your dual nature."

"Right couple we make, don't we?"

"I think we could both do worse, don't you?" What next? Next thing he'd be wanting to stick a great wodge of a jewel on her left hand, like Tom and Elizabeth over the weekend. She quite fancied the idea.

"Should I take that as a 'yes'?"

"Yes to what?"

His laugh was warm, sexy, and delicious, starting deep in his belly and coming out in a great peal of delight. "Anything you want, darling. Anything!"

Her happiness was ridiculous, a mortal—alright, a shape-shifting mortal with a long lifespan—made her feel this way. It had been years, centuries since this wild, lighthearted joy filled her soul. Wasn't too far different from the sensation of downing too much mead on an empty stomach, a mistake she'd only ever made once. Was Michael a mistake? No! Every finely honed instinct told her he was honest, honorable, and sexy as all get out.

And he loved her.

Don't forget that!

As if she was likely to!

"So where are we going, and what's this thing you have to tell me?"

"Silent Pool. We're almost there. I just hope there aren't a hundred picnickers disturbing the quiet."

Not a hundred. Just a couple of cars, their occupants walking around one of the most peaceful spots Antonia had seen in centuries. Ignore the cars, overhead airplane noise, and the rubbish bins, and she could imagine herself back in her girlhood, or at least somewhere in the fifteenth century.

"It's lovely!"

"I'm glad you like it," Michael said, coming close and settling his arm over her shoulders. "How about a nice stroll?"

They'd run through the night together; why not meander though the day? Matching her pace to his—or was he adapting to hers?—they walked in perfect rhythm to the edge of the pond, then around the shore, pausing in an odd, little rustic summer house that was definitely not fifteenth century,

"I see why it's called Silent Pool. There's no sound. No water rippling, not even birds singing." Uncanny. Elizabeth might have an explanation, but . . . "Is it supposed to be magical?"

"Not magical exactly. According to legend, a virgin drowned here trying to escape the advances of Bad King John, and as a result, it's been silent ever since."

"As good a story as any, and not unbelievable."

"You knew King John?"

"Not personally, but I lived through his time. And his brother's wasn't much better. Yes, there was the papal interdict in John's time that made things difficult for many, but back then, life was hard. If you had the patronage and favor of someone in power, it was easier, but for the vast mass of humanity, life was rough, and often short."

He tightened his hold on her shoulder. "Were you one of the poor then?"

"I was a traveling midwife known for my skills. Not wealthy, barely comfortable, but I had the support of the Colony. We had the advantage of immortality; epidemics don't touch us."

"The Colony?" Michael asked.

Darn! Love was making her incautious in more than one way. "There are other vampires in England, and we support each other as need be."

"I see." She bet he didn't, not really. "Many of them?"

"Michael, I'm prepared to reveal my nature to you, but I won't for the others." He nodded, accepting that. Why not? He understood about concealment.

"Just wondered. Can't help being curious."

She bit back the comment about what curiosity did to the

cat. None too tactful and . . . "Back in the pub, you said there was something you wanted to tell me?"

"Yeah, there is. I might have it all wrong. It's just your friend's car, the one the yob was trying to break into, was a Jaguar, an XJ8S."

"What about it?" She didn't go cold. Couldn't go cold. It wasn't in her physiology, but something very much like cold snaked up her spine. "Michael?"

"Don't look so worried. It might be nothing."

"If it were nothing, you'd have forgotten it right away, and you'd certainly not be telling me."

"Alright, alright." He shook his head, pulling away a little to run his strong fingers through his tawny hair. "It's a bit complicated."

"I can follow complicated things."

"I know that, Tonia," He shook his head. "Okay, listen. You know I go prowling at night." She nodded. Of course she did. "Last night, after you left early, I was restless, so I shifted and wandered toward the edge of the village. I was heading toward the main road when I ended up by those cottages beyond the station, and since by then, it was latish and quiet, I wandered into one of the gardens and stretched out in the shadow of the hedge. Just resting and thinking."

"The windows were open in the house, and I could hear two men. They were going on about something not working out, blaming each other by the sound of things and making a few uncharitable comments about the vicar and his wife. That made me really prick up my ears as I'd heard, like everyone else in the village, about the windfall of stolen jewelry that landed on the vicar's back step. So I perked up my ears and eavesdropped.

"It was obvious that these two were involved in it, and both blamed the other for messing things up. The detail that caught my ear was the argument about taking or not taking the Jaguar and one of them not getting into it to retrieve something. Thought it was too much of a coincidence after Friday night, so I'm telling you."

Bless him. "Yes, Stella's car is a Jaguar, but it's gone, towed away. She had a prang on the way down, and it's getting repaired." And bless Jude for his efficiency. A Jaguar morphing into a Mercedes would put anybody off the track. "Thanks for the warning. Do you often overhear things like that?"

He frowned a little. "Not a lot, just sometimes." He shrugged and paced back and forth—definitely feline in his movements. How did everyone miss it? "Tonia, this might sound wet, but I do listen in on conversations. Not out of nosiness, but to get a taste of life in a human household. I listen to families arguing, children playing, even arguments over TV shows. I was lonely until I met you. The closest shifter is in Kent, and he's a rather odd fellow."

She'd never thought of loneliness, but what if she didn't have the Colony? She walked right up until she was nose to nose, knee to thigh and breast to chest. "I'll fill your loneliness for you, Michael."

She would, and the Colony was going to have to lump it.

Chapter 14

Justin leaned back in the wing chair in Tom's study, looking out at the garden beyond as he sipped a glass of very good port. "This has been fun, Tom. We visited a couple of places I haven't seen in two hundred years."

"You should get down from the rural vastness of Yorkshire more often. Bring Stella and Sam to Town. There's more to amuse a child here than in Havering," Tom said, leaning back and resting his cheroot on the ashtray at his elbow.

True. "We will." He paused and sipped again, letting the dark liquid sit on his tongue. It was texture, not the taste, he enjoyed; that and the companionship of sharing a glass with Tom as they had for centuries. "Thanks for persuading me to stay another day. Much better than going back to Yorkshire and spending the day worrying about Stella and Sam.

"Instead, you'll go back tomorrow and worry about them."

"I have two operations tomorrow. That should keep my mind occupied."

"Does it work?"

"Hell, no! I still worry, especially after the car business

and the damn stolen loot, but we took care of it all, and Stella has plenty of common sense. In my mind, I know they are well and safe. It's my heart that questions. Most likely because I miss them." He gave a dry chuckle. "Funny really. Before I met Stella, I thought my existence was contented and complete; now I wonder how I lived all these centuries without her and Sam."

"It's that way with Lizzie. She drives me loony at times, but I'll forever owe Vlad a debt of gratitude for rescuing her and Heather. What if he'd passed them by, left them there?"

"He didn't."

They both went quiet, enjoying the companionship between old, old friends who don't need conversation nor discussion of the mixed emotions Justin once felt toward the one-time Lord of Wallachia.

Tom reached for the Bohemian glass decanter and handed it to Justin after refilling his own glass.

"I hope they're alright," Justin said, topping off his half-empty glass. "Besides, I need to get back to see Gwyltha. I'll talk to her about the ruddy car thief. She'll see it my way. How can she not?" If she didn't, they'd have a stand-up argument. Stella hadn't attacked. She was protecting her child. All the difference in the world.

"As fond as she is of Sam, she might just forget our code and her antipathy for the South and come down and take care of the fellow herself. You've nothing to worry about, Justin."

Tom was right. Not harming mortals did not extend to mortals who harmed and intimidated those under the Colony's protection. "I wonder where he is? Wouldn't mind a quick word with him myself."

"Unlikely we'll ever know. He's no doubt hiding out if he has the minimum of sense."

In the middle of another companionable silence, when the only sound was the distant traffic noise, Justin's mobile rang. "Excuse me, Tom. It's Stella," he said after a glance at the readout. He stepped out onto the small terrace that led down to the garden.

"Justin!" Was she anxious or just hurried?

He fancied he heard Tom's mobile ring, but he was too concerned about his wife and love. "How's things in Bringham?"

She told him.

"I'm coming back down there right now!" The village was a hotbed of evil!

"Please don't, Justin."

"Why on earth not? This on top of everything else should be enough to convince anyone to get out. If Antonia has a modicum of sense, she'll donate the house to charity and shake the dirt of Bringham from her feet."

"Listen, Justin. Please."

He listened. "The horrid business from Friday is over. The jewels are in the hands of the police, and our car is off and gone. You and Tom took care of everything. Sam was shaken. Heck, so was I! But we're fine now, and I promised him two weeks down here. Besides, is a crook really going to go around the villages looking for Sam or me? He's no doubt lying very, very low with the police after him."

Yes, he'd concede that point, but this new development added a whole new crimp. "It's not just that. You've got a dead body!" By Abel, it was like something out of an Agatha Christie: the body in the Anderson shelter!

He sensed her hesitation. Was he actually getting through her stubborn head? "I thought long and hard about this, Justin. My first instinct was to hightail it out of here, but I think it's much better to stay. At least a few days."

"Why?" Terse, yes, but if he said much more, he'd start ranting.

"Okay, Justin." It wasn't okay at all, but he let that pass. "It's Sam. I think he feels very involved, almost responsible about the outcome." Sheer nonsense, but he'd let that pass. "He's been talking to the detectives. He asked to talk to the crime scene team, and he's made friends with the policeman they left to keep an eye on things. Sam's really gotten into this, and he told me when I put him to bed he wants to be a detective when he grows up.

"Yes, I know he'll change his mind a hundred times before then, but he's fascinated. Not in a morbid way, but in a quest for justice. He wants to know who she is and to see the killer caught. I want to stay the two weeks we'd planned, Justin."

It was a plea, and it was next to impossible to refuse her. If he did refuse, she'd probably stay anyway. "I'm worried about you both, love."

"You think I'm carefree? It's been a crazy couple of days. but Sam is fine, and I really think if I whisk him away now, it will upset him more than staying."

"Don't forget the murderer loose in that darn village."

"I think the most likely murderers are Dixie's nasty, old aunts. I'm calling her to check their diaries just as soon as the police have some sort of time frame."

By Abel, she was, no doubt, spot on! The police should take her on. No, perish the thought! "Don't you start playing amateur detective!"

"I have no intention of doing so if I even had the time to. Elizabeth is teaching me how to build web sites." With that last word and an assurance that she loved him with all her heart, she rang off.

Justin looked up at the night sky and the buildings opposite. When had his life become so complicated? Since he fell in love and acquired a wife and son. Stella had forceful arguments. She had an abundance of good common sense. But none of that meant she was right!

He snapped his phone closed and stepped into the study

just in time to hear Tom say. "Hang it all, Lizzie! Use your gumption! That place is—"

Deciding Tom had his own arguments to press, Justin stepped back out and waited for Tom to join him.

"Well?" Tom said as he walked though the French windows.

"'Well' is not the word I'd use to describe the situation."

Tom snorted. "Cock up then!"

"Closer."

"Damn it all, Justin! How can you be so blasé about it all? Elizabeth, the woman who just agreed to marry me, won't do what I tell her!"

"They often don't, Tom."

"They need to! This whole venture is getting out of hand! They've barely been down there a week, and they're knee deep in stolen jewels, carjacking, and now murder!"

"Stella and Sam have only been there three days, and come to think of it, things were quiet before they arrived."

"That's not what I meant!"

Justin clapped his hand on Tom's shoulder. "I know you didn't, but do you really think ultimatums and directives will get you what you want?"

"What the hell can we do? This isn't over. There's more trouble brewing, I swear, and now Elizabeth, and Stella and Sam, are down there with a murderer running around."

"According to Stella—and I'll concede she's most likely right—the murderer or murderers are pushing up daisies. But, I agree, it is worrying."

"So we just sit here and let whatever happens happen?"

"Of course not!"

Tom pulled away and paced the length of the terrace and back. "What then? First it's 'don't tell them what to do as they won't listen,' and then you're worried!"

"Tom, my friend, let's go back in, have another glass of

your excellent port, and I'll explain what we are going to do."

Tom contained himself long enough to top up their glasses, but the moment he set the decanter down, he asked, "Well?"

"We join forces. I have to go back to Yorkshire tonight— I can't leave patients waiting—but I'll be back first thing Wednesday. I'll drive down so I have my own transport. You'll have to hold the fort tonight and tomorrow.

Tom gave a sideways look. "What exactly do you have in mind?"

"Surveillance is the modern word, I believe." That earned an even more skeptical look. "First, we call John Littlewood and ask him to lend us his house in Epsom."

"The place up on the Downs?"

"Exactly. He only uses it for the races. It's nicely remote but a comfortable distance from Bringham. We set up there and take turns keeping an eye on things. I know you need time to work, so we'll just play box and cox. As long as one of us is on top of things and the other is near enough to get there fast, we'll have a handle on things."

"And what will they say if they realize one of us is forever lurking around?"

"Will they notice another crow on the fence or an extra seagull on the lawn?"

"Not seagulls. They don't come that far inland in summer."

"You can be a peacock for all it matters, but one of us will be there every moment of the day."

"So you are worried."

"Worried, yes. Panicking, no."

Tom drained his glass. "I think I'm panicking. This being in love is hard on the nerves!"

*   *   *

"There you are!" Antonia walked into the small parlor off the bar where Stella and Elizabeth sat at a low table.

"Where we are!" Elizabeth said. "We could say the same about you. But we also know where you've been."

"Oh, hush!"

"And what you've been doing," Stella said. "It suits you."

"You're not leaving him anemic, are you?" Elizabeth added with a bit of a grin.

Nothing like friends to deflate euphoria! "Good evening to you too!"

She pulled out a chair and sat down. "Where's Sam?"

"Upstairs. He discovered the rooms have video games on the TV. I shudder to think what it adds to the bill, but it gives us time to talk."

"Good. There's something I need to pass on." She repeated, minus a few details, what Michael told her.

Stella went thoughtful.

Elizabeth was curious. "How did he happen to overhear this?"

That was the question she'd dreaded. Hard to answer and still keep Michael's secret. "I think he overheard it in a pub somewhere." As good a lie as any.

Didn't entirely convince Elizabeth. "Sounds a bit unreliable. Who were they? And was he sure of what he heard?"

"It's pretty clear to me they were involved or knew something about the robbery." Stella said. "If Antonia thinks Michael is reliable, that's good enough for me."

Thank you, Stella!

"So what do we do, if anything?" Elizabeth asked.

Stella frowned; Elizabeth reached for her glass of whatever it was and took a long swallow.

"I think we should wait and see," Stella said. "It is worrying, but assuming they are the characters who did the robbery, took my car, drove off with Sam, and tried to break into it, what now? That car is gone. If they got the registration number and can trace it, it will take them up to Yorkshire. Assuming they read the paper or listen to the news or local gossip, they know the jewels are no longer in the car. Why would they need to bother us again? I think they'd be more concerned with lying low than anything else. It never hurts to be careful, but . . ." She paused. "I do suggest we keep this to ourselves. No point in giving Justin anything else to fuss over."

"Or Tom!" Elizabeth added.

Antonia smiled. "Had trouble with them?"

Stella rolled her eyes. "Shall we just say that after he heard the latest development, Justin stopped short, but only just, of actually ordering me home."

"Tom didn't stop short. I told him to shove it!"

"This morning's discovery agitated them?"

Stella laughed. "That's one way to put it. I managed to convince Justin that a dead body, while distressing, isn't likely to up and endanger us, and as for his concerns about a murderer at large in Bringham, I believe the late Misses Underwood had a hand in it, and they are long since dead themselves."

"You really think they did it?" Elizabeth asked.

Stella shrugged. "As good a guess as any. We know they blackmailed people and ruined lives, and who else is likely to be burying bodies in their backyard?"

Depended on when she was buried. Antonia couldn't picture two old biddies hauling out a dead body, but perhaps Stella hadn't thought of that. "Are you sure you don't want to leave and go back to Havering? Would keep Justin happy."

"Yes, it would, but rushing back and cutting this holiday short will bother Sam more than staying. "

"Then we should be extra cautious," Antonia said.

"Never hurts," Stella agreed. "But with the place crawling with police, I think we're safe enough. We no longer have anything anyone is looking for."

"Does Michael know who these two characters are?" Elizabeth asked.

Tricky here. "I think he has an idea."

"Then he can shop them to the cops," Elizabeth said.

Easier said than done. "You're right." And it would never happen. How could he explain that he just happened to be under their window . . . in cat form?

"Hope he does," Stella said. "I just wish I could finger them for scaring the willies out of Sam. Not possible without explaining how I can run faster than fifty miles an hour."

Michael had similar difficulties.

"So we're staying and getting things done despite our significant others' objections?" Elizabeth said. "Not much they can do about it, but sit tight and wait."

"I can't see Justin sitting tight anywhere," Stella said, "nor Tom, for that matter. They know exactly where we are, and I bet there's an owl up there in a tree watching us."

"Tom likes owl form," Elizabeth said. "He shifted into one on Saturday."

"My point exactly," Stella said with a smile. "I don't think we have anything to worry about."

"Amazing how much mess they can make in two days," Elizabeth said, looking at the heaps of turned earth and the jagged edges of rusted metal that had once been the walls of the shelter. The entire area was surrounded with meter upon meter of blue and white police tape.

"Forget working on the new building," Antonia said with a touch of irritation. "I called Mark the builder. He's very philosophical about it; said they'd another job to go to and to call him as soon as we get the all clear."

"Which could be weeks," Stella pointed out.

Antonia groaned. "I can see it now—September rolls

around, and we can't open as we're still waiting for the police to close the case."

"Doubt it will take that long," Stella said. "Okay, the café is on hold, but it's an extra, not vital. If you go ahead with everything else—line up craftspeople, hire the help you need, set the advertising in motion—it could all be ready in time."

Did nothing get Stella down? Just as well. For a few seconds, Antonia had half-believed the colony members who thought her insane to invest time and money in Bringham. "I'm glad you're both here—and Sam," she added, smiling at him as he peered over the police tape. "Let's get inside and decide what we're doing. At least we can get in the front door."

"It's quiet," Elizabeth said as they pulled up chairs in the office and Sam wandered off to explore the house. "That's something."

"You really are a pair of blue-eyed optimists!" Just as well, Antonia thought to herself. "So what do we do, ladies?"

"Whatever we can," Stella said. "There's the web site. Can't do it on my own, but with Elizabeth's help, I can, and I can always proofread. We need to contact the people who will be answering the ads when they come out. We still need office supplies. We started but never phoned the order in."

"And there's still the walled garden to restore," Elizabeth said. "And the rest of the grounds could do with a good going over. The grass has been cut and the beds weeded a bit, but that's about it."

She was darn lucky to have their support, but still Antonia wondered. "Maybe this house is jinxed. A lot of odd things seem to happen here."

"Evil has happened here," Elizabeth said, her voice still and purposeful. "I can feel it, but I've burned herbs to clear away the taint. Plus, there's plenty of good and happiness. No reason we can't overcome the negative energy."

Stella gave Elizabeth a look of polite skepticism. Antonia held her peace. She well remembered the days when magic still held sway. "Why don't you take on that garden restoration, Elizabeth? Hire someone. You know what we're paying: local average, plus a bit more if we find someone really stupendous." That made her very happy. And why not? The area did need work, and it might be an added attraction. "Stella, why don't we go through the applications we have so far—split them between us, and see what they have to offer?"

Her dark eyebrows almost met her fringe. "I'm not sure I want to accept or refuse work; I might take in things you loathe or reject some fantastically brilliant potter."

Sneaky dig that. "I get your point."

"How about I go through the job applications and look at hiring the part-time assistants? That I think I could do. I know the sorts who work and the ones who fall sick when there's a rush on."

She bet Stella did, that she could spot a malingerer or a light-fingered sort at fifty paces. "Right, you go through the job applicants. I'll go through the craftspeople, and Elizabeth, you—"

"Take care of the garden. I'll see about an ad in the papers we used before." She looked around the room. "And I think we'd better return the thermos and teacups Emma left with us. It's been over a week; we've probably committed some dire social solecism by hanging on to them this long."

Good point. It had been a nice gesture, even if jam tarts weren't anyone's usual fare. "Go ahead and mention the tearoom. See if she's even interested."

"Why not let Sam come over with me?" Elizabeth looked at Stella. "Emma mentioned she had children in school. Maybe there's one Sam's age."

Stella nodded. "Why not? Might be good for him to have a friend while he's here. I was wondering how long exploring the house and gardens would keep him occupied."

Stepping into the hall, she called him from the bottom of the stairs.

He came running down, his shoes echoing on the uncarpeted stairs. "Guess what I found in one of the rooms, Mum?"

Stella went very still; Elizabeth jumped; and even Antonia felt tension tighten her shoulders.

"What, Sam?" Stella asked.

"The neatest thing, Mum. There's a door and stairs up to an enormous attic, and you can look out all over the garden and to the Green and houses miles away."

Elizabeth let out a sigh, Stella visibly relaxed. After Monday, they were all a bit skittish over new discoveries.

Sam ran down the last flight of stairs. "Yes, Mum? Okay if I look up there again later?"

"By all means, if it's okay with Antonia and you don't mess with anything. But now, Elizabeth needs your help."

Stella watched from the door as they left, Sam carrying the thermos and Elizabeth the tray balanced with cups and plates.

"Worried about him?" Antonia asked.

"You mean about the body, to say nothing about the Friday incident? Of course. Can't help it. Being a mother means you're hot-wired to worry. But I keep telling myself, he's handling it well; if he's upset, he can talk to me or Justin, and everything has worked out okay, apart from that poor woman they found."

"I'm beginning to worry about her. Somewhere, she has a family who never knew what happened."

Stella nodded. "But now, with luck, they will. What if she left children or a husband? It's so sad." She shrugged. "Worrying about her won't help anything, will it? Let's look at those applications."

She reached for the stack on the desk.

Not fifteen minutes later, Sam came running through the front door. "Mum! Can I go play with Peter? He's nine, and his Mum asked me to. Can I?"

He was followed by Emma and a fair-haired boy. "You're Sam's mother? I'm Emma Gordon. Would it be alright for Sam to stay and play a while? Would be doing us a favor— Peter's best friend moved away when school broke up, and there's no one else his age nearby."

That settled, Sam left with his new friend; Stella sorted the applicants into no, maybe, and *I hope so;* and Antonia picked up the phone to make appointments.

Elizabeth was debating web site or garden when there was a knock on the front door.

It was the young man from the garden.

"Sorry to disturb you, but you did say to ask before I went into the garden. Is it alright if I nip back there?"

"Fine," Elizabeth replied. "I'll come with you. I was on my way there myself."

She watched him out of the corner of her eye as they walked across the lawns. He was an odd young man. Mid-twenties at most. Tense. Hair a bit unruly. Good clothes; expensive even, but his trousers needed a good press, and there was a button missing off his shirt. Down on his luck, perhaps?

Once in the magic garden, he stood at the edge of the lawn and looked around. "It's so peaceful here."

"And it reminds you of your mother?"

He nodded. "Yeah."

She looked at him, her mind clicking. A young, able-bodied man at a loose end in the middle of the day. "Do you have a job?"

He gave her an odd, sideways look. "No."

"Would you like one?" Getting personal, but . . .

His look switched to wary. "Why are you asking?"

Male pride? Testosterone sensitivity? "You seem to really like this garden, you remember it as it used to be, and I'm looking for a gardener."

He stared at her a good minute. "You'd employ me?"

"If you're interested, and assuming you know roses from ragweed."

Another long silence. "I don't know much about gardening, but I'd love to work here, and I could call on Bert Andrews."

"Who's Bert Andrews?"

"The gardener for the Misses Underwood. He retired years ago, must be over ninety now. He lives with his granddaughter in the village."

Her impulse had to have been the goddess's inspiration. A gardener who loved the garden and knew the original one to consult with. "It's a deal then." She mentioned hourly wage and national insurance, not that he seemed concerned about money, and shook on it.

"When do I start?"

Nothing like eager employees.

"Tomorrow okay? You'll have fill in an application. Won't take long. Be sure to always go round the far side of the house as the other is all marked off with police tape."

"Yes,"—he frowned—"the body they found."

"Does that bother you?"

He shook his head. "Not unduly. With what went on in that house, it's not too surprising. They were rather nasty old ladies." Brits did go in for understatement. "There is the other way into the garden from the back. I could use that."

There was. "I know. The door is a bit rickety. Might need working on."

"I could have a go at fixing it. Do you have tools?"

"We have a toolshed. Check and see what's there. If we need anything, we can buy it."

"Mind if I ask why you want to restore the garden?"

"I'm a witch." His eyes grew wide. Might as well say it all. "Have been for several years, but I don't practice the craft the way the Misses Underwood did." That got a sharp look. "I follow the maxim of 'harm to none.'" Eyebrows went up at that. "I've never seen anything like the herb and magic garden here. I want to preserve it."

He nodded. Had she imagined the assorted underlying emotions? He was not happy about witches, at least of the Underwood sort. Not entirely unreasonable. The old ladies probably had some dirt on this young man. "Okay then. Start tomorrow, and you'd better come in and meet the boss."

"You're not in charge?"

"Just in the garden. Antonia runs the place and owns it."

He followed her though the front door. "News! I have a gardener!"

"That was fast," Antonia said, looking up and smiling.

"Not only that, he knows the retired gardener."

"It's your project; go ahead. Might as well fill in National Insurance and personal details while you're here." She reached for a form and, looking up, handed it to him. "You!"

James froze, his hand in the air, reaching for but not touching the paper. "Oh!"

"You're our new gardener?" Antonia asked, more than a hint of asperity in her voice.

"I was offered the job, and I accepted," he replied.

"You have a good reason for hiring James Chadwick?" Antonia asked Elizabeth.

Dear Goddess! Elizabeth couldn't believe it! How had she never asked his name? "Chadwick! You're Sebastian's nephew?" Elizabeth wanted to hit her head against the wall. The first person she hired, and she . . .

He pulled himself straight in the chair. "Yes, I am. Want to withdraw the job offer?" His voice was sharp, defensive. Understandable.

"Maybe," Antonia said. "Why do you want the job?"

This would be interesting. He thought a minute. "First, because I was offered it. Second, because I'd love to work in the garden. And finally, because I've never had a job and think it's time I did."

Stella looked as if she was about to pass out from shock. "Never had a job?" she asked. "Never? Ever?" Had to be beyond her understanding. She'd had little experience with the idle rich.

He had the grace to look away from Stella's astounded stare. "Never. After I left school, I worked for my uncle. You've probably heard what happened to him." All three nodded. "I take care of his affairs and his house, but to be honest, I like the idea of earning my own money, and as I explained to Miss Connor, that garden has memories of my mother. I'd like to restore it for her sake."

"She's dead?" Stella asked.

"So I was told."

Odd, but a catechism about a dead mother didn't seem apropos. Antonia shook her head. Wasn't often she was flummoxed, but . . . "Mr. Chadwick, Dixie LePage is a good friend." He visibly quailed. "So to be honest, you do not come recommended. If Elizabeth wants you to work on the garden, fair enough. Just earn your money and don't give me any reason to fire you, or I will."

He swallowed. Twice. "I won't."

He left, assuring them he would be there tomorrow on the dot of nine.

Antonia shook her head. "Honestly, Elizabeth, you know how to pick them!"

"Should have asked his name, I suppose, but . . ."

"You've got him. You see that he does his job and behaves. If he makes a pass at you, I'd advise you not to let Tom know. He'll make mincemeat out of that young man."

"Dixie warned us about him, right?" Stella asked. "Told us to watch out for him."

"Yes, she did," Elizabeth replied, "but so far, he hasn't tried to hit on me. Seems more pathetic than philandering, and either he really pulled the wool over my eyes, or that garden does mean a lot to him."

"Reminds him of the time they tried to fry Kit!" Antonia said with a snap.

"Maybe . . ." What a thought! "Maybe I'll ask him."

"Elizabeth!" Stella said.

"Best way to know, and if he really was involved, he deserves to fry. If he wasn't, best to know that too. Sheesh, he seems more ineffectual than anything else."

"Could be he's got you snowed," Stella said.

She hoped not.

"If he has, I think we can take care of him," Antonia said. "Dixie single-handedly did for Sebastian, and there are three of us."

Chapter 15

"Any news?" Justin asked as he got out of the car. "I've brought supplies. We'll need ample feeding for all the transmogrifying we'll be doing." He unlocked the boot and reached for a freezer chest. "Want to grab something? Tell me what's going on as we unload this little lot."

"Quite a bit," Tom said, hefting two containers. "Nothing urgent or unduly worrisome."

They put the chests down on the quarry-tiled floor. Justin popped open the first and started stacking the blood bags in the fridge. "Something has to have happened. It's been almost three days since we left. Don't tell me they've been sitting quietly crocheting doilies all this time!"

"No, but they have signed on two old ladies living up near the roundabout to knit for the gallery. Apparently, the Misses Black make Argyle socks, wonderful baby things, and Shetland shawls, and then there's the vicar's daughter, a rather horsey jolly hockey sticks sort, who came by and shared the inside scoop on what happened on the vicarage back lawn. Seems the vicar's dog chewed on some of the loot, and there was a bit of a delay while everyone waited with bated breath for the lost loot to reappear."

Tom was asking for a jab in the ribs. "Anything important? Disturbing? Worrying? Things that I need to know?"

He nodded. "There was one thing, but I'll wait until we unload this lot. Don't want you dropping one on the floor. Makes such nasty stains."

Justin straightened, blood bag in hand. "Tell me, my friend, or you might get one of these across your chops."

"It's not that worrying, just curious. That's all."

He tossed the bag on the shelf. "Tell!"

"You might want to sit down first."

"Just spit it out."

Tom gave a wry smile and a little shrug. "Well, Elizabeth, my love and my life, a woman I believed possessed of abundant intelligence and good sense, just hired James Chadwick as a gardener."

Tom had not been kidding. Sitting was a good idea. Grabbing the edge of the fridge would have to do. "She did what?"

"You heard it aright the first time. Not sure I want to repeat it." Rolling his eyes heavenward, Tom raised his hands, palms up. "I'm just reporting what I saw and heard. My reaction was much like yours. I was tempted to descend from the damn tree, transmogrify into all my naked glory, and ask her what the hell she was thinking."

"Why didn't you?"

"I hate standing on the grass in bare feet."

Justin sent a silent petition to the gods to give him strength, all but tossed the remaining bags into the fridge, and slammed the door. "What now?"

"Now?" Tom had needling perfected to an art! "Now you take your turn. I tell you, pal, this has been illuminating. I had no idea what was involved in setting up an art gallery.

They've been working all hours, Stella going in one direction, Elizabeth in another. Can't keep track. It's a two-man job."

"How's Sam?" He couldn't stop worrying about the aftermath of the hideous happening on Friday.

"He seems to be fine, but half the time, he's off in yet another direction. Most of the time, just down the lane. He's found a friend, and they dart back between each other's houses like a pair of hyperactive humming birds!"

The image was intriguing. "So he's been alright?"

"Definitely alright. Having a great time. Beats me how Stella kept up with him as a mortal. Almost did my wings in flitting back and forth from Peter's house to Orchard House to that darn hotel and across to the pub and back again."

"The pub? Sam's been frequenting the pub?" Tom called *that* unimportant? "What was Stella doing?"

"Keep your hair on! He's not turning into a juvenile toper. She was there with him." Oh, yes! Nothing to worry about! Tom turned with a shrug and a wicked twist of a smile and walked toward the sitting room. Justin was after him in a flash, beating him to the doorway. "Explain, please, what my wife and child have been doing in the pub?"

"This is the twentieth-first century, Justin. Sam has been eating the Barley Mow out of scampi and sausage rolls, while Elizabeth eats steaks for two, or three if she's lucky and Antonia goes with them."

He should have known. He'd been in the same pub with Dixie. It was nice enough and across the Green from the house. But it was hard to rid his mind of the nineteenth-century images of half-starved waifs buying penny glasses of gin because it was cheaper than food. "So, working on the gallery, lunch at the pub, and Sam playing with a friend." Sounded so innocuous, were they being ridiculously suspicious? No, not if Sebastian Caughleigh's nephew was in the mix. "We've got to do something about that Chadwick character."

"I agree, but so far he's done just what he was hired to do: pulled weeds, pruned bushes, and cut dead branches off the trees."

"You have to have missed something! Our pal Jimmy is better at seducing the local milkmaids than tilling the soil."

Tom stretched out in a wide leather armchair. Since he appeared to be settled for the duration, Justin took a seat in its twin on the opposite side of a rather ugly hunting print. An original, he noticed.

Tom nodded. "I agree, but so far, he's kept his nose commendably clean. As long as he doesn't hurt one of ours, he can deadhead to his heart's content."

"It's more than a bit odd."

"Agreed, and talking of odd, let me tell you what I've found out about our adamantine ice princess."

"Antonia?"

"Is there more than one?"

Tom paused, obviously enjoying stringing this along. Justin was tempted to wait him out, but darn it, he wanted to get down to Bringham, fully au fait with everything. "Spit it out, man!"

"Our Antonia has found herself a lover."

"About time, too, if you ask me. She's carried a candle for that frog Larouseliere far too long!"

"I think we can safely say she's over him. Don't really know why she pays for a room at that hotel; every hour she's not working, she spends with this new chap. He . . ." Tom shook his head. "I wish you'd check him out, Justin. There's something odd about him. Can't figure it out. You've been around so much longer than me; maybe you can."

Justin shrugged. "Let her be, Tom. If she's found a nice neck to nibble on, good luck to her. She's more than old enough to take care of herself."

"It's not that. He's odd, I tell you. Something about him doesn't seem right."

"I'll have glance his direction, but truly, Antonia is more than able to take on any mortal, and unless he bothers my wife or son, he can be as odd as he likes. You'd be better occupied worrying about that Chadwick specimen than Antonia's new fella." Tom didn't look convinced. But heck, Antonia was entitled to a bit of a fling. "Who is he?"

"A potter who's contributing to the gallery."

"Contributing more than his pots by the sound of things." A good gossip never hurt, but he hadn't come all this way to chat. "You've been out there all day; I'll take the evening shift."

The night was clear, the air still warm, and the moon not yet up as Justin glided on owl's wings over Orchard House. All was well and quiet; a police car drove by; sounds of TV and mortal voices came from the open windows of the houses down the lane. Across the Green, the Barley Mow had a car park half full, not bad for a weeknight. No sign of Stella's car, or the others. Giving the crime scene and the tape fluttering in the night breeze a last glance—sorry business, that— Justin headed toward the hotel.

He felt like a voyeur: Elizabeth was sitting up in bed, eating—did she never stop? She'd closed the curtains, but he caught a glimpse when the breeze blew them apart. Stella hadn't drawn hers. Light shone out into the garden. Justin couldn't resist alighting on a nearby branch and looking in. Stella was nowhere to be seen, but Sam was perched on the end of the bed in his pajamas, watching TV.

His son! Whom he'd protect until the day Sam aged and died. Sam! As if sensing his presence, Sam turned, stared, then smiled.

"Hi, Dad!" he said, slipping off the bed and tiptoeing to the window. How in the name of Abel had he known? "Brilliant to see you," Sam whispered. "Mum's in the shower."

Should have guessed that by the running water. Sam held out his arm. Accepting the invitation, Justin settled his talons as gently as he could on the soft cotton sleeve. "We'd better be quiet if you don't want her to know you're here. We're okay. She's having fun learning to do the web site, and I've found a friend, Peter. We've been exploring the gardens, and we started making a camp in the big boxwood by the drive. Everything's okay, honest. I miss you, and I hope you come back soon."

What a child! Mere mortal he wasn't! The shower stopped— time for a strategic retreat. Justin gave Sam's hair a gentle tweak with his beak by way of salute. Sam smiled back and leaned out of the window, holding out his arm. Justin spread his wings and launched into the night. Sam stood at the open window, waving.

His son. His child. The thought left Justin lightheaded a minute until he set his wings steady and soared.

Where now? Roof or tree?

He watched the hotel a while, but all was quiet, so he headed up to Orchard House and perched on the roof, noticing the cars leaving the Barley Mow and the lights going out in the houses by the Green. All peaceful there, so he flew back to keep watch over his family.

All was well. He heard Sam's sleeping heartbeat and Elizabeth's. Odd that ghouls' hearts still beat. Did they age like mortals? Time would tell. Sam would. Justin's heart might not beat any longer, but it ached knowing he'd watch Sam age and die. How much more must the prospect hurt Stella, knowing she would outlive her son and his children's children's children.

Not that they could change anything. Best take all the joy from Sam's existence they could. But how had Sam recognized him in bird form? Odd, very odd. An aftermath of taking Sam's blood last year? That should never have happened. Wouldn't have if he hadn't been unconscious and Sam hadn't been as persistent as a fighting cock. He'd even defied Gwyltha.

Justin had smiled when Stella had recounted the incident. After all, if Sam hadn't insisted, he, Justin, would have been a goner. Just as well, perhaps, that Stella and her son made their own rules.

If owls smiled, he'd be grinning like a fool thinking about his family. He settled for ruffling his feathers in the night.

Spreading his wings, Justin left his perch in the oak tree and headed south, sweeping over the common, his sharp owl eyes scanning the ground beneath, seeing rabbits and stoats hunting in the night and a mouse scampering for cover, perhaps wondering why this particular owl did not attack. Or did mice think that much?

A fox broke cover from a row of gorse bushes and ran across an open area of the common. Justin hoped the rabbits and ferret got safely to cover. Or did he? Didn't the fox need prey to survive? Didn't every creature? Wasn't that thief just protecting his own interests when he stole Stella's car? Maybe, but he made the mistake of upsetting Justin's wife and threatening his son. Offenses not lightly forgotten. Justin truly regretted not being able to deliver the thieves as well as the jewels into the hands of the law.

But he still might. Hope lasted a long time for a vampire.

A turn of his wing and a shift in direction, and Justin spied what mortal—or owl—eyes never would: a vampire running at speed.

Antonia he presumed.

Interesting, but even more so, beside her ran a large, tawny cat. It was none of his business, and Stella would no doubt tear him off a strip for nosiness, if she ever knew, but Justin let his curiosity lead him.

Keeping pace with Antonia and her feline companion, Justin followed as they raced across fields, through woods, and even skirted a private garden. She leaped the river while the large cat landed in it with a splash and raced to the far bank. Her laughter rose in the night air as the cat turned and chased her! What was going on? Women running with wolves was one thing, but it seemed Antonia had taken to taming wildlife as a hobby. So much for the fella Tom had claimed. Antonia wasn't courting, but animal taming!

And thoroughly enjoying herself by the sounds of things. The cat chased her a few yards until she turned and chased him back. Now that was odd, but given Antonia's powers, perhaps not surprising. They ran across open country for several miles before turning and skirting the woods by an estate, leaping hedges and jumping fences.

Antonia was happy, no doubt about it, and it was about time he returned to his family. Antonia Stonewright was old enough to take care of herself, even if she had acquired an unusual hobby. And where, come to think of it, had this feline come from? Pumas were not exactly indigenous to the Home Counties. And where did she keep it? Those old outbuildings at Orchard House were too decrepit to house more than mice. So what? Time to stop spying and go home.

He'd already turned, swooping low, and was heading back to Bringham Manor Hotel when the shot rang out.

Instinctively, he banked and soared, thinking he was the target, but Antonia's cry of horror had him swooping back. She'd been some paces behind the cat, but now she covered the space between them in seconds, bending over the downed creature as two figures emerged from the nearest woods.

"Got it!" one shouted. "Who'd have thought it!"

"You did it, Mike!"

Putting herself in front of the wounded cat, Antonia drew herself tall and turned to face them. "How dare you!" Her voice carried in the night air.

Astounded was a good word to describe their reactions.

They both stopped, lowered their guns, and came forward. "It's our kill, and this here is private land."

These two had no idea. They would soon. Very soon.

As they came forward, Antonia stood her ground. "I advise you to leave. Now."

"Leave without taking what we bagged?" the first one asked.

The second one stepped forward. Foolish mortal. "You leave him. We've been hunting this animal for years; he's ours."

Justin almost felt sorry for them, but when the first one aimed his gun at Antonia and said, "Leave it! It's ours!" it was time to intervene.

He swooped low, landed a few meters behind the pair, and transmogrified just as Antonia stepped forward and took the gun out of the man's hands. By the time Justin had resumed human form, she'd snapped it in two and tossed both parts across the field.

That caused a bit of consternation.

"Shit! Almighty!" the second one said.

Number one appeared dumbstruck.

But not for long. He reached out to grab Antonia just as she snarled, fangs at full drop.

At this point, they appeared to suspect they might have the disadvantage. They exchanged panicky glances. Number one backed away, but number two wasn't giving up. A few paces behind the other, he raised his gun, aimed, and shot Antonia in the shoulder.

Time, perhaps, to intervene.

Justin stepped forward, grabbed number two and his smoking gun, and spun him around.

The shocked expression might have been for Justin's extended fangs, or perhaps naked men seldom appeared in the fertile fields of Surrey. Either way, he screamed and fainted. Made it much easier to snap his offending weapon in two.

"Mike," Justin said, stepping over the limp body, "if you have the minimum of survival instincts, I advise you to run just as fast as your puny legs can carry you!" He added a good, loud snarl for emphasis, and Mike took his advice.

Quite a fast runner for a mortal, too. Must be the adrenalin.

"Just dropped out of the sky, did you?" Antonia appeared less then delighted, but maybe worry added the acerbic tinge to her voice.

"Nice to see you, too. Got a spot of bother? Your wound is healing, I trust?"

"Mine's fine, or will be in a short while. It's Michael." She turned back and knelt beside the injured animal. "I don't know what to do."

"You do pick unusual pets, Antonia."

She snarled at him, fangs still extended. "He's not a pet! And dammit! I don't know what to do for him!"

Justin knelt with her, his hand on the puma's shoulder as he examined the wound. "The bullet's in deep. If I could grab some clothes, I could help you get him to a vet."

Obviously the wrong thing to say!

She glared at him. "What could that do? Oh, Justin, you don't understand! He's a shifter! I can't take him to a vet. No mortal hospital can help him, and if they could, what would I say?"

A shifter. A skinchanger. It took Justin a moment or two to get that straight. "Then we need to get him out of the open. He may well heal as well as we do. Do you have any idea?"

"Why would I? We never got round to discussing bullet wounds."

Understandable. "Then we play it by ear. Getting him to shelter is the first thing. We can hardly take him back to the hotel. What about the house? Somewhere undisturbed and private where I can check the wound."

She shook her head. "His own house is much nearer."

As she lifted the cat in her arms, the unconscious poacher,

or whatever, stirred. Justin bent down, squeezed his shoulder, and whispered a suggestion to him, and he went slack in the grass. "He's taken care of. He'll be out for a few hours."

"I hope it rains on him."

"After we get your friend to shelter."

She'd been right about not far. And just as well that it was all across fields and woods. The sight of bloodstained Antonia carrying the wounded animal would have been more than enough to shock most mortals. The accompaniment of a naked man, would have been an interesting extra.

They covered the distance at a run, arriving at a clearing surrounded by a series of buildings. "He lives here?" Justin asked.

With a nod, Antonia went up to the front door. "Key's under the crate by the pottery door."

Whoever had put it there had no trouble lifting weights. Justin retrieved it and opened the door. Antonia walked in, holding her wounded friend close, and turned to say. "Come in."

Shapeshifting pumas lived modestly but comfortably. "Is there a bed we can put him on?"

"Of course." Snappy was pardonable in the circumstances. Justin shut the door and followed her into the bedroom.

She'd pulled back the covers, and now the cat was slowly bleeding on the sheets. He looked sick, and Antonia didn't look much better. She couldn't have bled that much, not from a single gunshot wound that must have already healed.

Justin crossed to the bed. "I have no instruments with me, but I'll do what I can."

"Thanks." Her eyes met his. If he hadn't known it was impossible, he'd say hers brimmed with tears. "Don't let him die, Justin!"

"Not if I can help it, Antonia; you have my word. Now, let me have a look at him."

The bullet had entered the shoulder, and appeared to be

lodged somewhere in his chest. Nasty. "Is his heartbeat always this slow?" If not, they were in trouble.

"It's a good bit slower than mortals."

"That's good news then, but . . ." He looked down at the wounded animal–shifter–friend. "Antonia, understand I'm going blind and ignorant here. He obviously doesn't heal like we do, but I doubt he has human metabolism either. I've scant experience with animals of any sort, other than the odd horse from time to time over the centuries. I'll do what I can. Everything I can, but . . ."

"Please."

"In case he suffers from sepsis, I need boiling water; tweezers or some sort of probe, all sterilized; pads and clean towels; and something to stitch him up with." Assuming he succeeded. She was out the door heading for the kitchen when he asked, "Let me borrow your mobile, please."

"I left it in the kitchen."

She had. Right on the counter. He picked it up, punched in numbers, and was answered by a sleepy-sounding Tom. "Sorry to disturb the first good night's sleep in two days, but get yourself over to the hotel and keep an eye on things. I'm rather busy."

"What happened? You alright?"

"I'm fine. Just ran into a little problem that requires my professional services. I'll meet you in the big tree by the hotel entrance later."

"You're watching the hotel between you?" Antonia asked as she lit the gas under a saucepan of water.

"We were worried. Too many odd things going on around here. And we've just had another one."

It was a measure of Antonia's concern that she just shrugged and filled another saucepan. "Water's on the boil. I'll fish out something to use as an instrument and sterilize it. There are clean sheets and towels in the airing cupboard. Rip up what you need. I'll help you in a minute."

Stack of towels in his hand and a clean sheet on top, Justin went back to the bedroom. The animal—he'd better start calling him Michael—opened one eye but didn't lift his head. His tongue lolled out, and the wound still bled.

"Sorry, old chap," Justin said, stroking his head. "We'll do what we can. I'm a doctor, an old friend of Antonia's; just lie still. You'll be right as rain in a jiffy." He hoped to Abel and all the gods he told the truth.

The shifter opened an eye as if to acknowledge Justin's words. His uneven breathing suggested he was in pain, and the darn slow heartbeat worried Justin. Not much he could do but staunch the bleeding until Antonia had those make-shift instruments boiled. He could hear her rummaging in drawers and opening cupboards, and he hoped she came up with something better than a potato peeler.

Chapter 16

Seemed like ages before Antonia returned with a dish of steaming water that she put down on the bedside table. "I did the best I could, boiled everything for twenty minutes the way we did during the last war. Couldn't find carbolic, so I added a bit of household bleach. Need more light?"

"I'll manage. I operated by candlelight during the Peninsular War." She'd been pretty inventive. No scalpel or forceps, but she had needle-nosed pliers, a pair of tweezers, scissors, and a couple of thin-bladed knives.

"Hope you've got what you need." She sat down and put Michael's head in her lap. "He's not well, is he?"

"Since I'm unfamiliar with the normal physical state of a shapeshifter, I really don't know. He seems stressed, as if in pain, and without anesthetics, this is going to make it worse, but I have to get that bullet out."

"Hold still, Michael," she whispered to the creature. "We're getting the bullet out."

The animal—Michael—the shifter whimpered a couple of times as Justin probed and poked. The damn bullet was lodged near a bone, After interminable minutes spent digging and twisting, Justin dropped the bloody bullet on a folded towel. "It's out. Now to clean him up and hope he heals." He wiped off the worst of the blood and gently trimmed the ragged edges of the wound. "You forgot needle and thread, Antonia; think you can find any? If not, we can hope for the best, but I'd like to close it up."

She came back in a few minutes with a handful of small bulldog clips. "Will these do? No sign of needle and thread; he must throw his clothes away when the buttons fall off."

"Better than nothing." He dipped them in the sterilizing solution, then carefully gathered the edges of the wound together, and slipped on the clip.

"Anything else I can do?"

"Get him some water, just a little. We don't want him to choke, but he's bound to be thirsty." He placed a folded cloth over the wound and, taking strips torn from a sheet, bound it in place. Makeshift indeed, but he'd seen worse bandages in his time.

Antonia returned with a bowl of water. "Here you are, Michael. Not too fast." As if he understood, he lapped slowly, finally resting his head back on the bed and closing his eyes. He seemed to sleep, or perhaps he was resting.

Either it had worked, or it hadn't. At least he'd done no harm. The bullet was out, and the bleeding had slowed. "It's a matter of time now, Antonia. We can take turns sitting up with him. Why don't you go and wash up; your clothes are covered in blood."

She looked down at her bloodstained blouse and slacks. "You're right. I'll have to borrow Michael's clothes, but he won't mind. And talking of clothes, you really need some."

True but . . . "I'll shift back and fly home. I'm not rummaging through another man's clothing."

"In the circumstances, I doubt Michael would mind, but please yourself."

She reached into a couple of drawers, finding what she

needed easily, and left the room. Moments later, the only sounds were the shower running and Michael's slightly steadier breathing. Justin pulled the duvet over him, gathered up the bloody towels and makeshift surgical tools, and went into the kitchen. He had blood all over his hands and arms, but a good scrub in the kitchen sink took care of that. Drying his arms and face on a tea towel, he went back to check on his patient.

"Who the hell are you?" asked the sandy-haired man standing by the bed. The naked, sandy-haired young man with a rough dressing on his shoulder. The bandage was too tight. Snug before, it now twisted into his muscle.

"I'm Dr. Justin Corvus, an old friend of Antonia's. I need to readjust your dressing."

"You need dressing! What are you doing here with no clothes on? And where is Antonia?"

"In the shower. She was rather covered with your blood, and she had an injury of her own." Which should be healed by now.

He sat down hard. "What happened?"

Justin sat at the far end of the bed. "What do you remember?"

He wasn't listening. "You said Antonia was hurt? When?" He stood again, a little wobbly but determined. "Antonia!" He raced out of the room, grabbing the door to steady himself but getting to the bathroom. "What happened, and are you alright?"

Antonia seemed snappy when disturbed in her ablutions, but by the sound of things, snappy switched quickly to delighted. They both came back two minutes later, Michael with damp hair and Antonia wearing a couple of crumpled towels. "I told you I was fine; you saw that for yourself!" Still snappy. "Let me dry off and get dressed."

"Good idea," Justin said. "Far too much nudity here. This is Surrey after all."

No one was amused. "Cut it out, Justin," Antonia said with a frown. A frown she seemed ready to share with everyone. Michael got it next. "Michael, I'm fine. But I'm dripping wet, and I'm getting dressed. If you have any sense, you'll get back in bed and let Justin check your wound."

"Just tell me why he's naked in my house!"

She had perfected the irritated frown. "For the same reason you are!"

With that, she turned and strode out.

Michael gave an exasperated "Damn!" and looked at Justin. "Are you really a doctor?"

"I am."

"What did she mean by naked for the same reason I am?"

"Think about it while I check your wound. You took a bullet, and if you move too much, it may start bleeding again."

It didn't, and it wasn't likely to. As Justin eased off the now tight bandages, he peered under the pad. The skin had healed. Easing off the clip to Michael's "Ouch!" proved it. There was a puckered scar, but the skin was clean, bright pink, and newly healed.

"You heal fast," Justin said. "Not as fast as Antonia, but very fast. You were in a bad way when we brought you home."

"What do you know about Antonia?" My, he was surly. Protective, too. On the other hand, how much did he know?

"We've been friends for years."

"And you normally meet her naked?"

"Only when performing emergency surgery on shape-changers who get shot."

That gave him a bit of a pause. "What do you know about her?" Persistent bloke.

"All you know, Michael, and more besides." Antonia said, coming through the door, dressed this time. She sat beside him and held his hand. "You can trust Justin. I do. Now, what do you remember happening when we were running?"

He thought a minute or two. "You were behind me, we were skirting the Bainbridge Estates and then . . . I was shot!" He went pale. "I was shot. What about you?"

"I was too, but it didn't bother me the same way. Vampires tend to heal fast. You didn't. You had me worried."

"It's the metal." He shut his eyes a moment. Opening them, he looked from Justin to Antonia and back. "You saved me. Thanks."

Justin inclined his head. "I'm glad I could. Your death would have deeply distressed my old friend."

"So you know she's a vampire?"

"Indeed I do. I've known her ever since she was transformed."

That had him thinking. "You're a vampire, too?"

"I am, but would be obliged if you kept that in confidence."

Michael held out his hand. "It's the least I can do, considering what you did for me."

"It was a trifle makeshift, but I am very, very glad I succeeded. May I suggest you avoid that corner of the neighborhood in the future?"

"I will. What happened to the man who shot me?"

He fled, after I snarled at him and snapped his gun in two," Antonia said.

That earned her a chuckle and a wide smile. "Sorry I missed that."

"Yes," Justin agreed. "Antonia in full battle cry is impressive." She had routed a good few Saxons in her time, and if she'd only been there at Bosworth, things might have gone differently for Richard.

"Not too sure who they were. Poachers, I suspect. The second one is out cold in the field. We left him there with a prayer for a thunderstorm to cool his predatory bent."

Michael leaned back against the head of the bed. "I really missed something it seems, but again, I thank you both."

"It's my job to heal when I can," Justin said. "In this instance, it seems I could." He stood. "Since you seem to be well and healed, I'll leave you to Antonia's care. I must go."

"Want to borrow a pair of trousers?"

Justin shook his head. "Thank you, but I'll leave the way I came." He turned back in the doorway. "One word though, young man. Speaking as one who has known Antonia for centuries and cares greatly for her, do not break her heart." On that note he made it to the front door. Once outside in the moonlight, he stepped away from the house, shifted, and headed back toward the hotel.

Michael could only half-believe what had occurred. The itching pink scar on his shoulder confirmed what they'd both said but . . . "He just happened to be there when I needed him?"

"Not exactly. Justin was in the village keeping an eye on his family—a long story that is not mine to share," she added. "He was flying home and saw us, followed out of typical Justin nosiness, but luckily was there when we needed him. He helped get rid of the two poachers, too."

"He's an old, old, old friend and a doctor?"

She nodded. "Yes. Several centuries older than me. He first learned his skills in the Roman army."

"I see." It was a lie—he didn't, but Justin had accepted that he was a shifter without turning a hair, and Antonia trusted him. "Must admit, coming to and finding a naked man in the doorway was a bit of a shock."

She chuckled. "I can see how it would be, especially with me naked in the shower on top of it all. We were all pretty bare at the time, but Michael, Justin is one of the good guys. Don't ever forget that."

"And I should trust him with my nature?"

"He trusted you with his."

He had. "What did he mean he'd come the same way I had?"

"Think."

He did. "He shifts?"

She nodded. "Another confidence you need to keep."

"You shift too? You never told me."

"I can't. It's mostly men who shift. We women don't as easily, if at all."

"You talk in plurals."

"There are . . . several of us. They keep their secrets too."

"So,"—he put his arm round her shoulder.—"you women can't shift. Pity that."

"Oh, we have our own skills, like flying or running as fast or faster than pumas, and . . ." Her hand slid down his chest. "Other things."

He grinned. "Good thing I've healed."

"A very good thing. Now, lie back, and I'll see if you are fully recovered."

Tom, a friend and ally to be relied on, was perched on a branch with a clear view of the hotel drive and Elizabeth's room. As birds, speech wasn't possible, but mind contact was.

"Took your time, didn't you? I rush over here, forsaking rest and sleep while you gallivant."

"Gallivant is not the word, my friend. All quiet here?"

"As peaceful as a sleeping hotel. I'm beginning to think we're both a bit paranoid."

"Or overprotective? Being in love does that to a man."

Tom gave the closest thing to a nod that a owl could manage. "Amen to that!"

"What say we do another last circuit, and if all's well, we retire to John's comfy little establishment?"

He didn't need to ask twice; Tom spread his wings, and

Justin followed. A quick swoop over the hotel and Orchard House—Justin resisted the impulse to double back and see if all was well with Antonia and her shifter—and they headed for Epsom.

Back in human form, fortified with fresh blood from the fridge and wearing the rather nice silk dressing gowns John provided in his guest bathrooms, Tom and Justin faced each other from the two leather-covered chairs in the comfortable sitting room.

"Alright," Tom said. "Tell me why you yanked me out of bed. What sort of emergency?"

Justin told him.

Tom listened, eyes wide, and giving the occasional gasp of astonishment. "She's taken up with a skinchanger? An animal?" he said when Justin finished.

"You'd be best advised to be tactful on the subject around Antonia. She is, unless I am totally mistaken, in love."

"With an animal? A puma?"

Tom did have a few prejudices to overcome. "I encountered him in both forms, and as a human, he was as coherent and intelligent as you or I."

"But he's a big cat!"

"At times. At others, he's a productive, tax-paying human running what appears to be a successful business."

Tom shook his head. "What next?"

"My friend, I brought a human child into the Colony; you introduced a ghoul; why not a shifter? Variety does appear to be the spice of life, as the saying goes."

"Gwyltha will throw a wobbly!"

"Gwyltha appears to be more and more adaptable in her third millennium."

"She's going to have to be to accept an animal as an equal!"

Not just Gwyltha—Tom needed a little flexibility, too, but . . . it would come. Couldn't fail to once he actually met

Michael. As they sat in the quiet, rain hit the roof in a sharp torrent. Justin laughed. "Antonia wished for rain to drench the poacher we left in the field. Seems her wish has been granted."

"It's raining!" Sam stared out of the window at the rain bucketing down. "Peter and I were going to make a fort in the orchard today."

"Why not make a fort in the attic instead?" Antonia suggested.

"Could we really?"

"If it's alright with your mother, and as long as you and Peter promise not to dig holes in the floorboards."

"We won't!" He turned to Stella. "Can I call Peter and tell him?"

"Sure. Tell him we'll come by and pick him up. Save Emma coming out in the rain."

Elizabeth stared out the window. Might as well call James and tell him to stay home. Wasn't much he could do in the garden in this weather. While Sam and Stella went upstairs to call and arrange things, Elizabeth picked up her mobile.

"That's fine," James said in reply to her suggestion he delay coming in. "Things are a bit busy here anyway. It's our turn to have the police up in our end of the village."

"What happened?"

"Are you sitting down? You'd better be as this is rich: Early this morning, I was woken up by hammering at the door. It was Sid Hayes, a local man often suspected of poaching. He was soaking wet, and kept insisting he'd been attacked by aliens. I called the police. Seems, after a bit of questioning, he and an accomplice he refuses to name were poaching on the Bainbridge estate when the so-called aliens attacked him and left him unconscious in the middle of a field.

"A truly interesting detail is that the police found the broken remains of two unregistered shotguns. Since the police can't find the aliens who allegedly produced and damaged them, they are throwing the book at old Sid."

"Two broken guns?"

"Snapped apart. Sort of adds weight to the UFO story, but the cops go by the laws of this country and planet. Who knows what really happened?"

Elizabeth could make an educated guess. Better have a word with Antonia. "Life's never dull here in Bringham, is it? See you tomorrow."

Antonia was in her room.

"Been destroying any unregistered guns lately?" Elizabeth asked.

The utter shock and then fury in Antonia's face wasn't what she'd expected. "He didn't waste any time spreading the word, did he? Did Stella tell you?"

"No, James."

"Who?"

"James, James Chadwick, the gardener."

"How in the name of Abel did he know?"

They were on different channels here. Elizabeth repeated her conversation with James. Antonia frowned. "So by lunchtime, the entire village will know."

"Know what?"

"Elizabeth, bear with me. This is a bit complicated, and Stella needs to hear as well. Wait until I have a chance to tell you both."

"Tell us what?"

"Hold on, please. I can't face explaining everything twice."

With Sam and Peter dispatched to the attic with a couple of large cartons and a supply of apples, Elizabeth closed the office door and leaned against it. "Okay, Antonia, I have been extraordinarily patient. Tell."

"Tell what?" Stella asked.

"Antonia has something to tell us. Right, dear?"

"What is going on?" Stella asked. "Am I the only one missing something here?"

"No," Elizabeth replied. "I'm missing quite a few bits, and Antonia promised to fill in the blanks. Seems last night a poacher was attacked by aliens, and one of them snapped his shotgun in two."

"You did that, Antonia?" Stella caught on fast.

"I broke one of them. Justin took care of the second one."

"What was Justin doing out in the fields last night?"

"Running around naked! Uninvited!" Antonia replied, pulling out a chair and sitting down. "That's what!"

Stella shut her eyes a second or two; lifted her shoulders and chest as if trying to take a deep, calming breath; raised her hands up, palms outward; and opening her eyes, said, "I know there was probably a very, very good reason for Justin to be running around the neighborhood naked and with you. Please tell me what it was before I rip your head off and then his!"

Antonia looked as if she'd like to take a relaxing breath too. "First, Stella, to preclude all head ripping off, Justin was uninvited and unexpected."

"He just dropped out of the sky naked, I suppose?"

"As it happens, yes. I'll explain, and then Elizabeth will have the ending. Or what I hope is the final word."

Elizabeth had to hand it to her—Stella was a darn good listener. Apart from "Oh, my God!" and "What?" a couple of times, she sat tight and said nothing until they'd both finished.

"So,"—she creased her forehead—"Justin and Tom are watching from the treetops to make sure no bad guys get us. Michael, the potter, is a shape changer, and the latest word in the neighborhood is that aliens have landed. In case I hadn't noticed, I'm not in Ohio anymore."

Antonia's mouth quivered at the corners. "Are you sure we're even in Surrey? With all that's gone on, the last week or so feels more like a trip to another dimension."

"Michael's okay though? He's going to be alright?" Stella asked.

"Thanks to Justin, yes. Seems it was the metal in the bullet that prevented Michael from changing back; otherwise he'd have healed, much like we do."

"So your new love is more than he seems," Elizabeth said.

"Aren't we all?" Stella asked. "The only 'normal' humans in the house are the two tearaways up in the attic." She shook her head. "You're right about this being a wild week. I won't say anything about what next, since there always seems to be something more. Is it us starting things?"

"Hardly. You can't be blamed for someone stealing your car, and it's not my fault I bought a house with a dead body in the garden," Antonia said.

"Has to be Mercury in retrograde," Elizabeth said.

"Yeah, well I hope he gets unretrograded fast," Stella replied. "If Sam wasn't having such a good time with his new pal, I'd be tempted to yank him, and Justin, back to Havering."

"You're going back next week anyway," Antonia said. "Might as well hang around to see what happens next."

"Heard there was a strange call out from Bringham," Detective Inspector Warrington said as Jeffers brought in a stack of interdepartmental mail.

"Alleged UFOs and aliens landed during the night. One poacher arrested. Illegal gun charges, and interestingly, two shotguns snapped in two, presumably by an extraterrestrial force."

"Right." Warrington reached for the top envelope. "We'll be called out to look at crop circles next!"

"Not in this weather. With a bit of luck," she added with a grin.

Jeffers left, taking her cheerfulness with her, and he started reading the coroner's report of the Bringham case. Long practice had him skimming the technical details and pinpointing the salient points: female, white, 20-25 years of age, had borne a child or children. Cause of death: Strangulation. Tissues being tested for possible poison. Estimated interment 15–20 years, perhaps longer. More precise time impossible to determine. No apparent physical problems. No jewelry or other identifying articles. Dental records enclosed.

So, a nice, healthy young woman had been strangled and shoved in an unused air raid shelter twenty years ago. At least he had somewhere to start. Stretching the time frame from twelve to twenty-five years, he asked for a list of all reported missing persons who fit the description.

Someone's missing daughter, wife, or mother had just been found. His job was to match them up and find the murderer. Might take him weeks, months, but he'd do it. The poor, nameless young woman deserved justice.

Chapter 17

Halfway through the morning, a van arrived loaded with folding tables and chairs and portable partitions. "I was told next week," Antonia said to the driver as he and a helper unloaded carton after carton.

"We found we had it in the warehouse after all."

"Wanted to see where they found the body, eh?"

The chap shrugged and grinned. "Don't tell them in the office, but you can't blame us for being curious, can you?"

She could, and almost told him so. Sometimes, she did not understand mortals. "I'm glad you brought it all anyway. How about putting it over there?" She indicated the onetime drawing room. "If you want to have a look at meters of police tape, it's around the side of the house. You can't get anywhere near anything."

"Right you are," he replied. "Sean," he called to the man standing by the van, "bring them in."

Would have been so much faster to tell him and Sean to stay in the van and call on Stella to help, but Antonia had long adapted to living with mortals, and this pair was a sight to behold. Between all the "Over here, Sean" and "Keep that

end up, Greg," and "Easy over there, now," they took ample
rests to look around.

"Fixed it up nice, you have," Sean said, taking a breather
between trips back to the van.

"You knew the house?" Antonia asked. A bit surprising,
but who knew?

"Not really. I was in here once as a kid. My gran worked
here cleaning for the Underwoods. Murder to work for they
were, she said." He seemed oblivious to any possible tact-
lessness. "Real odd they were. Used to argue something terrible with each other, my gran said." He shook his head at
the oddity of eccentric old ladies.

"How long ago would this have been?" Very much a leading question, but why not?

"Let me think. I were a boy, seven, eight, or so. Say
twenty years or more ago when she first started working
here. She stayed a couple of years and finally gave up. She
was getting on a bit, and they were becoming funny. She'd
turn up in the morning, and they'd tell her they didn't need
her. Got tired of it, she did. After all, you need to know when
you're getting paid, don't you?"

One certainly did. "Your grandmother still lives in Bringham?" Why ask—curiosity or an odd sense of unease after
the past few days?

"Nah!" He shook his head. "She retired and went to live
with my aunt in Bognor." Given the goings-on around here,
Antonia didn't blame her.

They unloaded the rest with even more huffing and puff-
ing, and after stopping only to peer at the scene of the crime
over the mass of police tape, Sean and Greg left, no doubt to
regale their cronies about the excitement surrounding a heap
of fresh dirt and a lot of rusty corrugated iron.

As she turned back to the office, Sam and Peter came
clattering down the stairs. "Hey!" Peter said, "look at all
those boxes!"

"Could we have one when they're empty, please, Antonia," Sam asked. "We could take them upstairs and make a real castle."

"I've got go home now; Mum said to be back by twelve, but tomorrow? Could we please?" Peter asked.

She was not tough enough to refuse two pairs of hopeful eyes. "Tomorrow. We need to empty them first."

"Let's hope it rains so we can play upstairs again," Peter said. "Your house is so much more fun than ours."

"But you do have a TV and Nintendo," Sam said.

"This is more fun. Bye!"

Peter ran off down the drive, splashing in the puddles.

Sam turned to her. "Thanks for the boxes, Antonia; they will be brilliant! Is Mum in the office? I'm hungry."

Nothing new in that.

James hadn't realized how much two days of work had lifted his spirits until he didn't have any. Yes, he agreed, there was nothing he could do in the pelting rain. But . . .

After coffee and toast—dry toast because he was out of both butter and marmalade—he went back to the stack of papers on Sebastian's desk and noticed the open deed box where he hadn't found his mother's death certificate. The more he considered it, the odder it seemed. Maybe it had been sent off for insurance and never returned? It had to be possible to get back copies. He booted up the computer; typed in Somerset House; realized that was no longer what he needed; but by following a few links, got the right site and an application form for a death certificate.

What could be easier? Other than the fact that he didn't know the date of her death or her age. Not for certain. He'd been six, when she'd left, run off, according to Uncle Sebby, with a man. How many months later had he been told she was dead? Six? Nine? The details had been lost the morass of misery and loneliness.

The form gave a three-year window. He typed it up, tapped in his credit card number, and sent it off. Maybe he'd just solved the mystery.

He thought back to the day he'd been told she was dead and Sebastian had gone off to the funeral. Why hadn't they held the funeral in Bringham?

He'd never questioned it as a child. Why would he? Grownups were always right. Or so he'd then believed. And his mother was gone. He'd cried himself to sleep for months afterwards, praying and hoping she would come back one day. Hearing she was dead had exploded that hope. She was gone for good.

Except no one had ever told him where or how.

He stood and stretched. He was going to have to wait days, maybe weeks, to get his answer. But meanwhile . . . He crossed the room and reached for his jacket. Maybe the church had funeral records.

Just as well he didn't have to go to work. He'd found another job to do. It beat shuffling old Sebby's papers or wondering what to do about that barn of a house.

He had no luck, at least not at the church. He'd been baptized, and so had his mother and Sebastian. Heck, they even had confirmation records for both of them, a sacrament he, James, had avoided by declaring himself atheist to the scandalized vicar.

After drawing a blank at the church and arousing the curiosity of the vicar's wife, he drove into Leatherhead and studied the local paper's archives in the library, turning up nothing after an announcement of her marriage.

Seems his mother had just disappeared and then mysteriously died.

On that note, he went home, watched TV until fatigue overwhelmed him, and went to bed, waking to sunshine and a clear sky. The grass would be wet underfoot, but he could prune, and he should go and talk to old Bert Andrews. James phoned him first, unsure what sort of welcome he'd get, but the old man's granddaughter was delighted to have someone —anyone, James suspected—come and sit with her grandfather. "He'll be glad of the company and the opportunity to talk about the old house. He's been going on about it ever since he heard the news about the body being found there. Terrible business, isn't it? Don't know what the world is coming to."

James forbore pointing out that the "terrible business" had occurred several years back and agreed to come over at ten. On the way, remembering old Bert had once had a weakness for Bass Ale, James stopped and picked up a half dozen bottles.

"Good of you," Bert said when James deposited the bag and bottles on the coffee table. "Nothing like it, is there? Tell Dawn to bring us a couple of glasses."

"Oh, Grandad, you really shouldn't, not with your blood pressure pills," she fussed without any appearance of expecting to be minded.

"Get along with you," Bert said. "Go and take your children to the park. We'll be fine and snug here."

"It's the dentist, not the park," Dawn said as she went out. "Won't be long, and thanks for coming," she said to James. "I hate to leave him alone."

As the door closed, Bert handed James a bottle. "Open it, will you? She's a good girl, Dawn. Can't deny it, but fussy. Her mother was the same; so was my Betty. Must be something about women."

Sensing that a request for a bottle opener would impinge on his manhood in Bert's eyes, James nicked the top off with his teeth, poured one for Bert, and another for himself. Taking just a sip to toast Bert James put his glass down on the table.

"So," Bert said, after smacking his lips and leaning back in his chair, the glass clasped in both hands, "you've taken over my job at the old house?"

"Yes, I have."

"Why?"

Good question. A mad impulse? A fit of sentimentality and nostalgia? Or because a pleasant young woman was prepared to take him at face value? "I was offered the job. The garden is really run to seed—nothing like it was in your day. They're doing the whole place up and wanted to include the gardens."

"You've got your work cut out for you, young fella. Not used to work like this, are you?" He looked at the sticking plaster on James's right hand.

"No, but I'm enjoying it. Working outside beats shuffling papers on a desk all day."

"Yer right there!" Bert took another drink, slurped, and wiped his mouth with the back of his hand. "Good stuff," he said. "Dawn gets me a pint once in a while, but I miss getting down to the pub." He shook his head and went quiet. No doubt remembering convivial evenings with his mates over a pint or two.

"About the garden," James tried again. "It's really overgrown."

"Best prune hard and yank out the weeds. That's all you can do, young man. Backbreaking work it is; not many nowadays care for it. Why are you doing it?"

"I used to walk there a lot with my mother. She's dead now."

He nodded. "Who was yer mother? One of the Underwood sisters? Was she the young one what ran off with a Yank?"

"No, my mother was Rachel Caughleigh. Rachel Chadwick after she married."

His gray eyebrows shot up. "Young Rachel? You were that little nipper she used to bring around?"

"Yes!" Old Bert remembered her. Did he know anything? "You remember her?"

"Just a bit. She used to come visiting the old witches. Always thought it a shame for a pretty young thing like her to spend so much time with old biddies. She were a nice girl. Polite, sweet, not like that snooty brother of hers. Now he come to a bad end. Hear about that, did you?"

"Er . . . yes, I heard."

"Bad business, but that's how things are nowadays. We had the National Service in my day. A year in the army would have straightened that brother of hers out, but no, he was . . ."

James already knew what Sebastian was, thank you very much. But his mother . . . "Remember anything else about her? I was young when she died."

The old man went quiet. "Sad that. Sent you off to school didn't they?"

Yes, for his sins. Or perhaps, those of his mother. "They did."

"Often wondered what happened to her. Nice little thing she were. Always polite. 'Mr. Andrews, may we come walk in the garden? I hope we aren't disturbing you,' she'd say. Nice little gel, polite. Sad what happened. Doted on you, she did too. Never could credit she run off and left you the way she did." He shook his head. "You were the apple of her eye."

So he had believed. "Do you remember what happened? When she died?"

Bert shook his head. "Just heard she had. Don't rightly remember exactly when I heard, but it were after I left the House. I weren't there much more than a few months after she ran off. They had me do a few big jobs: fill in the old pond, messy job that was, and cut down some of the old trees in the orchard—ones that no longer had enough fruit to be worth grease banding. Hard ladies to work for, they were. Wanted seventy minutes work for every hour they paid, but it was me job.

"Did a lot there, I did. Put up a tool shed they wanted. Planted blackberries over the old Anderson shelter and blocked up the door when they decided it was getting dangerous. Used to clip the hedges, too, until I got too old to get up the ladders. It were a good job."

Feeling a bit reckless and hoping it wouldn't do terrible things to the old codger's blood pressure, James opened another bottle. "Have another? I can't have too much. I'm driving."

"Weren't like that in my day." Bert shook his head. "In my time, if you went out drinking with yer mates, no one came after you with one of those breathalyzers." He took a long swig from his topped up glass. "Good of you to drop by. Good luck with the old garden, lad. You have your work cut out for you."

No doubt about it! And he rather fancied getting back and seeing to it, but James had pretty much committed himself to staying until Dawn returned from the dentist. Might be a long morning.

"You play dominoes, young man?"

"Er . . . yes." Or he had. Once upon a time. Couldn't actually remember when.

"There's a box on the sideboard over there. Go fetch them. Not often I get a chance to beat anyone these days." James fetched then, dumping his beer on a pot plant as he crossed the room.

To James's ignominy, Bert beat him eleven times before Dawn came back to release him.

With the wish that Bert enjoy the remaining beers another day, James made a beeline for his car.

What had he expected? Clear, concise directions how to take care of the garden? What a hope! All he'd got were a bunch of reminiscences and someone else who remembered his mother. Another confirmation of the unsubstantiated "ran off and later died" story.

Maybe he was clinging to a child's hope and belief that his mother had loved him. She had promised to be there when school was over but she hadn't been. She'd run off.

He was going on twenty-eight years old. Time he got over it.

He had a job—one old Sebastian would sneer at—but a job, and if he wanted to keep it, he'd better show up.

"We're a right pair of independent, liberated women, aren't we?" Elizabeth said the next morning. She and Stella were alone in the office. Antonia was stacking some of the promised boxes for Sam and Peter.

"What are we to do?" Stella replied. "It irks me that Justin and Tom decided to mount watch, but they are worried. Can't say I blame them; I am myself, and not that I'd tell him, but I feel better knowing he's close. Irritated, but much better."

Elizabeth smiled. "I'm just irritated, but I don't have Sam to worry about. I know I can take care of myself—no prob. But Tom is always so determined to do the job himself."

"But he cares, Elizabeth. He's crazy about you."

So ghouls did blush . . . interesting. "It's pretty much mutual." She looked down at her left hand. "Wouldn't be wearing this if it weren't."

"They drive us bananas, but life's far better with them than alone."

"You said it, sister!"

Stella couldn't, didn't try, to contain her smile. Elizabeth was like a sister. The sister she'd never had. Not only had Justin shown her what the love of an honorable man added to her existence and provided a future for Sam she'd never have managed on a dry cleaner's clerk's salary, but by bringing her into the Colony, she'd acquired the next best thing to a family, or rather, a law-abiding, nonfelonious family. In Antonia, Elizabeth, and Dixie, she'd acquired girlfriends. Even Gwyltha, the imperious and forbidding leader of the Colony, was someone Stella knew she could always count on. "So when are you and Tom making it permanent?"

"He was going for this weekend, but I told him he had to ask my father's consent. Not that Dad has much idea what's going on, but just in case."

"Is he going to say, 'Sir, I'm Tom Kyd, vampire. May I have your daughter's hand in marriage?'"

"Sort of. I rather fancy getting married at Devil's Elbow at sunset, but all the blood test complications rather put paid to that idea, so,"—she lowered her voice—"I want to get married here, in the garden, at the Autumn Equinox."

Stella still wasn't clear on all the pagan festivals and holidays, but this one she had heard of. "In the garden here?"

Elizabeth nodded. "That's why I want it cleared and cleaned up. Not the only reason. I also want to obliterate any traces of negative influences there, and what better way than this?"

All this talk about traces and influences was as much above her as auras and positive and negative energy. "Just give us the date; we'll be there. Promise. After all, you did say Sam was going to give you away."

"And meanwhile, we still haven't decided what we're going to do about our ever present men. I keep looking out the window at the sparrows and thrushes on the lawn and wondering which one is which."

"Can't see either of them going for sparrow. Bald eagle, owl, or heron perhaps.

"Or peacocks!"

Elizabeth's rather dirty laugh was cut short as the door opened.

"Sorry to interrupt," James said. "Antonia said I'd find you here, and I thought I'd better check in."

"Great." Elizabeth turned in her chair. "The garden's out there needing you."

He smiled. "I went by to see old Bert Andrews. He was full of reminiscences, but they were not much help. I'll go on pulling any grass in the beds and clearing the paths and cutting dead wood. When I get through, you'll have to tell me what next."

"Sounds good."

He hesitated as if about to ask or say something more, but nodded. "Right you are then."

As the door closed, Stella frowned. "Why does he do the job? He's rich. He has one of the biggest houses around. He pays a garden service from Leatherhead to do his own yard work and comes here to pull weeds."

"You researched him?"

"Not really. I was nosy, so I drove by his house and saw the truck parked in front. It's just odd."

"I think the reason he gave was why. He's never had a job and wanted to try."

"Maybe, but if so, why not start in his own backyard?" She would never understand rich people. Weird was not the word for it.

"Mum!" Sam and Peter bursting through the door put paid to her musings on the eccentricities of the rich. "Can we play outside? We saw James going to work in the garden, and if it's dry enough for him, isn't it dry enough to play outside?"

"I thought you wanted to make a castle in the attic?"

"We made one, Mum. It's brill, but outside is more fun, and we want to look for frogs."

"Any plans on what you'll do with any frogs you find?"

"Oh, yes, Mrs. Corvus," Peter said. "We're putting them in our pond. We've nothing in there, and my dad said a few frogs would liven it up and get rid of the green yucky stuff."

She hoped Emma was as enthusiastic about imported frogs. "Okay, just don't bring them into this house. Be sure to ask Emma before you take them in her house, and don't, whatever you do, go near the . . ." she hesitated saying crime scene, " . . . don't cross the police tape."

"Oh, we won't, Mrs. Corvus," Peter assured her with earnest, wide eyes.

"Promise, Mum," Sam added.

"Cross my heart and hope to die!" Peter added.

"Frogs," Stella said as the door closed behind them. "Maybe I'd better call Emma and warn her."

"Worry about it when they find any," Elizabeth suggested. "There's no pond or creek on the property. I think they're going to have a hard time finding any."

"For Emma's sake, I hope so. At least they are occupied and out of mischief."

"You have the most brilliant house and garden," Peter said as they ran around the side of the house toward the orchard. "Much more fun than ours. We don't even have an attic."

"We have an attic in our real house in Yorkshire," Sam said. "We had one in Columbus, too."

"You were so lucky living in America!"

Sam sighed. Whatever he said to the contrary, Peter was convinced that people in America visited Disney every weekend. "It was good." He missed Mrs. Zeibel, the neighbor next door he'd known since he was a baby. "But I like Yorkshire too." No point in trying to explain about not having a crack house down the road. Peter just wouldn't understand.

"Sure you didn't have a swimming pool?"

"Nah!" Only when it rained and the basement leaked. "Let's look for frogs. What do we put them in?"

"In our pockets, twit!"

"Twit yourself with bells on!"

"Can't catch me!"

"Can!"

Peter zigzagged in and out of trees, Sam close on his tail until he finally downed him with a rugger tackle. "Gotcha!"

"Pax! Pax! You got me. Let me up." Peter brushed his sweater down. "My mum's going to spiflicate me when she sees that."

It was pretty bad. "Let it dry, and we can brush it off. Won't show as much then." He'd ask Dad what "spiflicate" meant next time he saw him.

"Hope so."

"Sorry about it . . ."

"Never mind, my turn!"

Quick as a reflex, Sam turned tail and ran, Peter on his heels, until they both rushed through the opening in the hedge and into the kitchen garden, stopping a meter or so short of the bands of blue and white tape. "Pax!" Sam said, holding up both hands, index and middle fingers crossed. "We can't run here."

Peter conceded with a nod. "You think that when the police finish, your mum will let us dig it up? Maybe there's hidden treasure or vital clues the police missed."

"When the police finish, they're going to build a tearoom

there. Remember Elizabeth talking to your mum about it? We're already behind, and Antonia's worried it won't be ready when we open in September."

Adult deadlines weren't a major worry for Peter. "Shame really. Would have been fun to dig."

"There's always the walled garden. We could offer to help James."

"Not the same." Peter shook his head. "Was there really a dead body here? And you saw it?"

"Oh, yes, I did. She looked gross!"

"Really dead?"

"Very."

"I've never seen a real live dead body. Only on TV or in a film."

Peter didn't know when he was well off. "You haven't missed much."

"We could look for clues where they found her."

"Don't even think about it! We could end up in jail for crossing that tape." Did Peter have no sense?

Thankfully, he did. "Anyway, we don't have anything to dig with."

"We can look. Just as long as we don't cross the tape. We promised. Just looking isn't going near. Not really."

They paced the perimeter, stopping to peer between the jagged remnants of corrugated metal and the uneven piles of wet dirt, left as they'd been the day of the discovery. Toward the back, near the hedge, the tape ended.

"We could squeeze by there," Peter suggested. "We won't be crossing it, and we might see more."

They couldn't see much less. Clumps and humps of damp dirt were hardly thrilling. "Think we should?"

"I dunno. It's not crossing the tape. Not really."

Sam conceded the point, but . . . "Perhaps if we just stay against the hedge and look down . . ."

Sliding through the gap was easy; once they were past the

tape markers, there was precious little space between the overgrown hedge and the back wall of the old shelter. The earthen bank rose up steeply, and the brambles covering the mound didn't make things any easier.

"This was not one of your better ideas, Corvus." Peter said as he tried to disentangle a long bramble from his sweater and hair.

Sam tried to help. "Wasn't my idea."

"Was!"

"Let's get out of here. If your Mum's going to spiflicate you over the mud, she'll kill you if you rip your sweater up."

"You're right there."

Getting in was easier than getting out. Brambles that bent inward—and been relatively easy to pass—now blocked their way. Sam frowned. Mum had been more right than she knew saying not to come here, but if they called for help, they'd be in trouble for sure. "We need to squeeze by. Maybe if we crawl under the brambles."

"Or over them. There's a gap near the corner."

But it involved climbing on the curved wall of the shelter. "You go first."

"Scaredy-cat!"

"It was your idea."

And easier than expected: a scramble up the curved edge—that still stood—and a jump down, landing just beyond the tape. So they hadn't really crossed it. Peter managed it with ease. Sam followed, slipping once on the still damp earth and landing on his hands and knees, but he brushed himself off. "Glad we got out of there."

"You can see better from this side. Look."

"The side's all fallen in. Must have been the rain."

"How do you know?"

"It rained all day yesterday, twerp. We had to play indoors. Remember?"

"I know that! How do you know it fell in?"

"Because I saw it when they dug it up, didn't I? It's collapsed."

Peter accepted that, peering at the mound of mud and dirt. "There's something buried there."

"Oh! Go on!"

"No, Sam, look. Honest, there is. Look." Sam followed Peter's muddy finger. He was right. The end of what looked like a filthy box stuck out from the rough edge of the fresh dirt. "What do we do now?"

"We have to tell, of course."

"What if we get in trouble for squeezing round the back?"

Peter had a point, but . . . "We still have to tell."

"So you lads were climbing all over a crime scene and fell in?" Warrington gave them his hard stare. Poor little buggers were both terrified. No doubt their respective mothers had given them the "what for" in the twenty minutes it had taken him to get here.

"No, we weren't, honest," said the fair one with the muddy pullover.

"No, sir. We really weren't," the dark-haired one, Sam, insisted, shaking his head. "We really wanted to, but Mum said not to, so we didn't. Truly, we didn't."

"But we did—" the other one, Peter, began.

"So you did then." The truth always came out. Must be part of a policeman's job, scaring the truth out of schoolboys.

"No, sir," Sam said. He had a touch of an American accent. "What Peter means is that we did go round the back, but we never crossed the tape."

"Round the back? Where?"

"By the hedge," Peter explained. "Where the tape ends. Sam's right; we didn't cross it. Really, we didn't."

"Have a look, will you, Jeffers?" he said to the sergeant beside him. "Is there a gap?"

The two boys exchanged looks. No doubt crossing fingers and praying for good measure. Sam took a step nearer to his mother. Peter looked sideways up at his.

"There is a space, sir, and lots of footprints. Thick with brambles it is. No doubt the lads who set up the tape never imagined anyone getting through there."

So they had the truth so far. "What do you think that is?" he asked, nodding to the muddy mess and the two crime scene techs working on dislodging the object without collapsing entire side of the remaining air raid shelter.

"In there?" Pete asked, as if expecting a trick question.

"Yup. In the box, case, tin, or whatever it is. Any idea what's in it?" He still wasn't convinced they hadn't been up to something.

"Clues?" Sam suggested.

He was good at keeping a straight face. Jeffers had more trouble. She had to go over and check on the techs' progress at the crime scene. Warrington nodded at the boys. "I hope you're right."

"I hope it helps catch the murderer," Sam said, young eyes wide with hope. "I really, really do. I hope you get the bad guys and lock them up for good."

"We'll do our best, son."

"Good. I don't like bad guys."

Interesting. "Known any bad guys, Sam?"

He nodded. "Back when we lived in Columbus, two broke into our house and tied me and my babysitter up."

Poor little bugger! No wonder he looked so worried. Not surprisingly his mother stepped forward and put her arms round his shoulders. Nice woman. Sensible. Both mothers were. Let the kids speak for themselves, but stayed very close.

"I hope that never happens again, Sam."

"I've got my dad to look after me now." 'Strewth, the faith of kids! Terrifying really.

"That's good, Sam, Where's your dad now?"

He hesitated. Interesting. Separated? Would explain being down here with his mother. "He's a doctor; he has clinic in Yorkshire. He visited us last weekend. I miss him, but I'll see him again soon."

"I think they've got it, sir," Jeffers said.

Looked as though they had. All nicely done up in a sterile plastic bag. He hoped it wasn't some child's buried collection of old pennies.

"Sir," Sam asked, "do you really think it has clues in it?"

"Can't tell yet, son, but we hope so."

"One question, Inspector." It was the Stonewright woman. The one who'd called him. She seemed to run the place.

"Yes, madam?"

She walked round the others, coming within two feet or so, a short but imposing woman, a bit of a duchess, he suspected. "Inspector, do you know any more about how long that poor woman was there?"

Why not share it? It would get around the village, and it might jog a few memories. "Hard to say exactly, given that the body was enclosed the way it was, but we reckon fifteen to twenty years."

"Oh!" Peter's mother said. "Really? We all thought it had been there since the war."

Interesting. Village gossip often was.

"Couldn't have been."

Warrington turned to the speaker, a tall man, dressed like a gardener, who looked vaguely familiar. "Why not, sir?"

"I came here as as child. It was open then. I remember being told not to go near it. I think the old ladies used it for storage."

Very interesting. "Local are you, sir?

The man nodded. "Yes. I live in the village."

"Give Jeffers your name and phone number if you will, sir. We might need to talk to you." And he'd better go and

confront the ravening hacks of the press who'd followed him
out here like a bunch of vultures. Hell, there was even a TV
van. Ghouls!

Sam watched as everyone drove away. "Will they catch
whoever did it, Mum?"

"We can only hope, Sam," Stella said.

"What are we doing now?" Peter asked.

"You're coming home and getting a bath and clean clothes,"
Emma said. "Honestly, Peter, look at yourself. I ought to put
you in the washing machine."

"I wish we had a washing machine," Stella said as Peter
left. "Better take you back and change and go look for a
laundromat.

"It's a launderette here, Mum."

"Whatever it is, we need one. We might be gone all afternoon, but . . ."

"Go," Antonia said. "You too, Elizabeth. I think we all
need to get out for a while."

Chapter 18

Elizabeth grabbed her phone and called Dixie, catching her at home before she left for the Emporium. "I need you to check something for me."

"About the troubles?" Dixie asked.

"Yes. We have a time frame: fifteen to twenty years."

Dixie was quiet for a few seconds, then, "I'm game to look, but the dating in the dairies is often sketchy, and they might not have noted anything."

And might not even have been involved. "Thanks. It's a long shot. I doubt you'll see, 'We murdered a young woman this afternoon,' but there might be something. The gardener told us they used the air raid shelter for storage at one time. They had to know about blocking it up, and the old gardener remembers planting blackberries over it. Who knows . . ."

"With that lot, anything," Dixie replied. "I'll look and let you know if I turn up anything."

And if they did, would it help? Was worth a try though. "Thanks anyway."

Now what? Call Tom and demand to know where he was lurking? Or go into Dorking and explore the New Age and

Wicca shop she'd found in the yellow pages? If she got a move on, she could do both. After leaving a message on Tom's voice mail, inviting him to take her out to dinner and discuss getting a marriage license, she headed for Dorking.

"What do you want to do?" Stella asked Sam. "We've got the afternoon to go somewhere. The Castle in Guildford? Shopping? Any ideas?"

Sam thought a minute. He'd promised Dad not to tell about seeing him last night, but . . . "I think we should give Dad a call. I think he's worried about us." The way Mom looked at him, he worried he'd given Dad away. He had promised. "What do you think, Mom?"

"Good idea!" She gave him her very cheerful don't worry smile. So there was something wrong, and not just the new developments about the murder. "Want to get my cell phone?"

He went right into voice mail. Drat! "Dad? It's Sam, just calling to say hello and hope we see you real, real soon. Oh, and they found more at the crime scene today." That should get his attention. Satisfied, he snapped the phone shut. "He'll call back, Mum."

"I know, Sam. He will."

Mum was worried, too. Grown-ups! She should know Dad would take care of things. A vampire as old as his father could do just about anything, and Mum did pretty well herself. She had chased that car down and taken care of the bad guy, just as she had fixed two of them in Columbus. He shook his head. Grown-ups worried so.

After everyone left, James stayed. There was more than enough work to keep him busy for months, and on a day like this, it felt better to be outside pulling weeds than inside shuffling papers that he suspected he'd never get sorted.

And weeding was good for thinking. How long before he heard about his mother's death certificate? If one didn't turn up, what did that prove? And what about the thought that wouldn't go away since the detective had mentioned fifteen to twenty years? It was almost twenty-one years since his mother had left. They'd have thought him a lunatic if he'd said, "It might have been my mother." But what if it was? Maybe he'd kept quiet because he didn't want it to be. If it were . . . too many awful possibilities reared up. He yanked at a particularly stubborn tussock of couch grass. The roots went underground for a foot or more, lifting other plants as he tugged. He got it, tossed it in the wheelbarrow, and kept working

When he finally packed up, he had two barrowfuls of weeds and debris, an aching back, and a sense of deep satisfaction at the cleared bed. He also looked at the remaining jungle. It would take all summer to get this done, but why not? As long as they paid him, he'd come.

He put everything away, tipped the weeds onto his just started compost pile, and headed for his car.

A young woman was coming up the front drive as he rounded the corner of the house. "Hello," she said. "Is anyone in? I've brought some more samples." She carried a stack of bulky plastic bags.

"They all left early." She was familiar. He must have seen her around the village. "The house is locked up."

"Drat! I was passing and thought I'd drop them off."

"There is the side porch. You could leave them there. Should be safe enough."

"Thanks." When she smiled, her blue eyes crinkled at the corners, and a little dimple appeared in her chin. "Where?"

He led the way round the side. "It's hard to get through on account of all the police tape."

She gave a shudder. "How terrible this all is. The whole

village is talking about it." He bet it was! "I hope to God they find out who she was."

So did he. Although he wanted it to be anyone except his mother. "Here." He opened the glass door. "I'd put them in for you, but my hands—" He held them up, blistered and muddy. "Better not touch anything until I wash up.'

"You've been working hard."

"I like it." He pulled the door to. "They should be safe enough there until tomorrow. I'll give them a call and tell them you left them. What's your name?"

"Judy. Judy Abbott." She held out her hand.

"Better not shake."

Didn't seem to bother her. "It's 'clean dirt,' as my gran used to say." Her hand was warm and smooth as she gripped his. "And you are . . .?"

He took a breath. "Chadwick. James Chadwick." He braced himself for a fast withdrawal of her hand.

She must be new to the village. "How do you do, James? Thanks for your help. I didn't want to have to haul them all back." As they walked toward their cars, she looked sideways at him. "You live in the village?"

Here it came. "In The Grange."

"Oh!" Now she got it! "You're the nephew of that solicitor, Caughleigh."

"Yes." Why try to deny it?

"You really have a mess to sort out, don't you? At least according to my father."

"Your father?"

"He's the vicar."

Oh Lord! Time for a deep breath. Hell, that was almost a sigh. "I see." Only too well.

"Well," she stopped by her car, taking her key out of her pocket, "James . . ." She hesitated. Trying to decide how to excuse herself from speaking to him, no doubt. "I'm here all summer. If you ever need a break from gardening, give me a bell."

Took him a good ten minutes to realize she'd asked him to phone her! Would he ever dare?

After the others went their ways, Antonia drove straight for Michael's. She knew he'd be working, but after the events of the morning, she yearned for his common sense and assurance, and she wouldn't say no to a nice naked conversation. Her need for him burned like a simmering want. It should be humiliating to feel this dependence on anyone, much less a mortal, but in her heart, she didn't give a damn.

And did Michael count as mortal in the Colony's eyes? After the way she'd made an utter fool of herself with Etienne, vampire dishonorable, they should be darn glad she'd aligned herself to a nice, hardworking, respectable . . . puma.

She threw back her head and laughed. It was better than a low-budget film. The vampire and her big cat!

Michael was working in the glazing shed, dipping cream jugs in glaze and setting them on racks, when she walked in. He looked up the instant she crossed the threshold. "Antonia!" He stood, his face creasing with the sexiest of smiles as his dark eyes glittered. "I thought you were working today."

"I was." She put heavy emphasis on the was. "Things happened."

He put down the jug and, pulling off his thin rubber gloves, pulled her close. He smelled of heat and summer air, and his own animal scent. She wrapped her arms around him as she rested her head against his chest. "What is it, love?" he asked, his breath warm in her hair.

"Just one more thing going wrong."

"What?"

She told him. "I know this might help solve everything, but we could have done without the reporters and darn cameramen tramping over the shrubbery." She shook her head. "I'm beginning to think the whole venture is benighted and I should have stayed in Yorkshire and taken up pig farming."

He pulled back to look down at her, a hint of worry in his eyes. "From a purely selfish point of view, I'm glad you didn't take on the pigs." He stroked the side of her face with work-roughened fingers. "I'm glad you came south, and I so hope you'll stay." So did she! How could she consider leaving him? Would all hell break loose when Gwyltha heard? Did she care? Yes!

"Anything else the matter, love?"

She was not about to start explaining the complications and vagaries of vampire ethics. "I suppose today was just one more thing."

"But was it bad?" Good point. "If it helps the police identify the victim, isn't it an advance? Some grieving family will have a twenty-year-old doubt settled."

True. "I keep wondering what will happen next."

"What happens next is you help me finish glazing these jugs. We pack the kiln, get it going, and take a good, long shower and . . ."

She looked forward to "and." "How many jugs do you have left?

"Just a couple of dozen. I made extra for this woman from Yorkshire who asked to handle my pots."

She fancied handling a lot more than his pots. "Let's get going. How can I help speed things along?"

He handed her a pair of thin rubber gloves and showed her how to dip each jug. First, glazing the inside by filling and swirling the thick, white liquid inside each jug; then dipping it in a grayish liquid to coat the outside; and holding it with her fingertips, leaving the bottom bare.

It was easy, almost mindless work, simple and relaxing. By the time they had the whole batch glazed, racked, and loaded in the kiln, her mind had cleared, or rather been cleared of anything but her longing for Michael.

They finished by late afternoon, and Michael set the white cone in a dollop of soft clay and put it on the shelf, checking it was visible through the spy hole.

"All set," he said, turning the handle to seal the kiln before lighting the gas to start it heating. "We've got a few hours before we need to check it. Don't know about you, but I need a shower."

That wasn't all she needed, but it was a darn good place to start. She held out her hand, "Come on then, mustn't keep a lady waiting!"

His utilitarian bathroom wasn't quite big enough for two, but that wasn't really a disadvantage. Closeness was never a bad thing.

Not when the closest person was Michael.

They were inches apart, he with his back to the shower door, she against the wash basin. His body heat, the life-giving warmth she craved, came at her in waves. Antonia placed her hand over his heart; feeling the steady beat of life, she smiled.

"Well?" he asked, a smile twitching the corners of his mouth. "What's on your mind?"

"You," she replied, slipping a couple of his shirt buttons undone, "and how lovely you'll look naked."

"Great minds think alike." His hands settled on her waist and eased her blouse out of her skirt. Little tremors of anticipation thrilled her as his warm fingers brushed her skin. His skin was just a little rough, reminding her he worked with his hands. His sensitive hands, his inventive hands unhooked her bra and eased up and down her back, pulling her against him as he lowered his mouth.

His lips were hot with life, and at his touch, her body

flared in a wild rush of desire. As his hands came around to cup her breasts, she tore off his shirt, driven by a need to feel hot, living flesh beneath her hands.

He didn't object, chuckling as she pressed her lips to the soft golden pelt on his chest. He was so alive, so warm, so Michael, and her need half-terrified her.

What was it he offered that so filled a space in her soul she had never known existed? Why worry about that when his hands eased down, unzipping her skirt, and pushing it over her hips so it fell to the floor?

Stepping out of and kicking away the unneeded skirt, she took care of his belt and zip in seconds. Down to underwear, they embraced, hands stroking each other as they clung together, Michael pausing just long enough to turn on the shower before he wrapped his arms back around her and kissed.

His lips were so warm, so sure, so driven by a passion that filled her heart and soul. Her hands tunneled through his golden hair as her tongue found his, and they kissed with a wild fervor that left him panting and her grinning.

"Took your breath away, did I?"

"Smug, aren't you, my love? Just you wait. You may not gasp and pant, but I'm going to leave you shaking."

"Is that a promise?"

"From the bottom of my heart."

"What if I want a written guarantee?"

"No problem." He bent his head, and his lips brushed her shoulder. "I'll write it in kisses all over your delectable body."

What more could she ask? Her bra was down in the jumble of clothes on the floor. She slipped her fingers into the elastic waistband of his tightie whities. He was fast, but nothing beat vampire speed. Michael was naked, and very, very interested in the proceedings.

She ran a finger down the side of his impressively erect cock. "Lovely," she whispered. "Oh, Michael."

The steam from the shower filled the little room, leaving a sheen on his golden skin. She kissed his shoulder, lapping the sweet moisture, inhaling the earthy sexiness of his scent, as she felt his erection hard against her belly.

"Hold on, love," he said as he swept her up in his arms and stepped under the cascade of warm water.

Closing her eyes, she let her head fall back as the water ran down her face and over her breasts. Michael's lips closed on her nipple, and she let out a long, slow moan of utter joy.

"Like that, do you?" he asked, lifting his mouth just enough to whisper.

She nodded, knowing full well the silly smile on her face more than answered him. He kissed her other breast, his tongue teasing until the nipple stood hard and ready.

He set her on her feet and reached for the soap. "Turn around."

She faced the wall, her hands flat against the smooth tile, as he lathered up the soap. The clean, woodsy fragrance scenting the room as he spread lather over her shoulders and back, taking his time over her hips and her bottom. "Enjoying yourself?" she asked as his hands found the crevice between her bottom cheeks.

"Oh, yes," he replied. "How about you?" He was bending down now, soaping up her thighs and legs,

"Yes, rather! Got anything else in mind?"

His reply was to trail his finger along the back of her leg, over her hip, and up her side to cup her breast. His soapy fingers moved easily over the skin. "Definitely, my love. Turn around, please."

As if she'd refuse! She leaned against the tile, looking up at her lover, his lips parted as if ready to kiss, his eyes dark with desire and wonderful animal need.

How had she lived without this man, this wild creature of the woods, her lover? "Michael," she muttered as he spread soapy bubbles over her breasts and down her belly, his fingers gently opening her as his thumbs stroked her softest flesh. "I want you."

"Be patient," he said, a touch of amusement in his voice. "You're not ready yet, and I'm damn well not taking you to bed with soap all over you."

"All over me!" She grabbed the soap from him. "We'll see who has soap all over them! Turn around, lover!"

Laughing, he complied. "Getting feisty, are we?"

"You ain't seen nothing yet!"

"Tut, tut. Double negatives! Can't have that!"

Who in their right mind picked holes in grammar at a time like this? "What are you going to do about it?"

He took the challenge as an invitation to reach back and grab her between the legs. She was tempted to give in there and then, but why not do as he suggested, and prolong this?

She stepped aside just enough to elude his touch before moving forward. One hand pinned him to the wall while she teased him with lather down his back, taking her time as she soaped every available inch before pressing herself against him so her soapy skin slid against his. She eased her hands between him and the wall of the shower and slid her hands over his chest and belly. He pushed back against her, and she took the opportunity to close her fingers over his erection, easing his foreskin back and forth until he let out a sexy growl. "Trying to drive me insane?"

"M-m-m, yes. I think so."

"Enough!" He turned around, eluding her soapy grasp, as he pulled her close, her breasts flat against his chest and his erection pressing into her soft belly. "Time to move somewhere more comfortable, I think."

"In a minute." She stood on tiptoe and kissed him, pressing her mouth to his, seeking his tongue and his touch as she wrapped her arms around him.

Locked in their embrace, they stood under the warm shower, the water pouring off their faces and running in rivulets down their bodies to the floor.

The water ran lukewarm before they broke the kiss.

Neither felt the cold.

"You are incredible," Michael said, turning off the shower and reaching for a towel. "Here." He draped the first one over her shoulders and reached for another. "Better dry off." Arm around her waist, he steadied her as they stepped out onto the bath mat.

He reached out to rub her dry, but she stopped him.

Her hands eased down his belly as she knelt.

Stroking her fingers down his thighs, she smiled at his glorious erection. The sheer magic of his arousal never ceased to delight her. She was amazed at the life, the desire, the power that soared out from his wonderful body and the male strength nestled among his soft, golden curls. She adored the sheer loving arrogance and certainty of this man who knew he was loved and desired. Nothing in all her centuries had so amazed her. She ached to feel him deep, but just for now, she kissed the head of his cock, savoring the smooth skin and the sweet drop of moisture at the very tip. Michael angled his hips to bring himself even closer, and she opened her lips and slid her mouth down his length, taking him in deep, until her lips caressed the very root of his cock.

Confident in her female power, Antonia eased her mouth along his length. Then, fast as only a vampire could move, she swallowed him again. As his hands grasped her head, his fingers tunneling into her hair, she moved back and forth, her tongue easing along his length as her lips teased, stringing out his pleasure and her own rising need.

As her own desire all but peaked, she eased her mouth off him, sitting back on her heels to smile up at him. "Time we went to bed, don't you think?"

"Who needs a bed?" Grasping her by her waist, he lifted her, positioning her over his erection. "How about here and now?"

Too close. Too little space. Too steamy. Too . . . wonderful! As he lowered her onto his erection, she threw back her head, hitting the wall, but not caring one iota! Pressing herself down on him, she wrapped her legs around his waist and ground her hips down.

A mere mortal could never take the force of her strength. Michael gave a great laugh of joy and triumph as he pressed deeper. They were locked in a wild, carnal embrace, bound together by need and desire, delicious animal lust, and the deep-seated love that tied them together.

"All set?" Michael asked. "Ready?"

"Ready for anything you can give me!"

"That's what I hoped. Hold tight!"

She grabbed his back, clinging with all her vampire strength as he rocked his hips, pumping his erection deep into her, moving back and forth in a sweet rhythm of demand. Once she caught his tempo, she set her body in motion with his. In a wondrous unity of desire, they moved together, driving their own and each other's needs to a wild and hectic frenzy, their passion and desire building until they peaked.

Antonia dug her fangs into the base of his neck, the richness of his lifeblood sending her over the edge. Throwing his head back, Michael let out a deep, sexy growl; a cry of joy, satiation, and triumph as he climaxed, taking her with him. She was still clinging and shaking as he walked though the doorway and deposited her on the bed, leaning over her as the last aftershocks of her orgasm stilled.

"How was that?" he asked, his self-satisfied smirk leaving her in no doubt that he knew exactly how it had been and was justifiably smug at his prowess.

"Not bad."

"Not bad!" Another lovely, sexy growl, this time with a tinge of irritation and amusement.

"Not bad at all. In fact, bloody marvelous if you ask me."

"I was asking you," he replied, stretching out beside her and pulling the covers over them both. "Satisfied you, did I?"

"Like no one ever has. Ever."

His beautiful mouth curved into a slow smile. "Good, and I intend that no one else ever will, not while I live and breathe."

He did have the advantage on the breathing bit but . . . "I intend to hold you to that."

"Just what I had in mind."

They lay together in a tangled mass of legs, the scent of sex between them and a warm haze of satiation fogging her mind. How wonderful to come here and lose herself in his arms. Whatever the Colony might say, she'd stay by Michael.

"What's the matter, love? You looked as if you were frowning."

"Was I?

"Yeah, you were. Something wrong?" He brushed her hair away and kissed her forehead. "The trouble at the house still bothering you?"

She'd almost forgotten about the dratted murder. "It wasn't that."

"What?"

Maybe she should tell him. "I love you, Michael."

"I'd sort of worked that out for myself. You know it's mutual, right?"

"Oh, yes!" She kissed his cheek. "Without a doubt."

"Well then?"

Better spit it out. "I'm trying to work out an easy way to introduce you to the Colony."

"The Colony?"

"The other vampires in my bloodline."

He pulled away just a little, leaning up on his elbow. "Your bloodline? Like relatives? Kin?"

She nodded. "Yes. My community, if you like. We tend to keep together and support each other. Help out when needed, like when we have to disappear for a while or set up a new identity."

"I see." She bet he didn't really but . . . "And you think telling them about me will cause a problem?"

"I don't know for sure. We've added new vampires in my time, even a couple of ghouls, but—"

"Ghouls?" he interrupted. "Ghouls, as in living dead ghouls?"

"Yes, but they're not quite the way they're depicted in low-budget movies. They get us wrong, too."

"Obviously." He shook his head. "So your vampire colony admits ghouls and new vampires, but you think they may cut up rough over a shapeshifter?"

"I don't know, and to be honest, that's not my main worry. I want you, Michael, and my concern is to let everyone else know with the least fuss possible."

"Can't you just tell them? I clean up pretty nicely, and I'm reasonably presentable. As puma, I don't use the correct knives and forks, but as Michael the potter . . ."

She kissed him. "Love, you clean up wonderfully." She ran her tongue over his shoulder. "Deliciously. I just . . ." What did she want? Total acceptance by the Colony?

He went quiet beside her. Thinking. She could tell from the expression on his face. "How about we just take the bull by the horns? Announce we are an item, as they say, and see what happens."

What could happen? Gwyltha have apoplexy? It wouldn't

kill her. The others fall down in shock? Wouldn't give anyone a heart attack. "You're right. Why am I so hesitant?"

"What about other times? Haven't they known about your lovers?"

"Seldom. We tend to keep relationships rather superficial and mostly for sustenance."

"Oh." He pondered that. "I see."

She doubted he did, really. "On the whole, it's much, much safer for all concerned, but with you, Michael, I let everything go. I revealed my nature and fell for you like the proverbial ton of bricks."

"Damn glad you did, but I can see why you might not share the whole truth with everyone. Come to that, I don't broadcast to the world that I go furry at will."

"Maybe that's why we belong together. We both have a secret we can't usually share."

"And now we have shared, and you don't know where to go next?"

"I'm not going anywhere for now. I want to wake beside you and see the morning with you."

"How come sunlight doesn't turn you to ash?"

"Because it doesn't. A Hollywood inaccuracy . . . most of the time."

"What do you mean?"

"Some vampires weaken in the light and sleep to restore themselves. I don't know any who self-ignite." Although she'd wished for one to do so once upon a time.

"Listen, Antonia!" Michael said, his voice strong and confident. "I've been alone a long time. Now I have you, I'm keeping you. If your Colony makes bones over that, send them to talk to me."

She kissed him. Dear Michael, he meant it. What it was to be loved, not that he had any idea what he'd be taking on in confronting the Colony. "Being loved by you, Michael, is enough. The others will have to accept it; that's all."

"That chap yesterday, Justin Corvus, he didn't seem too surprised."

"Justin is a good man, and he stretched the Colony a bit himself recently. Maybe we should talk to him. But I'm with you, Michael, whatever happens."

"What can happen, love? We have each other."

Chapter 19

"Mum, Dad's really worried about us. We have to call him."

That had to be the third or fourth time Sam had said it. What was getting into him? "You worried, Sam?" Stella asked as she pulled into the car park in front of the hotel.

"Not really," he replied. "I know things are okay, but Dad doesn't, and he's worried. After all, Mum, someone was murdered here, and yes, it was a long time ago. I know you think it was the two old ladies and maybe that nasty Sebastian, and I think you're right, but we're right here. Dad isn't, and he's scared for us."

How in heaven did he pick up all that? And when did he suddenly get so smart? "What makes you think I think it was the old Misses Underwoods?" Might as well find out what else he'd picked up.

"Makes sense, Mum. It's their old house, their garden, and we know they did bad things. If they didn't do it—and being really old, they might not have—then I bet they knew all about it."

"You could be right, son." Right on the nail as far as she was concerned. This trip was turning out a mess!

"Call him then, Mum. Give him a bell, and tell him when we'll be home."

"You really want to leave? You were having such a good time with Peter."

"I am. He's great and I'll miss him, but Mum, it's time to go home. Couldn't we soon?"

Why not? This trip hadn't worked out as she'd intended. She had promised to help, and she'd done her share. Sam was right; it was time to go back to Yorkshire.

And Justin would no doubt be thrilled.

Justin snapped his phone shut. He was delighted and relieved that they were coming home, but not in the least pleased at this latest development. Yes, surely it meant the entire business would be resolved sooner, the poor woman identified, and everything settle down to normal—whatever passed for "normal" in Bringham. For his part, he'd just as soon they left today. He'd been uneasy about the whole business from the start. A holiday was fine, but why Bringham? Because stubborn Antonia insisted on setting up her new business there.

He shook his head. That was water under the bridge. No point in worrying now. After the weekend, they'd be safe at home. He had time to hotfoot it back to Havering. Stella need never know he'd been watching.

Sam would keep the secret. Amazing child there. His son.

Justin stepped into the kitchen, and opening the fridge, took out a blood bag, tore it open with one fang, and drank. Not much longer and . . .

His mobile rang again.

Drat! Gwyltha! "Greetings."

"Greetings to you, too, surgeon. What's happening down in that benighted village?"

"You mean Bringham?"

"Indeed, I do. No doubt it's sheer coincidence, but since your wife, our ghoul, and Antonia have been down there, Bringham has been on national news three times: dead bodies, the vicar's dog chewing on stolen gems, and the bit on the back page of the paper about aliens landing."

Hardly fair to blame Stella for any of that! Especially the alien landing bit. "Gwyltha, things happen. Crime is everywhere these days, and the body—and it was only one—was sheer chance. That's what happens when you start doing up an old house and pulling things down."

She still had a sexy laugh. It just wasn't a patch on Stella's. "Justin, I have 'done up' close to a hundred houses, and the last time I found a dead body in one was back in seventeen something."

Maybe but . . . "It will all sort out, Gwyltha. Police nowadays can find out just about anything. Anyway, Stella and Sam will be back home after the weekend."

"I see." He hoped not. "You're worried, too, and you want them home? About time, too, I think. Stella managed to demolish a Jaguar, too. Anything else I need to know, Justin?"

Damn! She must have heard that from Jude. "Not much really. Stella had a bit of a scare when someone was trying to steal her car, but she took care of it."

"She did, did she? Demolish anybody or just the car?"

"Gwyltha, nothing serious." Who was he fooling? "But it's more than I'm willing to tell on an open line like this."

"No problem. You can tell me this evening. Where are you? John's place?"

She would know, wouldn't she? He was beginning to understand Stella's irritation at being monitored. "We're here."

"Assuming that's not a royal we . . ."

"Tom's with me." Darn, bet she knew that already, too. "We just wanted to keep an eye on things."

He waited for a comment that never came. Silences could be more irritating than her inquisition. "See you this evening, Justin."

He had some interesting news to share when Tom returned.

Sam ran downstairs, intending to visit the stables. He still hadn't had the promised riding lessons, but given everything else that had happened, he wasn't about to grumble. In the entryway, he stopped in his tracks. A short, dark-haired woman stood in the doorway.

"Good afternoon, Sam."

Oh boy! Mum and Elizabeth weren't expecting this. "Good afternoon, Mrs. Gwyltha. You've come to visit?"

"I have come to find out what is going on," she replied. Her smile made her sound less angry. "Would you like to share a few details?"

"Don't you think you ought to talk to Mum?"

"I imagine you know everything your mother does, and perhaps more? Hm-m-m?"

His face burned. He'd promised Dad he wouldn't tell, but Gwyltha in the Colony was like the headmaster at school. "I only know one thing that Mum doesn't and that I promised not to tell. Sorry." It wasn't smart to make a vampire angry, especially one as powerful as Gwyltha, but he'd promised.

"Who did you promise?"

Deep breath. "Dad. It's nothing bad, honest."

"I believe you, Sam. Would you show me around the place? It looks lovely."

"It is. Antonia found it." Quick thinking needed here. Mum had enough to worry about without adding this. So . . .

"I'll show you around. I was on my way to the stables. Just wanted to get a drink first."

A bottle of Tizer in hand, Sam led Gwyltha across the wide lawn to the gazebo.

"Hardly the stables," Gwyltha said.

"They can wait," he replied. "What do you want to know?"

The encounter with Judy niggled at James. He'd probably read it all wrong, and besides, he had more pressing things on his mind than whether or not the vicar's daughter fancied him. He took a shower and changed from his gardener clothes, but he still felt on edge and strung out. Coffee would only make it worse, and the last thing he was about to try was alcohol. He settled for tea and went as far as boiling a kettle, before wandering back into the study, and staring out over the lawns. Funny really, he paid a prince's ransom to the garden care company to keep up the place and worked for pay in someone else's garden.

Something was off-kilter there. Hell, his whole life was off-kilter! If he ever got himself sorted out, maybe he'd take up gardening as a hobby, but Sebastian's sweeping lawns and rose beds lacked the fascination of crumbling walls and strange stone carvings, and the ever present memories of his mother.

He opened the doors and crossed the lawn to stand between two rose beds in full bloom. But the scent of three dozen bushes of Etoile de Hollande and Iceberg couldn't get the persistent thought out of his mind. It was too far-fetched. It was unlikely. But the "twenty years" reverberated in his thoughts. Twenty was close enough to twenty-one, and his mother had spent hours up at Orchard House, learning from the Misses Underwood. Learning what?

What if Uncle had been wrong, and she hadn't run off with an unnamed, unspecified man "from the village." What if she'd never left the village? The corollary of all those "what ifs" left him cold and angry.

The insistent ring of the phone drew him back in the house. Seemed the old shears and clippers he'd found in the shed and had left to be sharpened were ready. Might as well pick them up as drive himself batty here. The walk wouldn't hurt. Might even help him think.

He was coming out of the ironmonger's, clippers and shears under his arm, and not looking where he was going when he all but barged into Judy Abbott.

"Hello again," she said, shifting the shopping bags in her hands.

"Er . . . hello." She was lovely, like fresh-poured sparkling water in a crystal flute.

"Shopping?" she asked, looking at the package under his arm.

"No, not really." He was going to fuck this up, and . . .

"Picking up things I left to get sharpened." His chest was tight as a drum, and breathing seemed to hurt. This was ludicrous, but when she smiled and that little dimple appeared . . . Shit, he could swear he was blushing.

"Good are they here? I've some scissors Dad used to cut paper and are now useless. I ought to bring them here."

"They're very good! You should have them sharpened. They'll do a great job. Sharpen them up a treat, and you'll be very happy. Better bring them in soon as . . ." Damn! He was babbling like a blithering idiot.

"I'll do that." She fell into step beside him as he started down the High Street. "Is everything okay?" she asked after a few paces.

He should say "fine" and go on. He might have if he hadn't looked at her and noticed her eyes were the exact same shade as he remembered his mother's: deep, bright blue. It was the concern and kindness in them that did him in.

"No," he replied. "my life is the ultimate mess."

She nodded, as if understanding. "Would a drink help? My treat. It's only a hop down to the Blue Anchor."

"No!" Damn, that was rude but . . . "I don't drink."

"Good for you! I do, I'm afraid, and far too much. How about the Copper Kettle?"

They crossed the road to the teashop with its linenfold paneling and horse brasses. Ignoring the gray-haired waitress's attempts to seat them at a tiny table for two near the door, Judy sat herself down at a large table in the corner. "We need the space," she explained. "Lots of shopping."

She dumped her heap of bags on a spare chair and reached for a menu. "Hungry?" she asked.

Was he? It had been ages since his cornflakes at breakfast. "Yes, why not?"

"Seems it's poached egg on toast, beans on toast, cheese on toast, or a boiled egg. Bet that comes with toast, too."

Just like his mother used to make him for breakfast: a slice of toast cut into toast soldiers to dip in his boiled egg. He couldn't face it. Not now. "How about cheese on toast?"

"I'll go for the beans," Judy said. "Proper nursery or student food, isn't it?"

The teapot arrived with a promise that the rest was on its way. Judy stirred the pot and put cups on saucers. "Milk and sugar?"

"Both."

She poured and added milk and the one lump he requested. They were like two puppets, or a least he was, tightly strung, his mind moving jerkily and wondering why he was here.

Because she smiled as she passed him a cup. "Here you are." She stirred her own, lifting the cup as she watched him over the rim. "Cheers!"

He wanted to thank her for her kindness and outright

niceness, but the words were beyond him. He took a couple of sips of scalding tea and put down the cup. "I'm sorry I'm not good company right now." If ever.

"You're strung out and worried; that's why," she replied, taking another sip of tea and giving him a little smile. "Bringham does that to you. I know. I never stay more than a week or two if I can help it."

"Oh, no! It's not just that; it's . . ." and he let it all out. His mother leaving and dying, boarding school, his recent doubts, and the awful disinterment at Orchard House. His tea went cold, and so did hers, and they barely noticed the arrival of the savories.

"Good God!" Judy muttered, her eyes dark and glittering as if holding back tears. "No wonder you're on edge. If I had that much going on, I'd be a basket case."

"I think I am."

She shook her head. "Don't think so. You're perfectly coherent."

"Don't feel it."

"Stress does that to you, and you've been through the wringer."

At some point, she'd reached across the table and taken his hands in hers. He gripped her fingers. "I don't know what to do next."

"Tell the police."

She made it sound so easy. "What if I'm wrong?"

"So what? If you're right, they're much closer to solving things, and if you're wrong, you know it isn't her. Either way, you're better off."

"I suppose so . . ."

She wasn't going to let him put it off. "Do you have a picture of her?"

"There's several at home: wedding pictures and some photos of us and my uncle." Even a few with the father he didn't remember.

"Let's take one to the police and see what happens."

"Won't work. I mean, the body was old." He shuddered thinking of his mother rotted and gone.

"James, it will, " Judy persisted. "Nowadays, they reconstruct faces from skulls. They can match DNA and everything."

Of course! "Let's do it then!" She certainly galvanized him into action. "Let's go see that Inspector."

Judy drove down to The Grange in her battered little Toyota; James ran in, taking her with him.

"This is where you live?" she asked, looking round the vast entry hall.

"Yes, come on," he said, grabbing her hand and pulling her into the library.

She kept staring around while he tore a couple of photos out of an album and grabbed a picture in a silver frame. "This is your house?" she asked, sounding a bit skeptical.

He didn't blame her. "Not mine. My uncle's. I'm his trustee. I take care of things for him."

"Where is he then?"

He all but froze. Resisting the impulse to lie, he took a deep breath. "In Broadmoor." She was going to walk out; he knew it, and . . .

"God bless you!" she said. "No wonder you're feeling stressed. You have to cope with everything."

Bless her for not asking what happened. She'd put two and two together soon enough. "The bank handles most of it. I shuffle papers and pay bills and make sure the lawn is cut regularly."

"I don't know how you cope with it all, and then you work too? Well, let's at least try and solve one trouble. Grab your photos, and let's go."

They headed for Leatherhead.

James envied Judy her confidence and assurance. "What if he's not there?" James asked.

"We leave him a message that you have information that is vital to the case."

But was it? Only one way to find out.

"It's useless; you're useless," Dave muttered to John.

"What the hell am I supposed to do?" John asked. "I can't move without hurting, and these bloody painkillers make me feel as if I've been run over by a steamroller."

"I think a steamroller did go over your brain!"

Charming! John frowned. "You stop complaining. No one can tie us to the burglary, and if your cousin hadn't been stupid enough to go poaching with Fred Ellis, we'd all be as clean as a whistle. All I need is a cop asking me how I got hurt! I can't palm them off the way I can Mildred."

"Let them ask. Who's to connect Mike poaching on the Bainbridge Estate with a safe job in Leatherhead?"

"The cops aren't stupid. They know we did time together."

"Oh, stop it!

John stopped. He was tired. Damn pain pills! "Mildred was asking if you wanted me to get in on another job. She's already twigged we were up to something."

"Let her twig. What can she do? She isn't going to shop you to the cops now, is she?"

No, Mildred wouldn't—he hoped. He'd be a whole lot happier if there hadn't been that kid in the car. That boy could finger him. John half-wondered why he hadn't already.

He leaned back in the easy chair. Something was odd about the entire business. Dave might scoff and say he'd imagined things, but dammit, he hadn't! He wasn't on pain-killers then! That woman had jumped on the car and yanked him out of it, and he bore the injuries to prove it. But if he insisted on the truth too many times, they'd all think him loony.

"Gone quiet," Dave said. "Cat got your tongue?"

"I'm thinking, and you'd better, too. We got nothing out

of that job but a lot of trouble and my shoulder done in. If you'd only been there with the car when you were supposed to . . ." They'd been over this ground umpteen times, but John would bear the grudge forever, or at least as long as his shoulder hurt.

"Right. Would have been really clever to get nabbed for parking on a double yellow line. If you'd just waited for me to drive around instead of taking off across country and stealing a car—"

They could have picked at each other all afternoon, but the door opened and Mildred came in with a tea tray.

"Here you are," she said, giving Dave a look that spoke volumes of inhospitality. "I brought your tea and some fresh scones. Thought they'd be nice while we watch the news. I expect you want to get home, Dave."

How she hated Dave! Pretty rich considering the trouble she brought down on them last year through that damn coven! She hadn't even brought a cup for Dave. "Bring Dave a cup," he said. "He wants one before he goes."

Dave stood. "Don't bother. I'm going. See you, pal."

Damn Mildred didn't even show him out.

"You might have offered him a cup of tea! Not much to ask for my brother!"

"The sort of brother who'll have you in trouble again if you're not careful," Mildred replied. "He's no good."

"And who are you to talk? Meeting with those two witches when you thought I wouldn't know?" Got her there! Her eyes almost popped out in shock. "I heard them the other day. Emily Reed is the only person we know with a Honda. You talk about getting into trouble! You really want to get caught up in all that again?"

"I don't, and I won't!" She poured far too much milk in each cup and picked up the teapot. "I like to know what's going on, and the best way to do that is to talk to them. Ida had some news about the new people up at Orchard House.

One of them, an American, if you please, claims to be a witch. That's all."

He bet. Still, if she had secrets, so could he. "Just don't get caught up in anything; that's all."

She handed him his cup. "Want a scone with that? It's a new recipe Emily gave me."

"Sure it doesn't have hemlock or aconite?"

She scowled but buttered his scone for him all the same and cut it in two. He took a bite. Not bad either. He and Mildred had a snug little place here. If only he could be sure that damn kid in the car would never finger him to the cops.

Plate at his elbow and cup balanced, he sat quietly while Mildred turned on the telly. Why she insisted on watching the news every night he'd never know, but it was a small price to pay for her cooking.

"Oh, look!" she said. "That's Orchard House." There was a fast shot of a group of people, and a voice over explained that a new, and possibly important, clue had been unearthed close to where the body had been found last week. "Well, I never," Mildred went on. "It's that Elizabeth Connor, the one I told you about. Called herself a witch and wanted to join us. Fancy that, she's on the telly."

So what that the coven might start up again? What if Mildred had met with the other old biddies? Something far, far more important grabbed his attention.

There, with the erstwhile American witch, stood the kid from the car. He was here, in Bringham, and as long as the little bugger was around, he, John Rowan, couldn't risk going out his front door.

Something had to be done. That kid could queer the whole pitch.

Chapter 20

Warrington looked at the couple sitting across his desk.

"So," he said to the lanky, rather weedy-looking man, "you think the victim we found in Bringham may be your mother?"

He took a deep breath and glanced at the woman, who smiled encouragingly. "I think there is a very strong possibility," he replied. Hesitant chap, but who wouldn't be at the prospect of his mother being murdered and summarily buried?

"I see." Warrington glanced at his notes. Jeffers, sitting quietly in the corner, had been scribbling constantly. Would be interesting to compare thoughts later. "Your mother disappeared—ran off, you were told—twenty-one years ago. Right time frame, and she was reported missing."

"I was also told she'd died."

"But you never found a death certificate? We can check that faster than you can, sir, and we will." Warrington paused. "You remember her spending time at Orchard House studying with the old ladies. And they'd be?"

"The Misses Underwood. Faith and Hope were their names."

The names rang a bell with Jeffers. She looked up, recognition in her eyes. Interesting. "What do you remember about them?"

The young woman, Judy Abbott, let out a sharp laugh. "Sorry. Just came out. Everyone on Bringham can tell you a story about them, but go on, James."

"Yes, that's very probable, but I'd like to hear yours, sir."

James paused, wrinkling his forehead as if to sort out his thoughts. "I don't remember when I first knew them. I just always did. To a child, they were scary—sharp-voiced with prickly mustaches. Faith had long, yellow fingernails that I was scared would hurt when she poked at me, and Hope used to spit when she talked." He shook his head. "Funny, I haven't thought of that for years. They weren't really that old then. Sixties perhaps. The village all called them witches and . . ." Another pause. "They did practice magic, or so they believed."

Interesting. "And you believed this, Mr. Chadwick?" Long pause. Warrington had met that before: suspect trying to decide what to tell. Only this wasn't a suspect, but a law-abiding citizen offering information.

"I don't think so, but I did join the coven at my uncle's urging." This was getting off track, or maybe not. "My uncle, my mother's brother. He was my guardian."

"And he was?"

Another pause and a bounce of his Adam's apple as he darted a glance at the woman, who smiled reassuringly. Chadwick raised his chin and straightened his shoulders. "Sebastian Caughleigh."

Bingo! "I see." He wasn't sure he did, but he'd darn well delve into this until he did. But right now, that might just divert him from the current investigation. "So after your mother's supposed abandonment, you never heard from her again?"

"Never. I couldn't believe it. She promised she'd be there

when I got out of school, but she wasn't. I walked over to my friend's house and asked his mother to phone her. There was no reply. Finally, they called Uncle Sebastian in his office. He was out, but they left a message and he came hours later, or so it seemed. He told me my mother had gone. Just like that. I thought he was fooling, but he wasn't. It was a few months later when I was told she'd died. I never heard the details. When I asked, I was hushed, and it was only recently, sorting through family papers, that I realized her death certificate wasn't among all the others."

"You never went to her funeral? No one talked about it?"

"Never. I admit it seems odd now, but when you're six, you don't question grown-ups. I never did."

Poor little bugger, and now maybe, learning the truth. Warrington glanced at the photos Chadwick had brought. "It's impossible to tell just by looking at these. After twenty years, the body had decomposed a good deal, but our lab people can work up an identity from the skull." Chadwick winced. Understandable. "A DNA match is the most conclusive—that takes a couple of weeks—but a maternity test will settle all doubts."

They both nodded. Time to go on to the next step. "Before we put the taxpayers to that expense, perhaps, Mr. Chadwick, you'd be good enough to look over some of the items we unearthed today. Some had degraded too much to be of any use to anyone but the lab boys and girls, but we have a few."

James wasn't sure if he shared that hope or not. Would conclusive proof settle anything? Or just beg more questions? What if it was his mother? Who put her there? And if it wasn't, who else had been done in by the old witches? He didn't doubt it was them, aided, no doubt, by his dear uncle. "Inspector," he asked, "when my uncle confessed, did he mention anything about my mother? His sister?"

Warrington appeared to consider the question. "I don't

know, sir. I wasn't on that case, but we can look it up. You think he was involved?"

"There wasn't much in the village he wasn't involved in. And he was very eager to lead the coven. When the old ladies died, one soon after the other, he grabbed the lead."

The look the inspector gave sent cold prickles down James's back. Why had he said so much? And the Hades, why didn't Warrington say something? If it weren't for Judy sitting close—she believed him—he'd be out of here like a bat out of hell. Except the other one—the policewoman, Jeffers—now blocked the doorway.

"Here's what we have, sir." She handed a large plastic bag to Warrington.

"Thanks," he said, taking the bag and unsnapping it. He looked at James. "Might not be any help, sir. Maybe there's nothing here, but I'd be obliged if you'd see what you can make of these." He tipped a half-dozen sealed plastic bags onto the desk. "Most of the papers, driver's license and so forth, are being deciphered by the lab, but these were more or less intact."

James stared at the pile. Did he want to do this? What might it prove or disprove?

Judy reached for the closest, then paused, her hand in midair. "Okay if we pick them up, Inspector?"

"Go ahead. They're all sealed." He sat back, hands on the arms of his chair, and waited.

Judy spread the plastic packets out on the scratched desktop. "What do you think, James?"

That this was a flaming bad idea! But when he met her eyes, he could no more say it aloud than pull out his own tongue. "I don't know." And wasn't sure he wanted to, but he was here and . . .

"Just give them a look over, if you would, sir," Warrington said. "Most likely, they are all too far gone, but you never know . . ."

Judy pulled the first envelope closer. James peered at it: a decayed leather purse. Yes, his mother had had one with a clip on top like that. He used to like playing with it, snapping and unsnapping it, but half the female population of the British Isles had probably owned similar ones, and he had no clear memory of the size or shape.

The second held a rotted handkerchief, discolored and frail with age. Then a bag with a set of loose beads and a small corroded knot of metal that had once, presumably, been the clasp. Had his mother worn beads that day? He had no recollection one way or the other.

"I don't think there's anything here. It's all so old and dirty and . . ."

"Go on, James," Judy persisted. "Might as well look at the lot while you're here. You never know."

The corroded, cracked pen could have been anyone's. How many million Bic or Biro pens were there in the world? But the last tightly sealed bag, that had his throat tightening and his heart racing.

"Mean anything to you, sir?" Warrington asked.

Everything . . . maybe. Perhaps all mothers kept curls of baby hair in their handbags. Perhaps they all held one end together with red sealing wax and tied the other end with a narrow, pale ribbon that looked gray and filthy in the harsh light of Warrington's office.

Maybe. Maybe not.

As if sensing his turmoil, Judy reached out, resting her hand on his forearm. "See something?"

He nodded.

"Recognize it, sir?" Warrington asked.

James nodded again, needing a minute or two to get his voice back while his chest tightened and breathing came hard. "My mother used to carry a curl of my hair with her. She used to say it was from my first haircut. It used to be pale, white almost." And now it was dirty gray.

Warrington nodded slowly. "Thank you, sir. My sympathies if this does prove to be your mother. We still need to check the DNA, but we can certainly confirm or rule out the identification." He scooped up the sealed packets. "Unless by an odd quirk of fate, another young woman happened to have your hair in her possession that day."

"No!" He was certain. "She used to say she was going to keep it safe until I married and then she'd give it to my wife. She wouldn't part with it."

"Good point, sir. In either case, the maternity test will settle it once and for all." He stood. "Jeffers will call the lab and make arrangements for you to give samples. If anything else comes to mind, don't hesitate to contact me."

And that was that.

Darn good thing Judy was driving. James wasn't sure he could.

"You look done over and smashed up," she said as they got in the car. "You really think it was her, don't you?"

It took several seconds to answer her. "Yes!" He let out the breath he'd been holding. "It fits too well to be otherwise. I suppose lots of mothers carry baby curls, but that was pale, like mine was. My mother went missing about the right time. She spent days up at that house, and I could never believe she left without me, and she never called or sent as much as a post card. And what about the other details: no death certificate—hell. Sebastian kept everything."

He leaned back against the neck rest and shut his eyes. "If she was killed there, those two old ladies couldn't have done it alone. They couldn't haul a body out of the house and across the back garden. Someone helped them." He didn't want to say the name aloud. Seemed like summoning evil, but . . . "It had to be Sebastian. That's why I asked if he'd mentioned it when he confessed."

He went silent, the weight of this knowledge a suffocating load.

"What do you want to do?" Judy asked.

"Run away. Just drive and drive until we hit the coast, and then sit and think."

"Okay. Let me fill up first. Tank's almost empty."

His eyes snapped open as he looked at her in shock. "I didn't mean it! You don't have to!"

"You did mean it, and it's fine with me. Let me get some petrol and leave a message for my parents, then we're off. You pick—Brighton or Worthing?"

Gwyltha was beginning to understand Justin's attachment to this mortal child. Sam was truly extraordinary. But he had shared blood with a vampire. Even if he had no mortal memory of the event, his body and mind bore the influence. Interesting.

"You really shouldn't blame Mum," Sam insisted. "You really mustn't."

Giving orders, was he? Why be surprised? He'd already defied her once before to save Justin. Now it was his mother he championed. Stella and Justin were truly blessed. "I won't, Sam. Let me explain our laws: We prohibit harming mortals, yes, and exact punishment if any of our Colony willfully harms an innocent. But we also defend those under our protection. You are one the Colony protects. Not only was your mother defending you as her son, but she was also averting harm from a malefactor who threatened one our Colony protects."

"You mean me?"

"Yes, Sam, I mean you."

"Is a malefactor a bad guy?"

"Most definitely."

He nodded, satisfied and obviously relieved and having added a new word to his vocabulary. "Good. Dad's worried enough already." He paused, biting his lip. "Promise not to tell anyone I'm telling you this? I promised Dad I wouldn't tell anyone, but he didn't ask me to promise. I just knew he didn't want Mum to know what he was doing, and so I promised so he'd know I wouldn't tell her and he wouldn't worry about her knowing. But I don't think he'll mind you knowing." Complicated, but she followed and waited. "Mum doesn't know this, but Dad's watching us at night. I don't know where he's staying, but he came by the hotel last night."

"How was this, Sam?"

"He'd changed into an owl, but it was him. I knew. I think he's real worried, and he wants us home."

Interesting that Sam should recognize Justin so. Utterly amazing, in fact. "And you want to go home or stay here?"

"Oh, go home! It's been fun here between all the bad or scary stuff, but I'd like to be back with Dad." He broke off to wave. "Mum! Over here!"

And Stella came running, holding her speed to mortal pace, but not restraining her anxiety. "Sam?" she asked, "everything okay?"

"Oh, yes," Gwyltha replied. "Sam has been telling me about your eventful two weeks."

"I see."

Quite possibly. Stella undoubtedly knew Sam better than anyone else. "Sam, I waylaid you on your way to the stables; don't let me keep you from the horses anymore."

"You want to talk to Mum?"

"I do, and I believe she wants to talk to me."

He pondered the implications a moment or two. "Okay. Tell her not to worry so much. Dad will look after us." With that parting shot, he ran off before Stella had a chance to respond.

"So," Gwyltha said, motioning Stella to sit beside her, "Sam thinks you worry too much."

"He doesn't know the half! If I could still get ulcers, I'd

have one with the effort of hiding how much I worry from him."

"Ever thought he reads it all the same?"

"Yes! And that has me worried too!"

"Worry and motherhood go hand in hand."

Stella gave her a questioning look. "You were a mother?"

"No. I was spared that pain and missed the joy. They selected me to be changed instead. A husband and a family were never part of my future or my past." Why dwell on it? Better consider the present concerns. She'd already told Stella more than she'd intended. "The situation here in Bringham has you worried?"

"Yes. Too many things have happened. I wish, looking back, we'd left right after the the carjacking. Justin wanted us to, but I thought we'd be fine, that the problem was taken care of."

"It wasn't? Jude replaced the car, and the stolen jewels are in the hands of the police."

"That's taken care of, but what happened next? We dig up a dead body!"

"Yes, I heard about that."

"Sam saw it! Not what I call the perfect extra to a relaxing summer vacation!"

Poor Stella! "No, it isn't, but you know, my dear, I think Sam worries more about you being worried than about the unpleasantness. Children possess remarkable powers of survival and an incredible ability to compartmentalize these things. Yes, he'll no doubt regale his friends at school with every gory detail, embellish even, but then he'll push the incident away when something more pressing, like swapping marbles or playing conkers, appears in his life."

Stella nodded, acknowledging the truth of Gwyltha's words. "Maybe, but these are things to worry about. I just want us to get home and stay there a while. Sam starts a new school in September, and he needs time to get ready and be with his friends."

"He's going to Saint Aiden's then?"

"As a day pupil. Will be a long drive every day to York, but one of his best friends is going too. When he's eleven, he'll start boarding."

"To give security in his life when you and Justin have to move and set up a new one."

"Yes. I hated the idea at first, but Justin is right. At least this way, Sam will keep his friends."

"Motherhood is no easier as a vampire."

"You said it! That's why I want to get away from here. I'd do it tomorrow, but then I decided we'd leave on Sunday as originally planned. Justin will be here over the weekend. He and Tom have been mounting guard from John's house on Epsom Downs. Sam doesn't know that—no point in worrying him, and I only found out by chance—but I do feel better knowing they are both so close."

"We can summon more if you want."

"More of the Colony?"

"Yes."

"No." She shook her head. "We'll manage two more days. Is that why you came down?"

"Among other things. I wanted to see how Antonia's venture is coming along."

"That's going like a house on fire, apart from the delay building the tearoom. We're hiring staff and getting craftsmen and artists lined up. Have had some lovely samples sent it. People from all over the county are applying to join it. Should be a roaring success."

"Antonia's projects usually are." And talking of Antonia, unless she was very much mistaken, King Vortax's daughter was approaching right now. "She's coming, I think."

Stella all but gasped until she remembered the link between vampires. Antonia was Gwyltha's get. "She went to . . ." No. Better not tell. It was for Antonia to inform Gwyltha what Michael was to her when she chose. And what he was. "To see one of the local craftsmen, a potter who's selling his work in the gallery."

"I see." From her tone and the quirk of a smile, Stella suspected Gwyltha knew, or at least guessed, what had happened to Antonia. "Let's go and meet them."

Them? Stella knew better than to question Gwyltha. She'd half-expected to be taken to task over possible injury to the damn carjacker, and she'd had her arguments all lined up, but if Gwyltha wasn't going to bring the subject up, she certainly wouldn't.

They crossed the lawn to the front of the hotel, arriving just as Antonia and Michael got out of the van. Stella hoped Antonia knew what she was doing.

It appeared she did.

After a momentary hesitation, Antonia waved, turned to smile at Michael, and deliberately took his hand as she came toward them.

"I assume this is the interesting potter you mentioned," Gwyltha said.

"Yes," Stella replied. "That's Michael Langton."

"What is he?" Gwyltha asked. "Do you know?"

Quick decision here. "Yes, I know, but it's for Antonia to tell you."

"It certainly is."

Antonia gripped Michael's hand, as much to tap into his strength as to reassure him. "It's Gwyltha, our Colony leader." she whispered, knowing full well Gwyltha could hear if she chose. "You might as well come and meet her."

"I might as well, mightn't I?" he replied. "Do I have to ask her permission to court you?"

"Behave yourself!" They were way beyond that point.

"Gwyltha, welcome to Bringham," Antonia said, stepping forward and bringing Michael with her. "Let me introduce Michael Langton."

"Ah!" Darn Gwyltha for her all knowing smile. "How do you do, young man?"

He gave a little nod and took her offered hand. "How do you do? Antonia has spoken of you."

"I'm sure she has."

What did she mean by that? "We didn't expect you, Gwyltha."

"I heard disturbing things had occurred in the South."

"And some fine and pleasing ones." Everyone stared at Michael, including Antonia. He was stepping right into things. Why not? If she looked half as flushed and relaxed as he did, the whole world could guess how they'd spent the afternoon.

"Yes," Gwyltha replied, her mouth twitching at the corners. "I suspect this has indeed been a pleasant afternoon. Right, Antonia?"

Drat her! "Incredibly pleasant." She should have skipped the soppy smile and eye contact with Michael, but what the heck? No one had ever fooled Gwyltha, so why bother trying? "Are you staying long?"

"As long as needed. Any specific plans for the immediate future?"

"Antonia and I are getting married."

They were, were they? A glance his way got a wicked grin in return. Why not? Seemed half the Colony was getting hitched these days. Might as well.

"Congratulations!" Abel bless Stella! She stepped forward and hugged them both. Gwyltha might have managed more than that quizzical look. "Sam is going to be full of himself. He'll probably offer to give you away as well."

Gwyltha rolled her eyes heavenward. "What is it about the South that stirs things up in the Colony?" They all chose to treat that question as purely rhetorical. She looked them over again. "Any idea where Elizabeth might be?"

"I have an idea," Stella said. "She'll be back this evening."

"I will wait to meet her." Gwyltha replied. "And Michael," she said, giving him the full benefit of five feet drawn up tall, "What are you?"

"A shapeshifter, madam. I would gladly demonstrate, but perhaps not here."

"You are kidding, aren't you?" Antonia said, trying to duplicate Gwyltha's dignity.

He gave her a look of pure tease and affection. "Right, my love, as always."

"And what pray, do you think a shapeshifter can add to the Colony?" Gwyltha asked, way overdoing the imperious act in Antonia's opinion.

"That, madam, remains to be seen," Michael replied. "Time alone will tell. And we all have plenty of that ahead of us."

Chapter 21

Justin eyed Gwyltha over his glass. Praise to John Little-wood for keeping his cellar so well stocked! Nothing like a smooth port on the palate to ease a confrontation. Perhaps confrontation was a trifle strong, but she seldom left home unless she sniffed trouble. "You have concerns?" he asked as casually as he could while his mind raced over the myriad possibilities that might bring Gwyltha down from the North.

She sipped her port. "Yes," she replied after a pregnant pause while she put the glass down on a dark oak side table. "And my brief visit confirmed them."

"You've been in Bringham already?" Tom asked.

"I just spent a most interesting twenty-four hours there," she replied.

He bet she had! And she was about to share the wealth of her knowledge unless he, Justin, was very much mistaken.

"Things seemed well there?" Tom inquired. He was also playing casual and unconcerned. Did it well, too.

The respected leader of the Colony raised her eyebrows. "It's not quite as bad in your friend, Will's, Denmark, but you were both wise to stay down and keep an eye on things. Not that your respective wives and intendeds aren't managing quite nicely by themselves,"—she paused to permit a little smile to quirk one corner of her mouth—"and I'm not forgetting Sam."

"What about him?" Justin snapped, yes, but a man worried about his son.

"Sam is well," she replied, "but anxious that Stella is worrying too much, and,"—she paused again, wrinkling her forehead—"I am curious as to how he recognized you in owl form."

"Curious? I was flabbergasted! There I was, sitting out on a limb—literally, I may add—watching him through the window. He knew me straightaway, looked me in the eyes, and thought to me. Not a word spoken at first, not until I flew down and perched on his arm. But he knew me instantly."

"There is the blood bond between you," she said. "That may account for it."

"Surely that should work the other way? I have his blood; he doesn't have mine."

"True, and in all the centuries we've fed off mortals, I've never heard of this type of bond. Affection and tenderness, yes. Even carnal longing. But a mind link? Never!" She paused, thinking. "Bear in mind, you did not take from him; he offered his blood, knowing your nature. Insisted on it, come to think of it. He defied me, his mother, and Antonia. Plus, you were so weakened at the time, we feared your extinction. Maybe that had something to do with it." She shrugged. "Whatever the cause, linked you are."

"Yes." They were. Not that he was likely to complain. Who knew, maybe one day they would both thank Abel for the connection. "I wonder if it has developed as he has matured. I never noticed it before."

"Did you ever try to link with him?" Tom asked.

"Never occurred to me."

"Perhaps it is something you should work on," Gwyltha suggested, "once you are back home and settled."

"Can't be too soon as far as I'm concerned."

"Nor me," Tom said. "Elizabeth insists on working with Antonia, but at least she's agreed to cut it back to two or three days a week." He shook his head. "There's just something about that place."

Gwyltha let out a laugh. "Not boring, is it?"

"You obviously found it fascinating," Tom said. "What else did you find, besides the link between Sam and Justin? Come to think about it, how did you find out about that?"

"Sam told me. Just after he warned me not to blame Stella for any possible injures to the carjacker. Quite definite about it, he was." She smiled and shook her head. "I suspected he was about to pin me to the wall on that point, but Antonia strolled up and announced she was partnered with a skinchanger. That was just the first hour or so."

"The next morning, things got really interesting. The gardener was late. He left a voice mail for Elizabeth. Interesting gardener, too. At breakfast time, seems the entire village believed he'd eloped with the vicar's daughter. At lunchtime, he arrived for work. No elopement it seems, but apparently, a more formal arrangement is highly likely."

"'Strewth!" Tom shook his head. Absorbing all this took an obvious effort. "He must be up to something, and its not good, I'll be bound."

"Maybe not," Gwyltha said. "Elizabeth is inclined to take him at face value, and she is no fool."

And if he was dallying with the vicar's daughter, he was unlikely to be leering in anyone else's direction.

"So what now?" Justin asked, mostly out of deference to Gwyltha. He knew what he intended.

"Given the general level of anxiety all around, I'd suggest you arrive this evening and greet your respective households as if you've missed them for weeks. Stella is ready to leave. Elizabeth may want more time. She is knee-deep in plans, but might be happy to have you down there for a while."

"We should get there this minute." Tom was out of his chair and halfway across the room before Gwyltha shook her head.

"No. Arrive after dinner as planned. Knowing you are worried enough to stay near has caused Sam enough anxiety. No point in adding to it by rushing in like the cavalry in one of those Western films."

A good point, Justin supposed, but even so . . . "So we just sit tight for a few hours and then drive up?"

"And get them out of there," Tom muttered. "I should never have let Elizabeth come down here."

Gwyltha looked heavenward and shook her head. "Tom, when will you understand? You never will stop Elizabeth from doing what she chooses. She's her own woman, and that, my friend, is why you love her so."

Tom grunted, but didn't attempt to argue. Wise man. As always, Gwyltha was spot on, but at her age, why not? She was the oldest, the strongest, and the leader. Once, he'd loved her, and she'd shattered his heart, but now he knew what he'd felt for Gwyltha was a mere shadow of his love for Stella.

Strange how circumstances panned out.

They sat in silence with the companionship of old friends. Justin half-considered fetching another bottle of John's excellent port, but it seemed too much bother. A few bags of blood were more in order after all the shifting Tom and he had done the last couple of days.

Through the stillness and the quiet, a panicked cry shrieked though his mind. Sam! Justin felt his terror and panic, and he was out of his seat and shedding clothes as he rushed to grab a couple of bags before shifting.

"What is it?" Tom asked.

"Trouble! In Bringham. Sam called me! Follow me as best you can!

"I'll take the car," Gwyltha said, "and your clothes." She stooped to pick them up. "You two go on. I'll be right behind!"

If anyone had asked Sam, he'd have told them he just wanted the day to be over so he could see his dad. Dad as Dad, not Dad as the owl that hovered outside the window at night. But no one asked him.

Everyone was busy.

Busy being grown-ups.

Seemed everyone was getting married. Last night, Antonia brought Michael to dinner. He and Elizabeth split the uneaten vampire dinners, and Michael acted as if it were the most usual thing in the world. He couldn't switch plates as fast as a vampire though. But he'd done okay. Mrs. Gwyltha had watched Michael all evening as if deciding whether she liked him or not. That was Mrs. Gwyltha. A bit like a school teacher, really. But Michael was different, not vampire, not ghoul, but not quite like other people. Sam had wondered about it until later in the evening, Antonia had explained Michael was a shifter, a shapechanger.

Which was pretty cool and on top of that, Michael had promised one day to let Sam see him change.

One day.

After they got married, which would be who knew when? Seemed Gwyltha had to give consent, and so far she hadn't. You'd think someone as old as Antonia, and a vampire to boot, could marry whoever she wanted. Mum had explained last night about concerns about keeping the Colony a secret, as if Michael would go around telling! Sometimes grown-ups were hard to understand.

Sam kicked a pebble down the path. Peter was away for

the weekend, and he missed him. That was the one snag about going home—not seeing Peter again but . . . Sam sighed. He so wanted to get back to Havering. Too many bad things happened down here.

As Sam kicked another pebble down the front drive, a car drew up, and both James and Judy got out.

James was okay, a bit twitchy for a grown-up, as if he was always waiting for something bad to happen, but when he and Judy got out of the car, he was looking really happy, as if it was his birthday or something. "Hi," he said as they came up the path, hand in hand.

"Hello!" Judy said. "Is Antonia inside?"

"In the office. They all are. She loves the cushions you left. She said so."

Judy smiled at James, who grinned even more. "Smashing!" she said. "I'll go and see them." She squeezed James's hand before letting go.

James smiled back, all goofy and soppy. "I'd better get to work; I'm late as it is. There's a chunk I want to get cleared before the weekend."

Sam watched James go around the side of the house and Judy knock on the door, open it, and go in. Nothing to do here, and he'd bet anything Mom and everyone were talking wedding dresses and flowers. Might as well ask James if he wanted any help.

From his van parked a few yards from the Barley Mow, Dave peered though his binoculars. Damn his luck! The kid was there, but he had just toddled off around the house and out of sight. Shit! He'd been all alone for a good ten minutes. If only John had been here, they could have grabbed the brat, but no! He had to wander off and get something to eat.

That kid could finger them, or rather finger John, and if John got copped, Dave had no illusions about his brother keeping his lips zipped. John would shop their own mother to the rozzers to ease his own sentence.

Thing is the kid was only a kid. Maybe they should just get the wind up him so he was too damn scared to open his mouth. They'd be safe then. Maybe. Dave spat out the window. The way things had been going wrong recently, it was enough to make a con go straight!

"Anything happened?" John opened the driver's door and passed him a wrapped sandwich and a bottle of beer, wincing as he moved too fast. He was never going to forgive the kid for his wrenched shoulder.

"Better be careful, hadn't we? No point in getting done in for driving under the influence."

"One beer?" Damn, Dave, he almost sneered. "Can't handle it?"

. Who was he picking on? "The kid's gone round the back. We missed him while you were off for a piss."

"We'll get him."

And then what? Dave was not thinking that far ahead. They had to get him out of the way, but he didn't want to consider what John had in mind after they got the kid. Once they took care of the kid, he, Dave, was clearing off. John scared him. What with panicking during the robbery, stealing that car, losing the loot, and making up all that ridiculous rigmarole of a wild woman stopping the car and attacking him. Bizarre! Almost as unbelievable as the woman taking the knife off him in the Manor Hotel car park. Best not even think about that. He'd been stressed out and imagined it. Imagined the ruddy cat too! It was getting weird round here.

"Where did he go?"

"Who, the kid?" Dave asked, yanked out of his worries.

"No, the Lone Ranger and Tonto, you twit!"

"Who are you calling a twit? You berk! We'd never be in this bind if you hadn't shot that guard."

"And if you'd been waiting where we agreed!"

Dave scowled. That's what it all boiled down to. They had to get rid of the only witness. He still couldn't fathom how the jewels had ended up in the vicar's garden. Must have been the kid, who ran off after the car crashed. If he didn't know John better, he'd wonder if he'd made the whole story up.

"We'll get him," John said through a mouthful of cheese and pickle sandwich. "We can wait."

"Wanna stay here?"

"Get closer. The kid's round the house, right? Most likely playing in the garden on such a nice, sunny day. There's the dirt lane that runs up beside the walls and a handy side gate or two. Park there, and we'll keep our eyes peeled." Dave started the engine. "The minute we see him alone, we grab him."

"These are absolutely beautiful!" Judy smiled at Antonia's praise. "Even better than the earlier samples. Of course we'll take them and more. Why not make some smaller ones? We can price them lower, make them easier to sell, and hook people into coming back and buying the large ones."

"Smashing! I'll get going, at least after the weekend."

"Got a busy weekend planned?" Stella asked, looking up from the fax machine that was spewing pages.

"Sort of. It's called placating the parents." She hesitated but heck, they—and the entire village, she bet—knew James and she had been gone overnight, so why hold back? "They're a bit put out that I went off so suddenly yesterday, but that was nothing compared to their reaction when they heard who I'd been with. Seems my father's practice of Christian charity doesn't extend to James." She looked from one to the other in the pregnant silence. What did they know that she didn't? What was it her parents had just hinted at? "Anything I should know?"

By the look of the lot of them, volumes.

Antonia broke the heavy silence. "How long have you known him?"

Good point. "I met him yesterday morning."

"Not long then," Elizabeth said. "Know much about him?"

"I know he's all to pieces because he's worried the body they discovered is his mother's."

Nothing like causing a sensation. All three of them stared. Elizabeth let out a slow whistle.

"He's certain?" Antonia asked. "How did you know?"

"He told me. As for certain, the police are taking it seriously and doing a DNA maternity test." Their attitude rather got up her nose. James was going through turmoil, and they seemed more concerned about getting the grass cut on time. No! That wasn't completely fair but . . .

"Poor chap!" Elizabeth said. "He talked about coming here with his mother. I knew she'd died when he was young, but to think she might have been murdered and left there all these years."

At least Elizabeth was marginally sympathetic. "The connection with her disappearance only hit him after the Inspector mentioned twenty years. James's mother disappeared twenty-one years ago."

All three exchanged looks. Stella abandoned the fax machine, letting it whirl away untended.

"What do you know that I don't?" Judy asked. Might as well grab the bull by the figurative horns and find out. All these sly glances, pregnant with meaning, were getting on her nerves.

"You might want to sit down," Antonia said, standing and scooting her desk chair in Judy's direction. "It's a bit complicated."

"I can stand. What is it?" If they started in on James, she'd . . .

"Convoluted," Elizabeth said.

"Very," Stella added.

It was three against one, or rather, three against James. Hadn't he had enough strikes against him? Did these women have to start too? "Really? Complicated and very convoluted?"

Antonia walked around the desk and leaned against it. She was eye to eye. "I imagine you've heard talk in the village?"

"And ignored a lot. Round here, gossip tends to get expanded beyond reason. According to the local jungle telegraph, James and I eloped. We haven't!" Not yet anyway.

Antonia—she seemed to be spokeswoman, or chief attacker—went on. "You are aware of the connection between a coven of witches and James's uncle, Sebastian Caughleigh, who is now in Broadmoor?"

"Yes, and how the coven was originally led by the two old ladies who owned this house. When they died, James's Uncle Sebastian took over and got James to join the coven. His uncle was obsessed with power and control, and upset a lot of people before he finally killed a young man who worked at the Barley Mow and, in the end, broke down and confessed. I know James's mother disappeared when he was a child, and he believes she's the dead body you dug up here. James might not have been the local model citizen, but being reared by Caughleigh and bundled off to boarding school at seven, he hasn't turned out too badly, all things considered."

At least that silenced them a moment or two.

"You knew all that?" Antonia asked.

"And a ton more that isn't really your business. It's a good, long drive to Brighton and back. We talked."

"Antonia,"—it was Stella, who'd been quietest though all this—"I think Judy has a point, and whatever did or did not happen in the past, we've no reason to hold anything against James."

"Talk to Dixie; she might say otherwise."

"I agree with Stella," Elizabeth said. "I hired James as a gardener, and he's a great gardener. What happened in the past . . . "

The phone on the desk interrupted her. Elizabeth picked up, "Dixie!" she said, smiling, and the other two went quiet. All eyes on Elizabeth.

"What is she saying?" Stella asked.

Elizabeth held up her hand for the others to be quiet. She didn't want to miss anything.

"Did you get the faxes I just sent?" Dixie asked.

"They were yours? It's been running, but I didn't look. We got a bit sidetracked here.

"I sent nine pages copied from the diaries. I think they are what you were hoping for. Some are ambiguous, but given what we know, it fits. The police will want the originals, I suppose. I hate to part with them, even temporarily. Might bring them over myself."

Elizabeth's eyes met Stella's. "Check the fax; Dixie sent something."

Stella read the pages, eyes widening. "I'll say she has. This is . . ."

Antonia took the sheet, and, after a glance and a distinct raising of eyebrows, passed it to Elizabeth. She glanced at the first paragraph written in spindly handwriting. "Dixie!" Her voice echoed in her ears. "This is terrible! Incredible . . ." She went on reading. "Those old witches . . ."

"Bad isn't the word, is it?" Dixie said. "The more I read, the more I realize Gran did right to walk away from them and never go back."

Darn right! "Dixie, I'll call you back. We all need to read these. See you. Love to Kit." She hung up and looked around the room.

Judy couldn't stand it anymore. "What's going on?"

Antonia looked at Judy over the fax sheet she was reading. "This will take some time, I'm afraid. Want to come back later?"

She knew a brush-off when she got one. "No. If it concerns James or his dead mother, it concerns me." Call it instinct, intuition, what you will, she knew those faxes were about James's mother. She was tempted to rush out and tell him. Later. Right now, she'd stay put and find out what was going on. "I'm staying."

Prepared to stand her ground, Antonia's nod of agreement rather took the hiss out of Judy's indignation. "Fair enough," she said and looked toward Stella, who still held the stack in her hands. "Put them in order, please, and we'll all have a good, long read and then decide what to do with them."

"What's to decide? If it's evidence, it needs to go to the police."

Elizabeth looked up from reading. "Oh, they're evidence, all right!"

"What's in them?" Raising her voice. Yes, they had as good as admitted this concerned James, and darn it, if any of them started in again about his past, there would be blood shed on the parquet floor.

"It's not that simple," Antonia said, "and yes," she added, forestalling Judy's repeated protests, "we do want the guilty named, even if they are long dead and moldering, and for the sake of the living, we'd like the whole episode resolved. But we must be certain, not fire off wild possibilities to the police."

She was being fobbed off. No doubt about it. These three women sat on the solution to the whole nasty business and were trying to keep it to themselves. Not if she had anything to do with it! "Good idea." Judy forged on. "We should look at everything carefully. Stella has them all in order. Why don't we all sit down and read them?" She'd barely finished speaking when a sense of danger wafted through the room.

Whatever she'd said wasn't well accepted. Too damn bad. They were not shoving this in a drawer and forgetting it.

"I think you . . ." Antonia began.

Stella interrupted. "Antonia, Judy does have a vested interest in the outcome. You can't blame her wanting to know."

Antonia raised her eyebrows. "Who spoke about blaming anyone?"

"You advocated withholding information." Judy said, the tension in the room going up a few notches.

"I think we should let Judy read the lot," Elizabeth said, "but she must agree to keep it to herself until Dixie comes with the originals or we decide what to do."

"She's right," Stella added. "In fact, I think Judy's been incredibly nice. I'd have grabbed them if I thought they'd help Sam or Justin. Must be being British," she added with a smile Judy's way.

"Not really. There's three of you between me and the fax machine. If I thought I had a rat's chance of grabbing them, I'd have them and be out the door and down the drive by now."

Even Antonia smiled. For what that helped. "I see." She picked up the stack. "Are they in order?" she asked Stella.

"That's the order Dixie sent them."

Antonia flicked though them and looked across at Judy. "Alright. We all read them and you may too, but you agree nothing leaves this room until we hear more from Dixie. I don't want anyone going to the police with partial truths. When we point the finger, I want no uncertainty. No ambiguities. No doubts."

It wasn't what she wanted, but it seemed the best she could get. At least she'd see what was on those wretched papers. "Alright."

Antonia and Stella had to be graduates of one of those speed reading courses. They flicked through pages like nobody's business. Elizabeth read more at Judy's pace, but even so, it didn't take long for all three to get through the nine pages.

They waited for her to say something. Talk about disappointment! She'd really hoped this would sort everything out for James. "It's a lot of nothing. Talk of renewing vigor and calling up power, but what the heck does it mean? I bet lots of old people dream of restoring youth. Read any women's magazine. My father hankers back to days when he didn't have arthritis. It's just waffle." She'd halfway made a fool of herself for nothing.

"There's more here than you think," Elizabeth said, pausing as everyone looked at her. "Remember, they were witches."

"Everyone says that," Judy said. "It's talk! Like James's mad old uncle."

"No," Elizabeth said. "There was a coven, and they were witches. They practiced magic. I know. I'm a witch, too, but my path differs from theirs. I strive to do no harm. They had few scruples. We know a lot about them, Judy. Things it's better not airing. Some of their knowledge died with them, and a good thing too, but they make several references to 'The Spell of Youth.'"

"Just a figure of speech."

"Maybe it was, and maybe it wasn't, but I have their grimoire. Dixie gave it to me. I'm going to read through them and see what I can find."

"Forgive my ignorance," Judy said, "but what's a grimoire?"

"I was about to ask the same," Stella said.

Nice to know she wasn't the only one out of her depth. Seems she'd missed a lot being Church of England.

"A grimoire is a book of spells," Elizabeth explained. "Theirs is upstairs."

But not up the wide staircase that rose from the front hall. They followed Elizabeth up a dark, narrow stairway behind a door in the old kitchen. At the top were two attic rooms with pitched roofs. They were clean and newly painted but empty except for several packing cases, a few jars, and a stack of books on the wide table.

"Dixie had their things packed up for me," Elizabeth said. "Eventually, I'll ship it to my house in London. I planned to look at everything while I was down here, but I've been so busy." She reached for a thick, leather-bound book that resembled an old-fashioned family Bible, but as Elizabeth opened it, Judy saw the pages were covered with spidery writing.

All three of them stood there, waiting as Elizabeth flicked page after page. Until she paused, her finger marking a page. "Look at this."

They all crowded in. The ink was faded and the writing whirly, but the heading was clear: "Spells to absorb power." Underneath were headings: "From a mortal," "From a vampire," "From another witch."

"Oh, please!" said Judy, hope leaching out to nothing. "A vampire! They were nuttier than a fruitcake." She got the distinct impression the atmosphere in the room had gone tense and cold.

Chapter 22

All three stared. Antonia's eyebrows rose. Elizabeth shook her head. Even Stella gave her a odd sideways smile.

"Really! It's ridiculous," Judy insisted. "Honestly, who believes in vampires!"

Antonia shrugged. "Doesn't really matter whether we do or do not. What's important is that these old ladies appeared to. They thought they could harness a vampire's strength and power and, more to the point, that they could revitalize themselves by taking another's youth."

"If we take this to the police, they'll think we're crackers," Judy said.

"Is it more far-fetched than some of the things Sebastian Caughleigh confessed to?" Antonia asked.

Judy sighed. Was the woman serious? "Yes, and look where he ended up!"

"Did you know him?" Elizabeth asked.

"No. I've been away at school or Uni most of the time my parents have been here. I've heard talk, but it all sounded so far-fetched and obviously embroidered by village gossip. Or at least it did until James and I talked yesterday." Why did she get the feeling they were all agog to hear what James had told her? "I think that insane uncle wasn't the best person to bring up a small, motherless child."

It was obviously a sore point with Judy, and Antonia agreed absolutely, but this whole line of inquiry was spiraling out of control. To say nothing of a mortal intruding in on what was a Colony concern. Yes, the woman was romantically involved with James, but that rather posited questions as to her common sense. Whichever way one considered things, they had gone far too far. "I think," she said, "we should all agree to keep this in confidence until Dixie sends, or arrives with, the original diaries."

Stella and Elizabeth caught on right away. Judy was going to need a little urging.

"Judy," Antonia said, keeping her voice low but still commanding attention, "we cannot talk about this until we have conclusive proof. We must wait until we have the complete diaries before telling the police about this."

After a long pause, during which Antonia was beginning to think Judy was impervious to influence, she nodded. "Yes, we must."

"It would be of no benefit to have incomplete information dismissed or discounted by the police," Antonia went on.

"No," Judy agreed, "it would be of no benefit."

Stella and Elizabeth relaxed. She certainly had. "Let's go on back down," Antonia said. "We need to get back to work."

Once downstairs, Judy gathered up her things. "I like your suggestion of smaller and therefore less expensive cushions, Antonia. Maybe really tiny ones like old-fashioned pin cushions? I could use glass-headed pins as part of the design. I'll go home and have a think. After I say goodbye to James." Her smile left little doubt the position James held in her heart. Mortals!

"Get back to me as soon as you can," Antonia said.

"I will," Judy replied. "You're right about keeping the

other matter under wraps. What really matters is the DNA evidence." With a smile, she was out the door.

"Better tuck all that out of sight," Antonia said, nodding at the pile of faxes. "She was hard to suggest to, and if she catches sight of that lot, it might trigger her earlier resolve."

"You can hardly blame her for wanting to settle things," Stella pointed out.

"I don't 'blame' her, but my first concern is to protect us. How will finding his mother was a victim in some black magic rite settle anything?"

They got the point. Antonia looked at the door that had closed behind Judy and shook her head. "It always amazes me to see an intelligent mortal woman fall for a man so far below her."

'That's not really fair," Elizabeth said. "Okay. He's not a hotshot M.B.A. or Ph.D., but he's no one's fool."

"I doubt he has a single A level," Antonia replied, "and we know he was involved with Sebastian's activities."

"Since he was under that man's influence since he was tiny, that's not surprising," Stella said. "The line between law-abiding citizen and criminal can be very narrow at times. When we lived in a rough neighborhood and were surrounded by trouble, I prayed every night that Sam wouldn't be dragged in. There were kids in the elementary school selling drugs! I was so scared Sam would get sucked in."

"He didn't," Elizabeth said.

"Yes, but what if I'd been involved in the drug trade? What chance would Sam have had? James was raised by that madman, but he's straightened up since Sebastian was put away. He's got a job, not an executive level one, true, but he's not afraid of rolling up his sleeves and getting his hands dirty, and with Judy behind him, who knows? He might just turn out alright."

Stella still possessed a mortal's optimism. Antonia suspected James had done a good bit of dirty work over the years. "I hope you're right. Meanwhile, let's get busy. We're going to miss you, Stella, when you leave."

"I'm only an e-mail away," Stella replied, "and after all—"

She broke off as someone screamed outside.

"Sam!" Stella was out the French windows. They were all out the French windows, leaping over the blue and white tape and racing at preternatural speed toward the repeated screams.

Judy was several meters down the lane, wailing her heart out. "They've gone," she cried. "They took James and Sam!"

It all happened so fast. Sam's head throbbed from hitting the floor of the van. The whack the first man gave him hadn't helped either. He wanted to sob, but choked it down, trying to think. What was happening? He'd been helping pull weeds when a man burst through the old door in the wall and grabbed him. He yelled out, and James came running. The man shoved Sam through the open doorway, and another grabbed Sam's arm and yanked him along. Sam struggled and looked up at the man who held him. It was the man who'd stolen the car.

"You!" Sam said, kicking his shins as hard as he could until the man shoved a gun in his face.

"Do it again, kid, and you'll have a third ear!"

This was bad. Real bad. How could he call for Mum? He sensed the man meant it about shooting and was trying to decide how to get away when James burst though the doorway.

"What the hell are you doing?" he asked, racing forward only to lurch back as the gun went off, falling to the road with a cry and landing in a crumpled heap.

"No!" Sam pulled away, trying to go to James, but the hands held him too tightly. "You shot him!"

"Ain't the first time, kid, and you'll be next if you say another word." He pushed Sam backward. As he fell, a hand grabbed him. "Throw him in the back, Dave."

He went up in the air, the world spun, and Sam landed hard on the floor of the van. As he shook his head and tried to sit up, something hit him. James had landed right on top of him. The doors were slammed, and they were in the dark.

Moments later, after what sounded like a shout, the van moved off, bumping over the rough road. James coughed, and as Sam wiggled out from under him, he smelled blood. Fresh human blood. Lots of it. "James, they shot you. Does it hurt?"

James grunted and coughed. "Not too much, lad."

Another grown-up who lied. "Sorry, James; you were only trying to help me. These are bad guys. Real bad guys."

"Listen, Sam," James whispered. Sam hoped they wouldn't be heard over the noise of the engine. "You get that door open and jump and run. If you can get away, fetch help. I'm no good right now." He gave another cough.

Sam didn't think he could open the door without them noticing, They'd just stop and grab him again. That wouldn't work, and now, they'd turned off the rough lane and were going faster, and if he left James, they'd kill him for certain. "I'm not leaving," he said. "I'll get us rescued. Don't worry."

He couldn't bother Mum, and anyway, he doubted he could reach her mind. He never had before, but Dad had to be close. He'd sensed him near ever since the night he'd come to the window. Sam sat up as best he could and leaned against the side of the van. Trying his best to ignore the vibrations and bumps, Sam concentrated. *Dad,* he thought, struggling in his mind to reach his father. *Dad, help me! Please, oh please, Dad, help!*

Then it came faint but clear. *Sam?* Sam grinned and wanted to smack his hands together. He had his Dad. Everything would be alright. *Where are you, Sam? What happened?*

In a van. A white one. Down the lane by the side of the

house. They just turned right. Toward the common, I think,
Dad. Please come. Fast!

I'm coming, son. Hold on! His father was stronger. Closer.
Okay, son. I'm on the way. Who are they?

The man who took the car. And one I don't know.

That's alright, son. Just hang on. He did for what seemed
like forever while James coughed and wheezed. His breathing was raspy, and Sam was afraid he'd die. *Please, Dad!*

I can see the van, Sam! I'm right behind you, and Tom's
with me!

Things were going to be okay!

Stella led as they raced and caught up with Judy at the
end of the lane.

"What happened?" Stella asked, knowing in her heart that
Sam was in danger and scared.

"A van! They took James and the boy. Just threw them in
and drove off!"

"Did you see which way they went?" Antonia asked.

Judy gave a couple of little gasps but held herself together. "Right. Toward the common!"

With hundreds of places to lose people or bodies. Stella's
heart froze. "I have to get Justin. Then I'm going after Sam."

"Hold on!" Antonia said. Stella wanted to spit! She knew
she could catch up with the van, but not with Judy here.
"We'll follow in our van. Get it, Elizabeth!" As she spoke,
she grabbed Judy's shaking shoulders and held her close.
Not to comfort the mortal, although it might help calm her,
but to make sure she didn't notice the dark streak that took
off down the rough lane. "We'll get him, Stella. Don't worry.
Once we have the van, we'll give chase. Can you contact
Justin?"

Of course she could! She had a mind link with Justin and
should have made it sooner instead of panicking. Stella shut

her eyes and focused. She sensed him there one minute, but there was a shifting and wavering in their connection until Justin returned. *Stella!*

Justin, it's Sam, they've taken him. Heading for the common.

I know, my love.

What?! *How?*

Sam linked with me. Called for help the minute it happened. Tom's with me; we're going to get him.

At that moment, Elizabeth drove up. Judy climbed in, propelled by Stella, and Antonia got in the passenger seat. Before any of them had their seat belts on, Elizabeth was driving down the lane, racing around the corner, brushing the overgrown hedges, and ignoring the odd pothole. Stella snapped her seat belt on for form's sake—after all, there was a mortal next to her.

Judy was white-faced and still shaking. She should offer comfort, but she needed to link with Justin.

Do you have him?

Almost there. Once I catch sight of Sam, I'll tell you. He's frightened and keeps saying James is hurt. Shot.

Better keep that to herself. Judy looked just about done in. *Any idea where he is?*

His link is strong and clear. I'll reach him.

None of that made any sense, but she'd worry about that later. Had to be because the blood Justin took. Whatever it was, she thanked Abel for it!

Elizabeth sped on. The van bounced so much Antonia had trouble punching in Michael's number. It rang, and she willed him to be there and to answer right away. What if he were out in the clay shed and had left the phone off or . . .

"Antonia?" He was there!

She should encode this somehow with a mortal on the back seat, but darn it, they'd worry about that later. Judy was half out of it with worry anyway. "I need your help. Drop whatever you are doing. Someone—too long to explain now—has snatched Sam and James, I'll explain James later. They are in a white van heading for the common. We're following, but they have a head start."

"Want me to head them off?" Abel bless him! He knew what was needed without her telling. "Please. Justin and Tom are on their way."

"Which road are you on? The one that comes down to my place?"

"No. The narrow lane from behind our house." Elizabeth drove right over a pothole. "The rough lane behind our house."

"Lea Lane."

"Yeah."

"Bad that. It becomes a really rough road at the far end of the commons. A lot of rough bridleways there, and it's very wooded. Won't be easy on wheels. With four legs and my speed, I'll get there. 'Bye."

He was gone, and totally incommunicado since pumas didn't use mobiles. But he was another hope.

Judy grabbed Stella's arm. "Who is she calling? We should be calling the police."

"Never mind!" Stella said, snapped really, but Judy jabbering messed up focusing on Justin.

"Judy," Antonia said from the front seat. "Trust us. We'll summon the law in good time. There's nothing to worry about; just sit still and wait quietly."

Stella doubted that suggestion would take root but she had no more time to worry about Judy. Justin was back.

I see him. Tom and I are following them. When you reach the common, take the bridleway to the right. I'm staying with Sam.

"Elizabeth, Justin can see them! Take the bridle path to the right when the lane ends, and try to link with Gwyltha."

"Link with who?" Judy asked.

"We're getting close," Elizabeth said, completely ignoring Judy.

"I'm locked in a van with a bunch of loonies, and the man I love is hurt!" Judy said. "Stop right now, and let me out!"

Stella felt for her, but . . . "Judy," she said, holding her shoulder, "just sit tight and hush!"

Judy looked at her, wide-eyed, and went silent.

"What have I done?" Stella muttered.

"Doesn't matter. It worked!" Antonia said from the front. "We'll bring her back later."

Stella hoped they could. Judy looked fine; but was silent and completely still. Her worries about Judy didn't last long. Sam was ahead. Somewhere.

He's alright, Justin kept repeating. *Sam's unhurt but worried about James; he's bleeding and coughing.*

Maybe Judy was right—maybe they should be calling the cops and the EMTs.

Elizabeth slowed as the lane came to an end, and several tracks and bridleways lead across the common in different directions.

Stella leaned forward. "The far right, Justin said."

"You've got it!" Elizabeth steered hard right and took off down the rutted track.

Justin was overhead! Stella sensed him close by. He flew over the van, and ahead, she saw a pair of eagles swooping low and heading straight on.

Sam was worried. Real worried. Dad said he was coming, and he felt him get nearer, but the van was bumping on and James was coughing more than ever. Then the van stopped, and Sam went from worried to scared. It couldn't mean anything good. Doors slammed, and he scrunched his eyes against the light as the back doors were flung open. Two dark shapes stood by the open doors, and scared became terrified.

"Here we are, kid! The end of the road for you and your pal," a mean voice said. Sam couldn't tell which one had spoken as his eyes were still blinking in the sun. There was a growl, like a wild animal's, and a scream, a shout, and another scream. As his eyes adjusted, Sam saw a large golden cat had one of them pinned to the ground. It was the man who'd shot James. He was screaming as the cat raked his back with his claws and nuzzled his neck. It wasn't a friendly nuzzle. Sam couldn't help smiling. He looked for the other one. He was running to and fro, trying to shake off the two eagles clinging to his shoulders, or at least he ran backward and forward until he tripped and lay screaming on the ground.

"What's happening?" James asked, his voice weak and wheezing as he tried to sit up.

"We've been saved!" Sam said. "My dad's here and my mum!" James sounded and looked bad, but . . . "I'll be back," he promised and jumped down and raced towards Antonia's van as it pulled up.

Stella leaped out. Damn caution and mortals being present! She wanted Sam! She raced toward him as he ran. In seconds, he was in her arms, and she tightened her hold on his frail child's body. His mortal heart still raced with fear. "Oh, Sam! Baby!"

"Mom!" He held on just as tightly, clinging like a scared animal. "I was so frightened," he said. "Oh, Mum! They shot James when he tried to stop them. He's hurt bad, real bad. Dad needs to save him."

"Don't worry, Sam. Everything is going to be okay."

Eventually. Still holding Sam tight in her arms, she walked over to where the two still lay in the dirt and heather, writhing beneath their respective animal attackers, and gave each of the thugs a kick in the ribs.

Sam gave a nervous giggle. "Get 'em, Mum!"

Gwyltha came running up. Watched her kick them both and merely nodded. Just as well. "Never mind them, Stella," she said. "We can take care of them later." A touch of her hand on each one's shoulder, and they were out cold. "Now," Gwyltha said, "that's taken care of them for a while. What next?"

What next was Sam gaping at Elizabeth. He knew it was her, but she had red eyes, hands like gray claws, and a face that he wished the robbers had seen. It would have given them nightmares forever. "How do you do that?" he asked as her face relaxed and returned to the one he knew.

"Don't rightly know," she replied. "It happens when I'm really worried or angry."

"Neat!" Good thing James hadn't noticed; it would have scared him. "Mrs. Gwyltha," Sam said, turning in Stella's arms. "Dad needs to look at James. He's hurt. They shot him."

"They did, did they?"

"Yes!" He eased out of Stella's grasp and slid down to stand . . . almost steadily. "When they grabbed me, James tried to stop them."

"I see."

Stella frowned. If Gwyltha was going to bring up James's past . . . "He took a bullet for my child, Gwyltha!"

"Yes, Stella. I do not forget that."

"Nor will any of us!" Justin was back, butt naked and ankle-deep in the heather. She smiled at him, trying hard to ignore Tom, just a couple of feet away in the same inevitable state of undress. "I'll look at him, Sam. My clothes, Gwyltha?"

"In the car. I parked in the lane to avoid too many tire tracks."

They both ran off as blurs and returned in moments. Dressed.

"Where's Michael?" Sam asked. "He was here, wasn't he? I saw him. He was a big golden cat."

"He's by the trees over there," Stella said, nodding in Michael's direction. "I bet he doesn't want to shift without clothes to put on."

"Let me go and thank him," Sam said. "Dad, please take care of James."

"Do you need to ask twice, son?" Justin had his bag in his hand.

Sam grinned. "Great, Dad!" and ran off after Michael.

"I hope it is Michael and not a wild one," Stella said.

"Oh, it's him alright!" Antonia said. "I know. Sam," she called after the running figure, "tell him to hop in the back of our van, and we'll give him a lift home."

Sam laughed.

Talk about the resilience of youth! Stella looked around at the two prostrate figures, the fresh blood on the floor of the open van, and James, now on the ground, supported by Antonia and Tom as Justin bent over him.

And where was Judy?

Chapter 23

Sitting, being very, very quiet, in the back seat of Antonia's van, Judy was fully conscious and relaxed and apparently oblivious to the violence and preternatural activity of the past fifteen minutes.

"You laid on a very strong suggestion, Stella," Antonia said as they stared at the relaxed Judy.

"I just asked her to be quiet and stop fussing." Stella's throat tightened with worry. "I never imagined . . ."

"How very powerful you are?" It was Gwyltha who'd come up quietly behind them. "Seems Justin needs to take time with you to work on using your power. Strong emotion skews control. Better watch it next time."

Please! Let there never be a next time! Being a vampire did nothing to protect a mother from acute heartache and raging anxiety. Even if the focus of that anxiety was now sitting happily on a patch of close-grown turf, stroking a puma. It didn't seem to bother either Sam or his new feline buddy that he was covered in blood. "We need to get him out of here," Stella said. Any minute now, a troop of Boy Scouts might emerge from the woods, or a party of ramblers stroll down the rutted path.

"Precisely," Gwyltha said. "Get Sam away. We'll arrange things for the police, and let's hope the gun they used ties them to something else—hopefully, the guard they shot. That should cook them up nicely." She stood on the path surveying the scene like a general ordering her troops. "Stella, take Sam, get him cleaned up, and remove whatever memories need to go. Antonia, you go with her in the van; Elizabeth too. Justin, can that man be moved?"

Her curt nod at James twanged Stella's nerves. "That man took a bullet for my child!"

"Yes, Stella," Gwyltha replied, one eyebrow raised. "I am aware of that. That's why I'm attempting to save him." Okay, time to bite her tongue. "Well, Justin?" Gwyltha asked.

"Yes, but not far. He needs a hospital."

"And he will have one. We'll take him to the nearest one in your car. The story is that we were on our way to visit Stella and took the wrong turning. We ended up driving down here and saw him staggering toward us. He passed out, and you, doing your Hippocratic best, gave immediate first aid before seeking the surgical care he needed.

"Tom, you might as well go with Elizabeth. That van is surely big enough. We leave the two sleeping beauties right here with everything on hand to incriminate them."

"What about connecting them and James to Sam?" Elizabeth asked.

"Easily taken care of. James won't remember how or why they grabbed and shot him. It will be put down to shock-induced amnesia. His blood in the van will be more than enough to tie him to that lot on the ground."

"What about Michael?" Sam asked, walking up with the cat at his heels. "Can he ride with us?"

"I've a better idea," Antonia said, glancing at Gwyltha for approval before continuing. "Michael,"—the puma perked up his ears—"Stella will take Sam to your place to clean up. They can't go to the hotel looking the way he does. Is that alright?"

Michael made a sound like a loud purr; rubbed against Sam's legs, then Antonia's; and raced off toward the trees.

"Good thinking!" Gwyltha looked at everyone. "You all know what to do. Let's get going."

Tom took over driving after they dropped Elizabeth, Antonia, and Judy at Orchard House. Somehow, Judy's memory would be adjusted, and presumably, at some point, she'd hear about James's mysterious accident. Following Antonia's directions, they found Michael's house, or rather, compound. When Tom dropped them off, Stella stared at the outlying sheds and buildings. Michael waited for them at the open door, shifted back, and dressed as if he'd spent all afternoon working.

"This place looks super," Sam said. "I'm going to ask if I can explore."

"You're not doing anything until you get clean," Stella told him. Since his clothes were stiff with dried blood, he made no argument and willingly stripped off and got into the shower.

"Want me to burn his clothes?" Michael asked. "I doubt you can wash all that off."

Good idea, except . . . "What's he going to wear?"

"Ask Antonia to pick up spare clothes from the hotel, or he can borrow mine and roll up the legs."

Yes, there was a way round everything. "Burn them, please." Michael carried them off.

After making sure Sam had soap and a towel, Stella wandered back to Michael's sitting room. A glance at the clock stunned her. It had been less than an hour since they'd been sitting in the kitchen looking over those faxes.

She sat down, suddenly tired, worn, and weary. How must Sam feel? Shattered most likely, and darn it, she had to take away those memories. Not an easy task at the best of times, and now that she'd rendered Judy half-comatose, a really scary prospect, but who ever said motherhood was going to be easy?

Worry was part of the job description.

She wanted Justin. She needed his strength, but he was driving cross-country with his ex-lover and an injured man.

Alright! She needed to get ahold of herself. She was being ridiculous, and she knew it, but faced with Gwyltha, a nasty whiff of insecurity always hovered. An insecurity that made no sense. Not for one of Sam's mortal heartbeats did she doubt Justin's devotion to her or his love for her and Sam, and right now, she'd better shelve her insecurities and concentrate on Sam. He needed a mother in full control of her wits.

She made herself sit and relax until Sam emerged. Her baby, safe and sound, damp hair standing on end and wearing nothing but his underpants. They'd been the only article of clothing not bloodstained. There had been so much blood. She so hoped they had reached the hospital with James in time. Whatever he had or had not done in the past, he'd fought for Sam, and in Stella's book, that pretty much wiped the slate clean.

"I'm hungry, Mum. What happened to my clothes?"

"Michael's burning them. She didn't bother explaining why—a crease of his forehead, a quick think, and Sam had it figured out. "We'll fetch some more for you, and as for food . . ." She looked around the kitchen. Good thing shifters did eat. There were apples in a bowl on the countertop and a packet of cream crackers and a loaf of bread, and she bet the fridge was well stocked. "Wait and I'll ask when he comes back."

Michael obligingly returned in a couple of minutes, and

by the time Antonia arrived with fresh clothes for Sam (Michael had called Antonia to fetch them—nice man!), Sam was finishing his second cheese sandwich and starting on an apple. Resilience of youth wasn't in it! But Stella wasn't pushing their luck any further. It was off to Yorkshire tonight without fail.

"Well?" she asked them all after she'd bundled Sam off to cover his seminakedness. "Everything okay so far?" She realized too late that Michael stood right beside Antonia. What the heck? He was a good as part of the Colony.

"Fine," Antonia replied. "We got back to the house, took Judy inside, and wiped out what we needed to. Judy went home, planning miniature pillows and pincushions and utterly ignorant of the faxes and everything that happened after then until we got back to the house. As far as she knows, she never left it."

"Good." It had to be.

"Just a minute," Michael said. "You just took away her memories of the whole thing?"

Stella caught his shock and indignation. Antonia didn't seem to have. She nodded. "Yes. Best for everyone. No point in her remembering what would only give her nightmares. This way, once Justin gives the word, I'll call her and tell her James is safe and sound in Dorking Hospital, and she can rush over and bring him grapes and a bunch of tulips."

Michael's shocked eyes widened even more. "Have you considered the ethics of what you are doing?"

Antonia could explain things. Right now, all Stella cared about was getting Sam out of here. She idly wondered where Tom and Elizabeth had nipped off to, but she could make a pretty good guess. "You brought the van, Antonia?"

From defending the Colony to her lover to discussing transport was an obvious leap, but she looked at Stella. "The van?"

"Yes, the van. The thing you drive to get places. I want to

borrow it to take Sam back to the hotel, and I think you and Michael need a good, long chat without a ten-year-old in the audience."

"Point taken," she replied and held out the keys. "I'll see you later."

Judging by the atmosphere between them, it might be immediately . . . or days later. That was their worry. Hers was Sam.

"Come on, Sam. Time to get going."

"Okay, Mum. Let me get my shoes on."

They were bloodstained, but it couldn't be helped. She'd wash them off somehow. Later. "Alright, Sam. Say 'bye, and let's go."

He gave Antonia a big hug. "Come back for dinner," he said. "Elizabeth is going to need the food. She'll need extra after ghouling."

"Yes," Michael spoke cautiously. "And what happened to Elizabeth back there?"

Sam looked up at her, surprise in his eyes, then at Antonia. "He doesn't know?"

No, he didn't, and Stella was darn sure it wasn't her job to educate him. She glanced at Antonia.

Antonia nodded as if acknowledging the responsibility. "I think he knows, Sam, or at least guesses, but doesn't understand."

Sam scrunched up his forehead. "I thought knowing and understanding were the same. Sort of."

"So did I, Sam," Michael said. "But I don't understand. I saw her change, or at least her face and hands, but she didn't shift the way your father and the other man did. Or rather, the other vampire—am I right there?"

Antonia looked as if she could do with a couple of nice, relaxing breaths. She was going to have to manage without. "Yes. Tom, like Justin, is a vampire. As for Elizabeth, it's not my secret to tell, but since she showed herself to you, she told you herself in a way." She paused. "Elizabeth is a ghoul."

Stella gritted her teeth. Pity she hadn't yanked Sam away five minutes ago! Michael stared, dropped his jaw as his eyebrows shot up, and pretty much demonstrated that shifters could hyperventilate. "A ghoul!" His voice went up with shock, too. "A ghoul! The walking dead? The cursed slave of a vampire?"

"Of course not!" Sam sounded downright irritated. "Don't be silly! She's not cursed, and she's not anyone's slave." He shook his head as if stunned at how thick a grown-up could be. "Tom's always going on about how she never listens and won't do what he says. That doesn't sound much like a slave, does it?" He folded his arms and tapped the bloodstained toe of his sneaker. Michael had better watch it, or Sam would take him on.

What Michael did was absorb this carefully. "Tom? The second shifter? The one who came with your father?"

"Yeah," Sam agreed. "You know my dad?"

"Yes, Sam, I do. I met your father two nights ago. He saved me from severe injury, if not death. I owe him for that."

"That's okay. He does that a lot. He's a doctor." And was Sam proud of him!

Stella didn't try to hold back her smile. Sam was proud to be Justin's son, and she was proud to be Justin's wife. She needed to go find Justin, but it seemed Sam was in charge right now, and he would probably do a better job explaining things than either Antonia or she.

"Yes," Michael creased his forehead and shook his head. "So you're telling me, Sam, both your father and this Tom are vampires who shift and Elizabeth is a ghoul. But didn't you say she used to baby-sit you?"

"Sure, when we lived in Columbus and Mum had to work at Dixie's Vampire Emporium. I'm too big for a baby-sitter now."

Michael sat down. Good. She wasn't too keen on finding
out if shapeshifters fainted from shock and trying to absorb
too much impossible information. "You certainly are," he
said, making an impressive effort to smile at Sam. He then
looked at Stella, his dark eyes almost accusing. "What sort
of mother marries a vampire and lets a ghoul take care of her
child?"

"Hey!" Sam raised his young voice before she could even
try to come up with an answer. "Don't you dare talk to my
Mum like that! She's the best mum in the world and I'll tell
you what sort of mother gets me a vampire dad—a vampire
mother! So there!"

The last bit was verging on sassy, but since Sam had now
stepped close and wrapped his arms around her, she let it go.
Michael was going to learn fast around Sam.

"You're a vampire, too?"

Stella rather sympathized with his confusion. It wasn't
that long ago that she'd thought vampires were the stuff of
myths and legends. But heck, as a shapeshifter, he should
understand.

"You have an objection to vampires?" Antonia asked, her
voice sounding as if she'd chewed on powdered glass. "Don't
care to be around them, perhaps?"

If Michael had any sense, he'd pick his next few words
very carefully.

"That's not it, Antonia, and you know it. You, I accepted.
Justin, I owe, but finding half the village are vampires, well . . ."

"It's a bit confusing at first," Sam said, stepping forward
and patting Michael's shoulder with sympathy. Man to man
wasn't in it. "I was a bit amazed when I first found out, but
really, it's okay. After all, you're a shifter. You change into a
big, scary cat. What's the difference?" He gave a little shrug.
"You're all extra-human."

"What about you?" Michael asked, grasping Sam's free
hand. "How are you different?"

"I'm not. I'm just a kid who has to do homework and floss my teeth every night."

"But you have a mother and father who are vampires. Doesn't that make things strange?"

He shrugged again. "A bit, but most kids find their parents a bit odd at times. All grown-ups are. And besides, I have parents who are super strong and a dad who is so old he's super, super, super strong. I know they'll never let anyone hurt me. How many kids can say that for sure?"

"But this afternoon . . ." Michael began.

Sam all but blew him off. "Oh, that!" He shook his head. "I was worried about James because he was shot and bleeding all over me, but once I called Dad and he said he'd come, I knew he'd rescue us and I was right. Everyone came to save me. Even you. It's okay, really, Michael. The Colony all works together, and once you're married to Antonia, you'll be part of the Colony, too."

Michael nodded. Trying to grasp what came from the mouth of a babe, no doubt.

"Who says we're getting married?" Antonia asked, the edge still in her voice.

Sam turned to Antonia and rolled his eyes. Stella frowned. She was going to have to talk to him about that. "You know you are," Sam said, a mischievous grin curving the corners of his mouth. "After Mom and I go, you'll have a big argument and then decide it's okay after all, and you'll make up and get married. I bet you a new iPod you do!"

That was as good a point as any to get lost on. "Come on, Sam. Quit spilling Colony secrets. We need to find your father."

"Okay, Mom." Sam gave Michael another comradely pat on the shoulder. "Better be nice to Antonia; you got her in a real mood."

Stella made a record fast good-bye and left before she spoiled it all by laughing aloud.

* * *

Michael kept his eyes on the closed door, not on her.
Antonia clenched her fists. Things were nowhere near right
between them. "That is a child and a half," he said. His smile
implied he wasn't totally incensed.

"Isn't he lovely?" Sam was as good a point to start as any.
Better than most, in fact. "Stella set the Colony on its ears
when she announced she had a child. It's not often I've seen
Gwyltha nonplussed, but that was one occasion."

"How can two vampires bring up a child?" He spoke quietly, as if talking to himself, but she sensed it was directed
straight at her, her Colony, and her ethics.

"Just like any other parents: with love, a lot of prayer, and
a fair bit of exasperation and heartache at intervals."

Michael turned to her, face drawn, as he shook his head.
"They're vampires!"

"So am I, Michael." She suppressed a shudder at his ani-
mosity. They had to resolve this. How could he reject what
she was?

He thought a minute and gave a shrug. "I was about to
say that's different, but it really isn't, is it?"

Dear Abel, was he going to reject her and all she was?
"No, Michael, it isn't. We all suck blood. We all once died.
We will live a very, very long time. One day in the none-too-
distant future, Justin and Stella will be looking after Sam in
his old age and will watch him die, but meanwhile, they are
producing a rather splendid human being. What's so wrong
with that?"

He took a while replying. "Nothing, Antonia, love." At
least she was still his love. "Am I being foolish?"

Totally! But she'd keep that to herself. "Coming to grips
with the reality of vampires walking the earth isn't easy,
even for a shapeshifter." She couldn't resist making that last
point. Heck, Michael wasn't your average mortal on the
street.

"Young Sam seems to have no problem!"

It always came back to Sam. "He's a child. He half-believed in vampires. It was Stella who didn't. She was the one who had a hard time coming to terms with things. Sam just accepted the new situation."

"How did Stella become a vampire?"

How far should she tell? He was listening and trying to understand. "We don't usually talk about transformation to nonvampires, but since you already know what you do . . . Stella was shot by a street thug. Justin transformed her because he couldn't bear the thought of Sam being alone and ending up in foster care." His flinch perhaps meant she was getting through to him. "Stella was an only child; her only family is a mother in gaol. Justin turned her for Sam's sake, and she just about bit his head off right afterward from what I heard."

He nodded slowly. "I see." Unlikely really, or was it? Michael knew what it was to be different, after all.

"Were your parents shifters?"

He started at the question. Okay, perhaps she had changed subjects abruptly, but it wasn't that odd a question. "No." He shook his head and creased his brows. "More correctly, I don't know. One of them, at least, had to have been, I suppose, but . . ." She waited, knowing more was coming. Seemed ages by the ticking of the clock on the wall before he went on. "I was abandoned, in the style of a Victorian novel, on the doorstep of a convent when I was about two. I have no memory of it, but apparently, I was dumped there with a note pinned on my lapel, 'Please look after Michael. He's a good little boy.'

"That was it. Nothing else. The nuns, as nuns are wont to, took me in and put me in a foster home." He smiled, meeting her eyes. "No, no horror stories of abuse or neglect. The nuns gave me the name Langton, naming me after some benefactor of the convent in ages past. The Marshes, the family who fostered me, were a good couple. Mr. Marsh had been a roofer who fell and broke a leg and lost it to gangrene. He and Mrs. March survived by fostering children. There were usually three or four of us. Some came and went. She often had tiny babies for a few weeks before they were adopted, and others, like me, stayed years.

"I was just like the other children, or so I thought. I could run faster than anyone else. Got ribbons for it in school, and once won a cup at a district meet. I was thirteen, the youngest runner, and I beat out veteran competitors. I thought I might even be an amateur runner. Then I went off to Boy Scout camp that summer. One night I was restless, and I went out wandering in the woods in my pajamas. I felt jittery and bouncy—not altogether unusual for a thirteen-year-old boy—but then I started itching until I hurt all over, and I felt as if my skin no longer fit. My pajamas ripped, and I looked down and saw furry paws and arms. I was terrified and ran and ran and then came back to the same spot as if by instinct. It was hours later, and it turned out they were looking for me. I don't know how I changed back, but I did and pulled on what was left of my pajamas and walked back to camp.

"Got myself in trouble as someone had sighted a large, tawny wildcat in the woods just after I was found to be missing from my tent. No doubt the leaders were all terrified I'd been mauled or eaten. I was put to peeling potatoes and chopping onions the rest of the camp as punishment. It gave me lots of time to think about what had happened, and I half-convinced myself it had been a dream.

"That lasted until nine months later when I changed in my bedroom at the Marshes. I was nigh on fourteen and ready to leave school and get a job—there was no higher education for foundlings in those days. I clearly remember seeing myself in the mottled mirror in my wardrobe door. I scared myself silly. Then I realized it was my secret. No one else would ever know.

"I went to the library to find out about myself. There was a fair bit on werewolves, but nothing about shapeshifting cats. I learned I became a puma, but that wasn't much help. I often wondered—still do, come to that—if my mother knew what I was. Who knows?"

"Anyway, I had to leave school and take up a trade. Mr. Marsh had a cousin who was a potter in Farnham, not far from here. Funny how that drew me back. I was apprenticed there, at the end of its heyday as it happened. It went on for decades after I left, but toward the end, it only produced gardenware and flowerpots. In my day, the wares went up to Liberty's and Heals. So, I learned to be a potter. I was the only apprentice most of the time. I had a large attic to myself, and it was close to open country. When the need to shift came on me, I could change and run free.

"Later, after I finished my apprenticeship, I worked around the country at various potteries and spent my holidays in remote spots: on moors, the Peak District, the mountains of Scotland and Wales. Once in a while, I met another shifter. The first time, it stunned me; we recognized each other on sight, even in human form. We smell differently for a start. Can't tell you how wonderful it was to find there were others like me. We don't really keep in touch. Nothing like your setup, but we know who we are and we offer hospitality when traveling."

He stopped, looking at her intently as if to read her reaction. Her old, much battered heart ached for the adolescent alone, learning his real nature. And a thought went to his mother. Had she left Michael knowing his nature? Or had there been something about the toddler that scared her, so she fled? No one would ever know. Whatever secrets that mortal woman knew or had not known, all was now lost to the grave.

She gave him a little smile. They'd gone a long way from his concerns about Sam, but loving Michael as she did, she wanted, no needed, to know his origins, and he needed to tell her. She stepped closer and reached out, taking his hand. His fingers closed tightly over hers. "Michael," she whispered, "I love you."

There was a deep, wild gleam in his dark eyes. "I hope so."

"Don't you ever doubt me."

"It's not you I doubt, darling, but what about the others? Your Colony. Your Gwyltha wasn't exactly approving of me last night."

Men! Or rather shifters! She wanted to give him a big shove with her elbow, but she settled for grinning up at him. "Michael, you just helped rescue Sam. No one will ever question your worth again. Not that I ever did," she added.

His lips came down, warm and sweetly feral. She wrapped her arms around his neck and drew him close. How she wanted him! How she needed him! And how her body molded to his as his tongue found hers, and she responded with a wild need. They were like two wild animals—okay, one shifter, one vampire—alive with need and wanting and heat. Locked together by their love. She had never been this contented or joyous in her long, long life.

He broke the kiss to catch his breath. He needed to do that every so often after all. "Everything alright?" she asked, praying it was so.

"Almost," he replied. "You make me forget my worries, Antonia, my love."

"Something still bothering you?" She held him tight, as much to reassure herself as him.

"Yes, but I'm going to have to come to terms with things if I plan to stay around you and your lot, won't I?"

"We're not so hard to get along with, and after this afternoon, no one, not Gwyltha or anyone, will question your utility to the Colony."

"God, she reminds me of my old headmistress, proper old tartar she was."

"Keeping a bunch of vampires in line is harder than controlling a rabble of schoolchildren."

"Good point." He even smiled. Did she have him back, or was he still hesitating? "So, you come with the Colony as a package deal?"

Yes! "That's how it is."

"I can't offer the same. Shifters are loners."

"You offer yourself, Michael. That's all I ask." All she needed, come to that.

"I love you, Antonia, but I'm not sure I love your Colony."

"Can't we work on that? I don't live with the Colony, and I do want to live with you."

"You mean move out of that luxury country house hotel into my cabin on the common?"

It wasn't possible for her heart to clench or flutter, but it somehow managed both. "Why not?"

He took her hand and led her over to the sofa, settling her beside him. "We can sit here of an evening and talk about going hunting after it gets dark. I'll move in another fridge to hold your blood bags."

"I'd better get Sam that new iPod! Looks as though he won the bet!"

"Wasn't his bet about getting married?"

"And?" She grinned. "You don't want to make an honest woman of me?"

"The logistics might be tricky, dear. My existence is a trifle . . . opaque, shall we say? I pay taxes as a corporate entity, and the only way I got a driver's license was by lying about my age."

He still had a lot to learn. "Don't worry, dear. Tom will take care of it all."

"Tom? Elizabeth's fiancé?"

"That's right. He keeps all our identities up-to-date and apparently legal. Just let him know what you need and give him a couple of weeks."

"How does he do that?"

"I've no idea. He keeps on about how much harder it's getting each year, but so far, he's managed. I doubt it's all on the up and up, but it helps us cope. He'll sort out your affairs too."

"And I should trust him?"

"Why not? The rest of us do, and have for several hundred years."

Michael leaned back against the soft cushions and shut his eyes. She watched the light play on his beautiful, long golden lashes and the strong contours of his face. Blending her life to Michael's would not be easy, but worth every iota of effort. After a long silence, he opened his eyes and looked at her, a smile curving his mouth. "Right. Perhaps we should split the cost of that new iPod."

She snuggled into his shoulder and laughed. "Sometimes I think Sam is too knowing for his age."

"What do you expect, given the company he keeps?" The words might be hard, but his voice was light. There was no anxiety, no question. Just acceptance. Thank Abel! "So, everything taken care of. Just like that?" The last held a note of skepticism. They weren't quite at an understanding yet.

"We can check, but I imagine so. Justin and Gwyltha will see that James is fine and remembers only what he needs to. Elizabeth and Tom have taken care of Judy."

"And Sam too? You just wipe out their minds? Arrange things to suit your purpose!"

He was back to prickly again. "No, we don't 'wipe out minds.' We take out what they shouldn't remember in order to protect us all. Think about it. We want those louts caught and shoved into the clink, right? They'll be found. Prints will

match the robbery site with a bit of luck; they will certainly
be linked to James's injury; and I'll bet that gun will match
the one used on the guard. The police already have the jewels. Everything is taken care of nicely. Any mutterings from
the crooks about wildcats or attack eagles will be brushed
off. Yes, their injuries will get noticed, but not that much, I
don't imagine. It will be seen as a falling out among thieves.

"And about Sam, do you really think he needs to remember being snatched or James getting shot and bleeding on
him in the back of that dark van? And what about James and
Judy? James rambling on about a cat and the other two
might be dismissed as hallucinations due to stress and pain,
but Judy saw everything sitting back in the van. She would
be counted a reliable witness. Better leave her out of it.
She'll hear about James's injury and rush to his bedside.
They can get on with their lives, and so can the rest of us,
and two unpleasant specimens will be out of circulation."

He nodded, accepting the explanation, it seemed, at last.
"One word of caution, dearest. You do know that Chadwick
chap has a somewhat checkered reputation in these parts,
and Judy is the vicar's daughter and a decent woman by all
accounts."

"True, but she has her head screwed on tightly. Maybe
she is the influence he needs. Who can tell? It's up to the pair
of them."

"Yes." He was quiet for a few of his heartbeats, then
turned to her, resting his hand over her breast. Her body responded with relief, love, and wild sexual hunger. "I see," he
said as he slipped open two buttons on her blouse. His fingers were warm and gentle against her skin.

Gentle was very nice, but she wanted him fierce and loving. "What do you see?" she asked, setting her hand over his
steadily, beating heart and easing her fingertips inside his
shirt.

"That you have me utterly captivated. Been using some of those vampire mind tricks on me?" He had her blouse open, and his fingers swept inside her bra.

"Never needed to!" She yanked his shirt open and moved to straddle him.

He laughed, looking up at her. "Out to have your wicked will of me, are you, woman?"

"Of course!"

"I can think of more comfortable places than this old sofa." As he spoke, he stood, holding her by the waist as she wrapped her legs around him.

"Take me there then."

"It will be my pleasure, love!" He leapt over the back of the sofa and carried her into the bedroom, pulling back the sheets as he laid her on the bed. "This may take a little while . . ."

It could take all night as far as she was concerned. All night and the next few centuries.

Chapter 24

Sam was asleep, worn out from the day's events, and Stella was pacing the floor. She needed to hear all was well, and she hadn't. In her head, she knew things were just fine. Justin and Gwyltha between them could cope with the National Health Service and the entire Surrey Constabulary if they had to, but her heart was nowhere near as complacent.

She'd done her part, carefully removing all Sam's memories of the abduction and the aftermath. Best have him remember none of it. She trusted Tom and Elizabeth had done the same for Judy. Stella made another circuit of the room. A wild run across the common at vamp speed would help more, but no way was she leaving Sam.

Where the heck was everyone?

It was close to eleven. Aside from Justin and Gwyltha being gone and Tom and Elizabeth being off somewhere, Antonia was nowhere to be seen. Good thing that! It could only mean she and Michael were settling affairs in the very best way possible, and no doubt Sam was well on his way to winning a new iPod. Little monkey!

And she was well on the way to wearing a path in the fitted carpet when she heard footsteps on the stairs. Two sets of footsteps and no heartbeats! She had the door open in a flash and all but raced down the hallway. "Justin!" He returned her hug. She wanted shout aloud in her relief. She even hugged Gwyltha, something she'd never normally dare—their leader always seemed so unapproachable—but darn it, Gwyltha even hugged back. "Everything okay?" Stella asked. She just had to know.

"Let's get in your room first," Gwyltha said.

Good idea. There were mortals sleeping nearby. Once the door was closed, and her vamp hearing made sure Sam was still fast asleep next door, Stella all but latched onto them. "I want to hear it all, chapter and verse. Is everything okay?"

"I believe the Colony and Bringham will survive this." Gwyltha replied. Lots of help that was!

Justin did better. "James is fine. He has little memory of what happened, but he does remember being bundled in the van. Doesn't know why. He got fast and efficient medical attention. Nice chap there. Let me assist. We got the bullet out, and James has had enough antibiotics to take care of any possible infection. The police will be talking to him in the morning after the anesthetic wears off. We left him with a rather shaken, but affectionate Judy at his bedside.

"The first she heard of it was a phone call from Elizabeth telling her we'd found James staggering down the lane from the common, and he was now in hospital and asking for her. He wasn't, but it was a justifiable lie under the circumstances, and it brought her over posthaste. The police talked to us, but they seemed satisfied we were just two random tourists admiring the beauty of the Surrey countryside. I hope it stays that way."

"She doesn't remember anything that happened?" Stella asked.

"Not at all," Gwyltha said. "It was all well taken care of."

"Where are Elizabeth and Tom?" She'd been wondering all evening.

"Gone up to Town and then to meet Dixie. She's flying into Heathrow in the morning."

Good news! "Bringing the diaries?"

"Yes," Gwyltha said. "She decided to bring them over herself. Fastest way and safest. Seems they contain enough corroboration to sew up the local mystery you uncovered."

Wasn't exactly her, but she wasn't arguing. "Good! The faxes she sent over told it pretty clearly. Oh, cripes! Judy read all those faxes!"

"But she doesn't remember," Gwyltha said quietly. "Tom was quite thorough."

"Hope he remembered to take away seeing Elizabeth ghoul those thugs."

"You can rely on that. Protecting Elizabeth is his first concern."

Good point. Stella sat down on the bed. "It'll be good to see Dixie, and I hope this takes care of everything. I'm ready to go home. This place is hard on the nerves!"

Justin came to sit by her. "And who was it who insisted on coming here to give Sam a nice break and for you to help out?" Justin smiled, but she got the point.

"Okay, I did, and heck, I did help set things up, and when we get back, I'm signing up in York for a course in web design. I can set up in business and take it with me wherever we go . . ."

"Out to challenge Tom's skills?" Gwyltha asked.

As if! "Not in a hundred years! I don't want to hack into government databases. I want to build web sites."

"Good idea," Justin said. "The chap who does the clinic one makes us pay through the nose."

"You think I'll be cheaper?"

"Not cheaper, my love. Better value, and we can negotiate payment."

"All right, you two," Gwyltha broke in. "You do have an audience and a child in the next room!"

"Never mind." Stella gave him the naughtiest grin she could. "We'll be home soon."

"Not as soon as all that," Justin replied. "We have to hang around a few days to make sure Dixie doesn't need any help, and I want to make sure the police don't need a little nudge in the right direction."

"Finding those two red-handed wasn't enough?" Literally red-handed given all the blood James had lost.

"They found them alright," Gwyltha said, an amused edge in her voice. "Just as they were stirring—good timing there—and were looking around themselves in an idiotic and bemused style apparently, the law arrived and nabbed them nicely. I think they were in the back of a police car and headed for the cells before they had any idea what happened. Seems they both had records, the gun in the van is the same make and model as the one that shot the guard. They certainly have enough on them to keep them until they get confirmation from ballistics. And one other thing—the one called Dave decided to welsh on his partner. There really is no honor among thieves these days."

"How exactly did you learn all this?" She could guess, but . . .

"We stopped by the police station on the way back. The roof has a perfect design for perching on. Very handy." Gwyltha sounded as if she'd personally designed the roof for her own convenience.

So, seemed all was turning out fine. "Will be good to see Dixie again. Is Kit coming too?"

Justin shook his head. "He's staying behind. Seems he has a little neighborhood project he wants to finish off."

"More crime fighting?"

"Something about setting a trap for a pair of thieves who've been breaking into garages." Justin said.

She had to smile. "Good for him." Things had to be better in the neighborhood with a vampire on patrol.

"And," Justin said, putting his arm round her waist, "good for us, I think. We've done our bit to make Surrey a little safer, and, with a bit of luck, we have helped solve a twenty-year-old murder."

"If they accept the evidence in Dixie's diaries."

"They will." When Gwyltha spoke with that much certainty, who'd be nuts enough to doubt her?

"Good night, Gwyltha," Justin said, standing up and stepping over to the door to hold it open. "Your room is next to Antonia's, I believe."

"Any likelihood I'll have a neighbor tonight?" Gwyltha asked with a little quirk of a smile.

"Doubt it," Stella said. "If she's not back by now, we won't see her before tomorrow."

Gwyltha shook her head. "I don't know why she's paying for all these rooms; half of them are empty on any given night." With that, she bade them good night and swept off down the hallway.

"Good," Justin said as he shut the door. "She's gone at last. Time for a nice conversation with my wife." He crossed the room, eyes full of heat and desire.

Stella took two steps toward him. It was late, but not that late. "I love you," she said.

"I know," he replied, drawing her close. "You love me, you you missed me, and you are coming back with me soon, right?"

"Convince me it will be worth my while."

He smiled. She'd learned never to doubt Justin's smile.

*   *   *

Dixie's plane was on time, but so were umpteen others. Elizabeth couldn't help wondering if the entire traveling world passed though Heathrow at 8 A.M. every day, or was it just Saturdays?

There was an accident on the M5 and roadworks on the M25, but the delays gave Elizabeth and Tom plenty of time to fill Dixie in on the recent events. She listened, asking the occasional question and uttering the odd "Good grief!" or "What?" until they'd caught her up with the convoluted crimes and discoveries of the past couple of weeks.

"That place gets worse, not better," Dixie said. "Seems like the murder capital of Great Britain. Makes one long for the crime levels in Columbus." She gave a little chuckle. "Maybe we should come back one of these decades and let Kit sort things out back here."

"How is he?" Tom asked. A question he'd no doubt been holding back since they'd met her.

"Fine. Busy playing neighborhood vigilante and helping me in the emporium. He's also started writing again."

Tom all but swerved. Righting the car, he glanced over his shoulder. "Writing? He hasn't done that in centuries."

"He is now. He got so irritated at a mystery novel he was reading—one of those historical ones set in Tudor England— that he's started his own series set in Restoration England with Samuel Pepys as the amateur detective."

"Damn! He and Sam Pepys were a pair, I can tell you. Well, he'll get the historical details right."

Dixie nodded. "That's what he says. He does a bit of research every so often to check how his memory is holding up, and he's having a ball. He's also written a couple of one-act plays and submitted them to contests, but so far, no luck. One panel of judges even told him he should pick another pen name as his work could never equal his fifteenth-century namesake."

"Ouch!" Tom replied, wincing. "Miserable sod! I bet that one was a failed writer or a wannabe who's never finished a thing. What did Kit say?"

"He laughed, tossed the paper in the empty fireplace, and incinerated it with a look. Amazed me as I didn't know he could do that."

"He couldn't. Must be age increasing his powers," Tom said.

"I told him not to try it again. I don't want him burning down crack houses or anything like that. Too damn risky."

"He can control it, Dixie," Tom replied.

"Maybe, and talk about controlling things, is that an engagement ring I see on Elizabeth's left hand?"

"You bet!" Elizabeth waved her hand to catch the light. "Nice, isn't it?"

"When are you doing the deed?"

"Soon!" Tom said, not taking his eyes off the road.

Elizabeth rolled her eyes. They'd talked this over just last night. "At the Solstice. I want to get married in the witch garden at Orchard House, and it will take time to get it ready. We'll have to hire more people with our gardener recovering from a gunshot wound."

If vamps could choke, Dixie would have right there and then. She could scarcely believe her ears. "In the witch garden! Where they tried to kill Christopher?" How could she? How could Tom?

"Dixie, it's a sacred grove. Like a church or a temple. Sebastian desecrated it. I've burned sage and lavender almost every day to purify the space. Our gardener was cleaning it out. It will be beautiful and holy when we finish. Making our vows there will complete the circle of cleansing and rededication."

Maybe. But to her it would always harbor memories of Kit's blistered and naked body. Still, she'd keep that to herself; no point in raining on Elizabeth's and Tom's parade, or rather, wedding plans. "So it's been a good summer for you two."

"Yup." Elizabeth sounded so happy. "And we're not the only ones getting hitched."

"Who else?"

"Antonia."

"Antonia!" Marble maiden Antonia. Nothing would surprise her now. "Who's the lucky man?"

"You'll find out," Tom said with a hint of amusement. "One of the local legends."

Thanks, Tom! Pique her interest, then clam up! She'd have asked more, demanded more details, but he'd just pulled up in front of the police station that she remembered from her previous sojourn in Bringham. "I wonder if the detective Justin and I had dealings with is still here."

"Maybe," Elizabeth replied. "The one investigating our murder is called Warrington." Not the same one. Good.

He wasn't the same one, and he wasn't available.

"Sorry, madam," the desk sergeant said, "but Inspector Warrington is busy. Perhaps you could leave your package."

No way, José! "I'm not prepared to do that. Does he have an assistant I might speak to? I've just flown in from the States because I heard about the body unearthed in Orchard House. I think he will want to see what I've brought."

"Flown in from the States!" That impressed the sergeant and did the trick

In minutes, a young detective arrived, introduced herself as Detective Jeffers, and asked how she could help. At their mention of Orchard House, she led them to a cluttered office. "Inspector Warrington is in a meeting right now. He'll be here in a few minutes. Can I get you tea?"

They all declined and waited while Jeffers hovered in the

open doorway until Detective Inspector Warrington walked in, not appearing too enthused at being interrupted by stray Americans who had wandered in.

"You have information for me, Miss LePage?"

"Yes, I do." Mentioning her connection with Orchard House got a polite nod. Thumping two black diaries on his desk caught his attention. "My great-aunts' diaries covering the time period. I've marked the pertinent pages. You might want to have a look."

He still didn't seem too convinced. Sheesh, Brits! She picked up the top one, opened it at the first marked page, and pushed it over to him. Reading that spidery writing wasn't easy, but once he started, he was hooked, flicking from one marked page to the next before reaching for the second book and devouring that with an expression akin to excitement.

He put them down with an expression of mixed incredulity, horror, and satisfaction. "These are your property, Miss LePage?"

"Yes."

"How did they come into your possession?" She gave him the whole rigmarole of inheriting the house last year and selling it to Antonia. He leaned back, smiling affably. "If these are what they appear to be, Miss LePage, I thank you. We may have solved the murder. The entries here confirm the identity of the victim."

"It just refers to 'young Rachel.'"

He nodded. "Yes, but we have a local man whose mother disappeared in the same time frame and who had connections with the Misses Underwoods. Once we get the DNA report back, we'll know for sure." He paused, rubbing his hand over the worn leather cover of the top diary. "I'm indebted to you, Miss LePage, for coming all this way to bring these."

"I heard what had happened, and I don't think wrongdoers should escape, even if they are dead," Dixie said. She sounded frightfully prim and pious, but what the heck? She did believe that.

"I'm glad you do, madam, and I'm obliged. We'll need to keep these a while."

"I understand, but I do want them back."

"We'll take very good care of them." He looked toward the detective who still lingered in the doorway. "Jeffers, get Miss LePage a receipt, will you? Staying long?" Warrington asked, turning back to Dixie.

"No. Just a few days, but my friend, Antonia Stonewright in Bringham, or Mr. Kyd here will take care of them when you are through."

"Well, Jeffers," Warrington said after they had left, "sometimes it's luck or blind chance that solves a case. Fortune's been good to us this week. Yesterday, we nab the two thieves from the jewelry job, delivered on a plate as it were, and now we get the dots joined up in the Orchard House case by a visitor from the States who just happened to hear about it all."

"And, sir," Jeffers added, "I've been reading the transcripts of the Caughleigh case as you requested. Seems he made numerous references to 'Rachel' and 'doing his sister wrong.' With everything else he confessed to and nothing to tie it to, it got overlooked, but that about wraps it up."

He nodded. "Pity we can't haul someone in for it, but two are pushing up daisies in Bringham churchyard, and one is already in Broadmoor. And as for the Chadwick chap, he has to mourn his mother all over again with the added hurt of knowing his uncle abetted in her murder." He shook his head. "Sometimes, the world stinks!"

* * *

"Another vampire?" Michael asked as Antonia explained the rapid phone conversation, apparently with a friend who had just arrived from the States.

"Dixie. She sold me Orchard House and came over to give some old diaries to the police. Seems they pretty much point to the murderers of that young woman."

"Good." He meant it. It was good if that nasty mess was resolved, but that still left him with the recurring worry—would he ever get used to vampires?

"We're meeting them all at the hotel. Is that alright?" Was it? "I want you to meet her, Michael. Gwyltha and everyone will be there."

"I see." Unfortunately.

Antonia, his love, looked up at his reply and came toward him, arms open. "Just stop it, Michael! You're taking one stray comment of Gwyltha's too much to heart. Start listening to me, I love you! We are getting married. Repeat after me if you like, and get it through your thick, feline skull. After yesterday, no one will doubt you. And by the way, I love you!"

What else mattered? What else did he need? Vamps be blowed. He had Antonia. "Okay. Help me empty this kiln, and I'll wash up and be there."

"I'll help."

She always did. "Come on, then."

As he opened the kiln door wide, he tried to ignore the fact that he was soon meeting yet another vampire. His solitary life was over. Marrying Antonia was marrying the Colony. All in all, a fair deal. "When we go up to the Manor Hotel," he said, reaching in for a two-handled mug and handing it to her to put on the shelf to be glazed later, "might as well pack up all your things and bring them down here.

No point in paying for a room you're never going to sleep in again."

"Sure of me, are you?" she asked, tilting her head and smiling.

"Yes!"

GREAT BOOKS,
GREAT SAVINGS!

When You Visit Our Website:
www.kensingtonbooks.com
You Can Save 30% Off The Retail Price
Of Any Book You Purchase

- **All Your Favorite Kensington Authors**
- **New Releases & Timeless Classics**
- **Overnight Shipping Available**
- **All Major Credit Cards Accepted**

Visit Us Today To Start Saving!
www.kensingtonbooks.com

All Orders Are Subject To Availability.
Shipping and Handling Charges Apply.

**Sink Your Teeth Into
These Spellbinding Romances by**

Shannon Drake

Dead By Dusk
0-8217-7545-6 $6.99US/$9.99CAN

The Awakening
0-8217-7228-7 $6.99US/$9.99CAN

Realm of Shadows
0-8217-7227-9 $6.99US/$9.99CAN

Deep Midnight
0-8217-6837-9 $6.99US/$8.99CAN

When Darkness Falls
0-8217-6692-9 $6.99US/$8.99CAN

Beneath a Blood Red Moon
0-8217-6298-2 $6.99US/$8.99CAN

Available Wherever Books Are Sold!

Visit our website at **www.kensingtonbooks.com**

By Best-selling Author
Fern Michaels

Weekend Warriors	0-8217-7589-8	$6.99US/$9.99CAN
Listen to Your Heart	0-8217-7463-8	$6.99US/$9.99CAN
The Future Scrolls	0-8217-7586-3	$6.99US/$9.99CAN
About Face	0-8217-7020-9	$7.99US/$10.99CAN
Kentucky Sunrise	0-8217-7462-X	$7.99US/$10.99CAN
Kentucky Rich	0-8217-7234-1	$7.99US/$10.99CAN
Kentucky Heat	0-8217-7368-2	$7.99US/$10.99CAN
Plain Jane	0-8217-6927-8	$7.99US/$10.99CAN
Wish List	0-8217-7363-1	$7.50US/$10.50CAN
Yesterday	0-8217-6785-2	$7.50US/$10.50CAN
The Guest List	0-8217-6657-0	$7.50US/$10.50CAN
Finders Keepers	0-8217-7364-X	$7.50US/$10.50CAN
Annie's Rainbow	0-8217-7366-6	$7.50US/$10.50CAN
Dear Emily	0-8217-7316-X	$7.50US/$10.50CAN
Sara's Song	0-8217-7480-8	$7.50US/$10.50CAN
Celebration	0-8217-7434-4	$7.50US/$10.50CAN
Vegas Heat	0-8217-7207-4	$7.50US/$10.50CAN
Vegas Rich	0-8217-7206-6	$7.50US/$10.50CAN
Vegas Sunrise	0-8217-7208-2	$7.50US/$10.50CAN
What You Wish For	0-8217-6828-X	$7.99US/$10.99CAN
Charming Lily	0-8217-7019-5	$7.99US/$10.99CAN

Available Wherever Books Are Sold!

**Discover the Thrill of
Romance with**

Lisa Plumley

__Making Over Mike
0-8217-7110-8 $5.99US/$7.99CAN

Amanda Connor is a life coach—not a magician! Granted, as a publicity stunt for her new business, the savvy entrepreneur has promised to transform some poor slob into a perfectly balanced example of modern manhood. But Mike Cavaco gives "raw material" new meaning.

__Falling for April
0-8217-7111-6 $5.99US/$7.99CAN

Her hometown gourmet catering company may be in a slump, but April Finnegan isn't about to begin again. Determined to save her business, she sets out to win some local sponsors, unaware she's not the only one with that idea. Turns out wealthy department store mogul Ryan Forrester is one step—and thousands of dollars—ahead of her.

__Reconsidering Riley
0-8217-7340-2 $5.99US/$7.99CAN

Jayne Murphy's best-selling relationship manual *Heartbreak 101* was inspired by her all-too-personal experience with gorgeous, capable . . . *outdoorsy* . . . Riley Davis, who stole her heart—and promptly skipped town with it. Now, Jayne's organized a workshop for dumpees. But it becomes hell on her heart when the leader for her group's week-long nature jaunt turns out to be none other than a certain . . .

Available Wherever Books Are Sold!

Visit our website at **www.kensingtonbooks.com**.

Say Yes! To Sizzling Romance by
Lori Foster

__Too Much Temptation
   0-7582-0431-0   **$6.99US/$9.99**CAN

Grace Jenkins feels too awkward and insecure to free the passionate woman inside her. But that hasn't stopped her from dreaming about Noah Harper. Gorgeous, strong and sexy, his rough edge beneath the polish promises no mercy in the bedroom. When Grace learns Noah's engagement has ended in scandal, she shyly offers him her support and her friendship. But Noah's looking for something extra . . .

__Never Too Much
   0-7582-0087-0   **$6.99US/$9.99**CAN

A confirmed bachelor, Ben Badwin has had his share of women, and he likes them as wild and uninhibited as his desires. Nothing at all like the brash, wholesomely cute woman who just strutted into his diner. But something about Sierra Murphy's independent attitude makes Ben's fantasies run wild. He'd love to dazzle her with his sensual skills . . . to make her want him as badly as he suddenly wants her . . .

__Say No to Joe?
   0-8217-7512-X   **$6.99US/$9.99**CAN

Joe Winston can have any woman—except the one he really wants. Secretly, Luna Clark may lust after Joe, but she's made it clear that she's too smart to fall for him. He can just keep holding his breath, thank you very much. But now, Luna's inherited two kids who need more than she alone can give in a small town that seems hell-bent on driving them away. She needs someone to help out . . . someone who can't be intimidated . . . someone just like Joe.

__When Bruce Met Cyn
   0-8217-7513-8   **$6.99US/$9.99**CAN

Compassionate and kind, Bruce Kelly understands that everyone makes mistakes, even if he's never actually done anything but color inside the lines. Nobody's perfect, but Bruce is about to meet a woman who's perfect for him. He's determined to show her that he can be trusted. And if that means proving it by being the absolute gentleman at all times, then so be it. No matter how many cold showers it takes . . .

Available Wherever Books Are Sold!

Visit our website at **www.kensingtonbooks.com**.

From the Queen of Romance
Cassie Edwards

__Enchanted Enemy
0-8217-7216-4 $5.99US/$7.99CAN

__Elusive Ecstacy
0-8217-6597-3 $5.99US/$7.99CAN

__Portrait of Desire
0-8217-5862-4 $5.99US/$7.50CAN

__Rapture's Rendezvous
0-8217-6115-3 $5.99US/$7.50CAN

Available Wherever Books Are Sold!

Visit our website at **www.kensingtonbooks.com.**